DRAFTS OF A SUICIDE NOTE

Mandy-Suzanne Wong

Regal House Publishing

Published by
Regal House Publishing, LLC
Raleigh, NC 27612
All rights reserved

ISBN -13 (paperback): 9781947548824
ISBN -13 (epub): 9781947548831
ISBN -13 (mobi): 9781947548848
Library of Congress Control Number: 2019931662

All efforts were made to determine the copyright holders and obtain their
permissions in any circumstance where copyrighted material was used. The
publisher apologizes if any errors were made during this process, or if any
omissions occurred. If noted, please contact the publisher and all efforts will
be made to incorporate permissions in future editions.

Interior and cover design by Lafayette & Greene
lafayetteandgreene.com
Cover images and interior images © by Heather Kettenis

Regal House Publishing, LLC
https://regalhousepublishing.com

The following is a work of fiction created by the author. All names, individuals,
characters, places, items, brands, events, etc. were either the product of the
author or were used fictitiously. Any name, place, event, person, brand, or item,
current or past, is entirely coincidental.

Printed in the United States of America

My choices will work on me like poison until my humanity corrodes. They'll work on what's underneath until I am a monster. Maybe my existence amounts to an accumulation of debts, but maybe this is only partly true. I have lived like a shadow. Listen, please: lately I've had only one defense; even then, relief is temporary—I imagine dissolving in water.

AS1.
index card, 3x5", black-inked, laser-printed horror

I wonder what to call you. *You spirit, you disembodied creature, you dear, sweet, tantalizing phantom.* You're not just whatever designated word, whatever fleshless prefab vision is bound to fail you, even though all words are as enthralling and slippery as specters. As for me, everything in me amounts to the great void of the question we failed to ask; everything I am is falling in that chasm as if through the unrelenting emptiness of distant space that defies all knowledge. I am the question, and I am falling through it: the question of what we are. If you were always already gone and ghostly, can it be that everything you said is true? What strange gravity set us in the same orbit and moved us against each other?

Missing Woman Leaves 10 Suicide Notes.

I found it in an email digest from Bernews. The *Royal Gazette* led with the same story.

In connection with Aetna Simmons of Suffering Lane, St. George's, who was reported missing by her landlady last week Monday, a BPS spokesperson said, "Police can confirm that a stack of ten documents was found in Ms. Simmons' home. The content of these documents brings us to the unfortunate conclusion that Ms. Simmons chose to end her life."

One suicide note is an unfortunate conclusion. Ten is no conclusion but the opposite. *10 Suicide Notes?* That's a provocation. As far as I know, you can only die once.

What kind of gross excess is this: ten different suicide notes or ten replicas of the same? Vulgar excess or feverish excess? Is there a difference between vulgar and feverish? Say it's ten of the same. Like birth announcements. Invitations to a soiree. A newsletter for friends and family. Some people do that in lieu of Christmas cards.

"The Bermuda Police Service extends our gratitude to those who may have considered assisting in the island-wide search, which will be postponed until further notice."

Say the documents are all different. Ten unique suicide notes. Why not nine, like the Muses? What's so great about ten? An even number, five plus five. Stroke and circle. Ten fingers, ten commandments, ten Egyptian plagues.

Why bother with one, let alone ten? So you take leave of the living under a cloud of misunderstanding. What do you care, now that you're dead? And the article said *stack*. Meaning paper documents, not on a computer. Why go to that kind of trouble? Before killing yourself, you'd have to go to the post office, stand in line, *Good afternoon, I need some thirty-five-cent stamps. Oh, but this one's going overseas...*

I thought about this a lot. Driving to work. Parking in my exclusive spot. Being gentle with the door on my MG, green and seductive as jealousy and springtime. My job was to feed unwanted documents to an industrial shredder, so it's not like I had a lot to think about.

Ten suicide notes.

What does that even look like? Glass panes in a skyscraper? Pieces of ruined church lying down on each other as they crumble? *Dear*

Friends... But you may not have friends if you're writing this kind of note. *Dear Unfeeling World, Up yours. Signed sincerely...*

Aetna Simmons left ten unique suicide notes at Suffering Lane. Altogether they form a corpus. But in the most telling hypothesis, they're also a sequence in which each successive document replaces the one before. A series of drafts.

You know. A document wherein an author is doomed to discover that an unintelligible, even ugly reality has gobbled his or her intentions. This condition, symptomized by wailing and gnashing of teeth, is what writers call a draft. Remedies include the delete key, wastepaper basket, and starting over.

How do I know all this? I know the ten final dispatches of Aetna Simmons are all different from each other because I arranged to read them. I ordered photocopies with descriptions of the original inks and papers. How'd I get this stuff? Easy. I can get anything I want.

Inspector Javon Bean is a faithful client of mine. Built like a quarterback, whines like a toddler. Even e-whines: he's not on the Simmons case, can't get the file, people might ask questions. I said, "You're writing a book. *Unsolved Mysteries in the Bermuda Triangle.*" That took care of the questions. I said, "Next round's on the house." That took care of the whining.

Since it would be foolhardy to give my email address to clients, Javon locked us inside his spacious office. We sat at his pristine desk. I enjoyed, instead of windows, a large photograph of the inspector in dress uniform looking like he was one-up on things. Pictures of his children acquiring Sports Day ribbons lined up beside their father's image like ellipses.

He gave me an envelope. I gave him an envelope. He peeked into his envelope.

"On the house," he said, just to see if I'd developed amnesia overnight. I sat there and let that jackass look at me.

He actually squirmed. "Well, like the paper says, we sort of shelved the case."

"Not because you found her. Because you didn't find her."

"It's been ten days. And we haven't announced this, but you know the landlady? Jeesums, bye, she calls it in like, 'I think my tenant might've disappeared.' Might. Like it's just a few cents' difference between being there and not there. She up and died this morning. A stroke. Myrtle Trimm, eighty-one. Cleaning woman found her in her recliner."

Javon's got a bad case of the umums. *Sheumum, she up and died.* It's an endemic condition.

I asked, "What's she got to say? The cleaning lady."

"Two dead clients back to back? Ya girl must've started thinking they don't call this place The Devil's Isles for nothing. Next flight out, she was down the front of the line. With three of her mates." Javon got a knee-whacking chortle out of this.

"Any other leads?"

Aceboy looked at me like I'd asked a stupid question. I reminded him of the expense involved in producing certain pharmaceuticals. On the house.

"Mrs. Trimm didn't get her rent," he said. "Normally the tenant did everything like clockwork. Only time the landlady even saw her was rent days. But this month? Nothing. She wasn't there when Mrs. Trimm went to her apartment. Went down a couple times a day, three days in a row. Then she called us. Guess she needed money."

Skimming the case file, he added, "Tenant lived alone, no noise, no pets, no visitors. No car, no bike. TCD says she didn't have no license. Checked Immigration. No record of a work permit or Bermuda passport. US Immigration: nobody named Aetna Simmons been through their system. Canada the same. No UK passport was issued to Aetna Simmons, and no Bermuda passport with that name has been through London. No record in the schools. Nothing at the hospital. On her lease she wrote *consultant* as her profession, but no employer came forward. Saltus thought he had some evidence she'd had dealings with Clocktower, some insurance company. They never heard of her either, she didn't have no life insurance. No will, no debts."

"No body," I noted.

"Nothing for the coroner, nothing for the sketch artist."

"Nothing. Like she was already a ghost."

"First responding constable, that's what he thought too. Old lady, home by herself all the time, no husband. And no wonder, man. Cha. Saltus said she talked more to herself than to him. Only time she talked to him was to snap his head off. A police inspector's trying to ask her questions and she's snapping his head off. Minus a couple marbles, know what I'm saying? Maybe Aetna Simmons was her imaginary friend.

"But according to the file," Javon continued, "her apartment had a tenant at some point. It was clean, didn't look like nobody gone off in a hurry. Toothbrush in the bathroom. Clothes and stuff in the closet. Personal articles suggest a woman, not too fat, medium height. No fancy dresses, no business suits. Says here *casual wear*. Ordinary, you know? Just an ordinary lady."

Ten suicide notes and the man thinks she's ordinary.

"Look, is that it?" said Javon.

"No."

"Coming up on lunch, bye."

"Where'd they find the suicide notes?"

"I guess in the apartment." Lazy bum.

"Where in the apartment?" Should've said it to his face: ya just micin, fackin bum.

"Saltus signed out the photos. Gotta go from his report. *Found what appeared to be stack of suicide notes on desk in alcove in cottage adjacent to main house. Pink with white shutters. Furnished by landlady. No photographs or knick-knacks belonging to tenant—*"

"A cottage, not an apartment."

"Whatever."

No, there's a difference. In a cottage, she was isolated. In a Bermuda cottage of limestone and concrete with hurricane-safe windows, she could've screamed in the middle of the night, every night as long as she held onto life, and no one would've known.

"What else was on the desk?"

"Nothing."

Nothing. Almost just as I'd imagined. Ten suicide notes on an antique escritoire, alone in the soft light of a French library lamp leaning over them like a conscientious mortician. I imagined the notes in the center of the desk. But when I asked Javon, he said, "On the edge, left-hand side."

reverse were true, she'd have put the notes in the center of her desk, in front of the author's chair: I was here, I did this.

I destroy things for a living. Things like promises and secrets. Put them in the shredder, they come out in shreds. You want to think shreds are like old skin cells dropping from sunburned cheeks, but a shredded document is an amputated lip and a gouged eye. Documents bear witness with their bodies.

Humans bear witness with their memories, but memories self-shred. Without witnesses, you have no proof that you were ever anything. *Minu ga hana.* Not seeing is a flower. Reality can't compete with imagination.

The death of a document is never easy, never peaceful or silent, and never a sure thing. It takes a company like mine, serious equipment; you turn it into powder and then you burn the powder, but even then.

There might be a copy. Maybe someone took a scrap of damning evidence, turned it over, scribbled a note on the back. And the evidence survives. It sets sail on a new life beyond your reach. Your secret passes on, a ghost that keeps on coming back.

So why write anything at all? Because writing is a different kind of thinking from just thinking. Words appear under my hand. I see them and they see me. And I have to look. Excavating, I am the digger and the ground. And whatever's hiding underneath.

History knows uncounted private papers that lived second lives as "literature." *Diary of Anne Frank. Collected Letters of Thomas Hardy* (eight volumes). *The Heiligenstadt Testament* of Ludwig van Beethoven, quite apropos. These authors wrote for readerships of one or less. It takes a meddler like me to realize one man's to-do list is another's *Book of Disquiet.* Normally for such a discovery to occur, the author has to die first. In this, Aetna Simmons was obliging.

A series of drafts. Each meant to replace the one before as the comprehensive portrait of Aetna's final moments. At the same time, all ten narrate a longer story.

It begins with a cry for help (AS1) full of self-loathing and guilt, a plea in hope of being rescued from herself. Later she decides (AS2) that the escape she has in mind is death. But at this point, she doesn't quite believe it. She plays with the idea. Embittered (AS3), she starts getting serious. She drafts a credible suicide note that I can envision on monogrammed stationery or inside a card embossed with a hibiscus. She types it on a scrap of copy paper. And there's a chance that it's unfinished: maybe she's not ready after all. What she writes next is indirect (AS4); but if you get the reference, you know she's thinking hard about specifics: what will death feel like?

Now, is this the crux of the portfolio? Or are this page and the next irrelevant (AS4, AS5), mixed in with her papers when somebody Javon-like dropped a bunch of files? Maybe we'll never know. But I think Aetna's bitterness turned acrid, her thoughts obsessive. Serious ideations (AS6): detailed, organized, feasible. Enter rage and violence (AS7), and at last her intention is unmistakable (AS8). She tidies her affairs (AS9), scribbles the denouement all in a rush (AS10) like she's run out of time. Or she can't bear to give herself the time to change her mind.

One problem. The Ten are rife with contradictions. It's not a matter of imprecision. Her words, styles, even inks were scrupulously deployed. The problem is the fact that there are ten.

You wonder how she died, for example. AS1 suggests poison. Suicidological studies indicate poison as a favored method among authors of suicide notes. But you could also argue, based on AS6, that the author of AS1 displays a preference for a gunshot to the head.

And anyway, Aetna Simmons is nothing less than a suicidologist's worst nightmare. Their statistics show that seventy to eighty-five percent of suicides don't bother leaving notes at all, and of those who do, the intent is to issue instructions and explain themselves. But in her verbose obscurity, Aetna defies them all. She's a textbook exemplar of Pestian's intrapsychological theory of suicidal feelings, Joiner's opposing theory that such feelings stem from thwarted interpersonal relationships, and nuanced theories that agree and disagree with both. She suits almost all of Durkheim's and Améry's classifications. Anomic, egoistic, fatalistic suicide. Dozing and balanced and short-circuit suicide. Revenge suicide. Blackmail-suicide with a pinch of self-murder-by-ordeal.

One class she eludes. Altruistic suicide. This category is for people who dive in front of bullets meant for others. It covers *kamikaze* pilots, certain cases of *seppuku*. Dying for someone as opposed to dying-because-of.

Conclusions? Aetna Simmons had a cornucopia of reasons to quit this barbaric life. Love wasn't one of them.

Consider the following syllogism. Art is often made for audiences. The ten suicide notes of Aetna Simmons were written and compiled for an audience. Therefore the ten suicide notes of Aetna Simmons are a work of art after a fashion.

Note the similarities between the ten source documents and a collection of poems, an oeuvre, a musical suite, a portfolio. An artwork is a representation, a trace of some creative act. The creative act consists of an ideation followed by a flying leap into the unknown. The artist leaps at something—some language, some convention, a rock, a tube of paint—bent on taking it apart and building something dreadful from the wreckage. But she's never sure she hasn't launched herself into a void. She suspects all her daring will never lull the ravenous keening of her idea, and she cannot undo anything. This expression and dubious release, this destruction in creation's name, this is the potential that art shares with death.

Call this the Aesthetic Hypothesis: Aetna Simmons' suite-portfolio narrates and performs being-toward-death, the puissant consciousness that life is ruin. Each note is a frame in an open-ended drama, and the entire corpus is a movement that is paradoxically static, a performance and an object in a single effort to which the act of suicide is absolutely integral. She arranged to be nothing but ten papers in a column and the drama of their words. A Foucauldian might say it was a case of suicide as somebody's life's work, and as there could be no work more beautiful and bold, that someone was an artist.

What conspired to make me think and write in bygone modes that even now awaken stale regret tinged with fresh ire? My resentment and sense of drama were alive and unhealthy; and as for their conspirators, one was a dream, another was a storm. A third was a certain dearth.

Since Harvard I had suffered not a single worthy notion, nope. My thoughts were mundane and melancholy, often running in circles like certain shredder blades. Everything seemed superfluous, a way to kill time while I waited for who knows what. Was it that I'd outgrown the staid old scholarly forms? I don't think so. I tried my hand at fiction. You'd think I'd be good at it since I'm quite a character. But it got depressing. The drought played havoc with my nerves.

It was a relief when the ultimate memoranda of Aetna Simmons came along. Of course from her point of view I might've ruined everything. She wanted to pass out of the world, not to be immortalized as an accidental maestro of a literary form. But that ceased to concern me as other, dire matters took its place.

Which brings me to my dream. One night when my hypothesis was young, I dreamed about the last written words of Aetna Simmons.

I'm in a big American bookstore. I hunt for books with my name on the spine.

For the record, in the recurring-nightmare version of this dream, I don't find what I'm looking for. Not even in *Bargain Books*. I panic and run around because there's a giant shadow chasing me and laughing. I look for a place to curl up with my arms over my head. But I can't find that either.

That's not what happens this time. There's still a giant shadow chasing me and laughing. I'm still panicking and running around. And there still aren't any books with my name on the spine. But this time, frantic for a hiding place, I happen to dash behind *Noteworthy Paperbacks*.

All the Noteworthy books are black. No writing on the covers, no title, no author, nothing. Just this sort of lacquer that makes the books seem like pools of dark water.

I'm terrified of these Noteworthy books. I figure it's because I don't know what they are; I don't know what I'd have to do to make them *my* Noteworthy books. I'm expecting semicircles to show up in the pools, and they'll rise and become scales and spikes and the sinuous horned neck of a *ryuu*.

Maybe I only think that because each black book has a pair of built-in bookmarks, ribbons that start out red but change color, wriggling and flowing like the tentacles around the jaws of the sea-dragon. The very sea-dragon who attacked that diver in the old legend because she'd stolen the magic antidote for the agony of grief. Fleeing the *ryuu*, the *ama* slashed her breast open and hid the antidote inside it. I don't know who the nepenthe belonged to in the first place, the *ryuu* or the *ama*. And I think the latter died of self-inflicted slashes. And this isn't really how the legend goes, it's just how I dreamed it. But anyway, I'm convinced the bookmarks are sidewhiskers of a *ryuu* rising out of each black book which is really a shard of ocean. I'm about to freak out and run away.

But suddenly I know something else. I know, as I know now that I'm typing with my own two hands, that in those black books are the final written words of Aetna Simmons. And I'm no longer afraid.

I'm about to pick up one of them. I reach for a wet, oily spine. But there's someone behind me. I turn, ready to bolt, expecting the gigantic giggling shadow ready to eat me—

But it's Masami. Expressionless in a gray business suit. I debate running away. And maybe I'm about to. But she holds out her hand to me. She gives me a feather. Long as my arm and of a shimmering, uncertain, silverish color.

When I wake up, I feel like wasted time and space.

Which brings me to the storm. The ocean punished the beach. Longtails darted to their cliffside holes. Casurinas trembled. Heavy clouds sapped the colors from the flowers. People stocked up on tarpaulins and candles. The wind hurled itself at battened shutters like a desperate prisoner. Swells overwhelmed the wall of reefs around our island-archipelago, flooded the volcanic crater in which Bermuda glimmers like the wick of a candle. Surfers grabbed their boards and threw themselves at the feet of doom.

It shouldn't have been surprising that Martin canceled his trip. He'd postponed it once already. First it had to do with work, then the storm brought a puff of wind. Next thing we know, Martin's refusing to get on the plane. I wondered if he was toying with us, but Martin's not that subtle. I asked Nabi if he was scared of the Bermuda Triangle.

She said, "Go head, bye, get crackin."

Martin hung around about two weeks in which resentment turned me into a curmudgeon. Me: smart, sleek, spicy, life of the party, cavorting in riotous luxury beside the sea. My sublime ocean view looked like a bad drawing, my Miró and all my books became vapid. As I wandered my exclusive wasteland of empty hours, the last words in a vanished life became my days and nights.

I told Nabi I'd written an essay. Acegirl got all excited. "See? Told you it wasn't gonna last, didn't I tell you? You just stick with it, you beautiful genius, you."

Another night, another club, another idgit. Tony heard me loud and clear as I read the usual fine print. *What you are about to ingest/inject/inhale is a one-hundred-percent unique designer product that is unavailable anywhere else in the world. Resales and every other form of cost-carrying redistribution are nonpermissible. Cashier's checks, corporate checks, personal checks, credit cards, debit cards, gift cards, bitcoin, Wells Fargo, PayPal, Apple Pay, Google Pay, and whatever other idiotic schemes they come up with that aren't real money are unacceptable forms of payment. These are non-negotiable terms. Any violation thereof will result in the immediate termination of our relationship and, should violations continue, legal ramifications in which I will inevitably hold the upper hand. Please acknowledge your understanding of the terms and conditions at this time.*

I got to the club, headed for the bar, bestowed a shoulder-clap on a client who was deep in conversation and made a decent job of acting surprised. Fancy meeting you here, thrilling twist of fate. I pretended to be astounded, though he'd given me a small mountain of money that morning. We shook hands. I slipped him a black envelope the size of a local postage stamp. And he asked if it was true, was my father running for Parliament?

"Truth is, I hadn't noticed," I said.

The client, whose pupils were already negligible, took this as a terrific joke. Which it was, all things considered. That man was so parenthetical to my upbringing a half-decent editor would've gone ahead and struck him out.

I said, "Best make sure my passport's up to date, I guess." Another shoulder-clap and the dazzling grin of yours truly won roars

15

of laughter from the client and his interlocutor, the latter being a well-to-do individual who is himself in government and who later that night became another client.

Having acquainted him with Hallelujah, I'm dutifully nodding at some drawn-out tale of his, got the charm turned up to eleven, when Tony puts his arm around me like he owns me.

"Hey, yeah, Tony Trent, Paragon Re, how are you, if I could borrow my friend here for a just a second, have him right back to you in a jiffy, thanks."

Fast talker, fast everything. American expat. He was wining and dining the CFO from Paragon's Hartford office. I introduced myself as a partner in Bermuda's first CSDS-accredited, NAID-certified, MWMA-recommended, AAA document destruction company. I bragged that Bull's Head Shreds is the first Bermudian destruction company whose procedures have been formally acknowledged as FISMA-, FACTA-, and HIPAA-compliant, prepared to manage documents of top-level clearance. With an auditable, unbreakable, closed-loop chain of custody (CoC) that guarantees every assignment an internationally recognized Certificate of Destruction (CoD), we handle destructive security for the Bermuda government and corporate clients of all sizes, local and overseas, whom we serve with incontestable discretion. And you know, we don't just shred, we disintegrate.

"Empyreal!" said Tony, styling it as an expression of awe. "You must show Bill your MG. He's a collector."

"Cool runnings, mon!" said Bill.

I said, "Bermuda, not Jamaica. And Jamaicans don't talk like that."

"No problem, mon!"

Bill had a Dark 'n' Stormy in his hand. Tony looked for a manhole to crawl into.

"Now *that's* a piece of history!" said Bill.

My MG. That's where I named my price, Bill failed to bat an eye, and I delivered the fine print. Brand new client, I'd never have forgotten, and Tony was right there, watching his meal ticket fondle my car. Night after night I'm putting up with this shit. Bill slavered as he gave me four grand, and I gave him a blue jewelry box. The box had ten pills in it. Like small, exquisite pearls.

It comes with a spiel. I have a stance to go with the spiel. It's a stance like I'm conducting a minuet, and the clichés work every time. "Empyreal is a thousand times more luxurious than the most perfect wine. It's nuanced, subtle, puissant, and undeniable like the perfect woman. An exclusive experience which only the most discerning connoisseur can appreciate. Gentlemen, behold a glimpse of a higher plane, an elevated perspective where all the world is ripe."

Those idiots had no idea what I was on about. They nodded anyway. It's a tendency among my clients to agree with everything I say. This can be annoying though of course it's convenient. And opportunities for florid prose are rare these days.

"Now, what you tell yourself is up to you, but I cannot exaggerate. Empyreal is nothing less than pure perfection, which, being perfect, offers one question alone. Are you ready?"

Tony was like a bobblehead. Idgit made a purchase just for himself.

According to her obit, which included her final sendoff's date and time, Mrs. Trimm belonged to St. Peter's Church in St. George's. Her family chose St. John's for her funeral. This may have had to do with its central location in Pembroke, its proximity to the Anglican cemetery, or the parking lot out back, all of which St. Peter has to do without.

The lot overflowed. I squeezed my MG into a line of cars on the side of the road, hugging the cemetery wall. Inside I found a spot near the back with a pair of older ladies. We greeted each other softly and tried to look somber.

The ladies were in dark dresses with elaborate hats. They chattered in stage whispers, even giggled some. Understandable if Myrtle Trimm was anything like my relatives. And these ladies weren't necessarily relatives. Maybe they'd shared a seat with Mrs. Trimm on the ferry. Maybe they went to the same post office. Perhaps they were just in the neighborhood, starved for entertainment. For what reasonable purpose was I at that funeral?

The ladies looked around. One said, "Girl, if there's any of us here who's half as healthy as Miz Myrtle, we should all be dead."

"Got dat right. Goes to show, innit. De Lord says it's ya time, it's ya time."

I think I felt a bit like people who make pilgrimage to Stonehenge after reading Thomas Hardy, wondering what was in his writing besides writing. When Aetna Simmons disappeared, only one person showed a smidgen of concern, penurious though it may have been; one person willing to vouch that the woman ever existed. One note out of ten had a specific addressee.

The *Gazette*'s early reports on Aetna's disappearance mentioned Mrs. Trimm by name. Anonymity's barely more than a witticism around here in any case. The ladies in my pew speculated that the sudden loss of her tenant, her income's subsequent nosedive, the press and the police and all the strain were just too much for poor Myrtle. And as the organ began to play, one old biddy peeked around my chest and wiggled her fingers.

"Look, it's Clara. How are you, sweetie?"

I don't know why I looked. Maybe it's an instinct built into human genes, left over from the days when we hunted and were hunted in small herds on the savanna. All we had were our bare hands and inborn sense of community; one head turns, everyone turns, could be a saber-toothed tiger lurking in the grass.

Clara was more buffalo than tiger. But the other people. The man and the woman who slipped behind her as she stopped to chat with the old biddies. Panic sent a heat wave through my face.

They made their way to the front. The tall, sleek, black man was Barrington Caines. He's negligible.

But the tiny Japanese woman permitting Barrington to clear her path to the front of the church. She was bewitching even in her advanced years and severe trouser suit. All the men in her chosen pew stood as she passed. Barrington remained standing until she sat down.

Masami Okada-Caines. No mere tiger but a dragon. Her claws are dipped in platinum, her diamond-wrought fangs infused with deadly venom.

They didn't acknowledge me. They must've seen my car. Or maybe they forgot I have one. My hand kept running through my hair, a compulsion to make sure my face was hidden. The dragon has *oni* coursing through her veins. I was sure she'd turn and look. What the fuck were those two doing at a crazy old biddy's funeral? Who the hell was Myrtle Trimm?

The corpse gliding by. A shriveled twig inside a coffin. The face: unfamiliar, as it should be. The first I heard of her was from Javon. It was the first, I'm sure of it, but then why should those two give a damn? Discomposed, I almost missed the main event.

From what Aetna Simmons wrote, I'd deduced that Mrs. Trimm had an estranged daughter or sister, possibly living overseas. I was right: she had a daughter. The minister announced that he'd personally deliver a special tribute written by Myrtle's beloved Doreen, who I assumed was too broken up to do it herself. Masami glanced at her watch.

The plan was to sit through the service, get a sense of the atmosphere that Mrs. Trimm had left behind. Then hang around, mingle, drop a few questions. But I couldn't let the dragon catch my scent. Better leave now, I thought, get up, feign an attack of sobbing, but silent, silent, get the car—

I froze. In horror, I think, and anger. I wanted to leave the church with a whole lot of noise. I wanted my business phone to ring. Why not shove off from the pew with a clatter and a curse, begin my conversation before I reached the door? Let them turn, those two down in front, let them look and see my back.

I slunk away without a sound. No one noticed. My new plan was to get stoned and see what happened. I was on my way home to do just that when my phone rang. The other phone. Martin had finally gone to New York.

This is the routine. On Mondays, Nabi's husband goes to London or New York on business. The car stays at the airport until he comes back, Wednesday or Thursday night. Because Bermy is a geological dust mote, our laws about cars are like Chinese laws about babies. So Nabi, managing partner of Bull's Head Shreds, takes the ferry to work and lets me take her home.

This time it went like this. She didn't know I'd been to a funeral, so when she called she said she was sorry to interrupt my work. Two shredding specialists and a driver called in sick, she said; there was slack to be picked up, she'd just found out some lawyers wanted us for a big job as they prepared to move their offices, so it'd be great if I could come and spend the afternoon.

19

I said, "I miss you too."

I drove into the city, and on striding through the front door at Bull's Head Shreds I found myself inside an everything-proof plexiglass cube. Wayneesha, the receptionist, recognized me from her desk beyond the glass and activated a high-tech keycard reader, giving me the go-ahead to flash my high-tech keycard at Door #2. Having cleared Door #2, I chatted with Wayneesha, Wayneesha buzzed Nabi, Nabi buzzed me through Door #3. Behind Door #3 was a little chunk of hallway, Door #4 leading into Nabi's office, Door #5 to the secure server room, and Door #6.

Door #6. The heart, the stomach, and the guts of Bull's Head Shreds. Our Maximum Security (Level 6, thank you) Warehouse where a shredder big enough for a family of *Homo sapiens sapiens* to live in turned paper into dust.

Nabi saw me in the hallway from her three-doored whatever-proof transparent-plexiglass office. She also saw into the break room and everything in Max Sec. To get between the break room and the warehouse, people had to walk through Nabi's office. I don't know how she could stand it. Cameras were everywhere.

"Dr. Caines, I thought next year's Christmas gonna get here before you." Her voice sang out through the intercom in one of her pellucid and impenetrable walls.

"Muses live to be obeyed, Mrs. Furbert."

"Is that right? Well, so do I. Reinforcements for you, Bryan." She poked a button. Max Sec supervisor poked in turn from the inside. Door #6 popped open with a wail as of a giant alarm clock.

I bro-fisted Bryan, grabbed coveralls, safety goggles, dust mask, construction-worker earmuffs, and the barcode-scanning thing that once more read my keycard. Assigned the drop-off pile, I grabbed a file box delivered by some walk-in. Scanned the barcode that Wayneesha'd pasted to the box, which the scanner and our wireless network logged into my record, adding me to the box's Chain of Custody. I upended the box on the sloping conveyor belt that lapped everything up into the giant shredder's multi-maws.

All the while and none too softly in the background—cool and faintly whitened with the HEPA-filtered dust of the no-longer-remembered—a forklift fitted with a networked computer electronically unlocked the secure storage bins we provided to our customers, raised the bins like sacred offerings, and emptied them onto that same conveyor belt to be pulverized at something like ten thousand pounds an hour.

Credit card receipts, doodles, and some accounting firm's eight-inch binders full of mathematical arcana all hacked up together into paper chum. The shredder excreted it in indistinguishable minute particles, which the same machine gathered up and packed together into bales. The bales of nothing would go forth over the ocean to the Land of Milk and Honey to be reformed and sold as new, unmarred paper. Nabi says I shouldn't say "Land of Milk and Honey" in reference to the USA.

My purpose was to make sure no rotten carrots, flat tires, or dead babies came out of the drop-off boxes. They never did. I looked at used-up papers climbing the conveyor belt. I was grumpy and uneasy. Hadn't seen head or tail of Mrs. Nabilah Furbert in weeks, thanks to Martin and that stupid storm; hadn't been to work in a little while myself, sort of thanks to Aetna but really out of a desire to make my absence keenly felt. Whenever something like that happened, I tried to get ready for the worst and knew I wasn't ready.

On top of that, sightings of Masami and Barrington have never been good for my nerves. Why would Masami interrupt a money-making day for an old lady? And not just any old lady, a dead one and a stingy one who whined to the cops about a single month's rent. Myrtle just didn't fit the profile of the uncommon investor who gets Caines Asset Management to kowtow.

Could be political. Barrington had the look of the campaign about him. Then again, he never leaves home without that look. Personal, then? Another all-new plot to ruin my life? A connection buried so deep in my unconscious that I acted on it without knowing? Or a coincidence?

Ludicrous. Masami would rather lose a limb on purpose than accidentally appear to let a hair slip out of place.

I might as well indulge myself. Remembrance may be all I have left. In the car, Nabi said, real soft, "What is it, Dr. Caines?"

21

I didn't want to say anything. But at the traffic light on Dundonald, she said it again.

"What's wrong, baby?"

Her hand on my knee. And it seemed like a thousand years since I'd listened to her voice.

"Ran into my parents." I sounded like a kid with a scraped elbow.

Traffic light on Spurling Hill. She touched my cheek. Didn't make me say anything else. There's nothing she doesn't know, anyway, concerning that particular debacle. Nothing she doesn't know about anything authentic. We have only to look and we're defrosted. Down to the nuclei that we conceal from others behind titanium doors with umpteen foolproof locks.

Doors, locks, and little colored stones liquefied and diffused at the foot of Spurling Hill. It was painful, she seemed about to cry, I caught her hand and we both knew—two weeks without each other had damaged both of us.

We drove along South Shore. Bright blue sky, late-summer breeze. Bermuda's is an untamed beauty, disordered and sundry, off-the-cuff and uncontainable. Pink oleanders and orange hibiscus share the curb with cherries in red, yellow, and green, pink and purple ice plant, blue bells, match-me-can splashed with red and burgundy. Casurinas reach for leathery bay grapes, thick-leaved rubber trees, and royal poincianas, those vast trees with hoards of bright red flowers. Those to the south bow to the wind coming in over the ocean. Their trunks bend over the road, branches reach for their companions on the opposite side. The northward trees grow tall to meet the embrace of the southern, and the road becomes a tunnel. Sunlight sprinkles the cars like tears of longing from the branches. Beyond the trees, sandy beaches flush rosy with their love for the mercurial ocean. An ocean so clear I could see right to the bottom from the road. Monday through Wednesday or half of Thursday, everything was exquisite.

By the time we reached Southampton, we were almost calm, stroking each other's fingers. Nabi was herself again.

I should say one of her selves. I find their dynamic rather telling.

"You know, I think there's something going on with Wayneesha, I don't know what, but I'll find out. Baby, I'm sorry, I know you're writing, but with three people out sick I really need you to come in tomorrow—"

"Didn't I tell you I'd flatten out the world for you?"

"Yeah, go head. Get me a puppy I can keep at your place."

"What? No."

"I want a Bichon Frise. Martin's allergic."

"No."

"See what I mean? Giant rolling pin's heftier than it looks, innit." She has a delightful laugh.

Chatting again, she barely stops for breath; she's researching a hard drive shredder, a super-powered shredder that disintegrates computer drives as if they're paper; it's the latest thing; the thing is, it's expensive—like she doesn't want to tell me while I'm driving expensive—but even though paper documentation is still crucial, nowadays it's all about digital documentation too; and the NAID says nothing is more vulnerable than digital information in its end-of-life phase—and then her phone rings.

She went quiet when she answered.

"Hi honey. Yes. Okay. Okay." Long pauses.

This was the other Nabi. Gleaming and untouchable in a plexi-glass box.

She hung up. "Martin. Left one of his iPads home, wants me forward this and that. I didn't even know the man's got more than one iPad. Mercy. What was I saying? Oh, right."

And she was back. My Nabi was back, and I was triumphant. *He had no idea there was a Nabi who poured her heart out to me and told him nothing.* We went up to my flat.

"Kenji," she said against my chest.

I was underwater. The water was buoying me up as water does. When I broke the surface my lungs would fly open, grab the air, Nabi was the air, and my empty chest would squeeze—but it had been two weeks; what might she have decided in two weeks? My blood was thrumming in my ears; my arms were like crinoline around her, hesitant and stiff, caught between longing and fear.

Nabi said, "Long two weeks."

Luring me up as air does. And the sunshine at the surface.

"Sorry I didn't call back that time. It wasn't safe," she said.

She left her shoes on the mat. Glance at me over her shoulder, where I was still on my own threshold. That glance, I know it well. I see it all the time in the empty spaces in my days. When it comes in memory, it stings. But in person it's a wave big enough to throw me at the shore. I scooped up Nabi in my arms, we did the whirligig thing, her laughter bounced high and wild around the room.

That glance is reserved for just two people. It's a question, it's unspoken doubt. Even when she's wrapped in silk and pearls, ready for a night of stars and virgin cocktails, sometimes that glance slips through. Course I've never actually seen Mrs. Furbert all dolled up for a benefit or gala even though, if there is one going on, you can be sure she'll be there. I did get to see her just before she got married. Nabi was holding the flowers, the end of her train was fastened to her wrist, and her parents were in the room. In the back of the church. So I could only touch her hand. An encouraging, brotherly, damning-it-all squeeze. And that glance became a look of horror.

That night I thought I'd never get out of bed again. And, execrable dolt, I couldn't fathom why I'd think such an outrageous thing.

We ran out to *Ethelberta*, my rascal blue twin-engined Scout, which I'd really bought for Nabi although neither of us was ready to admit it at the time. I think Nabi thinks she's a bit afraid of the Atlantic deep, and maybe she is a little. Everyone should be a little. When the ocean decides to take us, it'll take us without warning. More inexorable than the density that buoys us up are the currents that will surely drag us down, such things answering to nothing but the moon.

But once we cleared Dockyard, I'd offer Nabi *Ethelberta*'s helm, and Nabi would accept. It made her laugh to see me put my feet up on the waterproof blue cushions in the pointy end. I'd sit facing the square end so I could see her laughing, beaming brighter than the sun-sparks in the water. We never knew where she'd take us. Some minikin dwarf island, a nursery for sea-things of all colors? A secret sliver of cove between Bermuda's cliffs? Challenger seamount where the humpbacks hold their concerts or the wreck of the *Vixen* where grand shoals of silver fishes would sweep and surge around us, of one body with the water?

"Turtle!" said Nabi. I turned too slow as usual, the little yellow head slipping below. She could've chosen any of those half-wild places, and on a Monday evening none but turtles would've seen us. Would've been another story on a Saturday, but we almost never had a Saturday.

We stayed away from populated beaches. Only by a miracle would we not have been recognized: this is Bermuda. We almost never dropped the anchor, never approached other boats. We waved exuberant hellos to strangers at a distance just like everybody, couldn't help ourselves; standoffishness would've made us stand out anyway. When we approached the marina, Nabi buried her head in a floppy hat with a huge brim. I'm an embarrassment, you see. Being in my company is an insult and embarrassment. Don't mind me, I never remarked on this, we never discussed the undercover shit, just did it.

That day the briny blue was a rich, royal color and the relentless rippling of millions of little wavelets with dark undersides murmuring of mysteries below. Nabi took us out to sea, way out past the wreck of the *Cristobal Colomb*, where about seventy feet of water was suddenly six thousand feet deep, something like that. I wondered which way she would aim the pointy end before she yanked the power. We always kept Bermuda hazily in view so we'd know where to find it. Nabi liked to turn us so it was in front, a slim but solid edge on the water. I would've put the island at *Ethelberta*'s back, rendering our horizon a vast open question.

We didn't need the drama of a color-changing sky. We didn't need a whole sun's worth of colors. Nor the adventure of waves shattering on reefs, nor dolphins and blue-finned flying fishes. Just the boat, the open, and the crew of the *Ethelberta*, yes, that would be us. Nabi spun the wheel, cut the engines. Our home lay before us, De Rock dead ahead and gray, giving up its multihues to distance. We ate Chinese takeout while Nabi filled in those lost weeks. Every hymn she'd sung, every customer she'd shredded for, the temporary traffic light on Harbour Road, Discount Day at Gorham's where she'd bought a new convection oven. I bathed in words like *girt big boxes* and *Cuisinart* borne like bubbles on her mellifluous voice. And then we didn't need words anymore.

Nabi made an armchair out of me, her shoulder underneath my

chin. We listened to the water buoying the boat and easing by us without knowing us. We watched the ocean moving but not changing, restive repose. And you know something? You have no notion how vital that moment was. To remember life is possible without needing to sleep through it. To be reminded rationality is possible without despair or dismay. I didn't want to move, but my breath moved. And Nabi turned. I looked at her with gratitude and trusted that she'd hear it, and she did. She kissed it softly back to me. The ocean held us suspended, aloft.

Sometime, something too distant to see, the moon or a mega cruise ship passing far away, set the *Ethelberta* rocking. It happened with us too often: some mild external thing reminding one of us our time was stolen. This time I think it was me. It was usually me. I turned Nabi around, we started kissing exigently—till somewhere in the tacit din of my anxiety she discerned that this was a brimover of fear, and we didn't want to love that way, out of fear.

She said, "Wait, Kenji. We're here now, baby." She tipped my head onto her shoulder.

You don't appreciate this quieting, you don't understand it. Since it wasn't an illusion, we had to hold it carefully. Like holding a butterfly. Just as rare. Just as chancy and necessary.

You're wrong if you think we were all serenity all the time. That kind of calm isn't like me.

How I wish it was. But it was fugitive, and returning to my normal was a horrendous blow. I lived on a roller coaster. Every time Nabi sent me soaring to the top, I never knew if the ride down was a temporary dip or the beginning of a flying leap off the rails. In practical terms, this meant every time I thought Nabi was about to speak, my heart slipped out of position. Peezed over to the right and stuck in that place in my neck where the air's supposed to come in.

This wasn't a feel-good feeling. It was scary. It was because I never knew if she'd whisper something nice, send me cross de pond to buy some pens, or pull all the turtles out from underneath the world. Imagine: Martin calls, her voice does that soft thing, then she hangs up. Then what? Pick up where we left off? Or *turn around, baby, this in't working, I gotta go home. For real this time.* As in forever.

And it wasn't just when Martin called. Every time Nabi began to make a word, I had to wonder if it would be a word for *never again*. Because there's never a good time for such a word, it can happen anytime. Email, SMS, on the phone, or in my arms. I was living on the edge of a precipice with one foot hanging off all the time. At the same time, what can I say? I could listen to Nabi talk accounts and hard drive shredders till the ocean swallows up the cliffs. Listening for her voice was the very definition of hope. So what I mean is, it's not like I wanted to back away, not like I even could. I couldn't bring myself to think my toehold on the edge counted for nothing. And since it was just a toehold, I didn't dare move a muscle.

Maybe dread and hope are almost the same thing. Like the distance between on-the-edge and over-the-edge is almost negligible but not really. So being with Nabi was bliss and anguish. Every sound she made was a terror and a treasure. I almost never breathed evenly. That's something Nabi didn't know.

❧

TO WHOM IT MAY CONCERN:

This is the only productive thing I've ever done: finish up
the fading that began when I was born, pushing change to
the limit of its power over me. Until I'm dead, my body is
capable of just a few predetermined alterations. To be
frank, it's boring and distasteful. Possibility will open up
its arms to me only once my heart stops beating.

I'm not talking about an afterlife. I mean whether I'll be
fish food or compost, I don't know, that's up to you. From
my standpoint, this means my final change is entirely
contingent, necessarily so. It's out of my hands.
Nonetheless, after the change, regardless of specifics, I
will be life instead of waste. Life for living things that
know better than we do.

You have my permission to sell everything if you feel like
it. The proceeds you may give to anyone except the
government and the Salvation Army.

Thank you for helping me take advantage of this
once-in-a-lifetime opportunity.

AS2.

White copy paper creased trifold like a business letter. "Everything
and every world *is* without reason, and is thereby capable of actually
becoming otherwise without reason" (Meillassoux).

I left a printout of my essay on the nightstand on Nabi's side. I woke to find her snuggling against me, reading. She drew my limbs around her like I was a giant shawl.

Waking up with Nabi. Nabi is worth waking for. Waking with Nabi is real waking.

"*Aetna Simmons' Final Words: Suicide and Suicide Notes as Works of Art.* Baby, you think that stuff is art?"

I explained about the audience, creativity, French guy who said that thing about something. During the night we had loved with diuturnity and our emotions all out of hand. Now my brain was full of fuzz. Her body brushed me where I can't be brushed and think properly. She looked dubious, but she read several pages over.

"Why'd she write ten of them?"

I mumbled about a tactile-performative statement.

"So it's art because there's ten of them."

Does the Aesthetic Hypothesis boil down to this? I decided to worry about that another time. When Nabi spoke again, there was something in her voice.

"You're saying her death is like the Mona Lisa. Like a Britney Spears song."

"No, not clichéd. The opposite."

"Like that book about the dinosaur who found a place where books can walk around like spiders?"

"Well, no."

"You said that book was the greatest, most original story you ever read."

"Well, yeah, *nikkou,* but—"

"So, best-case scenario, this woman's suicide is like a story of a dinosaur in a place where one-eyed goblin-thingys build underground libraries. Both great art, right?"

"There's more to it than that."

"Of course there is, sweet genius. But not the way you think. Baby, I don't know about this project, it's too weird."

I started to argue, but I wasn't well equipped; it was easy for her to hush me, cuddle me against the pillows, whisper, "It's not good for you."

She didn't mean my first good idea since *T. rex* ruled the planet was no good. I didn't reply. Nabi smoothed my brow and said, "I didn't mean it like that, baby. Just try a different subject. I mean, ten suicide notes? Whatever Aetna Simmons wanted to achieve, don't you think we're a little too sane to understand? I'm kidding, baby, don't look at me like that. What can anybody say? What happened to her is sad and creepy, and that's it. Come with me into town, give your brain an airing-out. After that, come back, sit down, and you'll come up with something else."

She kissed me before I could remark on the flaws in her reasoning.

I passed the day on bin watch. It involved loading forklifts, watching colored lights turn on, and not seeing or touching the documents inside the heavy-duty plastic bins. We have two trucks that take the bins to customers and pick them up. The whole time they're with the customers, the bins stay locked. They have narrow mouths like stingrays'; they can slurp just a couple pages at a time. Overall tamper-proof. When the bins come back to us, only the keycard-protected forklifts in Max Sec can unlock them. And that happens only when the forklifts raise the bins up high above our reach in the instant before turning them upside down, dumping their contents in the dumper that conveys them to the conveyor that damns them to their doom.

At lunchtime we previewed our first TV ad. Still photographs of the Bermuda Day Parade with idgits in backward baseball caps throwing confetti. Live action now: some kid picks up a piece of the confetti, shows it to his momma, who sees that it's a piece of someone's horizontally strip-shredded financial record. "This is somebody's financial record!" she exclaims. Only idgits strip-shred horizontally. Only the uninformed strip-shred at all. Momma looks shocked. She shows the confetti to her acegirl, who stands next to her; acegirl shows it to her husband, who looks bamboozled at the sky; and the woman next to him peeks at the tiny strip of paper over his shoulder.

Kid addresses camera. "Chingas, people! This is just fullish! Don't let this happen to you. Let the pros [pron., *de pröse*] deal wif it. Call Bull's Head Shreds. It's thur *job* [heavy diphthong] to keep you and ya customers secure. And they recycle everything [*arryding*]. You ask

30

me [pron., *ax*], it's a no-brainer. Bull's Head Shreds got you covered."
The screen fills with our logo and contact information.

It's not bad. For Bermuda. Probably as good as we'll get. It really
happened too, only it was New York, not Bermuda, and the confetti
was made from police records. I mention it because strip-shredded
confetti is a worthy analogue for the mess I've made of my existence.

I began to hate *Aetna Simmons' Final Words: Suicide and Suicide Notes
as Works of Art.* It was missing something. Some days, I saw this as
a challenge. Assured of my prowess as a virtuoso of research and
prose (PhD), reassured by the happenstance that Nabi would be over
in the evening, I thought on such days, *Lad, with thy dazzling quill thou
wilt illuminate the cave of life and death and make record of thine insights, and
journals everywhere will covet thine insights and elevate them on golden wings.*

Other days, especially weekends, the futility of things was pungent
and disgraceful. I despised all my clients and loathed my computer,
indifferent even to my automotive pride and joy. I needed medication to cope with the bleakness and the pressure of the pointlessness
of work.

We're too sane to understand, Nabi said. When it comes to suicide,
we are *a priori* incapable of saying anything beyond the obvious. She
might've hit on something there. Even though she only has an AD
from the College. In my research I came upon an author (an Austrian
who killed himself with sleeping pills, thereby securing his credibility
on the matter) who wrote that suicidal reasoning is beyond the reach
of every form of language. This is because language—consisting
selectively of the meanings, arrangements, and deployments of
words—works the way it does on the assumption that the reason
people speak to one another is *survival.* We think, communicate, and
give a damn just because we want to live. Life is the goal of all goals.
We desire it above all else. Unless of course we don't.

Then everything turns upside down. Not in the sense of an upended roller coaster that keeps everything intact in compliance with
the latest safety regulations but in the sense of an inverted fish tank
without a roof. Everything shatters into an unintelligible mess. Every
condition of being, like weightlessness and oxygen, spills out from
underneath the world. Living becomes impossible, so communication

31

is impossible. Words become impossible. The being for whom living is impossible, the suicidal intellect, therefore cannot be narrated or explained.

If this is correct, then a true interpretation of Aetna Simmons' writings is impossible, and my project was futile from the start. Maybe I knew that, just never thought about it. Or I kept on because I knew.

I sat in my leather chair by my Tiffany lamp at my seriously antique rolltop desk. Here in my private study, as in my living room, books govern the walls on custom-built, floor-to-ceiling cedar shelving complete with rolling ladders. The south-facing walls are windows bringing me the evanescent sea, shaggy casurina tops, and the salty breezes carving holes in the cliffs.

I googled *Aetna Simmons*. I learned there are six urologists in Simmons Place, Tennessee, who accept Aetna Health Insurance. I tried *Bermuda Aetna Simmons*. I found the earliest news stories on her disappearance. *Ms. Simmons is reported as having "dark" features and no distinguishing body marks.*

When the police lost interest, so did everybody else. She wasn't on Facebook, wasn't in the phone book. Good thing I have contacts. Lawyers, doctors, MPs, VPs, CEOs, bank people, church people, tech people, smart people who realize it's in their best interest to do what I say without asking questions. HSBC even has a guy I can speak to in Japanese. He and I comprise about fifty percent of Bermuda's Japanese-speaking population, so confidentiality isn't an issue. I texted the guy. He never knew Aetna Simmons. But he found her abandoned bank account in his computer. *SIMMONS AETNA P.*

On an irregular basis, Aetna received transfers from some numbered US dollar accounts in Grand Cayman and made top-ups to a local prepaid cellphone. She hadn't done either in some time. Her last electronic payout was to BELCO, her final light bill shockingly low at $148.57. Three days later, she spent $42.52 at Supermart, leaving behind a balance of about two Gs in her account and a supermarket's worth of people who didn't recognize her name. Another week or so, and Mrs. Trimm was griping to Inspector Saltus.

But if Aetna had time to settle up with BELCO and buy groceries, why didn't she make a down payment on her last month's rent? Some token payout might've discouraged Mrs. Trimm from so expeditiously raising the alarm over her $4,800.

$4,800 a month. In St. George's. That cottage must've been more like a townhouse: two bedrooms and den, I thought, renovated with amenities and probably a view, which according to her almost non-existent money trail Aetna almost never left until she left forever. Completely boring person, said the HSBC guy, never even went out to dinner. Unless of course she had accounts at other banks.

But my contacts at Clarien and Butterfield came up empty. She must've had money abroad, I thought, otherwise she'd never have taken that cottage. Do the math. The incoming transfers were of inconsistent amounts that approximated ten grand each. She got six such transfers every year on an irregular schedule with dry spells in between that sometimes went on for months. Perhaps the Cayman accounts were her own.

In my flat jam-packed with silence, I came upon an intriguing conclusion: Aetna's income was like mine. That's why she kept it hidden, bouncing between islands.

Consultant, she wrote. It's really not so farfetched. Consider the pharmaceutical broker, who's as much of a psychologist, marriage counselor, legal aide, and financial consultant as he is a therapist of another kind.

That put a new spin on things. Successful criminals must be consummate pretenders.

Take AS2. Aetna creates the impression she's got everything covered. She wants readers to have no doubts about her sanity. If living is *boring and distasteful*, here is someone who respectfully returns her ticket. Far from resentful, she looks forward to turning her back on everything. No, really. What happens to her next could be anything at all and she'll have no say in the matter. What could be more intellectually stimulating? She even seems to anticipate some vague form of physical pleasure from the transition into a corpse.

You could say AS2 is a misguided attempt at what they call a First Form Suicide Note. But you'd be wrong. AS2 does intimate isolation, hint at a lifetime of failure, and suggest Aetna's failures weren't entirely her fault, blaming instead the inexorability of *change*. All this is typical in a First Form note. However, where are the feelings of isolation? Does she just forget to beg for forgiveness? She doesn't even mention any specific problems. None of these omissions are typical. And *change* is every problem, not a specific problem. In AS2, the *final change* is also the solution. Clearly some confusion here.

It boils down to this. At this point, Aetna can't admit dead equals gone. Your-corpse-*qua*-fish-food is nonequivalent to you-*qua*-you until you unequivocally change the definition of *you* from, e.g., *brilliant but unappreciated scholar and love artist with a connoisseur's tastes* to *nothing*, because fish food isn't anything except a means of energizing fish, and the existence of fish can't lay claim to any more of a point than your existence can. Or mine, for that matter.

But Aetna isn't ready for that kind of humility. That Salvation Army crack like she thinks no one's going to care; it excuses her self-pity while at the same time she assumes a swarm of buzzards around everything she has, and it's a matter of pride, giving her corpse to the bugs instead. Scrambling for self-worth, she homes in on death like a coke fiend with her nose in a packet of Splenda.

And yet AS2 displays a rare sensitivity. Metaphysical, ecological, almost too philosophical for a genuine suicide note.

That's probably because it isn't a genuine suicide note. What's a suicide note but a promise?

Don't tell me you don't know anyone who's made promises they never meant to keep. Maybe they wanted to mean it, but they don't have it in them. It might require something too formidable for them to wrap their minds around, in which case all the best intentions in the world wouldn't add up to sincerity. AS2 might be this way. Or it could be a baldfaced sham. In terms of suicidal authenticity, a few among the Ten are questionable.

Where'd I learn the difference between a fake suicide note and a truthful one? Google. Where else? Suicidologists have spent decades on this question. Their best-known experiments compared "real" suicide notes, written by people who actually ended their own lives, with three kinds of "fake" note. Fakes included notes by "non-completers" who threatened suicide but never went through with

34

it, notes by "attempters" who tried to get the job done but wound up botching it, and notes written at the experimenters' request by nonsuicidal volunteers.

The studies concluded that both genuine and false note writers dole out full helpings of blame and guilt as they try to rationalize their decision to die. The sincere and uncommitted both look forward to death as some kind of release. But real suicide notes howl with anger and despair; desperation pours from them as from open wounds. They paint the suicidal plunge in hopeless and defiant smears. Fake notes may be emotional, but they describe the decision to die as a practical choice. Quick fix for financial woes, legal troubles, or failure and stagnation, as in AS2. Fakes shy away from the word *death*, preferring implications (AS2: *once-in-a-lifetime opportunity*). Real notes say it like they mean it because they really do.

These distinctions are stylistic. They're subjective. Unreliable. According to suicidologists, only one thing separates truly suicidal documents from deliberate or inadvertent feints and does it with the surety of a guillotine. A to-do list.

Water my plants; lawyer's phone number is X; safety deposit box is whatever; burn my Thomas Hardy books with me or I will haunt you till you die. Last-ditch impositions of this sort are key. Real notes have them, fake ones don't. Why?

A to-do list addressed to someone other than oneself signifies one's intention to go elsewhere. You're going out, the cleaner's coming in, you leave a note. *If the plumber calls, please let him in.* You send memos to your staff. *Turn OFF shredder at end of day!!!* You make lists for other people to take care of when you know you won't be around to do it.

Morbid thoughts do strike people who are sad enough to write them down but lack the determination to grasp their meaning. But to-do lists don't occur to such waffling melancholics because although they are depressed, they fail to grasp the fact that suicide means never coming home. Which means they're not ready for it. Fakes might be desperate, but if they can't imagine the world without them in it, they'll blow their cover by omission.

AS2's a good attempt but not quite good enough. The Salvation Army thing isn't an item on a list; it's a conditional statement, not an imperative. It mentions no specific articles, which vagary gives it the timbre of a jest.

But if you think the distinction's clear-cut, you've got the wrong impression. Like suicide itself, which overturns the ultimate priority, the science of suicide is beset by contradictions. For instance, it is clear to suicidologists that real notes are longer than fake ones and less likely to convey positive emotions. It's equally clear that fake notes are longer than real ones and more likely to avoid positive expressions. Those researchers who insist on the to-do list as a mark of suicidal authenticity are just as confident as those who posit that authentic suicides just want everyone to forget they ever existed.

To make matters worse, as one study pointed out, suicidologists too often assume that suicide notes reveal their authors' actual psychological states and sincere feelings even when authors knowingly or unconsciously try to conceal them. People who fall prey to this assumption overlook the reason why suicide notes have so much impact: they're written to be read. Every suicide note is a chance for an author to present an artificial self-image. In nineteenth-century Europe, newspapers published suicide notes. How many of those last campaigns did what they had to do to make their authors look like saints? My bet would be all of them.

I wonder if Aetna Simmons drafted and redrafted because she had no idea who she wanted to be. Drafting identities like dress patterns, trying them on, all at the last minute. Not realizing she'd lied until the next draft came along. Unaware that sometimes she was faking.

Or was she unaware? How innocent is a life lived in painstaking secrecy?

The idea that Aetna might've been a criminal was appealing. It set my imagination to racing through dark landscapes, cavorting unrestrainedly with what-ifs, flirting rashly with if-only. It made me a high-res portrait. A dark, dark woman, tall with tiny hips and round, juicy breasts and long fingers and a swarm of black curls, perfect, airbrushed flesh. Eyes like the bottom of the sea. A woman who feared no shadow because shadow was where she lived, where she was made. And she loved darkness because it defied the bright, impudent world. And so she was ever free. Her time was unconstrained, the

36

space in which she moved flexed and flowed with her body because that was how she constructed them. Freedom and resolve were her meticulous creations. She cultivated them as they nourished her to the end.

Nabi, on the other hand. My *nikkou* does the AIDS walk, the cancer walks, the End To End for charity. Tag days, bake sales, visiting at Westmeath. She volunteers at the Ag Show. Sings in the choir at Mount Olive AME, where she and Martin are in charge of the Sunday Bible Study Group. If she has something you need, she'll worry until she can give it to you. If she mislays an invoice, she asks God to help her find it.

But at Bull's Head Shreds, the managing partner won't stand for no nonsense. Wayneesha and those lot, drivers, suppliers, even customers; they try any bullshit, Nabi gives them what for. It's not easy for her; she's timid at heart. That makes her admirable.

Also terrifying. That timidity, I think it's why she won't leave Martin; she's too timid to hurt him or weather talk. It chills me to the bone, for I never know when timidity might transmute into terror, overcome her, rip her away from me. The question of a long drop opening up before me.

I'm a skilla when it comes to grinning through chronic anxiety. Nabi never sees it. Years of practice, you know. Practice being afraid of Nabi being afraid. Are the pills any wonder when you think about it? If Nabi did see it, then what? She'd giggle and say *bye get crackin, stop ya noize.*

Look at this shit. I'm so used to living like this I'm stuck in present tense, you notice?

ॐ

One afternoon I broke into my husband's computer. Little ol' me vs his company's firewall-this, password-protected-that. First time I'm seen the firewall, I got scared, had to catch myself. But come on, girl, quit micin, quick Thank You to Lord Jesus & I'm in. 1st I couldn't believe it. Ya girl's staring at the screen with my hands over my cheeks, whispering Bye-no-bye, bye-no-bye!! In the BRMS network, this little worker bee found some vicked booster rockets!

Can't think of any problem I couldn't solve from there. It's like the world spread itself out below me, a living map that I can change just by pushing a few buttons. The hackers' world is a shadow of the eyes' & ears' world. Hidden behind it, lurking almost in plain sight, & at the same time distant, above everything else. That other world can turn this one upside down without even really touching it.

I went deeper but not too deep. Scared to stay long. Cyberspace don't run on Bermuda Time! But I was too long anyway. Too much time being scared & then giggling when I wasn't scared. Martin didn't catch me, Honey didn't notice nothing. It was that other one, the new girl with the lightning tattooed on her head, the white-hat hacker on Martin's team. White-hat cuz what she does is legal (she says). She saw me. She knew right where I was.

Poor Martin came home all up a tree. I watched him run around to all the windows & wiggle the doorknobs, peeking in the keyholes cuz he thought somebody broke into our house. Or the cleaning lady stole the laptop I take with me every day & taught herself Python. Poor Honey, he was all over the place. I felt bad, stupid, vexed, scared again, & at the same time, I don't know, maybe the tension was too much, maybe I sorta wanted to see what he would say.

"Honey, it was me, all right?"

"What was you?"

"In your computer."

"No it wasn't."

"Yes it was, Honey. I'm sorry."

"But you don't know how."

"Well, yeah I do."

"No you don't. The person who did this used a very sophisticated programming language."

"Honey, you can learn that stuff online. Just ask that child with the squiggle drawing on her head."

My husband looked at me like I was something weird in the Aquarium. More than anything else, I think he was floored by the idea that I could learn something he'd call "sophisticated." But the weird look only lasted a second.

"Why?"

"I don't know. I didn't look at anything confidential."

Not much, anyway. But Martin got all vexed. He went into that mode that could've made him a preacher. Poor Honey was tired, he'd been traveling a lot, & I guess he had a right to be disagreeable, but he even brought up Psalms 55 (going too far in my opinion) & wouldn't let me get a word in. When he asked me why I did it, the man answered for me.

"Boredom, is that it?" He compared me to a kid trying to get attention.

"You're being real unfair, you know that?"

"But I pay you every attention. Anything you want—"

Sigh! "It has nothing to do—"

"Then what does it have to do—"

"Nothing. I said I was just looking."

"What, pray tell, were you looking for?"

Well, I wasn't looking for a fight. Our first in years, I was thrown right off my track. One good thing about the Psalms, they gave me time to think. Lord, take note. I spoke not a single lying word.

"A client told me, well, it's just a rumor. HSBC's into asset management & CAM, which Kenji's family—"

"I'm aware who owns Caines Asset Management, & they wouldn't dare. HSBC wouldn't either."

"The competition between them is really—"

"No it isn't. HSBC is a bank. CAM is not a bank. CAM invests. Nabilah, what you heard is gossip. You're blowing it out of proportion. It's not your fault, you're just mixed up. You're mixing up whatever this person said—"

"I'm not stupid, Martin."

"Then you know you should've ASKED instead of breaking into my system. You want to worry about somebody, what about me?

39

What about the security of my company's systems & the data that belongs to those who depend on us for confidentiality?"

Well, ya girl said more Sorrys than I can count, I promised I'd never ever do it ever again, I'd stop pretending to be a hacker forever & ever. Then I spilled some tears. Honey didn't notice they were hot & frustrated. We made up. Haven't quarreled since. I'm writing this down to remind myself of what I learned. & cuz you gotta write it down before you can shred it.

Maybe it wasn't smart to mention CAM. After that I had to steer M away from K. For some reason I thought about the guy who was steering the Sea Venture when that hurricane drove her into razor-sharp rocks. I've asked Jesus why I thought about that guy. I still don't understand since what I'm dealing with is really a much simpler thing. Like driving 2 bumper cars at the same time.

Oh, & here's what I learned from this little adventure:

1. Proxy server's not enough. Gotta mask in layers. Masks for the masks, shadows for the shadows, hiding places for the hiding places.

2. Finish praying 1st. Never hesitate.

Next time, I didn't get caught. Or the time after that or anytime after that. I hacked Kenji's computer too & found drafts of things he'll never finish, some of them just a few lines, poor Baby. This acegirl's ringin, as they say.

GIRT BIG bonus for M this quarter, yessai! So proud of him. Great night celebrating @ Lido, Elbow Beach. Talked about upgrading to BMW. Walked on beach hand in hand under stars. I made him make out with me, nobody around, mussing up his tie to tease him, Honey didn't like that but didn't want to stop either, that's what makes it so funny! So happy for my Martin. Keep telling him you don't have to worry so much, everybody loves you down that place. You go Honey! We're movin on up.

& when he finally realizes he's got a hacker (!) "on the outside" that he can trust to help him find the answers that much faster, even for shadowy questions he don't dare ask out loud? Well, you just wait & see, those lot gonna be begging to hand him a Directorship.

❧

"Did Aetna Simmons have a criminal record?"

Not the same thing, n.b., as being a criminal.

"No," said Javon.

"Why didn't you say that in our last meeting?"

Shuffling of papers. Shuffling in seat.

"You said you didn't find any photographs. So why did you send me one?"

"It was in the file."

"Ten suicide notes. That's what you told the press. You sent me nine notes and a photograph."

Shuffle, shuffle. Looking down at fingers clinging together. Disconsolate eyes, lacking focus. Rounded posture, barely able to prevent himself from curling up and sobbing until dehydration made him quit.

Hallelujah withdrawal. I treated him to a smile and spoke slowly.

"Nine notes. And a photograph."

"That's what we got."

"I had to surmise that the photograph *is* a suicide note in an alternate form. Would you agree?"

"I don't know, I guess so. Look, man, I sent you everything I could find, I swear."

Since he was about to cry, I let it go. Bleeding heart that I am.

Javon sighed, "Man, that shit you gave me."

"Crucial, innit."

"It's beautiful. It's the most beautiful shit I ever had."

"It's called Hallelujah."

"Hallelujah."

"Hundred bucks a pill."

"Fack." He shook his head, helpless and woebegone.

"Did Saltus double-check these Clocktower people?"

"Say what?"

"Clocktower Insurance. Their name's on her W-2."

"Double you who?"

People tell me I'm impatient. For the life of me, I don't know where they get that.

"That form you gave me? Remember? With her writing on the back? That form means Aetna Simmons worked for Clocktower the round faces has different amounts of yellow and purple shading. The tower rotates once every five seconds, so the effect is of the moon in four different phases. Except the moon's trapped in the tower with the hands of a clock etched into it.

This is the logo for Clocktower, Inc. They sell life insurance and health insurance. In other words, they take your monthly premiums and give you nothing in return unless you die or are variously maimed. I'm not going to list the contents of their website which, for anyone excited by insurance, is nothing short of riveting. It would be a crime not to let it speak for itself.

What it doesn't tell you is how Clocktower came to be worth billions. People must die now and again. Yet the company's share price is astronomical. You'd think dividends were their only expenses. They also don't tell you who runs the place. I mean it looks like all there is to Clocktower is five people. "Chief" people like Jim J. Falk, Chief Risk Officer and Executive Vice President. One would assume, since you can buy Clocktower's insurance anywhere in the US and file a claim almost anywhere in the world, that Jim has at least a couple underlings. I did learn that women hold twenty-four percent of Clocktower's executive positions and thirty-two percent of their recent hires were people of color.

Not that I was prepared to write off the Internet as a resource, especially since it was the only one I had, but in hours of scrolling and messing with search terms, Google made few interesting contributions. One was an image from some issue of *The Bottom Line,* a business magazine by the makers of our *Royal Gazette.*

Interesting really isn't the right word. *Disturbing* would be better. Even *brain-curdling.* You could've knocked me over with a feather.

On the evergreen lawn of Bacardi's Pitts Bay Road headquarters, the fountains do all kinds of things from geometric dances to impersonations of delicate forests. The building itself is a stone and glass structure inspired by Ludwig Mies van der Rohe. From across the street, it resembles a crouching animal about to spring, perhaps a scarab or a headless sphinx; and when the lights come on at night beneath the trapezoidal cascades flanking the shaded terrace, swaddled in dark glass and crowned by Bacardi's golden bat, the place is like the entrance to a city of tombs stuffed with treasure. It's easy to see why the Association of Bermuda International Companies chose Bacardi to host its annual dinner.

I've visited Bacardi many times. They ask me to attend all their glitzy events, especially when bored, cranky, thrill-seeking, or singularly rich bigwigs descend from the heavens abroad. Usually I oblige them. But never the ABIC dinner. Martin goes to ABIC dinners and parades his wife around in glittery outfits.

Little did I know these dinners were more hazardous still, oh yes, more perilous even than Mrs. Furbert in a gown without a back.

You can see I'm having difficulty coming to the point. The point is Jim J. Falk of Clocktower Insurance underneath the golden bat. He and another man, happily intoxicated, press champagne upon a black-clad woman. She abstains, of course she does, faced with *The Bottom Line*'s inquisitive camera. Her smile is the glint of diamantine fangs. The men are some of the masticated morsels which have become the leather in her Gorgonian wings.

Jim Falk, Barrington Caines. And the dragon is Masami.

I don't remember what I googled, the whole thing is too distressing. I shut down my computer, rebooted, did the search again. It didn't help. She was still there. So was the man who, whether he knew it or not, had paid a lot of money to a certain "consultant." Also the dimwit who tries to forget he's my father.

It was ever a surprise to come upon this man in the house where those who share my DNA, including him, once lived. Only when Masami was in the room would I bother with Good morning, *otousan, ohayou gozaimasu*, esteemed paternal entity. Which after a while embarrassed him, so he stopped noticing it. Whereupon I quit noticing him too. Since he never came to my defense even once, I consider him as good as null, not even null and void; *void* implies too much potential, *void* has actual philosophical significance. He might as well have not been in that picture. Had it just been him and Jim, I would've scrolled on by. The operative figure was Masami. The operative was always Masami.

I became convinced that Masami must be some kind of *ikiryou*, a poltergeist driven out of its living body by the demonic compulsion to make someone else's life a living hell. After all, Masami doesn't believe in destiny. What happens to you is your own responsibility, she says. A person dies in a moped accident because he was dumb enough to buy a moped, not because of bad luck, which incidentally doesn't exist except in sniveling excuses. So *unless* the Masami in that picture is an *ikiryou* who feeds on nothing but vengeance and hatred and exists with no other purpose but to torment me, Masami and Falk stuck themselves in front of that camera to flaunt their relationship. A relationship which at least indirectly includes Aetna Simmons.

I put my money on the living-ghost scenario. Why? Because it made that photo impossible. And it only stood to reason that the photo was impossible. What reason? Aetna was mine. My opportunity. Masami would not use her to entangle me in poison-coated wings. On that point I was determined. I tried to forget the photo.

My nightmares wouldn't let me.

I'm sure his momma keeps him busy, but still. Kenji's little brother's been coming round Bull's Head. Looking for him. First time was a Thursday, Baby wasn't in. It was lunchtime, M & I were going to Harbourfront, so Erik didn't get to tell me what he wanted. I figured he'd call K himself, & he did, but Baby didn't answer. He kept not answering all weekend. I know this cuz E came back the following Friday (Baby not in). Now, 1st of all, Iesha answers when I call/text her, but if she can't, if she's got dinner on the stove or something, she is not gonna leave me hanging all weekend! But men are different. Sigh. Those 2 have never done right by each other. So on the Friday, I took E to lunch. I thought if all he needed was to get stuff off his chest, maybe I could help & he wouldn't have to wait on K.

Hadn't seen that bye in donkey's. I mean Erik. The 4 of us got on well as kids, but the brothers by themselves? Lord have mercy. I mean, they're sweeties, but the mouth on Erik, Lord, come on. Ya boy's always chopsin away, I don't care where we are, his mouth is carrying on. One day Daddy took us all down St David's to that ice cream place, & even he just couldn't take it. K elbowed E & said, "Shut ya mouth, bye, chingas, no one cares about ya gossip."

"Dis what you call gossip is de national pastime, brah," said E.

"Let's drop you at de Flagpole, then. You address de nation while we lot go greezin."

Iesha & me almost died laughing, but I'm serious, E never stops. At the same time (you wouldn't expect this & I love my Baby all the same), the only humility in that family belongs to E. Except, just like his brother, aceboy knows he's a cutie. E got his momma's light skin, he dyes his nappy hair brown with reddish highlights like what's trendy in Japan, skipping around in HD color while Kenji, my tall, dark genius, takes on the whole world in black. Bush of springy-satiny black curls, smooth black arms like the best nights out on the ocean, fingers like kisses of shadows. & his delicate lips, his fine & slender nose. Eyes like Crystal Caves. I could stare into those eyes till the Lord decides to wipe the world away!

But! Sigh. I'm writing about Erik. When I asked E why he's anxious to talk to K, E said it'd been 3 years since they last spoke. I think he was ashamed. He told stories from their childhood. I knew all of

So there I was, tracking Clocktower through cyberspace and running from a semi-animate poltergeist. Having torn myself away from Clocktower's homepage, I turned one dark virtual corner after another. I stumbled on Tom Bukhari and Macy Moran in a bunch of old news articles and public case files.

Tom and Macy are dead. Fully dead.

Tom died in an accident ten years ago. Heading to work on the New Jersey Turnpike, his Benz was the loser in an altercation with a Mack truck and heavy fencing.

He was a stockbroker who'd beaten gastric cancer. Surgery, chemo, and more surgery, only to die under the back end of a truck, cancer-free.

In his system they found low concentrations of a sleep aid. Not enough to kill. Hell, it wasn't enough for a full night's sleep. Tom only needed four hours; he cut his sleeping pill in half every night. But his insurance company dismissed the findings of the coroner, who admitted that dead bodies never look stoned. Tom could've been higher than a satellite when he died and his carcass would've insisted on "low concentrations." So it was easy for the insurance company to envision a cancer-wrought paroxysm of depression in which Tom tried to kill himself with an overdose of pills. When that didn't work, he'd gotten in his car, perhaps in hope of leading a caravan of pilgrims to St. Peter.

Suicide doesn't pay, said the insurers. They refused to give Tom's widow the two million in "death benefits" to which she was entitled. The company claimed that by taking his own life, Tom voided his insurance contract.

Did I mention Tom was insured with Clocktower? Not that it matters in the grand scheme of things. All life insurers do it. Call it the suicide defense. By killing yourself, you defend them from having to pay out on your policy. It's called a suicide exemption clause, and it's legal almost everywhere: if you arrange your own demise within two years of signing up for life insurance, your insurers won't be liable for a penny. The idea is to prevent people from cutting their own throats before the ink's dry on their policies. Apparently poor people think that's a good way of providing for their families.

Tom's insurance policy was thirty years old when he died. As longspun and lovingly tended as his marriage to Sadira. Clocktower invoked the suicide clause anyway because most of the time, the suicide defense *works*. Who'd bother trying to wrestle an insurance company over one guy's policy?

Nobody. Just his widow. In a contest between a widow and a faceless corporate entity, do not put your money on the widow.

Overwhelmed with grief and shock, alone with nothing but the tears she poured into the vacant pillow at her side, Sadira insisted that Tom couldn't have killed himself. The guy died in a car accident. Cancer-free. Those things were indisputable. And Sadira swore she'd never seen Tom get depressed, not even when his illness was at its worst. She argued with Clocktower for two years.

She tried, anyway. They gave her the runaround, ignored her letters, quit taking her calls. In the miraculous event that she got to speak to somebody, she had to remind them who her husband was and what had happened. Relive it, in other words. The cancer, the accident, the postmortem, again and again. Clocktower figured all they had to do was wait. Grief would wither her until she forgot that she was right.

They underestimated her. Sadira got a lawyer instead of giving up. Clocktower's legal department knew they had no case. Those two years, they were just bluffing. Sadira's lawyer and the judge saw through it. But between Tom's death and the arrival of the check, three years wandered away. In those long years, Clocktower squeezed the widow's two million, invested it, made money on it. So when all was said and done, the company made a profit.

There's only one reason they're not fighting to this day. Clocktower couldn't prove Tom wanted to die on the Turnpike that morning.

It wasn't just the physical evidence. You want to think that stuff is objective, but it isn't. You could read that half a pill as one night's sleep or as a major underestimation of those pills. As for the car, Tom was alone. He'd never talked about suicide before, but who knows what he was thinking?

Proof of intent. It simply wasn't there.

Things worked out differently for Sisi Moran. Not too long ago, her mother Macy, a socialite and something of a bombshell, went

51

sailing with three friends off the coast of Florida. A squall came out of nowhere, capsizing the grossly wealthy twenty-somethings. Coast Guard picked up three of them, the ocean claimed their luxury pocket cruiser. Sometime later, Macy washed ashore, looking like a barracuda's breakfast.

Macy may seem immature if you consider her priorities (parties, clothes, men, and parties), but as the single mom of a three-year-old she did have some sense of responsibility. Enough to buy life insurance just after Sisi was born. That kid should've had a million bucks to roll around in. Instead, she got nothing.

In Florida, life insurance companies don't have to settle for two years. Suicide exemption clauses can legally remain in force forever. Hence Clocktower's party-line. Macy insisted on sailing even though the forecast warned of dangerous marine conditions. At best an inexpert sailor, she persuaded her friends to let her steer the boat. All in fun till the wind came up and she refused to turn back. Strange? So's the fact that only one person eluded the Coast Guard.

All four mariners put on life jackets. All, Macy included, were capable swimmers. So her death makes no sense. Unless she made sure that she would not be saved.

Burden of proof lay with Clocktower. How did they prove Macy wanted to die?

Physical evidence? There wasn't any (barracudas, etc.). Her friends didn't know if she swam toward the sinking boat or away from it. They were busy trying to stay alive in open ocean in a storm. Yes, they'd seen the weather reports, but Macy was loath to postpone the sailing trip because her three-month South-Pacific vacation was imminent. Her friends were adamant: all she wanted was to maximize her time with them before she went. Nobody believed there'd actually be squalls; weather reports are always wrong. Sure she took the wheel, but someone else took over when things started to look bad. It wasn't Macy's boat, for Christ's sake. It wasn't true that she'd refused to turn back; they'd all agreed. She was a strong swimmer but the storm was stronger. That wasn't her fault. So much for physical evidence.

In any case, intent is a state of mind. Psychological autopsy, they call it: reconstructing the deceased's personality, relationships, and final days with an eye to clarifying her motives and intentions. It meant interviewing everyone who might've been close to Macy and hoping they didn't lie. A million good reasons why anyone might lie on behalf of an orphan.

But that kid was her own undoing. According to Clocktower, Sisi was the motive. Macy took her own life because of her three-year-old daughter.

After all, Macy herself was young. Accustomed to fast living, she found her world upended by a kid come out of nowhere. Squirming, shrieking, seeping, seething little hellion who, neighbors attest, strained Macy's patience until the young mother burst into tears of despair. A child who therefore had to make do with a live-in nanny at all hours of the day and night. Macy's nerves were shot; she had to take not one but two strangers into her house, life as she knew it was over, and everyone expected her to be happy about it. There was one way out and Macy took it.

Clocktower's investigators based this version of events on interviews with the nanny and Macy's neighbors. Those who survived the storm told a somewhat different story. Macy, they said, was little more than a child herself, and maybe she could be melodramatic, but she loved that kid. She did her best to make sure Sisi would have a decent life no matter what happened, and if you don't think that little girl deserves it, you're etc.

Two conflicting stories. Public outrage building in Miami, pressuring the courts to do something about greedy bastards ganging up on toddlers. And then the nanny found Macy's suicide note. A pink envelope sticking out from underneath a dresser, a private dresser in the nanny's private room. Macy had been dead almost two months.

The nanny reasoned that the note had been on top of the dresser but fallen and slipped underneath. Though it was pink and only partially concealed, she'd managed not to notice it till long after Macy had fairly decomposed. Sisi got the blame for that too, by the way. She was so exhausting that the nanny sleepwalked through those two traumatic months. According to NBC, the note said things like: *It's not her fault but it's only the beginning and I'm already all used up. I'm not me anymore. I've already stopped living. I'll let her down but that is nothing new. She'll be better off without me.*

Vermeers and Picassos. Frank Abagnale, the great impersonator.

Aetna Simmons, forger of fantasies.

And Clocktower? Some unwritten rule, writing history before the fact: if someone's policy is worth, say, a million or more, then given favorable circumstances, the insured is presumed a suicide.

Favorable circumstances? Access to the insured's writing materials. A victim who at his time of death was capable of writing. No comas or catatonics. Perhaps for all big policies, Clocktower keeps a file on the insured's linguistic idioms, grammatical idiosyncrasies, level of education, literary affectations. Handwriting samples, day planners, likely addressees. Psychological autopsy but in advance. By whom is the client made to feel unworthy? What has the potential to drive him to depression? Is he prone to drinking, speeding, risky boating? Where are his failures? Whence come his frustrations? What would it take to break him?

Everyone's a failure and a charlatan. It wouldn't be hard for a denizen of darkness, who spends her days slithering between faces, to find out and reveal where and how someone betrayed himself. Not only a forger but also what we call an author. Someone who discerns what silences might say.

Still, if it was me, I'd have deployed Aetna's talents only when conditions promised a good outcome: the evidence is almost there, just needs a nudge from circumstantial to conclusive. Pills in the bathroom, corpse on the bed. All they need is a connection made explicit.

Reserve her for cases that would settle promptly with her help. Pay other claims so as not to draw attention to themselves. Two or three cases a year, that's all; Clocktower could save millions, keeping their secret weapon squirreled away all the while. Their rulings on every claim would appear incontestable.

Imagine she gets sixty grand per note. Three notes a year, she hides the money around the world and spends the bulk of her time doing as she pleases. She could write novels, scholarly ramblings, avant-garde poetry. She could wear Versace, buy rare books, decorate her cottage with Danish furniture.

Keep to your shadows, you supple conjuror of clues, free as a ghost. You are the shades of all those dead insureds, whom you've taken it upon yourself to become.

final days with an eye to clarifying her motives and intentions. It meant interviewing everyone who might've been close to Macy and hoping they didn't lie. A million good reasons why anyone might lie on behalf of an orphan.

But that kid was her own undoing. According to Clocktower, Sisi was the motive. Macy took her own life because of her three-year-old daughter.

After all, Macy herself was young. Accustomed to fast living, she found her world upended by a kid come out of nowhere. Squirming, shrieking, seeping, seething little hellion who, neighbors attest, strained Macy's patience until the young mother burst into tears of despair. A child who therefore had to make do with a live-in nanny at all hours of the day and night. Macy's nerves were shot; she had to take not one but two strangers into her house, life as she knew it was over, and everyone expected her to be happy about it. There was one way out and Macy took it.

Clocktower's investigators based this version of events on interviews with the nanny and Macy's neighbors. Those who survived the storm told a somewhat different story. Macy, they said, was little more than a child herself, and maybe she could be melodramatic, but she loved that kid. She did her best to make sure Sisi would have a decent life no matter what happened, and if you don't think that little girl deserves it, you're etc.

Two conflicting stories. Public outrage building in Miami, pressuring the courts to do something about greedy bastards ganging up on toddlers. And then the nanny found Macy's suicide note. A pink envelope sticking out from underneath a dresser, a private dresser in the nanny's private room. Macy had been dead almost two months.

The nanny reasoned that the note had been on top of the dresser but fallen and slipped underneath. Though it was pink and only partially concealed, she'd managed not to notice it till long after Macy had fairly decomposed. Sisi got the blame for that too, by the way. She was so exhausting that the nanny sleepwalked through those two traumatic months. According to NBC, the note said things like: *It's not her fault but it's only the beginning and I'm already all used up. I'm not me anymore. I've already stopped living. I'll let her down but that is nothing new. She'll be better off without me.*

It was enough. Believing her existence was just a living death, Macy meant to subtract herself from Sisi's life once and for all. One way or another, she meant to die, and in the storm she saw a chance to make it look accidental. She wanted to do right by her little girl. In a good mother that is only natural. But she still intentionally violated the terms of her insurance policy. If it weren't for the suicide exemption set forth in said terms, Clocktower's remaining customers would've had to shoulder higher premiums so the company could afford to honor high-priced claims like Miss Moran's. Suicide exemption clauses protect the living from the imprudence of the dead.

No judge could force the company to give Sisi anything. Not in Florida. For lawyers, juries, and judges, a suicide note is conclusive evidence. Proof of intent doesn't come any stronger. Soon as that nanny stumbled on that paper corner, every legal threat vanished from Clocktower's horizon. So why did the note take two months to come to light? Is it a coincidence that it appeared just as an enraged public and bloodthirsty media began to try to muscle Sisi's case toward the courts?

We'll never know. I've never liked toddlers, so those questions didn't interest me. My concerns were literary. I wondered who wrote Macy's suicide note.

No one talked about it. Not to the sensationalistic online sources which, for this mere civilian, were the only sources. But someone must've sent that note to a forensic document examiner.

Questions such as: Was it Macy's handwriting? Did she have access to pink envelopes? Was she the type to say *let down* or would she have gone with *disappoint*? Was this really a suicide note *per se*? Could it have been an excerpt from a diary, not a promise but a private outburst of frustration with the outburst as its own sole purpose? Was Macy really ready to die, or was this a cry for help? Did her words mean something more than what they seemed to say?

Faking. It happens. How hard is it to imagine pretending to want to die? You could start over somewhere. I could forget the charade I've made out of my life.

As for pretending to want to die on behalf of someone else, Clocktower had plenty of reasons to get someone to do this, and by tacit industry standards it wouldn't have been unethical. Policies get rescinded all the time for fabricated violations. Invented illnesses, events that never took place, a headache becomes an overdose, a storm becomes a suicide. Why not? I happen to know that people are always in the market for illusions.

The belated appearance of Macy's suicide note is rather convenient, don't you think? The sentiments are genuine. Suicidologists say that when someone decides her absence will make her dependents "better off," that's a sure sign of intent. It could also be the mark of a creative writer who knows how to do research.

Say Macy wasn't the writer. And Clocktower prepared that note, planted it when things got sticky. And a little pink envelope saved a million bucks plus profit potential. Do you feel a new hypothesis coming on?

If only Tom Bukhari had left a suicide note. That sneaky widow of his would've never had the chance to bleed the company of two million. Their legal department could've kept the suit tied up in court, held out indefinitely, arguing unresolvable questions.

Interesting that Clocktower hasn't made the news since Macy. Other insurers have. Usually because of lawsuits over unpaid death benefits or unfairly rescinded policies. I'm talking Allstate. I'm talking Prudential and State Farm. On the losing end of a class action, MetLife paid out five hundred million in death claims that should've been honored years before. So it seems Clocktower is doing something right.

It's unlikely that none of their customers have died. Given their track record, it's equally unlikely that they're handing out big checks to every orphaned widow who files a claim.

Hypothesis is a dangerous business. The allure of evidence is that of an Arabian lamp. One author, ten voices, an aberrant W-2. These things need hands. They need eyes and a mouth. They need someone behind them, flesh in their shadows.

Imagine her at her table. Always alone in a room that's always dark. A palette of pens and fonts, handwriting copybooks, phrases, inflections, tendencies, emotions. Like William Ireland, who penned letters by Shakespeare. Van Meegeren and De Hory, who painted

55

Vermeers and Picassos. Frank Abagnale, the great impersonator.

Aetna Simmons, forger of fantasies.

And Clocktower? Some unwritten rule, writing history before the fact: if someone's policy is worth, say, a million or more, then given favorable circumstances, the insured is presumed a suicide.

Favorable circumstances? Access to the insured's writing materials. A victim who at his time of death was capable of writing. No comas or catatonics. Perhaps for all big policies, Clocktower keeps a file on the insured's linguistic idioms, grammatical idiosyncrasies, level of education, literary affectations. Handwriting samples, day planners, likely addressees. Psychological autopsy but in advance. By whom is the client made to feel unworthy? What has the potential to drive him to depression? Is he prone to drinking, speeding, risky boating? Where are his failures? Whence come his frustrations? What would it take to break him?

Everyone's a failure and a charlatan. It wouldn't be hard for a denizen of darkness, who spends her days slithering between faces, to find out and reveal where and how someone betrayed himself. Not only a forger but also what we call an author. Someone who discerns what silences might say.

Still, if it was me, I'd have deployed Aetna's talents only when conditions promised a good outcome: the evidence is almost there, just needs a nudge from circumstantial to conclusive. Pills in the bathroom, corpse on the bed. All they need is a connection made explicit.

Reserve her for cases that would settle promptly with her help. Pay other claims so as not to draw attention to themselves. Two or three cases a year, that's all; Clocktower could save millions, keeping their secret weapon squirreled away all the while. Their rulings on every claim would appear incontestable.

Imagine she gets sixty grand per note. Three notes a year, she hides the money around the world and spends the bulk of her time doing as she pleases. She could write novels, scholarly ramblings, avant-garde poetry. She could wear Versace, buy rare books, decorate her cottage with Danish furniture.

Keep to your shadows, you supple conjuror of clues, free as a ghost. You are the shades of all those dead insureds, whom you've taken it upon yourself to become.

Onryou. An angry spirit. Dissatisfied but dead, it's helpless and frustrated. This is the haunting kind of ghost. It hangs around because some conflict binds it to the living world. People got the wrong idea about its death, let's say, so the ghost loiters and lurks, plagued by the agony of an unreachable itch. Everyone believes it perished in an accident, failing to realize the car ran into the truck on purpose; and as a result of this oversight, a poor insurance company has to dole out two million. It's so unfair the *onryou* cannot abide it, and it scours the world for a way to correct its mistake. Then *yokatta!* Here is Aetna. The *onryou* possesses her. It takes control of her genius and vocabulary. Through her, it engraves the truth upon the world. It explains that death was its own preference. It confesses that it violated the terms of its life insurance policy (though it never meant for anyone to get hurt, least of all Clocktower, which had taken such good care of its premiums over the years). It absolves the company of undue responsibility and with that discovers that its chains have lifted and dissolved.

Maybe I'm exaggerating about the *onryou.* Even without the supernatural angle, the Clocktower Hypothesis isn't an easy swallow: the last written words of Aetna Simmons are really suicide notes, or early drafts thereof, written on behalf of other people who at the time of writing were already dead. Having sold the notes for a lot of money, the author repurposed them in a subtle narration of her own being-toward-death as described in the Aesthetic Hypothesis.

I know—bye, get crackin. But it's not unheard of for people to leave multiple, authentic suicide notes. Virginia Woolf, for instance, wrote one note to her husband and a slightly different one to her sister. A guy named Gary Dubos left a couple versions of a suicidal poem.

But Gary and Virginia didn't have W-2s from Clocktower. If each note is a mask Aetna contrived for someone else, it's double camouflage for its secret author. The impression I'd formed of her grew inconstant and complicated, getting all mixed up with what little I knew of the crooked corporate world. Yet the Clocktower Hypothesis was the only explanation that made sense. The only way for all the evidence to fit together.

Ten suicide notes. Not a single signature. W-2. Macy and Tom. Grand Cayman.

A sliver of grass on top of a volcano.

Bermuda's strange potency. Whispering forests along disused railway lines. A temperamental ocean and impulsive winds. A city built in illogical enthusiasm for color. A mystifying dialect involving car horns in expressions of gratitude.

A feather of limestone no more than a mile across—why does the great ocean leave it open to the air? The simple act of standing on such a slim contingency as this, this accident of an inhabitable squiggle, is a marvel by itself. One can't help but feel better about oneself for being here.

Of course it's nothing but an enchantment, that feeling; it's the hocus pocus of the Devil's Isles, confected not with smoke and mirrors but wildflowers and sunsets. Still, I can understand why the pseudo-suicidal would want to live here, someone who makes her living by pretending to want to die. Aetna wasn't Bermudian; there would've been records. So it wasn't a matter of slinking back like dying salmon, hounded home by a lack of opportunity. It wasn't just secretive practicality, for while this nation is prone to being overlooked, Bermudians and gossip go together like Dark 'n' Stormy. No, what bound her to this place was the need to like herself sometimes. She wrote on behalf of greed for the ruthless and deluded. Bermy could have been her Hallelujah.

She chose *Simmons* because it would blend in. That would explain why no Simmonses came forward when she disappeared.

But *Aetna* isn't a Bermudian moniker. This one she chose as a symbol. *Aitne* in Greek, from *aitho, I burn*. The name of a nymph who took a suicidal risk. This nymph went round Zeus' gates and got some ease. After the fact, it occurred to her to worry about his vindictive wife. The terrified nymph prayed the earth would swallow her; and Zeus, having moved on to some other longtail, happily obliged. A mountain grew on top of her, Mount Etna of Sicily, hot and disagreeable. In that mountain, Hephaestus forged Zeus' famous thunderbolts whilst beneath it lay a woman imprisoned by her own terror and lust. The mountain pulverized Aetna's humanoid form. Her children, sons of Zeus, came forth as hot springs.

The crater in which Bermuda rests forms the summit of a submerged and extinct volcano. So Aetna Simmons got herself swallowed by one of the earth's corpses. The enchantment that fanned the flame of her vanity showed itself for what it was when the night came down. The island-archipelago's resplendent colors faded to the uniformity of nothing. Ghosts and might-have-beens rose up to hem her in.

In the United States, there's a little thing called a W-2. It has to do with "tax returns." As I understand, if you're caught without a "tax return," men in black will show up at your house and make you watch while they purloin everything you own. They'll drag you into the street and kick your ass in public, and while you're lying there bleeding they'll go into your house and lock you out. So I've heard.

The W-2 tells you what the US government gnaws off your paycheck before you even get to see it. It looks like a cage for a giant, rabid cougar; only that's your salary peeking out between the bars, mewling because it's about to lose a toe.

The reason I know so much about W-2s is that Aetna scrawled a suicide note on one of them. AS7. Red ink from a rollerball or gel pen pressed too hard. A message in blood on the walls of her prison.

But where her social security tag should be, the form has been conveniently decapitated, its top edge cleanly severed: Box A is missing. Box E has her name and the address of a company that forwards mail to Bermuda via commercial airlines.

The form wasn't dated, but at some point the US skimmed $25,714.29 off her salary of $85,714.29, leaving her $60,000. They took thirty percent, which means Aetna wasn't a US citizen or permanent resident. If you're one of those, they skim a little less. What's weird is that round number. 60,000. Could be a coincidence, or Aetna had some arrangement with her company.

Let's say she wanted $60,000 for services rendered. On account of the men in black, the company raised her basic salary to $85,714.29 so that after being skimmed she'd get exactly what she'd earned. If the company valued her enough to do that, then chances are they

> Friends: what's done is done.
> It's pointless to delay.

AS3.
Typewritten on white strip. The rest?

Aetna couldn't afford a family or friends, only co-conspirators. Crooked underwriters and actuarial assistants hidden inside Clocktower like sleeper cells. They wouldn't have known her well, hidden as she was herself. I imagine they hired her online. With empty wallet keening, she grabbed whatever she could find at freelancewrite.org. Anyway, real friends don't let friends suffer premature mortality.

Whoever they were (and this is really something), each of them could've received their very own copy of AS3. She typed several to a page and finished them with scissors: imprecise, slanting cuts surround the slender text. Perhaps the strips showed up in pigeonholes at Clocktower's headquarters. Sneaked in with the agenda for the next board meeting. Squeezed into tiny envelopes, perhaps accompanying flowers.

The text (nine words) may look like it was written in a hurry. It's nonspecific and ambiguous. *It's pointless to delay* turning herself in works just as well as *It's pointless to delay* the culmination of all ends. And *done* need not mean "done with life." It could mean "done with" something that the author leaves unspecified, confident that her readers will know what she's referring to.

But the whole phrase, *What's done is done,* has the somber toll of suicidal forgiveness and farewell blessing. It also sounds like George Eastman. Eastman invented Kodak film. In 1932, he shot himself in the chest after penning this contribution to suicidal literature:

To my friends: my work is done. Why wait?

Concise, effective, beautiful. The poise and careful emptiness of minimalism.

Eastman's note is easy to find online. Famous as the man himself, if not more so. To an aspiring virtuoso of the form, Eastman's piece would've been an inspiration.

Or a stumbling block. AS3 is too close to derivative. That could raise flags.

It's a fragment, that's what I think. An unfinished draft included in the Ten as evidence of her painstaking, frustrating process, which itself played a role in her journey toward voluntary death.

That's assuming she used the scissors just for kicks.

છ

Sometimes, under the influence, I wondered if we should stop. If I should be the one to tell Nabi we should stop, *what's done is done.* What if we were one of those things she kept doing only because she always had? What if, since we were a kind of backwards nine to five, the night shift of all things, not even a full week, we were never actually "now" as Nabi said: as a hallucination isn't "now" but is precisely what isn't happening even as you think it's happening? Were we just aging skillas pretending to live backwards? Is nostalgia ever enough?

P1, Warwick Academy. That's how we met. Nabi noticed that purple was missing from my rainbow. She asked if I wanted to borrow her purple. I said yes and thank you, but it was actually called violet, not purple, in the context of the rainbow. She said, "Well you don't have to be a smarty pants." Whereupon I, accustomed to those very words acerbically delivered by my slow-witted brother Erik (Nabi hadn't met him yet, she had no way of knowing), hung my head and said, "I know." She asked if I'd like to be friends even though I was a smarty pants, and I said yes. When Friday came, she announced she had permission to invite someone from her brand-new big-kids' school over to play. She wanted it to be me. Her mom called Masami and off we went.

You'd think a man lucky enough to marry Nabi, who with a flutter of her lashes can turn a hurricane into a peaceful afternoon, would recognize the boundless potential of commonplace events. But although Martin considers himself latitudinarian, he's selectively narrow-minded on certain points. He realizes that Nabi would give the clothes off her back to a stranger; but it never occurred to him that giving and gratitude, humdrum forms of satisfaction, might grow and change into something profound and singular. He thinks we're still just friends in a crayon-sharing kind of way. He thinks, in short, that we're stuck in P1.

Soon after I returned from Harvard, the three of us got together for dinner. Mr. Furbert observed my and Nabi's tendency to giggle like smallies. "It's like we're all back in secondary school," said Martin. "I like that," he said. "That's nice," he added. Martin went to Berkeley, not Warwick, so I don't know where he got off with this "we" business. It was my duty to point out the serious nature of the partnership that Nabi and I had developed. Look at all we'd achieved at Bull's Head Shreds.

What did Martin come back with but the summer team-building program? We fill our establishment with schoolkids to recreate the atmosphere of our own school days; we surround ourselves with children so we can act like them all summer. So he claimed. Nabi almost choked on her virgin piña colada.

She's proud of the summer program. She turned a penurious idea of mine (hire kids instead of temps during full-timers' vacations) into a community service. Together Nabi, Wayneesha, and Bryan teach a ragtag bunch of big-mouthed smallies about teamwork, responsibility, accountability; the vitality of information and documentation; the significance of confidentiality and trust; the importance of security and staying out of trouble. The kids are sixteen-plus, subject to drug tests, background checks, and NAID approval. Remuneration is generous, but problems with gangs or cops will result in termination. Nabi explains all this, makes the hooligans sign contracts, confidentiality agreements, Chain of Custody records just like every employee, just as legal and just as binding. This in't no supermarket checkout, Nabi tells them; we are handling information that for some powerful customers could mean the difference between poverty and prosperity. For some, like medical offices, we're their way of complying with very important laws; laws that have to do with privacy, compassion, and the right to be forgotten. As she told Channel Nine, Bull's Head Shreds had to get a special NAID dispensation to hire pre-diploma students in this unique program, which helps young Bermudians prepare for college in ways both tangible and intangible.

For Martin to toss it off as self-indulgence was just mean.

This point warrants further remarks. If you don't understand how Martin is, then the fact that his presence makes things start going shru de trees won't make any sense.

Some of it has to do with his profession. His company, Bermuda Risk Management Solutions, offers a Vegas-style buffet's worth of various services to other corporate types. I don't know what all those services are. I am not up on the nuances of risk management. I have better things to do than mire myself in Martin's gory details. I'm aware that he heads a mighty team of "corporate investigators."

It's exactly what it sounds like. He's a PI for the business world. Say you're a *Fortune 500* conglomerate. You want to hire a corporate cynosure to do some heavy lifting at the executive level. Lest his dazzling résumé blow the fuses on your judgment, you hire BRMS to dive into his shadows before you sign the contract. And that's not all. Looking to merge with another multinational magnate? Hire BRMS. In case what you took for an Apple turns out to be an Enron. Heading for the courtroom? Let BRMS handle your pre-litigation research. You'll know you've done your homework if they've done it for you. Think your CFO's got some fingers in the jar? Call BRMS. They'll conduct your fraud investigation with deadly precision and discretion and without setting your employees at each other's throats. BRMS: fast, neutral, meticulous, and impeccably hush-hush.

The investigative division consists of several teams like Martin's. His is the all-star team. He's team leader, big surprise, with two dozen underlings spread over London, New York, and Hamilton. Nabi claims he knows everyone and everything going on in the business world, even things that no one in their right mind would admit to knowing. You see, everything's a lead; every lead is some pathetic little animal that Martin's divinely ordained to hound back to its den wherein other little animals lie cowering. His touch of paranoia whips him on until the lead keels over and dies from exhaustion. The same condition convinced him there's a market for recorded video chats. So he'd rather spend half his life on airplanes than entrust his all-star strategy sessions to the likes of Skype. He's going to lead the entire investigative division one day, crowed Mrs. Furbert; every BRMS gumshoe *in the world* will answer to him, and the company will *have* to make him a Director. I'd like to make him knuckle *sushi* with *jujitsu* sauce.

In corporate circles, everyone knows Martin (if not quite as well as he knows them). People treat him as they used to treat policemen once upon a time. When underneath their tall round helmets, they seemed to carry comprehensive knowledge of what ought to be done with the world at large. When their dress uniforms and shiny accoutrements reeked of integrity. This treatment has gone to Martin's

us-versus-them rhetoric is turpentine on the fire of hatred between racial groups and damnation itself for mongrels who, excluded from every group, wind up as punching bags for all. Not that Barrington knows anybody like that personally.

I am no puppet of history, but reminding me of that man's self-righteous treachery is another easy way to become my enemy. It made a ravishingly handsome lady almost as repulsive as dead cats. Yet could I get up and leave, leave with nothing but the misallocated burden of Doreen's oppressors' guilt? Though with each sound out of her mouth, it became clearer she and I had no more than stale vinegar to offer one another, I couldn't let her have the final word. I had to find out what she was up to, trying to provoke me. For Aetna's sake I had to. And I'd pay for it in flesh.

I said, "Look, you've got the wrong idea."

"Oh yeah?"

"Well, take yourself, for example. What's your line of work? It's obvious you're well-educated."

"I'm between jobs right now. But no need to worry. Soon as everybody starts getting white people's opportunities, I'm sure I'll find something."

"And lose all reason to feel sorry for yourself?"

"Do I look sorry?"

"Right. My mistake. Regret and entitlement are different kettles of fish."

"Ever notice how many meanings *entitlement* has? All kinds of meanings that could mean nothing in the end. Like *claim*," said Doreen. While I tried not to look as mystified as the deceased tabby on the TV stand. "A claim could be a question of entitlement. Or it could just be a lie. You want to know something strange?"

"Go ahead and try and shock me."

"I've looked all over for her will. Momma's will. Can't find it anywhere."

"Her lawyer?"

"Didn't have a lawyer. No safety deposit box. I figure it's around here somewhere, meaning it's as good as buried. With my luck, she willed everything to Czarina."

My smart-ass rejoinder died upon my lips.

"Czarina?"

"In the window." Doreen pointed with her chin.

Everything in Mrs. Trimm's living-dining room was brown, brownish-green, or brownish-yellow, from the loveseat to the crochet throw to the thinning carpet and the recliner where a strange old woman breathed her last. At the far end of the room, yellowish curtains filtered the light from the window down to its brownest tones. I peered through the noontime gloaming, dust motes heavy with cat hair, to a tall Siamese. Seated in the window as upon a throne. Dead eyes doomed to watch that window till the skin around them rotted.

"Heard from someone at the funeral. Czarina was her favorite."

I followed Doreen to the window. We looked at the cat.

It was like viewing the actual handbag that gave birth to Wilde's Jack Worthing. Or something like that. You see, "Czarina" made a cameo appearance in AS9. Now here she was in the flesh, sort of. Looking with glass eyes through a window. I looked too.

Beyond Czarina's window was another window. Had I a glimmer of desire to risk brushing up against a taxidermied cat, I could've reached out and touched that other window. Beyond it I could see the top of a plastic chair, a little bit of plastic card table in front of it, and was that a printer? Dainty white shutters flanked the window. The outer walls were pink. It was Aetna's cottage. Birthplace of the Ten.

The furniture wasn't supposed to be plastic.

I looked a bit too long. Doreen said, "Did you know Momma's tenant?"

"No. Did you?"

Doreen shook her head. "She died too, you know."

"I heard."

"I get to go through her stuff too."

We watched the empty space that must've housed Aetna's computer, now another absence. The left-hand corner, that very corner, where ten suicide notes awaited their new dawn.

I said, "Want some help going through dead people's stuff? Looking for a will, I mean?"

"Now, why would you want to do that?"

Some conspiracy between Doreen's eyelashes and cheekbones

made her eyes seem half-lidded even when they weren't. Things like that could agitate a brethren. Also her unhurried smile as it clashed with a voracious gleam, the mark of an unapologetic gold-digger. Revulsion notwithstanding, I bestowed an undefeated champion of a grin.

Doreen murmured, "All right, then."

Why set up a dead cat to watch your tenant through her window? Dementia, perhaps? Or the rest of the world is even more demented than you are, and someone else turned your stuffed heiress-apparent into a spy?

Glassy eyeballs fitted with microscopic cameras in a lifeless feline head: crazy but not impossible. But for what? Only Clocktower would've known there was anything worth looking at through Aetna's window. Did they have an inkling that she might betray them? Even if they did, any video of her would incriminate them too. Besides, if they were sane, they would've put the cameras in the cottage. Not in the dead body of her landlady's cat.

Perhaps the landlady was the hinge on this whole thing. Maybe she played both teams. Clocktower's jailer and FBI spy. The woman was eighty-one but, I thought, if the daughter's demeanor said anything of the mother's, Myrtle was capable of a great deal.

If it were true, it would mean the FBI was onto Clocktower for some time. Now, the Americans are treaty-bound to share details of relevant criminal investigations with Bermuda and vice versa (I make it my business to know stuff like that), so if they were interested, Javon would've known. If that idiot had any notion of what was good for him, he'd have said something. He hadn't. Now Aetna's file was missing.

Thankfully, a junkie's word wasn't all I had to go on. I had Aetna's word too.

AS9 is the most enigmatic of the bunch. Frankly, it doesn't make much sense. When I learned that it refers to a taxidermied cat, it got even weirder. You could read it as a warning or an invitation of some kind. Czarina's name follows what may or may not be the vague hint of a disputable notion that all will become clear.

If Czarina couldn't watch Aetna through that window, Myrtle

could. Even if she didn't know what Aetna was up to, she saw it all happen. Maybe Aetna knew. A disagreeable old lady scowling daggers at you from two feet away is hard to miss.

Consider: Aetna's on the verge of the decision to die. She knows Myrtle knows the mechanics of her bizarre lifestyle if not the rationale. So Aetna bequeaths her something that fills in the missing piece.

Why? Why would Aetna paint a comprehensive picture of the end of her life and leave it to Myrtle Trimm?

Maybe she hoped Myrtle would go to the police. Care of a senior citizen, Aetna left everything they'd need to unmask Clocktower's agenda. Left without paying her rent, knowing once Myrtle hit the ceiling she'd unleash every detail on someone like the unsuspecting Saltus. Of course, that's not what happened. Maybe because Myrtle kicked the bucket without any knowledge of Aetna's bequest.

If such a thing existed, what form did it take? Was I looking for a thumb drive? Micro-SD card? Key to mysterious safety deposit box, wherein Aetna's laptop lay undiscovered? Where in that clogged-up nest of hairballs could she have hidden it?

Look to her, Aetna wrote.

That night I wanted Nabi so much I thought I'd go crazy. But Friday meant she was with Martin and I should've been working. I was too depressed to think of going out. I took a bit of Zo to make sure I got to sleep and avoided the nightmares.

While I was at Harvard, Nabi saw a string of guys. I made a lot of women suffer for not being her. We shared stories of those people, both to hurt each other and to preserve our friendship. I told myself she married Martin for the same reasons.

I've asked her to leave him. I've asked so many times. They've been married eight years.

Maybe you've noticed how hard I try to be a pessimist. In each potential heart attack between words, I try to brace myself like a wise cynic. I tell myself to keep my sails up and full of wind and batten down the hatches.

It doesn't help. Probably because I've got too much going on at the same time (heart shifting to windpipe, etc.). But I've got to try, at least put on a show of trying to protect myself. Even if I'm the only nitwit in my audience of one.

Maybe it's easier with chemical reinforcements. Then again, maybe it isn't. That shit has the tendency to encourage hope. But so do sunny skies. And clouded-over skies. And the cries of feral roosters. Nabi herself, dammit. Every time I try to steel myself against the possibility that her fidelity will tear my hull right through, acegirl just won't let me. She just keeps showing up. She's not here now of course. But cha, you know what I mean. Why did she persist, however intermittently, in showing up? This was something I couldn't ask myself too often, lest I think how many Saturdays she spent baking brownies for Meals On Wheels.

Nabi didn't have Harvard grades or Harvard money. She got stuck at Bermuda College with a job as a teller while I ran off chasing literary greatness. Martin was already at BRMS. He found some banking to do each Wednesday with clockwork regularity. And now, although he spends more time abroad than at home, it's as if those Wednesdays are a limit his wife can't cross. He was there and I was gone, that's a fact.

There is no limit that those who set their minds to it cannot undermine. Not the law, not the ethics of industry, not even mortality. Aetna was comfortable with that, as am I. Nabi never even let it occur to her.

Middle of Hamilton. No parking around for miles. Small me and smaller Erik are sent into the crowded post office with the historic mission of collecting a package for Masami. We say good afternoon to the black lady at the counter, who replies by shouting over her shoulder, "Miz Okada's package, somebody!" Small Erik says cheerfully, "Hey, how'd you know?" Clerk eyes us like we're snot: *Just a guess.* And everybody in the place busts out guffawing. I mean everybody. I mean loud.

On some visceral level, even Erik understood. The joke was us stupid mongrels thinking we could pass for the ordinary Bermudians we were. Humiliated, the little bugger started sniffling. No one noticed except me. I took his sticky hand and scowled at the clerk, which she found amusing. I scowled at the white guy who came out of the back room with the package. He said, "Here you go, sensei," and laughed some more.

Sometimes when medium-sized me lay awake stewing over this, I wished I'd said in booming Japanese: "Erik-Katsuo, please carry this important package for our mother. Only you are strong enough."

I never said any of that shit. I snatched the stupid package and we mooched out. Erik wondered why a grown-up would call me *sensei*, and I tried to explain he'd meant it as an insult; an inappropriate word flung at us to show that we stick out just like inappropriate words stick out. Erik didn't get it. Small and enraged me couldn't articulate it properly, so I told him to shut up about it and we never spoke of it again. Maybe Erik would've whined to Barrington; that would've been just like Erik. But Barrington wasn't around, probably schmoozing over cocktails. That would've been just like Barrington.

I forbore to whine, but I did unburden myself to my best friend. Nabi scowled and said she didn't really get it either, but she'd never laugh at me like that. Mean like that. Cross her heart and hope to die and stew and fry. And she took my sticky little hand.

Such behavior was a constant in our small-to-medium years. I mean this habit Nabi had, which never did her any good: standing up for me when I got picked on. Black kids said, "What are you, what's the matter with your eyes?" White kids said, "There's no such thing as a black He-Man/astronaut/paleontologist." And Nabi *made* off on those lot. She gave harder verbal licks than any teacher. She even wagged her finger and invoked Jesus Christ. When girls left her a note asking why she hung out with a bookworm, she showed me the thing and announced in the middle of US History: "Because Kenji in't a tired wuffless bimpert like you lot." She got instant detention.

And when I ask myself what I bring to our beautiful conspiracy, I might come up with laughs, luxury, and listening. I might come up with nothing on sepulchral days like these. Or everything I do come up with feels like so much tissue paper. As I sink lower and lower, sometimes I try pretending Bull's Head Shreds was my idea.

I sat in my Cambridge apartment with a cheapo-Office-Depot shredder. Preparing to leap the Atlantic for the last time, not a single sure thing headed my way, I systematically destroyed all drafts of unpublished crap that I'd accumulated during my Harvard BA, MA, and PhD studies.

That's a lot of crap. I said as much to Nabi through the phone I balanced on my shoulder while my dissertation decomposed before my eyes. "Girl, if I had a dollar for every fackin piece of paper I'm put in this fackin thing, fifteen fackin years of fackin freezing off my fackin ass, I'd be a fackin billionaire, that's what. Driving me full fullish. Listen, this is me: *dissolving bit by bit the structure of the previous world into the night in which all cows are black.*"

A paraphrase from Hegel. Nabi ignored Hegel. She was deep in thought. She said, not really having any idea what she said, "Bye, go head. Cows are smelly. Ever driven by Spittal Farm on a hot day? Lord have mercy." Then she fell silent.

Next time she spoke, she got serious. She made me serious too. Guess you'd call that inspiration. We'd say we did it so we could reap the fruits of our own sweat. For my Harvard years were years of pure drudgery for Nabi. She wanted something of her own, and when she spoke of it, for the first time in our long history she sounded desperate.

I was on the first flight I could find. At the airport I heard my name outside of Customs, and there was acegirl shoving her way through the crowd behind the waist-high barrier. I remember someone yelled at me for dropping all my stuff in the middle of the floor, but I was in her arms and we were sobbing over the barrier like a *Casablanca* audience. Then I remembered the bag with the illegal drugs in it lying on the floor in the middle of the airport, tore myself away from her (still bawling), grabbed my stuff while Nabi shoved her way the other way. We collided in the sun (waterspouts still going), but we didn't kiss until we were in the Furberts' Honda with the sunshades up. Our first time.

Only then could Nabi stop shivering enough to drive. The flat on the seashore, I'd just bought it on the web. It had no furniture. Martin was off the island, so Nabi stayed. We slept on the quilt she'd bought me when Harvard said hey why not. In the morning I presented the full sum of the capital for our business venture.

I told Nabi the money's mine. Deep down she believes I got it from Masami. Masami, who heard of our Grand Opening from some obsequious colleague, assumes the startup money came from Barrington. This is because Barrington is a born sucker. Barrington thinks I bullied Erik into a clandestine loan. Erik is certain every resource within a million miles of the Caines family, I mean down to the last penny, is monitored with supernatural precision by none other than Masami.

I didn't need to say a word. Speculation jumped on the hamster-wheel of familial dysfunction. Nobody knew my other partnership, which began in Boston and is still lively and plump, was underway long before Bull's Head Shreds.

Nabi made the arrangements. Lawyers, equipment, staff, certification. That stuff comes easily to her. We went through dozens of names. Natty Shreds, Serious Shreds, Docta Shredd. We went with Bull's Head Shreds when she found premises near Bull's Head parking lot in Hamilton. My father's sister had a niece on her husband's side whose oldest kid was pretty good at graffiti, so I had him do a logo. Mean-looking silver bull with horns like scimitars. These days Nabi does all the work. I go in when she needs help or we can't stand to be apart another minute.

The rest of the time, I'm supposed to nurse my literary habit. For some reason she's all but positive that someday one of my critical analyses will be a bestseller. In the meantime I'll have Bull's Head Shreds to see me through and my best friend rooting for me. That's the way she put it.

Do you see why I believed nothing would ever come between us? Do you understand why I took it for granted, why some Friday nights all but killed me?

You may find this hard to believe, but cheating on Nabi never occurred to me. There was the agony of pining. There was Zohytin. That's all.

❧

Baby used to say (he wasn't Baby yet, he was @USA so far away) certain projects dump hot pepper on your creative juices, then there's no stopping them. Like his Thomas Hardy thing so long ago, poor sight. "The Art Of Vanishing" (never thought of it like that till Baby said!), that was one of those things. It's just so funny how these things happen. If I hadn't done all this, I wouldn't have got inspired to think about Bull's Head Shreds diversifying! Already!

"All this." Like buying a bare hard drive in town & getting a program called Macrium that'd turn it into a bit-for-bit, bootable clone of any other drive (must do before messing around!). Like sending off for a "write blocker," a little machine that lets you read somebody's drive without changing anything on it (harder than it sounds). Never know when I might need that, plus it looked so cute & every forensic technician has one. Bought some books too (The Hacker's Manual), & in an hour I learned how to get somebody's bank account number off their computer.

I still couldn't tell if there was any meat in that rumor (CAM trying to sock it to HSBC). Guess I coulda looked harder, lingered a second longer just for the purpose. But the whole thing was like cannonballing into the ocean, knowing I was gonna be absolutely freezing & the current might be strong enough to yank off my bikini if I didn't outwit it, out-think the current, come on Nabi-girl. I don't think I blinked the whole time, Lord forgive me but I loved every minute!

Saturday already! Another busy one. Since Wednesday I'm been wanting to sit down with my book, but I'm hardly sat at all! Not complaining, mind you (Thank You Jesus for this day). Sang this morning with Mt O choir at Farmers' Market down Botanical. Lunch with M at Masterworks cafe. Honey was all happy, it was sweet. Too shy to join choir himself, Lord bless him, but he loves our singing.

I told him I'm starting a feasibility study on hard drive shredders. Martin said a HDS would be a great way "to get one up on the competition." Lord, I had to laugh. Competition? There's only one other shredding place on the whole Island, & it belongs to those sweetiepies up de country who told me the best secure collection bins to use. Anyhow, a HDS makes sense. I mean eventually. There's more old computers out there every day, & all of them know too much. But getting a HDS to Bermy? When you count shipping & customs (better find something to sit on, Lord), you could be looking at $100,000, depending on the shredder's features. But before I could get into all that, somebody from Argus came over & said hi. (I think he's from Argus. M's got so many people saying hi I'm been lost track.) Then Honey was dying to know where we'd found "All For Jesus," which he'd just heard us sing for the first time. Then the reading for this week's Bible Study, etc, etc.

Back on Wednesday night I was with K. Lord, I was bushed! We wanted to take out Ethelberta, but Baby saw I was too tired. We flopped out in the jacuzzi without even turning on the jets. Kenji rubbed my back, God bless him, & I rubbed some of that special soap into his hands (he was hauling drop-off boxes for me all afternoon). I got on my "favorite topic" (K calls it): HDS! I was still on it when we flopped out on the couch. Baby asked which HDS I like the most (like we're talking about shoes or suitcases, Lord bless him!), so I told him what I need to do & he said, "What's a feasibility study, Nikkou?"

Sweetie wanted all the details even though he don't have a clue how these things work. Suppliers, dimensions, where we might put the machine, how many customers we'd need to make it worth buying. Baby was lying down with his head in my lap when I mentioned the $100,000. But even after I said it, he just kept looking at me with total complete trust. Blew me away. I mean it. Kenji's beautiful dark eyes. Total complete trust.

He asked good questions too. Stuff I hadn't thought of yet. Like would customers want their old HDs leaving their offices? Somebody's HD has their passwords on it & that. As Baby put it, it's "total direct access to whatever." Point being that companies who handle lots of personal data might want the shredder to come to them. Instead of their old HDs rambling thru Hamilton where anything can happen.

"Idgit on a bike," said K. "Horse & buggy gets spooked by our girt red truck & there's an accident. People's hard drives all spread out in the street." I asked him was he saying we gotta shell out another $100K for a MSU truck that might as well shred paper too while we're at it? We want a truck that big, we're gonna have to wrestle government. Was he saying we need ALL of that if we want a HDS to make money?

K thought for a sec & said, "I know you can do it if you want to. But if you're not just asking me for moral support, if you really want a serious answer to that question, your feasibility calculations will get a lot more complicated. If you really want an answer, you have to see the question thru to its very end, wherever it may be."

Obsession comes so easily to K. Even so, what he said right then was true. Cutting corners is a bad idea, Nabi-girl, especially in this case. Still, I felt like whining, Yeah but don't we want it NOW??

I didn't. Got caught up. Checking out his eyes. To have anybody smile at me like that, no not just anybody. That complicated man. That brooding, abstract, impulsive man. While all that's going on is me. About trucks with shredders in them. My book knows how Kenji loves. He loves like a volcano, his love is explosive & comes from way down deep, so sweet & urgent it hurts us both sometimes. All of that was in his look, & well I overflowed, God bless my secret love, I forgot everything that was running thru my head. Clones, shredders, banks, dead people, all of it just flew away. I sat there playing with his hair, we didn't move or say nothing, & I knew I was bushed but I forgot that too & overflowed & started singing. This song I hadn't thought about in forever. Forgot the words too, just the tune, real soft, I couldn't stop it. That Jah Cure song about longing. I don't know why that song. But Kenji's smile grew into a great big grin, so I kept singing, & the more I sang the more I flowed. & Kenji, Kenji glowed. My restless lover with the crystal-cavern eyes, lying still and all unguarded right there underneath my hands. My Kenji, he just glowed.

❧

I got to St. George's around two the next day. Saturday, I believe. Doreen opened the door. My jaw dropped. The cats were gone.

"Ever spent the night with twenty-three dead cats? Try it for a couple weeks," she said.

Creepy. Disgusting. Insanitary. I get it. But the cats were gone.

"There were more in the bedroom. Like sleeping in a freak show. I couldn't take it anymore. Felt like part of the collection."

Czarina, the favorite, was nowhere in sight.

"Couple guys in that building have a truck. Took them to the dump. Best two hundred bucks I ever spent."

Now I'd never know.

I had to admit the absence of the cats left me better equipped to notice things. Like the flowery cushion in the recliner. Myrtle's library: a pair of dining chairs with paperbacks on them. All crime novels, all black authors. Above the loveseat were three mildewing images. Stern-faced Myrtle in her younger days. Front Street in the 1930s, lined with horse-drawn carriages and cars with befringed canopies. A drawing of a woman in a long, dirty dress, her head wrapped in cloth, a slave.

To the left of the dining set was a small kitchen. At the back of the kitchen was a door.

"My room. We'll start there."

It was full of plastic bins and little plastic filing cabinets. No bed or dresser; they'd gone to the cottage long ago. Doreen said, "Why let them sit around when they could make some money?"

Thus began her search for Myrtle's will and my quest for anything that might shed light on Aetna's life.

I tried to draw Doreen out, fishing for a deeper sense of her and through her of her mother. I didn't get far. We talked horror movies and American football, savage spectacles that could amuse us both for hours. But for the most part she was taciturn. She focused on her task with what Hardy would call *the hard, half-apathetic expression of one who deems anything possible at the hands of Time and Chance except, perhaps, fair play*. Sometimes she'd mutter something to relieve the tedium of decades' worth of BELCO bills, album after album of unfamiliar faces.

"There's a system here," she said. "I just get that feeling. Everything's filed in some way that put it all at Momma's fingertips. If we figure out what she was thinking, it'll all start making sense."

It didn't.

"Keep it in neat piles," she said. In case her relatives wanted a crack at it. "They get one week to decide, then it goes to the incinerator. Gonna rent out this whole place."

Nobody would want that threadbare, cat-infested place. I didn't say anything, but my eyes were starting to water. I was knee-deep in bulletins from St. Peter's, some of which were older than I am. We had yet to find anything of interest. And Doreen was sidestepping my questions. If anything, she and Myrtle grew more and more mysterious.

For one thing, I thought, as a sneeze threatened and died, why would Masami and Barrington have anything to do with anyone who lived like this? The sneeze rose up and conquered. I sprayed Bingo cards everywhere.

"Had one of those coming for about an hour," said Doreen.

The occasion wasn't right for martinis. But then Doreen's sense of propriety was skewed all over. She made furious martinis. A lesser man might've started swaying after only one. We drank on the doorstep and listened to the birds. A puff of breeze, the first cool whiff of evening.

I looked at Aetna's cottage. Small and fragile in the armpit of Myrtle's hedged-in property.

There wasn't any space in that cottage for rare books. Her equipment alone; she must've gone around tripping over it. The place should've been a storage shed.

What happened there? Would your Momma get involved with criminals? Why in hell did you have to throw away that cat? Couldn't ask Doreen that stuff without giving too much away. She aimed point-blank, but she was sensitive to subtlety. Subtlety, I thought, was my way in.

I was wrong about that. I was wrong about a lot of things.

"Can't wait to get out of here," Doreen muttered.

"And go where? The States?"

"Well, yeah. Civilization."

I figured she'd been back and forth a lot, possibly for college, and

91

willed our dialect away. She looked around with the wide eyes and gritted teeth that can afflict expats who fail to adapt to life on a rock in the middle of the ocean. Rock Fever, we call it. So I said I'd spent however long in Massachusetts. It turned out she'd visited Boston. She preferred New York. One thing and another, Patriots and Jets, next thing I know I'm pontificating on literary scholarship, throwing out the name of my ill-fated dissertation, *Phenomenologies and Ontologies in Thomas Hardy's Novels.*

"Who's Thomas Hardy?"

"Late nineteenth-century English—"

"Wait, a white guy?" She gave me the kind of sneer that connoisseurs reserve for sellouts.

"He was a damn good novelist."

"Meaning you'd never get a job if you researched…name some African female who's never been on Oprah."

"That's not true," I said, with no evidence whatsoever and considerable evidence to the contrary. The professorial life I described to Doreen was the dream-life of books. A creative life, a pensive life where thought and prestige went hand in hand.

"Go on," she said during a pause. The more I talked, the more thoughtful she became, studying my face like she'd suspected all along a Harvard don lay hidden there. I expected her to jeer at my idealistic visions which, knowing me, I probably didn't believe in even as I uttered them. But she didn't jeer. She said, "That's really what you want?"

I couldn't answer that. Maybe I'd said too much already. But what did any of it matter, I thought, since none of it was real? The problem was I thought I had the measure of her, lonely and tough, wishing she were even tougher; but neither of us was sure of me. What was I doing there? I didn't know what I wanted. I wasn't sure how far I'd be able to go. I never knew what I was going to say until I said it, and I had no idea what Doreen saw. It was obvious she was probing me for weak spots. She wanted to know the worst of me without having to earn it, and that meant she had an agenda. Either that or she was a subtle kind of sicko, which couldn't be ruled out. Maybe I didn't have the measure of her.

The bigger problem was, I let her do it. Even though I'd sworn eternal enmity, sworn not to let her get the upper hand, and promised myself all this not twenty-four hours before because I'd already let her poke a historical nerve. Why? Because she knew exactly which nerves respond to poking. She'd guessed. Like a seasoned con artist. Which was no excuse for letting her. And every time I tried blaming Nabi for it, I felt like I was the one playing myself for a chump.

"If that's the case," Doreen said, "being marooned on this island is a far cry from a dream come true for you."

That depends on whether it's Monday or Saturday, but I couldn't get into that. I found myself looking into an empty plastic cup. Doreen took it.

She wore the same high-cut shorts she'd worn the day before. I watched them as she went into the house to fill the cups. She leaned against the stoop as she drank.

"So what're you working on now?"

"Well, nothing. I work for CAM. Marooned just like you said."

In my student days, when I told people I was in Comparative Literature emphasizing English classics and new metaphysics, Bermudians would respond along the following lines: Bye, why you gotta write somethin tired? That kinda stuff *been* dead. A Jamaican client: *What bad man got to say bout white man's book?*

Well, books are very hard to kill, and they're not just for white people, but there's little use in arguing. For one thing, you won't get any help from your colleagues. They'll assume all you're good for are postcolonial studies, ethnic studies, or Caribbean studies, never mind that Bermuda's still a colony and isn't in the Caribbean. I've even been told that people from the Commonwealth are too polite to argue big ideas.

Well, I know de deal, I'm heard every iggrunt remark there is to hear under de sun and therefore, however, in conclusion, did it anyway. It wasn't worth the pain, but in a way that's why I had to do it. Or so I thought, you know. Smooth out the road for others. I was young then. Doreen knew better.

We went in after four martinis. Might as well have been lemonade for me, that's how I am. But it made Doreen talkative.

93

She didn't say anything useful. I gathered Bingo cards. She talked about New York. Best city in the world, blah blah; and even there, she said, a black person could find themselves shoved against a police car for walking down the street. To this day discrimination soured every industry from politics to opera.

I listened for a while. There was something about her voice. I wouldn't call it musical, not like Nabi's. *Nikkou's* voice is melody, made for melisma and soul. Doreen's didn't have soul, but it had depth. And a weird lack of depth. Low in pitch but also low in tonal variety. It was creepy and off-putting. And dampening, sort of. It made me want to sit there and not move and not say anything. A hypnotist's voice, that's what it was. A voice for chants and incantations. If there was such a thing as a dark sound it was this: Doreen's Obeah-woman voice.

And you know, everything she said was quite correct. So is some, not all but some, of what Barrington says. White guys do get all the breaks. But because he's Barrington and I'm traumatized-mongrel me, I can only take so much one-sided sermonizing. Even from preternaturally alluring women. I prepared the rant that undergraduate-me would use to shut Barrington up. In rare moments when he deigned to take the phone from Masami so he could deliver a brief on curbing my foolish ambitions.

"Well, look, you're right," I ranted. "Discrimination's rampant. But it's not just about black people or women or New York. Right here in Bermuda, Philippine people, male and female, are treated like second-class outcasts. You want to talk racism, gotta talk about that. Want to talk about sexual discrimination, talk about dubbing same-sex marriages a threat to safe parenting. That's one step shy of calling gay people child murderers. Talk about Bermuda-born kids of Portuguese parents—these are white people now—being ineligible for either Bermudian or Portuguese citizenship. Some MP wanting to stop a qualified Bermudian from becoming a magistrate because the brethren was of Indian descent."

At this point, Barrington would say, *Bye, I can't talk to you. Your problem is you never had it hard enough; wanna learn the hard way, go on, knock yourself out.*

Doreen said, "Why anybody needs used-up Bingo cards is beyond me."

"And, yes, talk about black Bermudians being underpaid and passed over for big jobs at Bermuda-based exempt companies. Then talk about worldwide fear of immigrants. Point is you can't just worry about your own demographics. Or pretend this foolishness only happens someplace else. What about people who don't fit any of the boxes?"

"You could just ignore it all and think about Thomas Hardy."

"Or build a house of Bingo cards."

"Or religious pamphlets," Doreen grumbled.

She relocated a tower of pamphlets to a garbage bag. Besides the Bingo cards I'd spilled, there were more inside the bin. I shoveled them into the garbage bag with uncalled-for aggression.

"At least thinking about Thomas Hardy doesn't do one bit of harm. Besides, he advocated gender equality even though it cost him his career. He was an animal activist too."

"So he'd be mightily impressed with somebody using his novels to screen themselves from contemporary social problems," said the offspring of a cleaning lady obsessed with taxidermied cats. "To top it off, you're practically handed everything you need to become a college professor, a cultural force—"

"Cultural force."

"—that helps disseminate new perspectives. But instead of doing anything with what you're given, you slouch back to this piece of rock—"

"Excuse me, multiple joined-up and very pretty pieces of rock."

"—and laze around as what, CAM's errand boy?"

"Let me ask you something," I said. "How many activist organizations do you belong to? Be honest."

"Not the point." Doreen shrugged. "Anytime a marginalized—is that inclusive enough for you?—a marginalized person succeeds, despite all social prejudices, in whatever they set out to do, that's a victory for everyone."

"I'm not so sure that follows."

A more seductive shrug you've never seen and never will. And the smile to go with it? The knowing grimace of a thing biding its time like a lobster trap? For what? To rile me up? What could she have to gain by riling me up?

I said, "So what're you doing unemployed instead of getting back on the horse and fighting the good fight? Why dig around for your inheritance when you could struggle for every penny?"

"Every little bit helps." I almost thought she'd wink.

No other woman on this planet is less likely to wink. But do you know, in all her too-personal digging and political going-on, Doreen's tone of voice never altered even a little? She wasn't robotic, but I mean she didn't get loud, her voice never hardened as voices do when they're excited. There was no lightness in it either, not at all. Yet I found myself wondering if she took everything she said as a joke. This riled me even more. I'm far from averse to a little haha, but what kind? To what purpose? How could it be that I was uncertain how I'd feel if she was joking?

It was a good thing I found the pillowcase just then. Frustration and I tend to egg each other on.

At the bottom of the bin, now empty of Bingo cards, I found a green pillowcase. And it wasn't the bottom.

Under the pillowcase was a long, flat box of reddish-gold Bermuda cedar. It had an ornate locking mechanism of tarnished brass. Not something you could jimmy with a paperclip. We tried.

This box was the reason we'd spent hours wheezing among moldy shopping lists. Doreen was convinced. I was dubious. To me the box looked like a fancy carry-case for poker chips.

But with Czarina gone, what else was there? We wrestled that box till we'd snapped a butter knife, chipped a screwdriver, and exhausted all the expletives in the dictionary. I persuaded Doreen to take the fackin thing to a locksmith on Monday and in the interim take a break from Myrtle's dust. Start on the cottage, I suggested.

"Long as you come lend a hand."

Did yours truly do the smart thing and reply, *Not on your life, you bitch?* Of course not. I said, "All right." I returned her slinky grin, poison for poison. Doreen waited for me to say something more. I said, "Guess I'd better say goodnight." Like I regretted it.

Truth is, it was getting late; I was having thoughts of ramming Bingo cards down someone's deadly throat; I had the long, empty-handed drive ahead of me; and by the time I got home I was mad enough to throw a punch at one of my bookcases.

I didn't hit any books. I missed. Just left a little skin on the near edge of a shelf. Go figure.

But before that. All right.

Myrtle's dining table. Cedar box and broken tools scattered over the tablecloth. Doreen and I looked at each other. She said, "Want to stay?"

I was having thoughts of ramming, etc., as above. I knew the wisest course was to never see that woman again, never again expose myself to that creeping, probing voice of hers. But, the devil take me, I did want to stay.

And I really didn't.

I said, "Not tonight."

Around three in the morning, I got fed up with longing. I let Zohytin draw a blind over the empty side of solitude.

The Middle Passage. Belowdecks my father's ancestors were stuffed and crushed as so much cargo like *iwashi* in a can, like cows in an industrial slaughterhouse. Cars on a car carrier have more personal space than the slaves kidnapped from Africa and shipped across the Atlantic. They made the whole journey flattened. Literally stacked on top of each other. In his speech as Guest of Honor at the Warwick Academy Prizegiving, Barrington said that to get into your "berth"—which was never wide enough for any breathing human, never deep enough either, so you sailed three thousand miles with the berth above you practically up your nose—you had to bend over backwards and wriggle in headfirst so you could land on your feet when you wriggled out again, provided your legs hadn't atrophied. To move even an inch, you had to become a spider.

"This wasn't living," Barrington said. And still says year after year. He's never not a Guest of Honor someplace. And he's not one to overvalue originality. "It was limbo."

Between life and death. Between earth and hell. Limbo was where Christians said non-Christians had to go instead of heaven. So if you were Igbo or M'pongwe, if you believed in juju instead of Jesus, you never actually finished dying when you quit breathing. Your *shiryou* got stuck between opportunity and damnation. You carried on undead but without hope. Trapped in the Middle Passage for all eternity.

Barrington's overcoming-slavery speech was the most he ever said to me in one sitting. Well, you know, I was sitting. He was at the podium. I sat stiffly among my classmates (arranged in order of height, so Nabi was far away) till they announced the recipient of the Academic Achievement Award. Then I had to go onstage and shake my father's hand for the first time. He gave me the silver trophy which I could only keep for the summer. I had to return it to the school so someone in the next class could win. That idgit shook hands with my father too.

Caribbean slaves made a dance called the limbo, having no idea that people would one day consider it a rational way to party. The limboist bends over backwards and tries to wriggle forwards beneath a horizontal stick while it gets lower and lower. Sometimes they set the stick on fire. After they put the fire out, they let inebriated tourists have a go.

I make a point of leaving parties before the limbo starts. The idea of the ceiling getting lower and lower is too much for my nerves. When I shook Barrington's hand, I looked up at him and found him grinning at the audience. We were up there together all of five seconds, and ya boy never looked me in the eye. Whatever, this was no surprise, not even then. Barrington is never more than beside the point.

The point is, every time I let myself think through certain existential questions, I have to think about limbo. Because that's where I exist.

Stuck in a middle passage. Neither here nor there nor gone. And if I didn't know Nabi, I'd think she got a kick out of it.

On Sundays Nabi and I make codfish and potatoes on the stove of my imagination. Truth be told, I've never seen Mrs. Furbert on a Sunday. Church takes up most of her day and her husband takes the rest. If it hadn't been for him, I'd have gone to hear her sing. Mount Olive AME is just down the road from me. I saw their car in the parking lot as I slipped past on my way to St. George's.

Doreen had on a tank top and fresh pair of diminutive shorts. I said, "Good morning. No politics."

Her smile wasn't a smile. It was bored. Some little rage simmered below it. And perhaps some faint repulsion. Or I'm projecting the repulsion. The varnish on her rapacious look seemed less voluptuous than the opposite. I thought of a fish. A cold, slimy, hard-eyed bottom-feeder. I allowed myself a smirk and said, "Girl, let's don't waste each other's time." She pushed past me; I stepped back to avoid touching her.

In my embittered mood, I thought uncharitably of *amemasu*: that obese, ugly fish that gobbles everything it finds. At night it climbs ashore. It turns into a woman. A hot and hard-eyed woman with cold and slimy skin. She awakens people's hunger. And once they've spent themselves with her, she eats them. Then I thought I was too charitable. Doreen's boldness of the day before wasn't a demon's preternatural energy but a delusion of a helpless, frustrated human who couldn't shame CAM's errand boy into groveling at her feet. I made a point of watching her from behind as she unlocked Aetna's cottage.

And I let my chance to escape flutter off into the hedge.

To say Aetna Simmons' cottage wasn't what I expected would be an understatement.

In Europe, certain buildings have plaques on their outer walls. *Here Ludwig van Beethoven Scrawled the Pseudo-Suicide Note known as the Heiligenstadt Testament.* This tiny pink cottage, far from anywhere, deserved such commemoration.

"Not much to do here. Don't think Momma would've given any valuables to a tenant." Yet Doreen opened the nearest drawer and peered inside.

No luxury townhouse. Fine. I still expected the tools of a modern forger. I'd formed an image of Mission Control: Printers of every make and model whirring on a metallic, floor-to-ceiling grid. On another wall, typewriters. On a third, pens and inks, the Mont Blancs and the Bics. International copybooks, manuals of handwriting analysis, paper of every sort. Such things were the masks under her masks, the baroque carnival masks she wore under her *noumen*.

99

Her words were her *noumen,* her operatic outer masks. She had to make sure someone would authenticate them *before* anybody thought to check for graphological anomalies. Or watermarks that could identify her printer. Authentication hung on her skill as an author, not as a mere forger.

Still, she should've had *something.* There wasn't a single shelving unit. Besides the crude all-in-one printer-scanner, there wasn't a scrap of equipment. No books. Not even one. Instead there were shades of Myrtle Trimm. Same tile on the floor. Same exhausted quality to everything. By the kitchenette were a café table and two chairs from Myrtle's dining set. No living room or foyer. Soon as we passed through the door, we were at the kitchenette, bumping the ramshackle café table a footstep outside the study.

Despite all this, I didn't breathe for at least a minute.

I didn't want Doreen to pick up on my excitement. She might tell her relatives, it could get back to Masami; Bermuda is such that all of it was possible.

I call it a study out of respect for the work that happened there. It wasn't a room, just a corner of extra space, a consequence of a misshapen wall. There was a card table with one of Myrtle's plastic cabinets under it. A wire-framed stand as a sort of credenza. Doreen opened a drawer in the cabinet; and as she bent to peer inside, her head was level with the place—the actual corner of the actual peeling card table—where Javon's co-inspectors found the remarkable documents that made prisoners of my thoughts. The folding chair behind the table: that was where she sat. Where Aetna Simmons rested her body while her mind gamboled beyond the boundaries of life and death. I stood still and tried to sense something of her. Just a whiff of her courageous and decisive spirit.

It was in vain. Doreen let me look into the drawers, but they were empty. The printer-scanner-fax on top of the credenza was full of unremarkable, white copy paper.

Cup of cheap pens on the table. Potted cactus. No papers; the police had them. Grocery receipts, Javon said, that was all.

In the document destruction business, you meet four kinds of people. People who keep everything and file it chronologically in fireproof cabinets. People who keep everything without meaning to do so; these people end up with stuff all over the place. There are people who keep a few important things and toss the rest. And people who throw everything away. What one throws away says something of one's being-in-the-world.

Aetna tossed it all. Nothing was sacred. Only ten flimsy little things. The printer was just too big to go with the trash.

Yet she must have kept her laptop; her nursery and her archive and her menagerie. Perhaps she'd hidden it, I thought, somewhere in the cottage.

Doreen rummaged in the kitchenette, came up with a wok, a colander, and mismatched bowls. I looked through the window in the study. I saw Myrtle's cedar box on her dining table. I saw the empty space where Czarina had kept her vigil.

The doorway to the bedroom squeezed between the study and the kitchenette. I found a twin bed, neatly made, lamp at the head and dresser at the foot, an armoire shoved awkwardly into a corner.

I checked the dresser while Doreen was in the kitchen. No computer. I found uninteresting underwear, pajamas, and socks. No teddies, no lacy bras, no thongs, not a single negligee. Disappointing but not nugatory: she wore Nabi's size in the bikini cut Nabi likes, although *nikkou* prefers brighter colors. Clothes in the armoire were inexpensive. Her palette tended to brown and gray with the occasional maroon. There were jeans and slacks, a skirt or two. No dresses. Nothing sexy. But she was obviously compact and comfortable with her shape. Again like Nabi, who, however, likes to show her curves and rightly so. In the bottom of the armoire were a sorry pair of black wedges and some tattered sandals.

What kind of human female negotiates the age of consumerism in just two pairs of shoes? Nabi has at least a dozen, and that's just counting the ones she stashes at my place.

Made me rethink the money. What if it really was sixty thousand a year, not per assignment? Five thousand a month, her rent was forty-eight hundred; and the money in Cayman was Clocktower's, not hers. All the risk hardly seemed worth it.

"Find anything? Perhaps a key or combination for a wooden box?"

Doreen in the doorway. Dare in her stance.

"There's something back here," I said. I hadn't seen anything.

I pretended to dig in the corner of the armoire, started to say I was wrong after all, and then...

It just didn't fit. My hand hesitated above a small brown bag.

"That's cute. Let's see," said Doreen.

It was worth about eight hundred dollars on Front Street. Aetna would've had to stop eating for four months.

Louis Vuitton's Speedy 25 Minibag in Damier Ebene leather. I'd researched it for Nabi's last birthday, eschewing it eventually for Louis' Speedy Bandoulière 25 in a midnight-blue leather known as Infini ($2,500). She carried it everywhere. Told Martin she'd bought it for herself.

"Nice," said Doreen. She took the bag.

She shook it.

I've thought a lot about the sound that snagged Doreen's attention. That sound would've been like the breath of a mouse. I've come to the conclusion I never heard it.

"What's inside?" said Doreen. She held out the bag to me.

I said, "A lady's purse is her sanctum." And dipped into the Damier Ebene.

Driving to St. George's, I'd formed the sentimental idea that in Aetna's cottage I'd find some kind of keepsake. The first clue. Something meaningful only to me. A tangible link between Aetna and me alone. Perhaps a book with a shiny black cover. Who knew that what I found would bring my life crashing down?

It was such a little thing. It rolled around in the handbag like someone lost without a flashlight in a deep cavern. The uninitiated would've pegged it for a tiny pearl.

I was glad I was sitting on the floor.

"What is it?" said Doreen.

The time when canniness and discretion would abandon me to frenzy lay in the unforeseen future. Swallowing a dozen impassioned curses, I said, "It's a pearl. Fell off a necklace or something. Probably fake."

Doreen held out her hand for it. Rolled it between her fingers.

It wasn't a pearl. It was Empyreal.

Doreen put the thing in the pocket of her shorts. She wanted a break. We went back to the house, she got out her shaker, and this time the drinks were stronger.

Fact: I know every one of my clients by name and by sight. I'm not bad at voice recognition either. Fact: According to the fine print, no one but yours truly could've sold Aetna that pill.

The facts left room for four possibilities. (1) A friend hooked her up. (2) She visited Boston and among its multitudes ran into one particular person. (3) Somebody violated the fine print. (4) She was a client whom I had known for years by another name.

The last was easy to rule out. None of my clients possessed the wherewithal, creativity, or organizational capacity required to pull off a double life, and no other disappearances were mentioned on the news. (1) would've required her to go out once in a while and spend money, which by all accounts she never did. (2) involved going through the airport with the stuff, and I can't imagine Aetna signing up for that; she was waist-deep in risk already. Addicts are capable of a great many things, but if she was an addict, she'd have had at least a full box of Empyreal and a ton of cash ready to hand. Furthermore, I knew her. Her intellect was not that of an addict.

"You're quiet," said Doreen.

"Should we check out your old room?"

I put up a convincing front, opening a bin at random, seeming to check the contents. But I spoke little. I was too angry. My enterprise was a cutting-edge machine, and now here was some vandal trying to plant a virus in it; if one pill had gone over to some black-on-black market, maybe it wasn't alone. I ransacked the archive in my head, each name, each voice. I looked myself in the eye by looking in, and I said, *You stupid woolgathering screwup.*

Then Doreen found the bank statements. She blinked like what she read was too idiotic to believe. "That woman gave Momma forty-eight hundred a month for that cottage."

I clambered over bins to Doreen's side. She gave me a narrow sheaf. "Any more in there?"

Back issues of *The Daily Bread.* Programs from the 1980 Bermuda Festival. A dozen statements from the Bank of Butterfield, one for each month of last year, chronologically arranged. There were the deposits. $4,800 a month. This correlated with Aetna's record at HSBC. She held on to the cottage at that ridiculous rate, suffocating between hedges and high walls, always, always scrutinized through that oppressive window.

"The market can't be that bad. The cottage isn't worth that, is it? Be honest," said Doreen.

"Divide by four. That's what it's worth."

Doreen took the statements and glared at them one by one. The balances ran over six figures, yet she made no comment. Didn't even crack a smirk. Or she did, and I failed to notice. I was pawing through my memories of suave conversations and expensive handshakes. I pushed my hands into a bin, then the one beside it and the one next to that, and dammit tried to think like a scholar. If my hypotheses were lines of poetry, I thought (not with any real logic), then somewhere a third line waited to be discovered, so altogether Aetna's situation would form a Dantean canto. Somewhere in that house, maybe right there in Doreen's room, that third line resounded. I told myself I heard it as one hears a distant echo; embedded in it somewhere was the reason for that stray Empyreal, and to hear it properly I had to damn it all and dig. Maybe all I heard was ire buzzing in my ears, but I couldn't stop flipping through Myrtle's old *Gazette*s any more than I could prevent connections reaching out to one another in my head, fusing with a spark, and reaching out once more.

Myrtle knew what Aetna did, I concluded. Somehow she knew enough to keep Aetna in that cottage under any condition, and for Aetna it wasn't simply inconvenient. It reduced her small fortune to a shoestring budget, fattened the risks she took a thousandfold. Blackmail, yes: a threat made present every moment as a face in the window. Aetna heading for Supermart, Myrtle watching till she disappeared around the hedge. Myrtle unlocking the cottage, Czarina sniffing and snaking round her heels.

A woman of the shadows, who shunned every convention because she loved freedom above all. A woman like that under the avaricious thumbs of Myrtle Trimm and an insurance company. Every human being who drew near to Aetna's close, umbrageous world was a greedy so-and-so bent on yoking her to them. She would've gone out of her mind.

I'm not sure of the chemistry, but it's easy to imagine certain designer compounds bringing on a stroke in an eighty-one-year-old. Empyreal makes cocaine look like a spoonful of sugar. It makes Hallelujah look like Centrum Silver. It dissolves on the tongue without scent or taste, so it could've gone into the milk or the Ensure, something Myrtle was sure to ingest not right away but eventually.

So there was time. When Myrtle succumbed, Aetna was already dead. And so a certain grisly theory remained far from anybody's mind.

It was enough to make me freeze with my hand in a jar of tarnished spoons. Once I'd overcome the urge to hurl the jar at the nearest bin, I assessed alternate theories.

After Aetna died, nothing Myrtle said could've done Aetna any harm. In fact Aetna may have *wanted* to expose Clocktower as her final act on earth. The mere presence of the Ten testifies to this, in which case she had no reason to kill Myrtle.

Except of course revenge, that old poisoned spur. Myrtle made Aetna's life a living hell. What if she left behind her story—all of it, say, on some flash drive—hoping the truth would mortify the nosy old witch right before she met her end, so she had time for remorse and nothing else?

Or Clocktower killed them both and with a little help made Aetna look like an assassin.

So, Dr. Caines, how's it feel to be an accessory to murder?

"What is it?" said Doreen.

"Nothing. What if the key's in here? You know, for the box." I upended the jar of spoons. Their noisy clatter did little to relieve my desire to snap them all in two.

I felt like someone had spilled yellow paint on one of my tailored suits. If ever it came out that Myrtle Trimm had died from a misapplication of a certain shortcut to enlightenment, I'd find myself disavowed by my conservative supplier. In Bermuda, unwelcome scrutiny is anathema to doing business. Aetna was dead, leaving no one else to take the rap. In short, this could ruin me.

One good thing: Myrtle was already in the ground. If she'd had an autopsy, nothing came of it. Otherwise it would've made the news. The conjecture that her stroke was anything but natural rode on the potential of Empyreal that wasn't there. The presence of a pill in a handbag in a corner of a dead woman's closet is in itself no evidence for the onetime existence of another pill which, if it existed, would hopefully have dissolved in the other dead woman's bloodstream.

I was putting spoons back in the jar (no key), wondering how I might sneak the pill out of this house without arousing the daughter's suspicions.

Doreen said, "Something's wrong, I can tell."

How could she tell? I affected an idle demeanor as I unfolded embroidered aprons from the bin. Beneath them were yellowed tablecloths, the scintillating feathered cape of a Gombey dancer.

"Your dad was a Gombey?"

"How should I know? Never met the bastard. I asked you a question."

"The answer is nothing." Bits of mirror winked out of the cape, sewn into the velvet among embroidered birds and lilies and long ribbons. I started to lift the garment from the bin, and Doreen grabbed my hand.

"Something spooked you in the cottage. If it's something about Momma, I deserve to know."

Her voice was low, her face unlined. But something in her eyes seemed to be on fire. In that moment her beauty was that of sunlight setting the ocean ablaze: look at it an instant and you'd look away blinded. Dazzling was the mirror that seemed to reflect my own anxiety from the depths of her black pupils.

It made me hesitate. How much could she see? Was she a demon after all with the power to see right through me? Never in my life had a stranger threatened me this way. Even Nabi and I had to learn each other. It took time even in our childish eagerness. And still, of my dark, pearl-studded territory—which I feared Doreen could stumble on even if I sent her on a wild goose chase—Nabi knew absolutely nothing.

In a way it was Masami who made me press on. I imagined Doreen having nightmares just like mine, starring Myrtle and an undead Siamese cat and all the same questions: *What has she done, what does she*

106

want from me… Myrtle's daughter creeped me out and mixed me up, but she didn't deserve that, I thought, nobody deserves that. Christ, what a sucker.

"Okay, look," I began. "Nobody would pay that kind of money for that cottage. Unless something else was going on."

Doreen's nails threatened to break my skin. She was shrewd; a moment's thought, and it was she who said the word. "Extortion."

"The tenant, Aetna Simmons. Did your momma ever tell you anything about her?"

"Estranged, remember?" Doreen dropped my hand, delved into her pocket. "What's that got to do with this?"

Empyreal. So tempted to grab the thing and swallow it.

Doreen said in her hypnotic way, "You know what I think? If this is a pearl, then it's a real one. It's not junk. I think Momma had all kinds of stuff like this. Her CAM portfolio is the tip of the iceberg. Somehow the tenant stole this, meant to stash it till she could find enough evidence to sue Momma for extortion. Everybody died before she got the chance. Except you."

She turned her fishy eyes on me. "You're here to learn how much of CAM's money Momma tainted."

Doreen's alone. Smart, quick, ambitious, fearless. Powerless. She's out of a job, desperate for money, probably for a long time. Then a momma whom she doesn't care two pennies for dies on top of an invisible bonanza. If only it wasn't "tainted," it could spell the end of Doreen's woes. If only Myrtle hadn't been whatever discarded or repelled Doreen in the first place.

That's how it looked to her, I figured. I figured it felt like the puny raft she'd made of broken mizzenmast and torn-up poop deck sweeping out from under on a wave. I am familiar with this feeling.

I'm not saying I felt sorry for her. It's just when door after door keeps slamming in your face, even doors supposed to lead to those who give a shit, including doors inside your head, you forget how to tell an open door from a slammed one. So I mean, I felt sorry for me, not her. Maybe a little sorry for her. Doreen didn't look cowed or teary, not even angry; she looked smooth, dark, solid, and unfairly, corrosively beautiful. I imagined her, Myrtle's DNA raging through her, taking the ersatz pearl to some jewelry exchange to sell for cash and ending up humiliated. I imagined Doreen's relentlessness driving her too far. Knowing the pitiless way she went about asking questions, it was easy to imagine her barging into CAM, demanding explanations from Masami and Barrington. Both of us were vulnerable. That's how I saw it.

I said, "Honey, that's not a pearl."

"And therefore you said it was?"

"Because, look, it's a pill. It's a designer drug. It's the Bugatti of designer drugs."

Better that she find out from me than anyone else. A police lab tech, say.

"Extortion and illegal drugs. My Momma."

I could only shrug. I knew that feeling too, having looked up at the CAM mountain.

"Eighty-one years old. Too cheap to buy herself a car. Just to make sure we're talking about the same person. I mean, I just get this feeling that you're about to tell me you think Aetna Simmons got sick of being taken, used this stuff to give my mom a stroke, and then committed suicide. Am I right, Kenji? You think Momma was murdered."

Doreen looked as cool as cheesecake about it. The pandemonium in my head was rather otherwise.

I began to wonder if she might be a cop. I tried to explain the pill wasn't evidence. Really there was no evidence that there'd been a murder, no hard evidence of anything except that Aetna Simmons knew how to have a good time. But Doreen argued at every turn. Motive, means, opportunity, etc.

"How would she have known which drug to use to kill Momma? From what you're telling me, this stuff is so rare it's not in any databases. Guess she could've asked the dealer."

"Doreen, I know you want closure and all that," I broke in.

"News to me, seeing as there's no such thing."

"At least you want to believe the best about your momma."

"Why? She sure as hell didn't do me any favors."

A moment of a smothered sigh. I needed Doreen on the defensive.

She wasn't about to make it easy, and I should've taken note of that.

Easy to say so now, of course. *The owl of Minerva takes flight only when the shades of night are gathering.* Hindsight and all that jazz.

"I'll cut to the chase," I said.

"Good idea."

"Aetna disappeared before your momma died. What if she killed herself—"

"You want to say she killed herself for the same reasons I'm saying she might've killed Momma. Because Momma bled her dry, because she ran out of money and got sick of being scared of what Momma had on her. Momma was so hungry for money losing her tenant sent her right into a stroke, which served her right because—"

"Look, I didn't say that."

"Because in the end, Momma was the only criminal around for miles. An extortionist. Her victim crawled off somewhere to OD and dropped one of her tablets in a purse that stayed behind. Is that what you want to say?"

It was. It really was.

Except the last bit. I mean Aetna OD-ing on Empyreal. That had never entered my imagination. I'm not kidding.

I was already perturbed, and this just made it worse: "How the hell do you know that? How the fuck do you know what goes on in my head? It's creepy. It's *my head*, for fuck's sake." I shut up, tried deep breaths; it was no good. And Doreen didn't answer right away. A beam of dingy sunlight eked between the curtains over her shoulder, battled through the dust and murk only to fade in the dank air between our bodies. I followed her gaze to the place where the light died.

She said, "We're the same. Not all the way but on some level. I don't have to know you to figure that out, I mean it's pretty obvious." She started to turn away. I reached across and grasped her wrist.

"What's obvious?"

"You want to think I haven't noticed, but you and I, we're spending a lot of time dancing around something. That's because we're used to being that way. Our shadows run deep. They go right to the bottom."

Those were her words exactly.

"Since that goes for both of us, you may as well forget about hiding anything from me."

She set her jaw as though she stood on a hill above a battlefield, tall and proud and grim. The anger I'd nursed all afternoon started to burn. Slowly at first but then, as I realized how unfair everything was, from Empyreal to Masami to Nabi and Louis Vuitton, and this stranger who presumed to sit there oozing gorgeousness and lust, daring to know me, that anger detonated to engulf them all and wrap me in a shockwave of despair. Doreen began to suck the fingers I'd curled around her wrist, and I believe I meant to shove her. I didn't.

Sunday is the Lord's day. That means it's full of joy each week before it's even started. My husband told me that.

One day, soon after we met, Martin took me to a lovely seminar at the Bermuda Bible Institute. "The Wisdom of Paul: Don't Give Up." Romans 6, Colossians 1, Martin loves St Paul. Galatians 6:9, that's one of his favorites: "Let us not become weary in doing good, for at the proper time we will reap, if we do not give up." After the class he took my hand in his strong fingers & said it again. "Don't give up."

Face it, acegirl: I was unhappy. K had gone to Harvard, I was trapped at the bank. He & I talked or texted all the time, so I tried to pretend I didn't have to miss him, but I wasn't any good at it. I tried to be myself (a janitor at work called me Smiley-Face), but I wasn't. I was a teller, dispensable & bored to tears, while my best friend got to go off & make something of himself. Martin's taking my hand, saying what he said, let me know that he knew. He knew better than I did even though I hadn't told him. & he wanted me to be OK.

Next thing I know, M & I are an "item," he's moving from St Paul AME to Mt Olive (Mummy & Daddy were over the moon!), & he & I are running Sunday Bible Study! Now I get to watch him find all the Good Book's possibilities & point them out to people in the Book & in the world. He sees the Joy of Promise everywhere. That's Faith, & Martin's Faith is pure & inspirational. Take that poor man the other day with the midnight ice-cream cravings, Lord have mercy. Honey whipped out his cocktail of Corinthians & Galatians, his kind & stirring voice warmed & sparkled all at once & almost made me cry.

Now he's traveling so much, that voice only comes out on Sundays. After the service when our little group troops into the hall, that little bit of social awkwardness which often troubles Martin just evaporates. We relax. He is inspired. He knows all the important translations & his interpretations ring out elegant & confident. & he always finds a way to work in his message just for me: Don't Give Up. We are comfy, he makes jokes, people laugh. They love his earnestness. It's pretty sexy actually. & I'm the one who gets to take him home. He's what my Faith dreams of. He's the beauty & the joy in Faith. & he's always back by Sunday, Honey's very proud of that.

One summer long ago, K's first summer back from Harvard (I hadn't met Martin yet), K was different, a little sad & trying not to be. Just like me, really, but we didn't understand yet. I took him to church, thinking it might help. It was Baby's first time to attend a service. I grew up on Sunday services. But poor K & E, I don't think their momma believes in God. I don't say that to be mean, it's just she took a lot of flak for taking Mr C away from his faith & not bringing up the children in the church, it sort of sidelined the whole family in the community. But my momma didn't think she could argue with her, so anyway. Kenji in suit & tie. Yes, girl. Mmmhm. Real sharp.

We were 18 or so. Mummy & Daddy looked nervous & Iesha was smug. The sermon was Matthew 5, the Beatitudes & "Love your enemies." & after, K & I went walking around Fort Scaur. Usually our conversations travel deep & far into the nitty-gritty. This time he just kept saying, "Yeah, it gave me a lot to think about." I pushed & prodded even tickled him, & K surprised me by getting annoyed. Turned out he got hung up on Bertrand Russell (I looked him up later, God have mercy on his soul) & verses 28-30-ish: "But I say unto you, that whosoever looketh on a woman to lust after her hath committed adultery with her already in his heart. & if thy right eye offend thee, pluck it out & cast it from thee..."

I got all hot in the face like I hadn't breathed in awhile. But I got annoyed too & sort of panicky for no reason. That made me more annoyed. I'm telling you, we didn't understand. I said, "It's just a figure of speech."

"Well, you know, I offend a lot of people," said K. "A born Bermudian who in't a 'real' Bermudian cuz I in't black enough. I'm too black for Japan. I've been called dirty in both places, you know that, dirty meaning what? Offensive. The Americans point out how un-American I am every _____ day & how dangerous it makes me. Now you're saying eye removal is some kind of figure of speech for what these lot should do to me?" He said it lightly like a joke. Like it made no difference to him.

"That's not what Jesus meant."

"Course not." & Kenji grinned. I thought he was going to put his arm around me, but he didn't. He bumped my shoulder with his shoulder & said, "You know what? That service was the best thing I've done in months. You know why? Cuz I did it with my best friend."

K never talked about Jesus again. I talk all the time, I couldn't stop even if I wanted to, & Baby never fails to encourage me. He encouraged me & Martin to take over Bible Study when the group needed somebody. He let me practice "O Holy Night" out on his balcony when I was due to sing solo at the Christmas service. He said, "Nikkou, you make Mariah & those lot sound like bad auctioneers."

But he won't talk about the Bible. He'll listen, he'll tease just enough to make me laugh. But he won't do nitty-gritty. It's cuz our friendship's safe haven. All those years he was away, we never argued once. We don't want to mess it up by disagreeing. Iesha says I was a coward not to wait for him.

But it's Martin who's the strength & courage in my Faith. Without Martin & in poor misguided Kenji's shadow, the Word Of God would look like nothing more than black & white. Without Martin there'd be no Sunday Bible Study Group, I couldn't carry on without him, all our friends & our pastor would cut their eyes at me! & how can I Give Up on our Lord Jesus? No, I can't.

I mean, it's not like I really have to choose. M's good for me, but so is K. K's always searching for new perspectives & ideas, a total contrast to M's unswerving Faith. But it's a good contrast! & You'd rather have a sinner than a sinner without Faith, wouldn't You?

❧

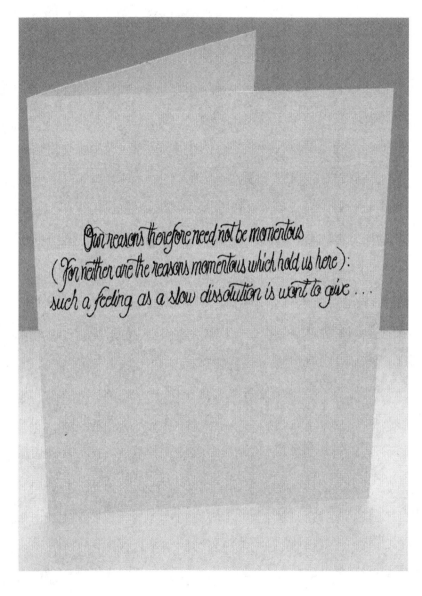

AS4.
Calligraphy on greeting card. Color: "creamy beige" (JB).
Stoic humility, costly naïveté.

114

A man with a toga and distracted expression strolled beside the Mediterranean as boats with billowing sails glissaded through the peaceable sea. *Even if I were not an old man,* he wrote, *I could not have helped feeling pleasure at this.* And such small pleasures were all he required out of life. Almost.

Life is not incomplete if it is honorable.

That'd look good in embroidery on a cushion, wouldn't it? Too bad it wasn't really Seneca's point.

His point was that if living isn't good, healthy, stimulating fun (and don't forget "honorable"), then it simply isn't worth it. Living just for the sake of living might as well be death. It's about quality, not quantity. And if quality is lacking, well, then *one must leave off bravely, and our reasons therefore need not be momentous; for neither are the reasons momentous which hold us here…*

I found him in AS4, the content of which Aetna borrowed from "On Taking One's Own Life," Seneca's seventy-seventh *Moral Letter to Lucilius* (c. 62-65 AD). His letters aren't like hers. They're not suicide notes. Whilst they do advocate suicide for the sick, the decrepit, the miserable, and those who'd rather not join them, Seneca's letters are meant to be therapeutic. Philosophy, he said, is a healing power.

Drawing from a classic text would've helped Aetna conceal her identity. But it also would've precluded any specific simulation. Seneca's was not the face she needed. The archaic tone, the *wont*, the perspective is ancient, distant, the true author well-known, the message too general. As someone else's missive, document examiners would never buy it. You want to say it wasn't for them. You want to say this one was personal.

Or it wasn't. A greeting card that stands up on its own so the message greets the reader like the name on a place setting. Inside, the card is blank.

But consider its place in the narrative of the Ten. In AS4, she philosophically denies the fear of death that torments every animal. She denies the *momentousness* of life and its demise. Considers the feeling of the transition, a peaceful *dissolution* (cf. AS1 and AS2). She has Seneca the Stoic establish learned precedent for her overcoming of brute instinct with cool reason.

I'm ready, she is saying.

She wasn't ready. She had six notes left to write. And she was still dreaming. I mean, *slow dissolution*? That's what Seneca thought too.

Despite his toga and eloquent vocabulary, I'd hesitate to call him a reliable source on this matter. First Nero accused him of conspiring to kill the emperor, who at the time was (yes) Nero. He sentenced Seneca to die; the latter chose to slit his wrists. But he didn't do it very well. His cuts produced an anticlimactic trickle. He cut his legs too. Didn't help. So he sat down and dictated something philosophical, something very important, no doubt suffused with insight, that has since been lost. When he got impatient, he took poison. It paralyzed the poor man's limbs but failed to do him in. Fed up and exhausted, he decided on a hot bath. There, at long last, Lucius Annaeus Seneca choked on the steam and perished.

He and Aetna shared a wish: if only I could die and death could be this way. This isn't *I am ready* but holding her hand over hot water, not yet touching, just assessing her courage. AS4 is a feint. Like my wasted weekend.

It's no wonder I was out of sorts on Monday morning, having been through all that foolishness only to learn nothing new. All I managed that weekend was to place my professional and private lives on the tip of my nose, bend over backwards, and fail to escape feet-first as the ceiling started lowering. This could not be rectified until I'd traced that peregrine Empyreal.

Four people may sell my products without violating the fine print. They are the concierges at Bermuda's most famous hotels. First stop: Jasmine Lounge, Fairmont Southampton Princess.

The lounge had a few tourists but not many. Americans don't care for finery anymore. The Jasmine has begun to feel less like a tea room and more like a high-end diner. The cutlery is rolled in napkins, and the first thing on the menu is a pulled pork taco. But for all that, it is easy, sitting there and sipping out of bone china, to imagine oneself back to the glory days of tropical colonialism as lush palmettos crowd against the picture windows and a carpet of English roses fades under your feet. I ordered the house blend and added, "Tell Gino that Dr. Caines is here." The concierge came running to my table, greeted me with a loud embrace as though I were a long-lost brother.

Here's how it works. When a tourist wants to party, he tells Gino. Gino helps him choose the product, tacks on a commission for himself, and collects. Then he texts me using a code based on Jasmine's appetizer menu. I stop by the lounge, enjoy a cup of tea, and since Gino and I have been old friends since the day we met, no one thinks anything of it when he joins me. We exchange gossip and a few other things, and he deals with the tourist, who has no clue that I exist.

Gino's not allowed to keep a stash at the hotel. If I suspected him of stashing or if he placed too many orders to be credible, I'd report him to the cops: possession with intent to sell. Besides, what I do is a service to my nation. My products are so exquisite, so unique that tourists have been known to visit this place several times a year for the sake of tiny, arcane things in velveteen boxes. With his job on the tip of the recession's tongue, Gino appreciates all this.

He read about Aetna on Bernews when she disappeared. Before that, he'd never heard of her. And he hadn't served any one-night-only guests. No locals, in other words, playing tourist just to place an order.

I had another cup of tea at the Hamilton Princess, another at the Rosewood and the Loren. No concierges had anything for me.

In a darkening mood I stopped at the Louis Vuitton store on Front Street. The sun was out, the harbor clear and blue, and it was Monday. Should've been lovely. But when I came face to face with a glass-enclosed Bandoulière Infini, everything in me grew heavy.

I decided that the weekend was Nabi's fault. I looked at the bag, feeling pissed off and pathetic. A well-pressed individual came up to me and said, "If it makes you feel better, the matching wallet's only seven fifty. We have the mini-agenda too. Five hundred, I think?" She dropped her voice, adding, "The agenda makes a great I-miss-you gift. Just so you know."

Had some evil sorcerer turned me into a billboard? Had the keys to my painfully crafted, multi-layered façade somehow just appeared in women's inboxes around the world? How did I manage to smile at Vuitton's crispy sprite? "What about an I'm-sorry gift?"

"The wallet. Definitely."

"I'll take both."

At the counter I attempted to pump the sprite for information. Vuitton products come with lifetime warranties, so I figured they must have a database of buyers. I complimented the sprite's little haircut, and she agreed to look and see if my lady really bought the Bandoulière or if it had in fact been the Speedy 25 Minibag.

"Aetna with an A," she said. "You know what? I don't see her. I hope somebody didn't trick her into buying a knockoff. Do you know there are people who actually do that?"

"I can't believe it."

"No, really. But the good news is you're sure about the color. The Minibag and Bandoulière both come in Infini, so either way, you're straight."

It was possible that whoever bought Aetna the bag also bought the drugs. Possible that she bought it herself under another name. Her real name perhaps, which in spite of all I'd done I still did not know.

Doreen called. She wanted to meet up, said she'd been to the locksmith. I didn't feel like talking. I let the call go to voicemail.

Chemically and economically, Empyreal is unconducive to daily consumption. The worst addict I've ever met couldn't stand to use it more than twice a week. The stuff is just that good. A ten-tablet box should last at least a month. I reasoned that anyone who reordered too soon could be selling. I do not, however, maintain sales records. That would've been stupid. The plan was to shake up every repeat buyer of Empyreal and observe whatever spilled.

Not a healthy plan. Implementation was stressful. It took effort not to growl at the best of clients as they all began to look like greedy bastards out to ruin me. This set in motion a familiar spiral of existential questions which did nothing to improve my disposition or expedite my other inquiries.

ME: Dr. Caines, why did you become a drug dealer?
MYSELF: So I could have a dangerous secret.

ME: Is that all?

MYSELF: Rather talk about how my family betrayed me in my time of need, crushing all my dreams forever?

ME: No thanks. I've heard all that before.

MYSELF: Exactly.

ME: Can you describe some of your products? Or would that ruin the surprise?

MYSELF: They're all synthetics. Hundred percent original, invented and manufactured by [NAME REDACTED], the famous medicinal chemist up in Boston. He's done work for [INSTITUTION REDACTED] and [PHARMACEUTICAL COMPANY REDACTED], other places like that. Besides Boston, you won't find our products anywhere except Bermuda. He and I like to keep things intimate, you know, on a scale we can supposedly control. But do you know I sell more than his Boston broker?

ME: Go long, bye.

MYSELF: [Laughs.] I'm telling you. Americans like coming here to get hooked up. Adds a whole sort of exotic flavor to the experience. And the locals, you know. It's easier for them to get to know me and the products than it is for Bostonians to get to know my counterpart there. This has to do with the size of our community. Anyway, our most popular products right now are Empyreal and Hallelujah. But I mean you have to understand this is an industry that changes very, very quickly, even quicker I would say than the tech industries, but of course I wouldn't quote me on that. What I mean is that Empyreal, for example, might be our biggest thing right now, but tomorrow or the next day some hotshot will make some kind of discovery, and the next thing you know such-and-such compound, the backbone of the drug, will become illegal—well, like [chuckles] impossible-to-get illegal—which means the chemical composition of Empyreal will have to change and I'll have to start calling it, I don't know, Imperial or something. What's important is staying a step ahead, which to be sure involves keeping the compounds innovative but requires first and foremost preventing inconvenient discoveries.

ME: And what do you personally bring to the operation?

MYSELF: Well, okay, what's missing from designer drugs like Bath Salts, which come in little plastic bags looking like bits of dried fruit? Or what's missing from Spice, another so-called designer drug that you can buy in what? Convenience stores? Excuse me? What's wrong with this picture?

ME: It does sound kind of tacky.

MYSELF: Thank you, so we agree on something. What's typically missing from designer drugs is the design. Design in the sense of style. Class. Sophistication. And for high-end clients, that's *so* important. That's what I bring. My clothes, my car, my intellect, the kind of elevated conversation that I'm capable of, even my face—which will always be exotic no matter where I go—all of it says to the client: this is a guy like Bruce Wayne and Mr. Spock. Like Beyoncé in *The Fighting Temptations*. Too much class to be here, and yet here he is. Clients want the attention and approval of people like that. Just being in the presence of that kind of cooler-than-thou, so to speak, puts people in awe of themselves. I flatter them just by being around, and I make them want that feeling to last. So there's the marketing side of it. I'm a sort of preview to the product.

[Flicks dust mote, perhaps invisible, off of spiffy suit.]

There's also the security side. Here in Bermuda—in the US too, only it's more pronounced here because our bureaucratic machine isn't big enough to cover itself entirely—if you do something in style and with a big old grin, right in front of every camera you can find, you will get away with it no matter what it is, even if it's putting other people's children up for sale. Like for example: little Filipino girl rips off BF&M for seventy-five G's; she does it in secret, so it looks underhanded and smells dirty. She gets caught, sent to jail. Meanwhile Premier So-and-So *been* milking the whole country for way, I mean, *way* more than that and faces no repercussions, *zero*, because he does it in style. Not to mention Minister Whatshisname harassing that lady like a pervert and going international with it on social media, broadcasting his contempt for Bermudians by telling us he figured we'd all get the joke. Anyway, nobody wonders what I'm doing waltzing into Parliament in the middle of a Friday afternoon *because I look good.* A man looks good in Parliament, why shouldn't he be there? I'm not saying I'm not discreet, I was born discreet, but you want to go hiding stuff in paper bags under a rock, tell some idiot come pick it up in the middle of the night, that's how you get caught.

You mix up with the gangs, you end up worse than getting caught.

ME: And the recession?

MYSELF: Cha. Listen, bye, I won't lie to you. The 1980s, 1990s, when kings and sheiks visited Bermuda and rented out entire floors, when college kids came out in droves for spring break parties and international companies installed their biggest big-shots in Tucker's Town, that was the time. I would've had a yacht. People would've had to come to *me*, make a fackin *appointment*, and I would not have been caught dead dealing with Javon Bean, Tony Trent, low income, low on brains, obsequious little animals. But Empyreal and I, we were born too late. At *least* the last five governments screwed this island and left her naked and bewildered with nothing but her beauty and an utter dearth of true allies, written off even by the people who set down our flag. The screwups and the screwed remain, picking up the pieces, growing desperate. Makes the risk that much greater, doing business that much harder. And do you know we've got a reputation now? I mean, [NAME REDACTED] and I do what we can, trying to change it, but it's a struggle. Bermy's got a reputation for high markups on low-quality products. Ditch ganja, going crazy with the baking soda, you know.

[Pause.]

ME: I've asked you this before, but if you don't mind I'd like to go over it again in light of what happened this weekend in St. George's. That all right with you?

MYSELF: By all means. Chances are it's been on my mind too.

ME: All right, then. Is it worth it, Dr. Caines? I mean really. You are decidedly alone. There's this sort of ghost of a limb that you and [NAME REDACTED] cultivated, sort of, halfheartedly? Maybe that's not the right word, but you went out alone on that gossamer limb. Yet it's more his than yours, I mean [NAME REDACTED]; he's got the compounds and the formulas, so if that limb fell apart, he could move on, but you'd have nothing. You're on painkillers, aren't you?

MYSELF: On and off. Mostly off.

ME: Rule number one of pharmaceutical brokerage. Don't become an addict.

MYSELF: You're in a fine position to wag your finger at me. Zohytin's a prescription drug. By prescription only. As in not in our catalog, understand? And I'm not an addict, I said I'm mostly off.

ME: It's a drug for dying senior citizens. Real stylish.

MYSELF: You need a slap upside the head, you know that?

ME: So my question?

MYSELF: [Sighs.] Is it worth it?

ME: Well, is it?

MYSELF: [Sighs.]

Nabi asked me to wait for her. She needed a sit-down with Wayneesha. She thought my presence might intimidate her young receptionist and assistant, so I sat in my car beside the harbor. I thought about handbags and drugs and the ceiling closing in. Finding myself thinking of Doreen made it worse. Till Nabi called and I jumped up, sped up Queen Street, zigged to Par-La-Ville and then the roundabout and Bull's Head; Nabi spied the MG and started bouncing up and down, high heels and all, hopped in and cried, "Hi, baby!"

She squeezed my hand in both of hers, bubbling me up so I felt like Coca-Cola and couldn't hold it in. "I got you a present."

She gasped. "You got a puppy?"

"No. No animals."

"Boo. What is it?"

"You'll see when we get home."

"What is it?"

I refused to say another word even when she tickled me. She bugged me all the way home, where I gave her the keys and said, "You get to unload the car."

"Wow. Thanks." She opened the trunk, saw the package from Vuitton, and squealed.

"That one means I miss you." I had her in my lap as she unwrapped the little agenda.

"I miss you too. Baby, you can't afford all this."

"Sure I can." Bull's Head Shreds pays me quarterly dividends.

"Thank you, baby, it's perfect."

"The other one means I'm sorry."

"Sorry for what?" she said as I used my cheek to rub her shoulder. "Sorry for what, baby?"

"For, I guess… For everything, I don't know."

"What's that mean?"

I tried to get off the subject by kissing her throat. That's my way of pretending limbo is a myth. But Nabi turned and watched my eyes. As if to magnetize the truth and draw it out of me.

"I'm worried about you, baby."

"I'm okay, *nikkou*."

"What's going on?"

"Nothing. The same."

"You mean you're still working on that suicide note thing?"

I couldn't say no. Nabi frowned.

She put her arms around me, her head against my shoulder. "Kenji, you remember when you got your bike?"

She meant when I turned sixteen, couple months before she did. I rolled my new Yamaha out of the garage, picked her up, and we zipped and dipped across the island, one end to the other with bugs getting in our faces. West to Dockyard, east to Ferry Reach, the wilderness of St. George's parish.

Nabi looked so cute in her black crash helmet. We lauded the triumph of my bike, our new, shared freedom. We anticipated college, launching ourselves into the world beyond our narrow isle. We spoke excitedly of Europe, particularly Greece, where I'd once been with my family on the way to Japan.

We sat on a low bridge, looking down into the water for bioluminescent sea-worms. We'd go to Greece, we decided, give tours at the Acropolis and Mount Parnassos, and have chocolate chip *tsoureki* with *ouzo* every night, and the Yamaha could come too! Our conversation flew to the apogees of the world and deep recesses of our minds. We shared a bunch of secrets we hadn't realized we still had.

I should've kissed her. It would've been our first time. Nabi looked at me like she was expecting something.

Of course I'd tell myself we would not have risked our friendship for anything in the world, not even the chance to make something more of it. Truth is I jabbered about glowworms out of pure cowardice.

Couple weeks later we were at my house, GCSE cramming underway. I convinced Nabi that she needed an A* in French if we were going to Europe; she grumbled that she wished Warwick offered Greek instead. Then Masami came in; I don't know how she got onto this subject, but she made it clear that Europe was no place for kids like us. Erik and I were destined for America, and Nabi, decreed the all-knowing maternal figure, would remain at Bermuda College.

Nabi and I looked at each other. "Let's go. Now. To Greece. Right now, Kenji," she whispered. And I'll always remember how her eyes grew huge as Masami called us to dinner and another opportunity vanished into time's shifting mists. Nabi never mentioned Greece again. Not even on that night, almost twenty years later, when all she meant was that there should be no secrets between us.

That night I watched her sleep. Naked on her belly. My hand moved through her hair, black and shiny like a night in which everything is clear. And I ached to wake her and ask why she'd given up on me. Especially if she wasn't going to give up altogether. Purgatory was becoming unbearable to me, but I couldn't help wondering if Nabi found it somehow sweet. Limbo sweeter than Greece. Like it says in *Desperate Remedies*: *With all, the beautiful things of the earth become more dear as they elude pursuit; but with some natures utter elusion is the one special event which will make a passing love permanent for ever.*

It was a sick idea. It was unworthy of Nabi. So I guess it was just like me.

Took forever to fall asleep. Stuck on Hardy's word, *elusion.*

Panic in the labyrinth—I forgot where I was trying to go and woke up with a cry before Masami cut me off. Nabi was shaking me.

My first conscious instinct was to jump up and secure the hurricane shutters against a nonexistent wind. Nabi pressed down on my shoulders and I struggled—I struggled because I thought she was Doreen, and had she been Doreen, I now believe I would've called her something else; but she turned on the lamp and I saw her, my Nabi's frightened face. I clung to her as one dangling from a cliff would grasp the edge.

Almost drove my fist into the bathroom mirror. Instead I turned on the water, sneaked out to the library where I keep my Zohytin, cut a pill into four pieces, and took one. I splashed my face, went back to bed. Nabi made me lie on my chest, my face in the shadow of her body as she propped up on an elbow, rubbing my back.

Zo dissolves anguish into aches. Rage and the agony of regret melt into terrifying sadness into anguish, which by then should be easy. *After great pain, a formal feeling comes... Chill—then Stupor—then the letting go... The Nerves sit ceremonious, like Tombs...* Emily Dickinson must've dreamed Zohytin.

Nabi kissed my temple and said, "That dream's not about your momma, is it."

I couldn't think of anything to say.

"You know how I told you not to write about that suicide thing anymore? You know how I said it wasn't good for you?"

I remembered. I remember every word that comes out of her mouth and some that she can't bring herself to say.

"Well, baby, that's when your nightmares got so bad. These aren't like the bad dreams you had before, these are night terrors, Kenji. Baby, thinking about dying, even other people doing it—it's not healthy. What've you been doing since we saw each other last?"

It trickled out. Well, most of it. Clocktower, Masami, Myrtle Trimm. I didn't talk about drugs or say much about Doreen except that she was a dismal soul who needed money—

"Wait wait wait wait. Wait. Hold on," said Nabi. "You're telling me Aetna Simmons was writing fake suicide notes for an insurance company so they wouldn't have to pay death benefits."

"Clocktower, right."

"But she quit for some reason. And decided, Lord have mercy, to expose the company. By leaving evidence on a flash drive or something that she—I mean, that she hid in her landlady's stuffed cat?"

"Czarina," I said. "Only the daughter got rid—"

"*Inside* the cat. Like, she stuck the thing down the dead cat's throat."

"For fuck's sake, Nabi, fuck the cat."

"Oh, I know you didn't just talk to me like that, no you didn't."

"Those two women might've died because of this. For all the fuck I know, Masami knows about it."

125

"You better calm down and apologize before you say another word. Because, baby, I'm here trying to help you, I'm *been* trying to help you, I'm been very patient, and I have to say it sounds like you're using obscene language to my face."

I grabbed one of the pillows, threw it hard across the room so it struck the Miró.

"Kenji!"

In certain situations, a quarter of a pill doesn't cut it. Clearly this was one of them. I threw out my arms, Nabi shuffled close.

"Baby, I thought you were kidding! I mean about infiltrating that woman's house—and the dead body of the—"

"It doesn't matter. You matter, it doesn't matter."

"Then why are you doing it? Why are you still doing it even though I asked you to stop?"

I couldn't answer that. Not with the truth. Anything else, in that moment, I'd have given her gladly. But I couldn't answer that. I thought of Ferry Reach and heard myself say, "I have to finish something. You know, for once."

That's not what I wanted to say. I don't remember what I wanted but it wasn't that.

"Well, baby, some things don't have nice clean finish lines with ribbons and all that. Kenji, all this stuff, if you listen to what you're saying, what if—if it's not true—or even if it is true, I don't know, what will you do?"

I hadn't thought about that. I twirled some of her hair around my finger and I said, "Maybe I'll write a novel."

Maybe in that moment I meant it. Nabi had this way of making me feel I could do almost anything.

"That's a good idea, a novel."

"I'm sorry," I whispered, and Nabi let me kiss her.

"But look, if that's what you want to do, then you have everything you need. You've got a story all lined up, you don't need to do any more searching."

"I love you."

"Do you believe me now? That it's not good for you?"

"I said I love you."

"I love you too, Kenji. So look, you always say that when something has to be written, it just has to; but promise me, before you do anything else, promise you'll think extra hard about whether this thing really has to. And talk it out with me, okay? Promise?"

"I promise."

By mid-morning I'd no intention of doing any such thing. For the rest of the night we loved with urgent trepidation. We kept at it until we were so exhausted there was no way I'd be having any dreams. But Nabi dragged herself up at six as usual. And then I cornered her in the walk-in closet.

"Leave him," I said.

"Baby, this isn't the time."

"Please."

That day she wore deep turquoise, which set off the Infini. She looked at me with the pain of someone being torn in two. But also with the kind of pain that you'd reserve for puppies left to starve behind a fence. She smiled through it and touched my face. She let her clothes brush me (I wasn't wearing any) and said, "We'd have to go away."

"I know."

"I couldn't stay here if I had to risk bumping into certain people on the street and everything."

"Yes."

My heart moved. My breathing stopped. Yes, I'd run after her naked to relaunch an appeal that was no news to her at all. But it had never got so far before.

"Yes, so what about the business?"

"We'd be okay."

"What's that mean?"

"It means sell the business."

Clearing my throat when horror flooded Nabi's face.

"Sell Bull Head's Shreds," she breathed. "Just like that."

"We'd be okay for money."

"Is that so?" Now her eyebrows came down like storm clouds over the horizon. "Kenji, do you realize Bull's Head Shreds is all I have of my very own?"

"Come on, that's not true—"

127

"Martin's the one who Brought All The Assets Into The Marriage."
His words, not hers.

"Everything else is really his. And baby, face it." With visible effort, she gathered her exhaustion and exasperation, she tucked it all into an imaginary bubble and blew away the bubble in an empty kiss. *Pfoo*, bubble, fly away; she'd learned it in a self-help book. Then she smiled like a new morning, for one more pernicious moment filling me with hope. I grasped her hands, she even laughed, just a whisper of laughter.

"Face it, sweet genius. Without the business we'd be broke as one-legged tables."

"No, Nabi."

"That's right. Broke. Both of us, you beautiful man, you."
She kissed me on the nose.

"What about the HDS? Diversification, everything. You don't want to give up everything we built together."

"That's not all we built, Nabi."

"Aw, you're a sweetie." She checked her phone, dropped it in her Bandoulière. "Where're your car keys, baby?"

I said something such as, "On the...right on the—"

She found them anyway. Came back, looked at me like she needed to say something. She kissed me for a while. And when she spoke, her voice was all messed up, like mine.

She said, "Bye, you're *done*. And the sun's just coming up."

Her smile was an exertion. She poked me in the chest.

"And it's your own fault, innit," she said. "Call me when you wake up. Or if you have that dream again. Next time you gonna tell me exactly what you dreamed, step by step, no excuses, hear?"

She kissed the wallet and the mini-planner, dropped them in her bag, patted it with the hand that bore her wedding ring, hung her briefcase over her shoulder. I hadn't moved, I was still staring at her, I mean here she is telling me to give up for her sake on the only decent work that had ever come my way and flatly denying that she'd ever do the same for me. I was so dismayed I could neither pull away nor make a sound as she took my hands, led me back to bed. As she arranged the blankets round my chin, her phone rang out like a blow to the head.

She said, "Hi, honey," and kissed my forehead. And left me with her phone pressed to her cheek, sending monosyllables to Geneva or wherever. And the ceiling came crashing in.

Every time that bastard calls from abroad, Nabi starts with the same bullshit. Why, everything's just fine honey, work's good, nothing of note on the news. She made a joke about it once: she could make a tape recorder talk to Martin, he'd enjoy it. Here I am trying to conduct an important conversation with the woman, panicking fit to faint, and fucking begging her; and acegirl's got the crust to actually answer her phone, like my panicking fit to faint is something she could put on hold or just forget to notice while she said yes to Martin again and again. I should've grabbed her phone and smashed it. Whatever kept us coming back here to take each other's clothes off, I should've smashed that too, smashed up all our hope.

I didn't. I lay like a watermelon dropped from a great height.

My Zohytin hides in a hollowed-out *Collected Works of Thomas Hardy*. I took two more of the pieces I'd cut up during the night. Then I thought to hell with it and took the last one. Giddy and floating, I reread a scene I knew by heart: self-righteous Angel Clare spurns his pretty new wife Tess, who offers to kill herself if it would end his unfair scorn. I slept a while and then, wasted, I called Doreen.

Sometimes tug-of-warring bumper cars gets to be a bit much. Them byes seem to think I'm got nothing but them 2 to fill the space between my ears. Tonight from NYC my husband tells me I'm got a real talent for "administration," meaning I should leave actual thinking up to him. I disobeyed him. He don't know it cuz I lied to him too, Lord have mercy. Scare of the century: something Kenji said made me wonder if I'd done it right, if I'd left traces after all. I've built my whole life around getting rid of traces, making sure documentation doesn't live to do damage. All sorts of what-if in my head as I dived into the bank again. I fixed it, double-checked, & this time it was right. ("Give thanks to the Lord of lords, His love endures forever!") The problem was a ":". That's how it is in this shadow world. Everything stands on the head of a pin.

Worrying what K's up to. Aceboy never says it, but I know he's disappointed that I never had it in me to throw caution to the wind, fling people's expectations back in their faces. But he did, & it worries me, how far he might go. & now this thing with Iesha!! She said (again), "Nabilah, I warned you better watch yourself now. Matter of time, etc." Well, Iesha don't know nothing. Merciful Lord Jesus, help me not to "blow this out of proportion" like one of them byes would do. It's nothing, I hear You telling me it's nothing. I know my Baby. Maybe I was too flippant with him earlier, but what else could I do? I mean, my gracious, what was he thinking, what more does he want from me??!

I don't mean (forgive me, Lord) about Martin, Kenji made himself quite clear about Martin, but that's a different thing. That's just men's egos & plain old jealousy. I'm talking about BHS. I'm saying all I've done & made that has to stay a secret could lead to my little enterprise, Bull's Head Shreds, taking a big step forward that this little worker bee wouldn't have dared to dream that it was ready for. & that's a good thing. Kenji said it's a good thing! He said he knows I could do it! HDS, MSU, the whole kit & kaboodle. So then what, he just forgot? He just forgot he said I should spend $200K cuz BHS is doing well & it could do even better? The man says "I know you can do it" & turns around & says "sell the business"??!!! Why not stick me on a speeding moped & then stick a lightpole out in front of it?!

Now, I know he didn't mean it, Baby was just upset, he was

confused. He woke up screaming, Lord have mercy. But that's cuz of the suicide thing, & Lord I asked You to protect him. Save my Baby, Good Lord Jesus, from the horror of those deaths. (10 suicide notes, mercy, what was SHE thinking?!) You know how Kenji is, You know I can't have him carrying that around inside him. You see, he doesn't actually need me to wreck my marriage, he certainly doesn't want me selling out on my career, all that was poor K being too freaked out to think properly, & You know my Baby loves to think. So. See what I mean? You gotta help him.

What am I gonna do meantime, You ask? I'll pray harder. I'll forget that Kenji didn't see how he'd hurt me, I'll forget he said all that stuff about M & BHS. I'll do my feasibility study. I'll be optimistic. ("For the hope of future joy, sound His praise thru earth & Heaven.") The thing is K thinks nobody understands his creativity, not even me, I could see it when I told him (again) to lay off the suicide thing. How bad would it be if I just said: Baby it's true you really can't go there, but I do understand, I really do, like nobody else in the whole world, & there's so many different ways to feel it! Wouldn't that light K right up? Wouldn't that fix everything? So Baby wouldn't feel like there's something he's missing? Then maybe he'd quit worrying about Martin? Course since he's K he'd ask me why, how come my "creative understanding" is so perfect, & I'd say…???

What if I said I made a girl.

Oh Lord, not that kind! My gracious! Iesha's always telling me I should let Martin "child me up" (she don't say it like that, of course) cuz then I'd have to "settle down & be sensible" (that's what she says). Like having people screaming the house down half the time, school fees, school uniforms, video games, pediatricians, hamsters, vomit on the floor, chicken pox, hair lice, pinkeye, music lessons, swimming lessons, etc etc etc, so you're as constantly broke as our Mummy & Daddy is anything close to sensible. No Thank You on that kind, Lord. One thing I will never be again is broke. After Auntie Time with my nieces I'll go home to my nice unmortgaged house. 2 byes in bumper cars is more than enough for me.

When I say "made," I mean on my computer.

NABILAH. I know. But I'm worried. Remembering just a little

131

will give me a boost. & that'll help me think better. Where's the harm? My book is only mine.

I did it all by myself, pretty much. My laptop went tappity-tap. Then I wrote a letter giving me permission to pick up her driver's license. I went to TCD. I took a number. I watched the silent TV ads for Carnival & walk-in medical care. Then they called her name & I got up.

A name that belongs to a person who existed only on that little piece of pink & blue plastic that TCD gave me then & there.

Until I tappity-tapped a little more. Then I collected her authentic birth certificate from the Registrar General. All they had to do was print out a duplicate of the one she never had.

She? You know I'm not that stupid, book. Let's say the name I made up & tappity-tapped is Seabird. Let's just say. Now let's say I fill out a couple forms & take a picture & send the forms to England. Then a passport comes in the mail.

Let's pretend it says Seabird. Now pretend it's my picture.

I can now go anywhere in the world, leaving Nabilah Simone Robinson-Furbert & all her sins & man-troubles behind. & it's all authentic, everything. These days you don't need a body to be somebody. All you need is a couple pieces of paper. & make sure you're in the computer.

Now, that's enough. I feel better now, don't I.

Zohytin is pure hydrocodone. One pill is equivalent to a handful of Vicodin. Zo is most effective when broken into pieces and consumed a little at a time. Taken simultaneously, two pills could send a juvenile or unconditioned system into respiratory failure.

Some years ago a broken arm landed me in Cambridge Hospital's ER. The Vicodin they gave me brought no relief at all, cursed at birth as I was with an unnaturally high tolerance for narcotics. Cocaine's as exciting as stale flour; Hallelujah and Empyreal only make me sneeze; a keg of vodka couldn't give me so much as a snicker. So, tormented by my shattered limb and a growing roster of clients who wallowed in euphoria while I stood by and suffered, I sought advice from a colleague, a pharmacist at one of Boston's leading hospitals. This colleague recommended Zohytin, having personally conducted multiple experiments. And relief from misery is joy, however fleeting it may be!

My colleague and I came to an arrangement involving Zo, Empyreal, and not-for-resale licenses. We conduct our annual transactions when Nabi sends me to New Jersey for paper clips and envelopes, whose dirt-cheap prices make the Land of Milk and Honey the Land of Milk and Honey. I volunteer for these Atlantic hops, breathing not a word of my northern side-trips.

Weeks may pass in which Hardy's *Collected Works* sit unopened in the library. When Martin goes on back-to-back excursions. In reckless stolen days when our love overpowers Nabi's conscience. But those days are outnumbered. A quarter-pill takes the edge off. Double it and there might be the possibility of laughter.

While studies show that the body begins to depend on potent opiates after a week or two of consistent use, hydrocodone, if overzealously consumed, can bring unpleasantness. My attempt to commit to an all-consuming addiction, when I moved back to Bermuda and realized certain things undeniably and far too late, was thwarted by just such unpleasantness. It's probably just as well, since addiction practically guarantees brushing up against withdrawal (one's supplier takes an inconvenient vacation etc.), and withdrawal from Zohytin is worse than anything in the nine circles of hell.

I told Doreen I was curious about the box but hungover and think-ing about calling in sick. I've never been hungover in my life. Truth is I was high. I thought Doreen sounded scrumptious. I thought a hangover sounded awesome. Myrtle's box had all the excitement of a gambling cruise. But it had been a while since I'd taken so much Zo. It made me feel a little sick, which only served to remind me that the current niftiness of things was artificial, so I still considered putting a pillow over my face. The thought made me titter but defeated the purpose of being high. Defeat makes me angry, so there you go.

"I hear Empyreal is good for this kind of thing."

"Coffee's better," she said. "I'll come over."

"Nah. It'll take forever on the bus." I didn't want her in my place. I said, "I'll come to you."

"You don't want to drive like that."

"Sure I do."

"Let me guess. You told her what we did. Already." Doreen snig-gered like a roll of thunder.

"It wasn't like that. In fact it's none of your business. In fact I never said there was anyone to tell. So where the fuck you get off to, thinking you know something—"

That made her laugh. The sound drove me right into a fury. I hung up on her, threw on clothes, threw a shoe when I remembered that Nabi had stolen my car, threw myself on my old moped—which I hadn't ridden since I'd purchased the MG, I was just lucky the Yama-ha had gas and hadn't rusted—barreling eastward, I almost nodded off thanks to Zo, and that made me fackin mad since it meant I really was pathetic. It was at the roundabout in Paget; my head dipped and the bike wobbled, old Johnny Barnes jerked me awake, probably saved my life with his plangent voice. Waving his spindly arms at every Tom, Manuel, and Lolita who drove by, waving his boater, hol-lering to hoots and toots of gratitude, "Good morning everybody I love you morning morning I love you everybody!" Not crazy, I don't think, just a self-made institution, a remnant of Bermuda's glory days like a patch of pink paint on a ruined house; a whirling fixture at that roundabout since before I was born. I wanted to shout, Der in't nothin good about it, ya fackin wuffless fackin bimpert! But I was busy speeding and trying to keep my balance, so when I got to St.

George's I was riled indeed. Doreen came out of Aetna's cottage wearing a sports bra and skintight little exercise shorts. I pushed her back inside and tried to throw her on the card table, which would've been stupid. She shoved me into the bedroom where I crushed her against the dresser, she pushed back and slammed me into the armoire, we sort of ricocheted onto the bed.

As we bumped around and moaned, Zo drew fuzzy pillowcases over the sensations, causing me to push Doreen harder, making my thoughts flutter and burst like roving blisters. I kept seeing Aetna Simmons at the Unfinished Church: the ruin that had never been other than a ruin, a gathering of incomplete arches and columns, gray limestone with weeds eking out a weedy life between the blocks. Windowless, abandoned, sky for a roof, and walls that never meet. Forsaken on a hill not far from where Doreen and I gorged on each other like adolescent vampires. Aetna was on her back, draped over the stub of a plinth like Tess at Stonehenge. She wore the pale linen of the damned, her black hair whipped her face in spirals, curling not like Nabi's soft loose waves but in tight springs that wound about her to her waist. She looked up at a flash of lightning, defiant eyes blacker than the angry sky. A storm roiled in her irises, growing vast and violent as she lay straining against it, keeping it at bay while it grew inside her with the urge to scream and at the same time all around her as the suffocating emptiness of death; her twisting turning into writhing as the struggle overcame her and when she opened her mouth the storm came out, cracking the sky with a ravenous roll of thunder. Water exploded from her, the ocean itself gushing over her as she arched in agony, water and more water, the entire savage Atlantic made rabid by the storm—and I knew, when she was spent, she'd rise up and walk into that merciless ocean, straight-backed and steady. Before she went she looked at me, seeming to know more than anyone would ever know. She shook her head as if to say, *It is a waste, what can we do, nothing for it but to be brave and let it go.* And off she went, down and down forever. She never so much as lifted a hand to me. Yet the eldritch strength that clasped me to Doreen seemed to come from Aetna and the sea, not Doreen's kickboxer-legs. I pushed my face past hers into the mattress underneath us. When I gasped I devoured the fragrance of the dead.

We walked to St. George's Square. I was coming down and none too happy about it. The air was muggy, which didn't help. We sat outside Gojo's with a pot of tea, expediting a coincidence that would decimate my world.

Doreen seemed fixated on a family of tourists who played with the stocks on the far side of the square. The kids put the parents in the stocks and took a picture. Then the kids went in the stocks.

I asked about Myrtle's cedar box. Doreen harrumphed. She'd come into a windfall, and she was unimpressed. Cool as a cactus. This was dangerous. At the time I found it as thrilling as it was chilling. Which just goes to show.

Some fifty years ago, Myrtle opened an account at Bank of Butterfield. She started with a quarter-million dollars. Doreen had never seen a penny of that money, never known of its existence till the locksmith cracked the box.

Throughout Doreen's childhood, Myrtle was a cleaning woman for St. George's Town Hall and St. Peter's Church; her bank statements corroborated this. Forty years ago she moved the bulk of her savings to CAM, which did extremely well by her. Couple years later she retired after a quarter-century of mopping. Even then she barely touched her savings. Lived almost forty years off the income from her rental property.

The little pink cottage was rarely without a tenant. The rent was unobjectionable at first. It went through the roof four years ago, a hundred and fifty percent. The deposits just kept coming. Also around four years ago, Myrtle received a one-time transfer from Hong Kong: fifty thousand smackers. Then, like fifty grand wasn't enough, the old harpy squeezed the life out of Aetna Simmons.

Maybe CAM suggested that she try the Asian markets, Doreen thought, but it was too much trouble, too confusing, so Myrtle sold out quickly, all at once. I don't know squat about investing, but it sounded good to me.

The box had years' worth of bank statements, pie charts that cartooned her CAM portfolio, financial correspondence; a yellowing letter from Masami and Barrington thanked Mrs. Trimm for placing her assets with them. The box was full, couldn't hold a breath of air. That's why we found last year's statements in a bin.

From a nylon backpack she'd slung over her shoulder at the house, Doreen produced a postcard.

A gleaming Horseshoe Bay, Bermuda's renowned strip of sand, where Nabi and I once somersaulted with the waves. Where we'd played at being pirates on the hunt for buried treasure. Doreen turned it over.

I leave everything I have, except my Life, to my daughters. "Mind the Pennies and the Pounds will Take care of Themselves." Myrtle Josephine Trimm (Final Will and Testament).

She had beautiful penmanship. A strong, even script with flourishes on the capitals.

"Daughters. Plural. Only one kid ever lived in that house," Doreen said.

It happens. People make children and abandon them. I know this better than anyone, and I doubted very much that Doreen's heart bled a drop for the sister who'd grown up without her momma. Instead I surmised, watching her expressive eyelids narrow in impatience, she was miffed because she'd spent a lifetime putting up with Myrtle only to have to share her inheritance with a stranger.

"It's not dated," I observed. "There aren't any names."

"Not even one."

"You could just not mention this. Even if you feel you should, you're probably in the clear. It's too vague for anybody else to make a claim."

"You don't think this has something to do with Aetna Simmons?"

I'd been watching an albino pigeon pecking at a loose stone near my shoe. At the sound of Aetna's name, I looked up and the bird flew away. Doreen's eyebrows lifted as though I'd missed an obvious connection.

A woman with an obscure past tracks down her biological mother who, for reasons unknown, probably to do with money, had abandoned her as a small child. The mother manages to raise a different child, Doreen, and has no idea what became of her first mistake. The mistake takes up residence on her mother's rental property, perhaps intending to keep watch over her in her old age. Daily the younger woman wrestles the question of her true identity. Should she reveal herself or let Myrtle treat her as a mere lodger? Her greatest fear is that she might be rebuffed; for never in her life has Myrtle made an effort to look for her.

Aetna wasn't the sort of person to pine for recognition from her mother. Then again, who can help but desire such a thing? Everywhere she went, she masked herself in anonymity; but when she found Suffering Lane, she found the mask becoming suffocative. All those years of not knowing if the woman who gave birth to her had ever loved her. When she found Myrtle at last, maybe she couldn't resist revealing who she really was.

Maybe the need for acknowledgment was overpowering. Maybe Aetna told her everything, even about Clocktower, a thorough husking of the soul. Catharsis overran her better judgment. So when the worst happened, she never saw it coming.

Myrtle took it all in. When she was alone, she sat down with her calculator. The profit margin on another descendant was negligible. Blackmail, complete with an insurance company jammed into a corner, was another story.

It would explain why Aetna stayed. Why she chose that pinched little cottage in the first place. Four years trundled by. Despite all her pleading, she remained nothing to Myrtle but the goose that laid the golden egg. Ignored, betrayed, exploited for too long, Aetna learned of a new designer drug. She murdered her mother. And then she terminated what must've seemed a superfluous existence.

138

Well I was gonna crunch some numbers for my feasibility study during lunch to take my mind off K so I wouldn't call & wake him if he'd got to sleep at last. I was antsy, I was worried, I just wanted to sit by myself in my office, nice & quiet with everybody gone, just in case Baby called me, when guess who came tickling at my door?

Erik! Ya boy did not look happy. Well Erik always looks happy. I only knew he wasn't cuz I know K. The tension that shows up around his gorgeous cheekbones. E doesn't have the gorgeous cheekbones, but today he had the tension & so did I, so I accepted when he offered lunch. He didn't mention seeing Kenji's car. Then again, E'd double-parked outside, not in the parking lot, so maybe he didn't see it. He ran us round to Mad Hatters, chopsin all the way. So it wasn't till we were inside that I got to ask, "Kiki, is there something you need Kenji to do? Or something?"

Ya boy hollered out & hugged the maitre d' like he hadn't seen her in forever (Erik's at Mad Hatters every other day or night). He said, "What hat you picking, mochi?" All the crazy hats hanging from the walls & ceiling. I don't know why they creeped me out today a little. E grabbed something huge with sequins & feathers, & I laughed (I didn't feel like it). He said, "You want a sweet little bonnet, innit."

"No, bye. My hair." Thinking I'd be seeing Kenji soon.

"You mean handsome Mr Martin don't care for hat-head? Who'd'a thought!"

E got the giggles. It don't take much. I felt a little cheap, so I said, "Martin's off the Island."

"So that's why your pretty little chin's down on the floor."

I said I'm used to it, just tired. But thinking about M got me thinking about K & worrying all over again. Iesha hadn't called yet, so all I had to worry about right then was suicide notes & night terrors & Baby being unreasonable. I got this dumb idea like maybe Kenji had been the one to reach out to his brother, maybe Kiki had heard something from him or about him, something that made him worry too, even after years of radio silence. So I blurted, "Is Kenji OK? I mean, is something wrong?"

For a sec Erik looked horrified & I realized (forgive me, Jesus) I should've said Are YOU okay. Kiki was the one reaching out to me, after all. But before I could say sorry, he laughed. "Like I'd be the 1st to know. Cuz Big Man On Campus (Kenji) goes out of his way to stick up for me all the time. Go head, mochi." E stuck up his hand to order alcohol. Still laughing but with an angry pout on his face. While we were waiting for our food, he took a gulp out of his glass & then, right out in public, he asks me if my husband ever cheated on me with my sister.

Lord have mercy, I said, "What?!" Kinda loud but I mean aceboy was serious! He even still looked angry. I whispered, "No! & you got some crust, etc." & ya boy got the nerve to get all whiny.

"OK but say they did. Just say. Would you slap him or her?"

Now Lord, I know what I should've said. I should've calmly said Neither & advised Erik to pray on his relationship with K & ask You for perspective & guidance. I'm hung around them byes for years, I know all this had to do with was the conflict inside E, wanting attention from his brother & envying him at the same time. I know this conflict is the Devil's work inside poor E, & when he was a kid it helped him blame K for things K didn't do. I know it was the same old problems rearing their same old ugly heads, & I should've been sympathetic instead of vexed. But I told You I was up a tree already. Now here's both O-C brothers looking for conspiracies in every corner & getting me stuck in the middle! Suddenly I felt scared of a million different things at once & couldn't tell what they were. Have mercy on me, Lord, it all came out as anger. Stupid to boot. I told E there's no way his boy of the hour would interest K, & that's something I know for a fact.

"No boyfriend right now, mochi. Too many good people left after government passed that law disgracing Bermy on the global stage."

"So not a boyfriend but some man you think is cute saw Kenji on the street, found out Kenji's your brother, told you your brother looks nice, & you got jealous, innit."

"No." Erik pouted like a kid, meaning I'm right. Sigh.

"Even though you're just as nice. Check you looking sharp today. Looking boasty."

"Well I guess that's true." Sometimes these lot drive me fullish.

"K's type in't your type anyway."

Lord, what nonsense! But it helped. So we talked about other stuff, well Kiki talked, talking always helps him. & well, Gal. 6:2,

140

"Carry the burdens of others…" But after that lunch I was ready for my BED. Tried getting on with what I had to do, couldn't get nowhere. Listening to E (like he's contagious, Lord have mercy!) just worried me even more: what if K took everything I said all wrong, what if my tone was wrong & Baby felt something I didn't mean, what if he ran with it the way he runs with things & ran smack into a wrong conclusion like maybe he should let that girl who looks at him at MarketPlace look a little longer? I'm a fool, Lord Jesus, I'm a grownup Managing Partner acting like a silly tweenie, but I just had a bad feeling. I don't know, just a bad feeling. Plus a feeling like I get when I'm trying to Double Dutch with my nieces, which I'm bad at cuz I'm slow. Like I can't see the ropes & can't figure out which way they're coming if they're coming. I had this crazy thought of what would "she" do, the digital & paper girl whose made-up name isn't Seabird, & now that's just ridiculous. Then I knew what I had to do.

I wrapped up the transaction I'd posted wrong 3 times. I packed up all my stuff. & cuz I know Kenji's love is my safe secret place, a rare sure thing in this uncertain life, I knew the only way I'd calm down was if I went to him & Baby held me nice & quiet.

That's when Iesha called.

&

It didn't feel right.

Or maybe I just didn't feel right. I felt like the sugar spoon that falls behind the drawer, forgotten except when it makes the drawer stick. The view back there was dark, paneled in self-pity. I gave the postcard to Doreen without a word.

"She's the one," said Doreen. "That means you'll never prove Aetna Simmons was anything but generous *to her own mother.*"

I didn't care for the smile that twisted Doreen's mouth as she watched me over the rim of her cup. The grimace of someone who's got one up on you or thinks they do or thinks they've caught you in a lie. But she said, "Where do I get the feeling you already knew that?"

From my lack of reaction to her stupid postcard which, by the way, I now believe to have been set in my path in order to draw me out. Doreen's question hardly merited a response, although she thought otherwise. She put down her cup with vigor. I was glad it was ceramic and not china.

"What is it you want, Kenji? If you're not looking for an extortionist, what are you looking for?"

She couldn't have said anything more cruel. At one stroke and out of context, that question brought home the lesson of the walk-in closet: no matter what lay between me and my horizon, the horizon was empty. No use in looking for the lighthouse or the sun, but like an idiot I looked anyway. From the middle of St. George's Square I looked for what I might have missed in a long kiss and a movement of eyebrows in a closet on the opposite end of the country, where I'd chased down Nabi naked (me not her) to plead for hope. The absurdity of being there and not there with Doreen brought back the sensations of being in the bowels of a wooden boat on a hurricane-tossed ocean with nothing but heavy fog and driving rain in all directions, and then I wanted only to be in bed with the covers over my face.

I said, "Where's the Empyreal?"

"The drug?"

"Give it to me."

"Why?"

Before I could overturn the table in a fit of rage, something happened that I never could've anticipated. And yet I should've. It changed everything.

Bermuda's capillary roads twist and coil in on themselves, often doubling back. Finding yourself faced with where you started even as you move away from it is far from uncommon. So is running into someone at exactly the wrong moment. Just as randomness plucked her out of the unknown, destroying her blissful obscurity as a haven for cahows and shipwrecked pigs, the Devil's Isle takes revenge by visiting coincidence upon its human occupants, often to their peril and embarrassment.

Hands on my shoulders. Whiff of perfume. "Working hard, I see." A dulcet voice. An echo of a sparkle that would've turned any other day into a winning ticket.

I have Zo's comedown to thank for my failure to leap from my seat, endangering the tea set. Instead I took the beringed hands and said, "Iesha, girl, where you been to?"

Iesha Douglas. Nabi's older sister. The only person in the solar system who knows the score. On certain occasions, when despite their untimeliness we cannot stay away from each other, Iesha covers for us. She tells Martin she requires Nabi for an evening of Girl Talk or Auntie Time with her twin girls.

I stood up and hugged her, introduced her and Doreen. Iesha's with Davison's, the souvenir chain. She normally works at Dockyard in the tourist season, but that day she was filling in for someone in St. George's.

I refrained, just barely, from asking about Nabi: had Iesha heard from her, was she angry, would Iesha cover us for a week or two so I could take Nabi to Greece and persuade her not to come back? I confined the conversation to Iesha's progeny until she strutted off with Nabi's buoyant step.

Where Nabi's soft and round, Iesha's taller, angular. She wears her hair in rows, Nabi flaunts sumptuous waves. Those absences of similarity were enough to conquer me. I watched Iesha walk away, folded my napkin in silence.

"Kenji," said Doreen.

"I've got to go."

"You didn't answer my question."

"What if I can't?"

"Bullshit."

"You shouldn't keep shit like that in the house."

"Shit like what?"

"You know what I mean."

"I'll give it to you if you tell me why you really came here. I mean the first time."

"Hon, you're acting up over nothing."

We walked to the house in silence. Should've gone straight to my bike, but Doreen pulled me inside. I don't know why I let her do it.

"Why don't you trust me?" Her hands were all over me.

"How many times have we done this, and I still don't know a thing about you?"

"What you got in front of you is all there is worth knowing. Be nice this time, all right?" She kissed me slowly as though she gave a damn.

I whispered, "Why? You a cop or something?"

"No. More hurt won't help anything, that's all."

The zeal of loneliness was in every move she made. Sometimes I held onto her too tight. We let our deprivation feed on itself through one another. So when it was over, I felt restored and desolate.

Doreen fell asleep with her head on my chest. I didn't want that, but I saw no way out of it. We were in Myrtle's bed. Everything smelled like dead cat. The light fixture on the ceiling had insect corpses in it. When I couldn't stand it anymore I said, "I have to go."

"No, you don't," sighed Doreen.

I lay still a bit longer, hoping she'd fall asleep and I'd have time to hunt down a certain tiny thing.

But she sighed again. "I may have a sister whom I never knew."

Wrapped in my own ruefulness, I perceived but a glimmer of the strange new light that Myrtle's postcard cast over Doreen's whole world.

"Help me find her," she whispered.

"Aetna's dead, hon. I'm sorry."

"Help me learn about her then. You will, right, Kenji?"

"I guess." In actual fact, I felt proprietary about Aetna. "Look, I really have to go. Stuff going on."

"Call me." She rolled under her mother's quilt.

I poked around in the clothing we'd dropped on the floor. I checked the nylon backpack and the pockets of her shorts.

"Kenji."

"Yeah?"

"Next time we'll make that trade."

See? She tortured me and I encouraged it. As the door closed, I could've sworn I heard her chuckling.

It's been about an hour since I wrote down all that stuff about Doreen. When I couldn't write anymore, I called Nabi. She didn't answer, I tried three times, no, four times. I felt myself starting to panic and that's no good because when she calls me back I'll be useless if I panic. I took some Zo, called again. Nothing.

To continue. I had sex with a revolting and enthralling predator who pretended to need me. I was back on my bike by three o'clock. And the day's accomplishments did not end there. After Doreen's parting jibe, I was determined to find out who had the balls to ignore my fine print. Anywhere besides De Rock, policemen might have qualified. Here, though I couldn't hold out hope, well, I had to try.

I have a thick handful of clients in the Police Service. They're all of high rank, so they spend most of their time in their Court Street offices. My unexpected visit rattled them. I wasn't in a mood with which anyone dared trifle, especially when greeted with a *kyuusho jitsu* handshake. I made them wheeze out the fine print as their eyes watered. What with all that and the possibility of eavesdroppers, no one gave me any crap.

Granted, few of my badge-toting clients can afford Empyreal. All the more reason for them to strong-arm other clients into making "donations," which the badges could attempt to use to supplement their incomes. Their primary market would've been one another, but stupidity could've made them try their luck outside the station, so I visited them all.

Including the dimmest dim bulb of the bunch.

By the time I reached Javon after several worthless interviews, I was in the mood to beat the idgit senseless. Cha, this nonsense was as nerve-wracking as it was ridiculous. Though I didn't hand out details,

145

the conclusion that I'd run into competition wouldn't have required cognitive exertion. They'd find the fool, make him undercut my prices, eradicate my indispensability to Court Street. I'd be vulnerable, they'd spread the word, and this is Bermuda.

Javon shoved back his chair so fast he collided with the wall. "It wasn't me I swear to God on my *kid's life*, Kenji."

One of the others must've pinged him with a warning.

"What wasn't you, Javon?"

Stage-whisper: "The fine print, Kenji, I never—"

"Wherein it says what exactly?"

Javon's rendition of the fine print was remarkably comprehensive. He'd probably been prepped. But when I let go of his hand, he asked which product was the problem. So it began. Already.

"Did you hear me say there was a problem? I didn't mention any problem. Maybe you need to lay off the drugs, Javon."

"No, Kenji, listen. There's no problem. In fact I was just about to call you. I'm a little short right now—"

I turned to go.

"Kenji, you—slow down, bye, goddammit! You as bad as my wife, you know that? I'm trying to tell you I got information for you."

Javon trotted round his desk to beat me to the door; he locked the thing and started talking. Two of us and the doorknob in a muted huddle. Perfectly unsuspicious-looking.

"Now, look. Can't say how I found this out, but the file on Aetna Simmons? You know, walking off like that? Well, Commissioner Wallace got it. Yeah, that's right. Saltus found out, went and asked him for it back 'cause he forgot to initial something or other, and Wallace said don't worry, case is closed, it don't matter. He wouldn't give over the file, Kenji, not even to Saltus. So here's what I'm saying. I'm not asking you to tell me nothing, I'm just saying. Whatever interest you got in this? It in't worth it."

Thrown out with the trash, devoured by the K9 unit, turned into a coloring book by someone's misplaced child, all that was conceivable. But the commissioner? Spending his own time on the death of a nobody?

Wallace had declined to state his reasoning. I couldn't approach Saltus, who didn't know me from Emperor Akihito and needn't be tempted to make inquiries. I couldn't ask any of my other Court Street clients anything about Aetna now that our connection had become incendiary. But it was possible the instigator wasn't at Court Street at all.

The commissioner's priority wasn't to resolve the matter but to quash it. Otherwise he wouldn't have turned Saltus away. Unless Wallace had some hidden skeletons, he must've repressed the file on behalf of someone else who did.

Someone wanted Aetna to vanish for a second time. Banished to the void where undocumented ideas go, as if they'd never occurred to anyone.

Javon knew no more about the file, but he did have more to say. "I didn't know this till, like, yesterday when I found out by accident, but my godmomma's daughter used to be married to the third son of Myrtle Trimm's father's second cousin. The guy's a private constable working out of Somerset. Now, like I said, if I were you, I would back away from this thing altogether. But if you want, I can get you a meeting. He knows you by name, you know, connected with the Bull's Head thing, so I told him you're my second cousin-in-law."

Here my acolyte took a deep breath and tried a grin.

"You're writing a book," he said. "*Unsolved Mysteries in the Bermuda Triangle.*"

I was in a tight spot and a rotten mood, but Javon was showing some initiative. And I'd become aware that if things kept going the way they were going, I might someday need him almost as much as he needed me. So I let him have that one. I bumped his fist with mine. "*Touché*, my brethren. Do it."

It's said that in Bermuda, the black-skinned Trimm, Ming, and Ingham families took their names from Trimingham, the white English settler who held their ancestors in bondage. He also fathered some of them. So poor Doreen had more relations than she realized. Sheer numbers could prevent their awareness of each other. Thus I had no right to expect Private Constable Neil Ingham to know any sensitive details about Myrtle Trimm's tenant. That he'd send everything I

147

thought I knew tumbling like a bullet train off an unfinished bridge I had no inkling whatsoever.

After I left Javon to bask in his own usefulness, I figured I'd have about an hour and a half before Nabi arrived at our love nest. PC Ingham was about to go off-duty when Javon called him. We decided to meet for drinks at the Somerset Country Squire, about ten minutes from my place. Once I'd ridden there from Hamilton, Ingham would have just shy of an hour to tell me that he'd never heard of Aetna Simmons. Or so I thought.

Nabi says visiting Somerset Village always gives her a bit of a pang. I suffered one myself at the Squire's outdoor bar overlooking Mangrove Bay. She and I were born in time to watch this historic place begin its struggle with deterioration. The quaint building opposite the Squire, for example, became, with its pretty double-staircase, another gratuitous branch of HSBC. It used to be a cozy outlet for Bermuda's great department store, which so happened to be called Trimingham's. The clan's white echelon founded the store in the 1840s. It became an institution only to fall victim to a scheme of HSBC's which, while the twenty-first century was still getting its feet wet, drove Trimingham's out of business. Nabi and Iesha used to walk to the Somerset outlet with their mother, spend a few moments each week browsing ladies' clothes and souvenirs just for the sake of time together. Sometimes, when we couldn't get a ride from school (CAM's interns did their best to embroil themselves in something vital by three thirty), Erik and I went along. He liked the china painted with Bermudiana. Nabi and Iesha tried on hats and fascinators, striking saucy poses while I played at taking pictures.

A couple of times it was just Nabi and me at Mangrove Bay. Under the resentful aegis of some aspiring investment guru, who probably wished we would drown, we constructed Sand-Acropolis and Sand-Versailles. Now the sea was like a marble that unraveled itself as it rolled over the sand, bleeding its solidity into the water until it seemed hard enough to walk on. Late-afternoon sunlight illumined the shallows all the way to the bottom, where hundreds of rotund clams burrowed into the beach. Sparkles tickled the edges of the empty punts anchored in velveteen seagrass.

Tall trees make a cabana of the parking lot that fronts the bay. The lot belongs to a post office; you can check your mail right on the water. But it's become a hangout for junkies and drunks. Recently Nabi's parents gave up their PO box because her mom got tired of boozy propositions. A dozen doddering fools lounged there that very day. PC Ingham spared them not a glance when he rode up on his Vespa.

This little man barely came up to my shoulders. He was spry, quick with a grin, downed a pint in three gulps. Educated and intelligent, made a fair show of attentiveness. But minutes in his company revealed that incessant reverberations of the man's own voice left room inside his brain for no other input. That meant he'd be a pushover and with any luck a fount of information.

That said, as soon as I set eyes on him, I should've known he was apt to throw me for a loop. For while Myrtle and Doreen were black as sin, this relation of theirs, Neil Ingham, was white.

"Well, what's history but a bloody mishmosh of discrepancies? Some people will have it exactly as you described: common ancestor, bastards everywhere, black and white, carved up the old man's surname. That's what I believe, mind you. But other people would just as soon not be related to me if they can help it and that's quite all right; me ex-wife tells me I'm awfully useless round the house and I always seem to kill the goldfish. I don't think anyone's researched the matter properly, or if they have they haven't said a bloody thing to me, so for all I know Inghams and Trimms are as different as De Silvas and Da Costas. And by the way, do use my Christian name, won't you? I've gone off and forgotten the PC up at the barracks."

Delightful little fellow. The pair of us got on swimmingly. Had the bloke not been a copper, as a drinking mate he would've been top hole. "You spent some time in England," I observed.

"Born in Bermuda, shipped to Eton at eleven, fighting my way back ever since, finally made it last year, and I have yet to recover from all that bloody English rain. I can still hear squelching noises coming out of my shoes."

I warmed him up to Aetna Simmons by asking his professional opinion.

"Well, the poor girl's dead. There's evidence enough for that. But to be perfectly candid, finding her will require an act of God. And so far He's not shown much of an interest."

The constable described a case, a few years old, which he'd followed from England. A man went to sea and his empty boat washed up. The man himself was nowhere to be found until weeks later, when divers found his body tangled in the underwater roots of mangrove trees.

"Not police divers, mind you. Members of the community with boats and scuba equipment. The whole thing was very public, a lot of Bermuda got emotionally involved. All because the man had a family who wanted him back. They were persistent, they kept everyone working and hoping. This girl has no such advocate. Which means, I'm afraid, Davy Jones shall have his way with her."

"What's the gossip in your family?"

"You've spoken with Doreen, I assume? Good, it's just that I'd prefer not to discuss anything she'd just as soon keep to herself. Because honestly of all the people in our jumbled-up family—which may or may not be a family, it all depends on whoever happens to be present at the time—Doreen's the only one with whom I'd eagerly manage a chat and a cup of tea.

"To be honest, no one really took much notice of Aetna Simmons. Doreen said it was just like her mother. Take a perfectly sane and decent lodger and run her into the grave. She put me in touch with her mum and some of her cousins in case I could be of service. Rather smug lot, the cousins, fond of spiteful gossip. There was a particularly nasty story—all in fun, of course, but not really in good taste—in which Myrtle harangued the poor thing till she decided to take poison, and when she was dead, Myrtle had her stuffed and propped up in a chair so she could continue to regale the woman's corpse with religious sermons and resentful criticism. Every time Myrtle launched one of her discussions, the ghost of that poor lodger wrote another suicide note." This story gave the little constable a brief teehee.

But he went on, "People never were kind to Myrtle. She was a very angry woman, incorrigibly resentful, and people resented her right back, especially poor Doreen. It was she who told me about her mum's religious mania. Just another thing about her that made childhood impossible."

150

"And your own impressions?"

"Well, I never met Myrtle in person."

"You didn't?"

"No, she didn't care to speak with me, only with the other fellow. Saltus, I believe it was. She said she felt more at ease among policemen of darker skin tone. And really I quite understand; one can't deny the racist history of one's profession. Plus there's no such thing as a Trimm-Ming-Ingham-Trimingham potluck or Christmas-carol singalong. For one thing, we'd need to borrow the National Stadium. I met Doreen in England. We happened to sit next to one another at a conference on criminal psychology at the University of Kent. The session was rather exciting, so in the discursive enthusiasm for which I am well known I couldn't help but engage her in discussion of the topic. She's awfully nice, Doreen, isn't she? We hit it off at once, then discovered that not only were the both of us from Bermuda, but we were also likely to be relatives!"

I bought another round ("Awfully good of you, mate") and Ingham bubbled on. Much of what he said I can't recall; it was as though he'd dropped a pebble in the sea, causing a ripple that grew with time and distance into a tsunami, engulfing the narrow sandbar where I stood.

Two words. Criminal psychology.

I started making plans. The smartest thing would be a long vacation far away. But there was Nabi, and I'd have to move my inventory. Hundreds of thousands of dollars in illegal pharma. My stomach filled with acid, I'd slept with the woman, gods help me—my cell phones had passwords, but a smart cop might know how—might know everything—it was all I could do not to sink my head into my hands.

And then Neil said: "…which of course is why her mum resented her. It's not to do with Doreen's father—who was a Gombey dancer, so of course, you know—rather it's plain evidence that we really are a family! All of us! But Doreen's mum didn't want that; she took a trending ideology and swallowed it right down. What nonsense. *Real Bermudians are black, all other colors amount to greedy foreigners*—and I believe I've just mangled one of your father's campaign slogans."

151

"Please don't remind me."

"My god, there was no one here at all till the *Sea Venture* got dashed up on the reefs! In any case, Doreen's mother treated her as though she had something horrid to atone for, as though she, her own daughter, were some kind of Edwin-Epps-like figure who chased her mother round the house with a cat o' nine tails."

Ingham paused to wet his palate. And in my astonishment, I said, "What? I mean—sorry?"

"Can't make it any clearer, mate. Doreen is Myrtle's daughter, there's no question. But Myrtle had very dark skin. Doreen's white."

All I managed was a stare.

"I'm quite serious. She's as pasty as I am. Got yellow hair as well, her mum hated her for it. She made a prison out of Doreen's childhood. Really. I don't at all blame her for not coming to the funeral. The house and her mum's things, all that can wait; I mean the old woman can't get any deader."

My hands went up. Stop, they said. As Neil blinked at me, I tried to conceal my consternation by ordering more beer. When I found my voice, it stuck in my bone-dry throat.

"Doreen wasn't at the funeral? I mean, I—she and I just emailed. I assumed—"

"Well, she didn't want it spread about. But look, I mean from her point of view. She's finally got free of her mother, she's worked and worked, got her scholarship to Kent and then on up to Cambridge. Her oral examinations were the day of the funeral, did she tell you that? A doctorate. At forty-three years old. I mean decades of work, doing the program bit by bit when she could afford it. At last the end's in sight and what happens? Her mum, healthy as a horse until her final moment, decides to jump ship. I mean, come on! It's as though she was determined to use every breath in her body, right up to the very last, to prevent Doreen from feeling absolutely free. Well, the poor thing had job interviews scheduled up in London after her exams. After that it's graduation. Next week, I believe. I told her not to bother."

The copper set his jaw, daring me to raise a challenge. How could I? I had no breath.

"Myrtle's got nephews and nieces. She's got cousins coming out of every crevice. It was one of them handled the funeral. And of course I've made myself available. So, yeah. All of us decided Doreen would do just as well to go about her plans and get herself settled in a job. I mean the market isn't exactly forgiving at the moment. And a woman in her forties? Just entering a profession? It'll be hard enough for her as it is. The house and all that business will just have to wait. You appear not to agree."

My expression betrayed me for the umpteenth time, obliging me to backpedal before I put the question to him straight.

"Are you saying nobody's been to Myrtle's house at all?"

"Well, to lock the place, of course. The cleaning girl did that after they took Myrtle to the morgue. Other than that, no, no one's been down there; the family decided to wait. We're not about to go peeking underneath the old girl's furniture for wads of cash. Even if there were any, we've all agreed. It's Doreen's prerogative. And anyway one of the cousins gave the keys to some solicitor, I don't know which one. I say, are you all right?"

My head, you see. My head toppled sideways when the blood drained out of it. Luckily my hand was there to catch it.

I don't remember how I got away from him. I didn't even notice my car parked in front of my building. I recall flinging myself at my desk, throwing open my laptop. No Doreen Trimm at Cambridge, but university websites always list current doctoral candidates, sometimes with photos. Cambridge: Department of Psychology: candidates in psychology—Doreen Eastbridge.

Myrtle's obit had a photo. I'd saved it, I brought it up. Myrtle's puffy cheeks, Myrtle's small, round chin. Myrtle's wide nose. All of it but the lips. The lips at Cambridge were too thin, the eyes were beady like the mother's but pale underneath large spectacles. And the coloring was wrong. Pallor and pink and blonde. Myrtle's daughter, yes, with the surname of some English husband.

So who was that in Myrtle's house?

Who ran through my undersurfaces, drawing power from my putrefying agonies of defeat, and dug in with her ankles at the base of my spine?

Some gold-digging relative? My instincts railed against it. My body refused to allow me to believe it.

My back stung with scrapes from the armoire. My mouth felt bruised where she'd shoved herself into it. Beneath the aftertaste of beer were traces of her tang.

I'd threaten her, I thought. The truth or else. But no, I hung up. What would I threaten with? My client's godmomma's daughter's ex-husband?

I threw the phone. Delivered some kicks to the underside of my desk. Wondered what the fuck I'd gotten myself into.

I decided to wait for Nabi in the jacuzzi. When my stomach quieted, I'd come up with a plan. Once I had a plan, I'd put it all out of my mind for the night. *Zaru soba* for dinner while Nabi talked about her day. Movies on the couch. I'd fall asleep with my head in her lap.

It was not to be. First I couldn't calm myself. I felt like pieces of my life were tumbling around me in a shower of broken cutlery. I have never been played the way that woman played me. It made me ashamed to be in my own presence. How could I believe anything I thought anymore? This made me sort of panic, and I had to take more Zo. With a hazy meadow between myself and me, I discerned the only course.

Get something on UnDoreen. Preferably the truth. At least enough of it to do damage. Begin again, not with what she'd said, what she'd done to me; begin with void and shadow and ask, *Who would do this?*

But instead of clarifying avenues of thought, my brain set off flares of anger and disgust, refusing to forget that if I'd begun the day in a sorry condition, I was finishing it in a state worse than contemptible. Unable to strategize, I found my phone, started to call Nabi, beg her to come home. Before I dialed, I noticed she'd left me a voicemail.

"Hi, baby. It's about, let me see, two thirty? I've been worrying about you all day long so I decided to wrap up the afternoon early, but… Well, Iesha needs me to babysit. She just asked me, it's totally last-minute, so she can't find anybody else. Anyway, so both of us came by, dropped off your car, and I—I came up to check on you,

154

but... Well, you're obviously not here. I hope that means you're feeling better and you got some sleep. Maybe you went for a swim or something, but I... Okay, listen, baby. Kenji. I'm really worried, okay? You're not here, you haven't called me, and this morning you were so upset—Look, I gotta go, Iesha's waiting outside. But I'll be at her place, I'll call you later. Or you can call me anytime, okay? Love you, baby."

I played it a dozen times. Transcribed it here word for word. Her forced cheerfulness giving way to tension, impatience, a moment close to tears, and then—then nothing. At two thirty I was with someone who pinned my hands to a dead woman's bed and seemed to scoop me out, starting at the back of my throat. It crossed my mind to sink below the water and stay there.

AS5.
mute b/w ruin, semi-glossy

I'm about nine, watching Masami's finger wag. Everything you do is a reflection of something greater than yourself. You have an obligation to achieve your utmost potential and so bring honor to the family, the school, and the pair of island nations that give you life.

Menboku. Eyes, face, reputation, prestige, dignity, honor. *Ikka no menboku to naru.* To bring honor to the house. *Menboku wo hodokosu.* To bring honor to oneself. *Mi wa ichidai na wa matsudai.* Life is for a generation, but a good name is forever.

And yet: "The opinions of others are often worthless. The house of Okada-Caines is beyond boundaries and borders and the prison of prejudice." Thus spoke Masami. Barrington said: "Listen to your mother."

In efforts to explain this kind of paradox, history just doesn't cut it.

Being a Japanese woman precluded Masami from building her corporate empire in Japan. That's just how Japan was. So she followed Barrington, youthful and hellbent, into Mid-Atlantic exile. She nevertheless believed (all evidence to the contrary, and every time she said it I thought, Cha, you coulda fooled me, don) childrearing to be the exclusive purview of the woman of the house. With help from Filipina maids, after-school programs, classmates' parents, CAM's interns, and the chauffeur.

And that's just how Barrington wanted it. Barrington had too much to do to bother with sons. Top of the list was proving to Masami, his exotic pet (who called him *shujin* and swore up and down that he was the bona fide head of the family) that he, yes, he, Barrington Caines, was CAM's *de facto* bossman. He failed. Nobody out-muscles Masami in business. Even Erik could've told him that. Eventually the *sumou* wrestler of greed belly-slammed Barrington's pride. He threw himself on the mercy of the dragon and vented his frustrations on Bermuda's politics. Which really is a shame because by that point I was old enough to appreciate what he harangued about but not fortified enough to dissociate important issues from Barrington himself. After all, this was the guy who evinced greater affection for the Bermuda Industrial Union than he did for his sons.

Research indicates that Japanese parents expect offspring to imitate their behavior. Yes, I tried to get JSTOR to explain. When I had access to JSTOR. When people at Harvard still liked me. I consulted the great digital oracle of scholarship in panicky moments which really called for a life vest. Like when Masami said: "You will have a limited time in which *ikka no menboku to naru* in the way that you see fit. If the time expires and you do not succeed, you will be made to do so in the way that I see fit. Rather a sturdy rooftop tile than a broken jewel." Barrington said: "Give Back To Bermuda."

Research also indicates, in addition to an elevated rate of paternal absenteeism in Bermudian families, that Japanese mothers do not punish their children or force them into things. Rather a child learns to fear his mother's disappointment. Bermudian parents, likewise, have been shown to prefer discipline via anxiety and guilt over all other tactics.

Then again, I'm sure any Japanese person could find a million reasons why Masami ended up in exile, corporate empire notwithstanding. And no one who finds out I'm Bermudian ever believes it. JSTOR was flummoxed too.

All this came up for the first time when I went for an MA-PhD instead of business school, which meant throughout my tenure as a grad student, I had to endure being told that the literary arts were not my calling and the fact would hit home sooner or later. For two years I suspected Masami of telling my professors to discourage me. I wasted so much time trying to catch her in the act. I'd come up with leading questions designed to make people let slip that they'd accepted a bribe from the Okada-Caines family despot. When I qualified to enter the PhD program, she observed that I had two degrees from Harvard but had yet to publish a single word, and she thought professional writers would consider that a failure.

That's when I began to understand Masami's notion of success. (Barrington's too, but whatever.) If I thought about it too much, it seemed paradoxical and murky. But it was really quite simple.

Money.

I lived in a shabby place in Inman Square. I had a Harvard teaching fellowship with such a meager salary you'd be justified in calling it charity work. That winter I fell down some steps in my apartment building. Broke my arm, had to quit waiting tables at the Harvard Faculty Club. And the fellowship covered tuition but not health insurance. I couldn't work off campus without breaching the draconian terms of my visa. I depended on Masami's stingy annuity, which would've gone to pay tuition if not for the fellowship. Either that or starve.

My apartment was on the second floor of a three-story, barn-like structure. The stairwell was always dark. Everyone clung to the walls, even those who'd lived there longer than I'd been alive. And they were all artists. Ever preoccupied, they tracked in mud and snow. The landlord never cleaned it up. That's why I fell. There were rats. The landings stank. I think something died in one of the corners. Nobody wanted to get a flashlight and find out. Nearby was the Zeitgest Gallery where I rubbed shoulders with the avant-garde. Composers, concrete poets, installation artists, and a sort of docent with a pigeon on her head. The pigeon seemed to look at me with pity.

Picture a blob of a man who never leaves his apartment. He's a genius-level chemist with consultancies at MIT, Harvard, and a bunch of pharmaceutical companies. He lives on the third floor of a certain rat-infested hovel in Inman Square. He's divided the lower stories into six closety flats. He leases them to financially challenged introspectives, usually artists. And oh yes, he makes designer drugs in his apartment. Nobody minds. It's that kind of building. Most of the tenants are too loopy to realize. Just a whiff of the lobby is enough to do the trick.

During a particularly low point in my life, that chemist was my landlord. He became my mentor, too. We discussed Hardy, Meillassoux, Badiou, my tale of *menboku* and woe. Thought at first he wasn't listening, bent over some petri dish or a centrifuge. But he said, "It's not about honor. It's about praise and gratitude. It's about people going gaga over you, groveling for your attention. You want that, come work for me. Grovel they will and pay you for the privilege. In Barbados you must have—"

"Bermuda."

He was just getting started on the mercantile aspect of his operation. He had one other broker, a stock trader living at the Ritz on Tremont. The idea of a Bermuda market titillated both of them.

159

They said I had the looks, the cultivation, and the attitude to make a success of it.

"I mean, visiting the Bahamas obviously—"

"Bermuda."

But I had no desire to return to the island. I trained with the Tremont guy and looked for clients at the universities.

Money, yes, but that took time. I began it because it was glamorous and cold-blooded. *Menboku ga nai*: without honor.

In case you're wondering, it would've been pure idiocy for me to call this guy at Inman and ask him if he'd hired a second Bermudian broker. First of all, he would've consulted me before the fact. Second, that question would be tantamount to an admission that I'd lost control of my turf. Let me make myself clear: *cautious* does not begin to cover it with this guy. If he thought there was one iota of a chance that I'd exposed us to unnecessary risk, my brokering days were over.

That's why in lieu of drowning I dragged myself to this ridiculous party at Dockyard. It was a function for accountants. They had soca and limbo. Needless to say, I turned down the invitation the moment I set eyes on it. Cozy night with Nabi or the back end of a conga line?

But circumstances changed. Hauling myself out of the jacuzzi and getting high enough to hug people cost me quite an effort, the end result of which was a hideous mistake; but there was nothing for it. While soaking I received a distress message from a client, begging me to attend the party and bring the girl with the green eyes.

Code for Empyreal.

It was one of the coveted apartments behind the National Museum, perched on ocean's edge at Bermuda's last western frontier. Seventeenth-century limestone, cannons from the period, tunnels, black iron gates. A view of open sea, coruscant cruise ships lumbering from New York and Fort Lauderdale to moor at our Royal Naval Dockyard. And a sky swept clean by oceanic winds. An effulgent throng of stars, an opulent celestial sphere almost lent an insinuation of elegance to the Accountant General's Cuban-cut aloha shirt, the punch bowl, and the pineapple cubes run through with little paper parasols.

I was in no mood to appreciate any of this. Neither was my client, Gavin Moniz, who met me in the parking lot and followed me around like a bad smell.

Gavin isn't an accountant. He crashed the party because I'd told him that as much as I respect him as a too-rare introvert, I am tired of delivering to his messy bachelor pad. The place smells like stale spinach. Start mingling, I told him, or get someone to clean. He elected the former and the gathering of accountants.

I went along with it because Gavin lives by Empyreal but can't actually afford it. I've known him to spend weeks sleeping at his office to avoid his landlady, having given me her share of his paycheck and then some. I didn't think he had the stomach for brokering, but addicts often have hidden caches of nerve.

It also happens that Gavin is a corporate investigator. Not too many people know him; he's one of an anonymous team that gathers info, writes reports, and leaves the finger-pointing to the team leader. Being in need of information, I wanted to speak to him at length, so the idea was to get the other clients over with and then retire with Gavin to some corner. But Gavin was convinced I'd forget him if he didn't dog my every step. I knew no one would talk to me if I had that fool pinned to my behind like a placard. That may be why I didn't learn a thing. Try as I might to banish him to the punch bowl, he was insistent. That's how he'd been taught to treat a lead.

You see, Gavin's with BRMS. His team leader is Martin Furbert.

That's where things got tricky. With his Empyreally enhanced creativity, Gavin could probably come up with several takes on any particular question, and he wouldn't betray my confidence. Martin, however, runs a ship so tight it could fit into a bottle. Hence Gavin's dependency on controlled substances.

I needed an oblique angle that not even Martin could use to tie Gavin's inquiries to me. I told him I'd come upon an opportunity to do business with someone at Clocktower (no specifics), but I suspected that the company was under investigation. Something to do with death benefits (no details). I was sure Gavin could appreciate that I didn't want anything to do with anything that might put me in the path of some undercover copper. I wanted names, records, anything of interest. Didn't mention UnDoreen, but part of me expected that Gavin would find her grinning in front of stars and stripes with a shiny little shield on her chest, and that part of me wanted to kick something. Preferably myself.

It was ridiculously easy to get Gavin to agree. I didn't even have to comp him anything. Stupidity, dependence, that's really what I sell. Not just me either, to be fair. There's a monkey on everybody's back. That's why capitalism works.

It didn't take long for Gavin's shenanigans to go awry. The next afternoon, a Wednesday, I was at my computer skimming a soporific article on states of mind in geriatric criminals. The piece was researched and prepared by a team of psychologists at Cambridge University, among them Doreen Eastbridge. There I was, shaking my head every few sentences—not at what I read but at the fact that anyone would impersonate this manifestly boring person, that I (yes, I) had not only slept with whomever I'd mistaken for this individual but also, thoroughly duped, enjoyed myself shamefully—when there came an email from Gavin.

hey, far as i can tell ur in the clear, some issues re death benefits and couple other payouts, but all insurance companies have those, they never like to pay, lol, mostly settled out of court, some in front of judge, a couple pending but no open investigations, no suspicions of fraud, not that anyone recorded anyway, no search warrants, no statements, fyi u prolly already know this but clocktower invests premiums with cam so anyone insured with them is also paying u :) guess u want to sell me a policy :) i'm kidding but u better keep us healthy, doctors and undertakers are $$$$:) safe, g.

I reproduce this here as the tackiest email I've ever received. It wasn't just tacky in its maltreatment of the comma. It wasn't just the offensive presumption that I was complicit in whatever CAM was up to. I *distinctly told* that jackass to specify via text message, *not email*, a convenient hour, *nothing else*, at which we might meet in person to discuss what he found. Nothing. Else. On top of that, the idiot emailed me from work. I could've strangled him.

Having spent some time spewing curses in every dialect I knew, I groaned aloud when my phone rang. I looked at it and cursed some more.

Putting it off would've only made things worse.

"Hey, Martin. Zapnin, bye, y'all right?"

Clenched teeth. Tight grip on clump of hair.

"Kenji, yes, how are you? Things are going well. Quick question for you. Gavin Moniz."

This is where Martin and I differ. He's precipitously direct, I'm quite a bit more subtle.

"Martin, aren't you in—"

"New York, that's right. Guess Nabilah must've told you. I get back tomorrow. Now Gavin Moniz, you know him?"

"Yeah. We met in Boston. Think I told you."

"Right. BC for him, Harvard for you. I just want to know how you got one of my employees to do your dirty work."

Pause. Deep breath.

Martin and Integrity. They are synonyms. Justice and The Facts, yes? Okay. Now, Nabi swore he knew nothing about the time she spent at my place. She was of the firm conviction that any tension between me and him stemmed from nothing more than differences in personality.

I'm different from a lot of people. But if the accusation came from any one of *them*, I'd have sidestepped it with finesse and made assets of my adversaries before we hung up. With Martin, I came to a boil in no time flat. "Gavin's not your employee. He works for BRMS. And what he does in his spare time is none of your concern."

"Kenji, in the real world, there is no such thing as what you call *spare time*. So what Gavin Moniz does is every bit my concern. He's a member of my team. He answers to my orders. His career is in my hands."

"I should think it was in his. And in any case—"

"You should think. Period."

"Martin, if an original thought met you on the street and said hello, you wouldn't know it."

"I beg your pardon, you—"

"And you're not *my* team leader. Period."

This is how Martin and I communicate. He steals some of my phrases, I ridicule some of his. Little slap here, little dig there. We often talk over one another. Think boxing kangaroos.

"Now you and I both know"—a favorite assumption of his—

"that when members of my team access certain secure databases, I know about it."

"You spy on them."

"The server notified me. It's my prerogative. Look, your address came up. I'd expect you of all people to respect information security."

"I'd expect you to respect people's privacy."

"*Respect* for my company's resources, especially given that, as you and I both know, you are *not* a paying client—"

"What's this about, Martin? Gavin touched a nerve, innit."

"No, it's not that, Kenji, it's—"

"Some big top-secret case?"

"It's the principle, all right? Gavin Moniz will have no further involvement in the Caines family soap opera."

"Soap opera. Daytime or prime-time, Martin? I ask because I wouldn't mind seeing it myself."

"What're you talking about, Kenji?"

A sigh, Martin feigning weariness. Like he hadn't instigated the whole thing.

"You've aroused my curiosity," I said. "See, I'm pretty close to positive that I've never discussed the Caines family with you."

Silence. Just briefly. Then he tried to parry my question with a question. "What's your interest in that insurance company?"

"What's yours?"

"Why Gavin? You and I both know that if you needed something from BRMS, you should've just asked me."

"What kind of case is it, Martin?"

This went on a little longer. We got nowhere.

Nabi and I had been apart thirty-six hours and so much had happened that a frightful apprehension shook me when I picked her up from work—how alienated I was from myself. Even worse, she was quiet. And that set off a clanging in my head like the Town Crier.

"What's wrong, *nikkou?*"

"Nothing."

"Don't even worry with it, trying that with me."

"You never called me last night."

164

"Figured your nieces kept you busy. You know, since you never called me either."

Was this just teenagerish ire? Yes. Was this adolescent drama spurting out of two cognitively developed adults in puerile squeaks? Yes, it was. I knew that. Nabi knew that. We knew it was humiliating. But you see, I was ready to snap like a twig underfoot. And imagine the sheer torture of Nabi not saying anything all day and then not speaking all the way home. Dying in my own Middle Passage, a matter of slow implosion. My stomach burned, my throat dried up. Soon as we got home, I planned to head for the library and sneak a book into the bathroom, let *Collected* Hardy galvanize my inner pessimist.

Nabi got to me first. She touched my arm as I was taking off my shoes. She wrapped her arms around me as far as they would go. I kissed the top of her head and said, "You first."

See, I thought this was acegirl's warmup for an apology. The breezy way she'd stabbed me through the heart in my own closet where I'd followed her unarmored. The sunny way she'd sashayed into the day while I suffocated in sorrow. I held her and waited for what I was due.

She said, "No, you first, baby."

Now, my fuse was somewhat shorter than usual. I deserved an apology, I wanted it, and I was tired of the runaround, tired of fuck-ups and dissemblance and excuses. From the woman I love, a little candor isn't much to ask. I decided she was trying to goad me into some kind of confession so both of us would end up apologizing and courtesy would force me to accept her apology without making a fuss after she so graciously accepted mine. Childish? Absolutely. Convoluted? Indubitably. But think about what I'd been through! Anyway, I wouldn't have it. Yes, I'd been up to no good, but that just wasn't the point. I found myself wanting to accuse her of something just to get the apologies rolling. It didn't have to be Martin. I knew that line of questioning would only make things worse. I took it anyway.

"Did you go telling Martin what Masami and those lot did to me?"

"Baby, of course not. You told me that stuff in confidence."

"Well, aceboy said—"

I didn't get to finish. Maybe it was just as well. All I had was

Martin's reference to the "Caines family soap opera." This was no indication that he knew too much about my business; he was merely stating the obvious. But anyway, Nabi flipped.

"You talked to Martin? I mean, but, Kenji, what're you doing talking to Martin, I mean *without me*? Baby, what's going on?"

Poor *nikkou*! I understood too late as usual. She was afraid I'd gone to Martin in the fraught aftermath of the walk-in closet, told that sea-pudding everything, and destroyed every reason for living. Her dismay was genuine. Like everything about her. And that's what I get for letting everything she may or may not say drive me to the very brink of scared stupid. I should've just backed down. Apologized, let Nabi say what she needed to say. But you know my state of mind, I was too wound up already.

I stiffened and said, "Nothing like that. You really think I'd do something like that? Throw everything away?"

She said, "Kenji."

Not exactly a denial. Cold slithered down my back, I felt the upper hand slipping away (I'd never had it in the first place, I was just being a bully), and I thought this was just too much and didn't dare let her say anything else. I cut to the chase instead.

Nabi knows all Martin's people from insipid BRMS get-togethers. She knows Gavin went to Boston and there made my acquaintance. What kind of acquaintance? That part she doesn't know. But if he sold me out to Martin, Gavin would never work again and he knows it. So I was up-front. "Look, I asked Gavin Moniz to find some info for me, stuff about Clocktower."

"You got BRMS involved in this?"

She seemed appalled. Like I was the one running some kind of conspiracy.

"Not BRMS, just Gavin. The guy did me a favor. It's none of Martin's business, he just stuck his nose in, calling me, talking about some Caines family soap opera. Bye's got some crust."

"So you didn't tell him about the suicide note business."

"No. He's a poky snobers and that's all there is to it."

"That's not all, Kenji. Far from it. You're on his radar now. He'll get suspicious. He'll be watching."

"Sounds like he already was."

But she sighed and shook her head, pressing the bridge of her nose like a manager who's found somebody's expensive mistake. She spoke to me that way too. "Why'd you stick our necks out like that, baby?"

"Like what?"

"Martin could find out about us."

"Told you I didn't even mention—"

"You didn't have to. I can guess how you handled that conversation."

"How *I* handled it?"

"And knowing Martin, his antennas are way up. He could find out, and for what? You put us at risk for what, for Aetna Simmons?"

She said *Aetna Simmons* in a tone straight out of the freezer. And I'd begun to feel like I was falling, so I grabbed it.

I said, "You're not jealous, are you?"

Pathetic. I know. I even tried a depraved grin. Fortunately Nabi didn't give it the time of day. I could've puddled with relief when she said, *"Duneenwurrywifit."* This translates roughly as *forget about it, you can't be serious.* She added, "Bye, look who's talking anyhow."

She sat on a kitchen stool, squeezing the back of her neck. I fell over myself to massage it for her. Her shoulders were stiff and hard as those wedges in the road; west of Somerset they're speedbumps, east of St. George's sleeping policemen. I put kisses all over Nabi's face till her smile broke out, she couldn't stop it. She held me from behind, her cheek against my back, as I made her a cup of tea and put rice in the steamer.

"Baby, I didn't say nothing to Martin. You know that, right?"

Course I knew it. It came down to this, Nabi thought: Martin was trained for flying leaps between circumstances and potential conclusions. Some such daredevil excursion must've brought him soap-operatic visions. I nominated Masami. Nabi's counter-theory was so freakish I spilled the oyster sauce and drenched the vegetables.

Let me back up, explain the circumstances. It won't take long.

My brother was stalking me. You might call it cyber-stalking since I hadn't actually seen my brother, only his countless texts and emails.

167

He wanted me to join him for a drink. My brother. Erik-Katsuo Okada-Caines.

The same individual who called me a snob and claimed my black shirts embarrassed him in public. Years of silence and then, out of the blue, some days before the ruined vegetables, the guy starts getting cozy with my inboxes. I ignored him. He was persistent, that's the Masami in him, so I marked him as spam.

Now for the endangerment of the oyster sauce. According to Nabi, on the previous afternoon, while I was being stupendously, athletically hoodwinked by UnDoreen NonTrimm, Erik turned up at Bull's Head Shreds. For the third time in barely as many days.

Looking for me, he said. He'd texted, he said. He'd heard nothing back, so he thought he'd check me at work.

Impatient. Thank Masami for that. I imagined my brother tapping on Nabi's door, manicured fingers wiggling at her through the glass. Pink Bermuda shorts, bright green tie and knee-high socks, a flaccid smile intended to showcase his practiced timidity and mental quietude.

"You were already having trouble sleeping," Nabi said. "That's why I didn't tell you."

"What the hell did he want?" I was now running around with paper towels.

"I'm still not sure exactly. You know how he is, baby, he'll talk half around the world before coming to the point."

This is true. Give Erik five minutes, he'll complain about everything from the color of your tie to the color of his tie to his star sign to the Premier's horoscope.

"Thing is, the first time he came by, Martin was there." Nabi helped me mop up the stove. "It was lunchtime. We're half out the door, Erik's trying to come in. Martin heard when Erik said you weren't returning his messages. Guess he jumped to the conclusion that there's something going on."

"Whole lotta nothin."

"Poor Erik."

"Poor Erik? He ended up right where he wanted, and girl I guarantee it he in't suffering."

"Well, he's anxious about something. Looking for his brother like he needs—"

168

"He needs a slap upside the head. There is nothing I have that he could possibly want. Masami put him up to spying on me or some shit."

"Language."

"Sorry, *nikkou*."

"I don't know. He seemed… Anyway, Martin must've sensed something. Him and his people-reading skills."

I was set to make a crack about the walking polygraph when something struck me. "Nabi, if Martin had a case, you know, to do with CAM or the stuff I'm working on, you'd tell me, right?"

She poured at least a cup of sugar on those saturated veggies, trying to make them bearable. She took them to the table. Then she took the rice. She came back and took my hand. "If it was your family, of course I'd tell you, baby. Provided I had anything to tell. Which wouldn't be too likely, you know that. Martin's not supposed to say things about his clients."

"But if it looked, you know, like his work and my work might sort of coincide. Clocktower, for example."

She dropped my hand. Turned away, pulled out a stool.

"You'd tell me, right, Nabi?"

"You've got enough for a novel."

"What I've got are questions. Look, is Martin on this case or what? Is he investigating Clocktower? Just tell me. Is that why you're being like this?"

"You need to leave that poor dead girl alone, Kenji. If I can't make you realize that, well, I don't know. I don't know what to think."

She was walking away. The counter, where she'd dropped her bag. Her phone was ringing.

"Don't give me that look, baby. I'm not trying to frustrate you or something. I know too well what it feels like. Yes, Martin?"

"What's that supposed to mean?" I said.

"No, I'm all right, you know, just a hard—"

The bastard cut her off. I went and slid my arms around her.

The way Nabi looked at me. Was it helpless? Searching me for some assurance and trying to get a word in with Martin. I tried to search her too. I whispered, "What is it, *nikkou*? Let me." But she

169

shook her head. I drew her close, put my lips to her brow, stroking her back.

"I don't have the invitation, Martin. If you don't have it either, what do you—no, Martin. I'm not saying you never had it. If you think you got it, then you got it—What? No, I'm not Questioning Your Integrity, when have I ever—Martin. Please listen, all right? I'm just saying if we can't find the invitation, we won't get in. Fine, I'll call them. Whatever. No, no, I'm not, I told you last week I didn't feel up to going, but you wouldn't—Yes, Martin, I just said I'd call them. Now goodnight. I'm not upset, I'm tired. Yes, I'll see you tomorrow. Okay. Okay. Have a safe flight."

She hung up. For a moment I held her, whispering, "It's okay, you're with me. You're okay, *kiseki*." But she pulled away. She put her phone into her bag. She sat down at the table and thanked God for His gifts of nourishment and grace.

She mumbled to her bowl. "Don't think I don't know you haven't told me everything."

How is it that the extent of her fragility eluded me?

Reaching for each other in the dark across the abyss of the unspoken. Which of us was more afraid? Me, I thought. My façades were crumbling. My brother was stalking me. My star product had found its way to what might've been a murder scene. And I'd slept with someone who, let's face it, was sniffing undercover for somebody. Aetna, my vocation, my vision, so long awaited. Gavin's hint that Masami might've held the strings on it from the beginning. And the only real truth in my entire life, hiding her truth from me. Without her I'll have nothing, you realize that.

In my arms, sometimes she slept, sometimes prayed. Caressing my chin, my shoulder, thinking I was asleep. I heard her say, "Lord, protect my Kenji." Christ, I should've known.

Nabi, forgive me. I've texted her: *forgive me.*

It shouldn't surprise you that my nightmare was scarier than ever. Books, labyrinth, helter-skelter. And Masami had a stain around her mouth, red-brown. The feather was shiny and rigid. I awoke in the usual style, my fists at my temples; I swallowed a parade of nasty

170

words. Nabi said, "Talk to me, baby," as she massaged my chest out of NASCAR qualification range. But reality pressed in just like those labyrinthine walls. I turned on the water in the bathroom while I went peezin to the library for a pill.

When I returned, I put my cheek in the curve of Nabi's breast. I closed my eyes and said in a voice reduced by shame, "I'm in a maze of books. None of them are mine…"

I owed it to her. When I finished, she considered in silence.

She said, "The books are black because they can't be read."

"They're Aetna's suicide notes."

"They can't be read," said Nabi. She sounded distant though her hand moved softly up and down my arm. "After you see the books, you run into something terrible. Something frightens you so bad it takes your momma's shape and you can't escape it. Because of the books."

I sort of wanted to tease her. Dr. Freud, your replacement has arrived. But my voice would only form a feeble comment. "I'm not frightened of Masami."

Nabi just patted my shoulder. "You know what you gotta do."

"What?"

"Forget the books."

What more did that warrant than a sigh?

"Baby, Aetna Simmons went to stand before Jesus. What happens to her is up to Him."

"Maybe." I summarized my conclusions based on what I'd learned. CAM and Clocktower both had a lot to gain from Aetna as long as she stayed hidden. Erik was probably a spy, dispatched to Bull's Head to find out what I knew or even make threats, sent by the *ikiryou* whose spectral eyes shadowed my every step.

Nabi's hand stopped moving. As I recall, so did her breath. She said in a strange voice, "Kenji, that's your mother."

I shrugged. Apples don't fall far.

"On *Martin's radar.*"

Martin and his radar. I propped myself on an elbow so I could look at Nabi's face. She gnawed her lip and stared at the ceiling.

"What is it?" I said. "We've been all right for years, haven't we? Trust me, he doesn't know anything."

171

"You don't get it, baby."

"He has better things to do than try to mess around with me."

Nabi wanted to say more, I'm sure of it. She didn't, just looked scared. She kissed me in that fearful, grasping way; like wheeling around the rudder and making a break for it even though we knew we couldn't outrun the darkening sky, the clouds solidifying into labyrinthine walls that would dam the ocean into rapids tumbling through ever-narrowing tunnels. Like trying to outrun time, that's what. When a light flashed in the dark, her phone sounded the alarm: morning was upon us, it was time for her to go; and enwrapped in panic I said, "Don't," and she said, "Come. Come with me, baby, and stay close."

അ

We got to town & K said, "Call Iesha. Come back tonight." I was getting out of the car. I closed the door again & looked at him. & I knew from that look that what Iesha said was nothing, I knew from how he'd held me in the dark. Mercy Lord I found myself holding his hand again & he said, "Come back & stay, Nabi."

Lord what could I do?? He had the kind of wild look that makes me worry, but it's Thursday & I can't be micin Thursdays, the day's business gotta be wrapped up by the time Martin comes cuz the poor sight's gonna be tired, just off the plane and everything, & this particular Thurs we had that "function" to go to, Lord have mercy I cannot rock that boat just now. I looked at his eyes aching (I mean K) & I was aching too. 1st thing in the morning & we're both all up a tree. I had a not-good feeling K wasn't just asking for one more snuggle but something else, something I can't do. It wasn't the right way to answer, it was like being tricky about it, & that wasn't what we needed, but it just came out, "Don't you love us just the way we are, Baby?"

I don't know what I meant by that. Maybe I meant the way we love is all-the-way but still sort of innocent. I mean Baby sorta puts me on a pedestal sometimes, don't he? So what if he knew I hacked TCD, HSBC, my own husband's computer? What if Kenji found out I'm a schemer & then didn't feel like "flattening the world" for me no more? If it's got room to breathe, our love will stay complete. So it's better that we're not together all the time (& I can't believe I'm saying this & it would've never got into my head if I hadn't taught myself Python & made a bodiless girl!).

I didn't say none of this to K. Baby looked like he didn't know which way's up all of a sudden, & his voice was so quiet, he said, "& what is that, Nabi? What are we exactly?"

Well, come on now, what kind of a question is that?! I mean it, Lord, I mean K really wanted me to answer! You could tell by his face, couldn't You? So why not send a little spark my way?

I didn't know what to say. All I could think was Lord have mercy get us off this subject. I smiled at K all gentle & foolish. I played with his fingers & said we're both making too much of this. I said it's cuz we're tired, he's not sleeping, so everything looks warped etc. I said if I saw my momma waving girt big ostrich feathers at me every night, I'd wonder about some things too. Kenji didn't laugh. I laughed for both of us, just softly. It was mug to try a joke right then. I said, "Sorry, Baby, you know I'm just teasing. Come on, let's get to work, we got a whole day together."

He had his eyes closed for a sec. Praying for strength, like that. Except I know Kenji doesn't pray.

What was that closed-down second, Lord? You want me to ask again tonight like I did last night, I'll do it. I'll ask You every night & thank You every day & praise You & ask You again the next night & the next: spare him.

𐐞၈

Half a moment it hung in actual air. Our bodies, my MG, the parking lot, the stone buildings of the capital were all around it. Other people could've heard it if they'd been near enough. People opening the car wash, the fitness center. For that half-moment, the question was actually in the world. *What are we?* And so it was an opportunity. A soft mattress or a sword could've materialized to stop me falling through myself and in the next half-moment give me my modality once and for all; my *how am I* and *am I really*, all that ontological bullshit. But Nabi laughed, she laughed, which means the question fell on deaf ears, as good as never asked. Falling on deaf ears, a question keeps on falling. If I'm doomed to keep falling until I've dripped completely out of my particulars into the horror of a living emptiness, then the decisive question for this falling body is no longer *What*. The falling question, the prime mover, becomes *How long?*

I forgave Nabi for laughing. I watched the forklift and waited for a chance to slip outside. I went to my MG and helped myself to my on-the-go stash instead of walking in front of a bus. Then I went back to the forklift. And when Nabi smiled anxiously at me, my insides were downy enough that I could smile downily back. I remember that much. As long as I didn't imagine it. I watched other people's histories grind down to nothing.

We decided I shouldn't be there when Martin picked her up. But the wrenching hour came and Nabi didn't want me to go. She touched my face and I kissed her on the sidewalk outside Bull's Head Shreds.

It was stupid. I know. The middle of Hamilton. Just a small kiss, not a protracted affair. Still, I know. But Zohytin made me reckless, I felt like everything was falling apart, Nabi was acting like she was out to sea in a punt. We had to grab onto something.

Nabi hung onto my arm as she walked me to my car. She shut the door on my MG, turned away with an enervated wave. Instead of leaving her to Martin and a bunch of strangers she didn't even want to see, I should've stuffed her in the car, driven straight to the airport.

Cowardice? Maybe not. This time I had a halfway-decent reason. When Nabi and I were on our way to the parking lot, I thought

I glimpsed somebody at the end of the street, moving on a course perpendicular to ours.

It was UnDoreen. Or someone with her shape and haircut in a business suit. Or a hallucination due to stress and paranoia. Or a ghost. Either way, she knew my car. And I didn't want her anywhere near Nabi.

Ghosts are everywhere. Don't underestimate them. They take many forms. They can be words, they can be *ikiryou*. They can be things. Papers, fonts. Images.

A picture is a ghost of a moment that has disappeared. You take a snapshot of something when you want to trap its apparition in a bygone time. You freeze an abandoned building so you can savor its despair. Its hopelessness is a phantom which, captured by your lens, will never be torn down or repaired.

I bring this up because the picture that forms a turning point in Aetna's journey—call it AS5—became significant to me when cracks appeared in all my structures. My relationship with that picture was never good. It defies my hypotheses by not saying anything at all. It's like an outlying point on an otherwise perfect graph.

Can it be a suicide note without any words in it? But what are words before they're words? Before we know how to read them? What are *kanji* but pictures, shapes drawn on a page? Geometry of the letter A: symmetry of a rooftop.

I returned to AS5 when I was out of ideas and beginning to falter. I'd considered the possibility that it belonged in tenth place, summing up everything. Or in first place like a cover. Neither seemed right. Aetna had an eye for symmetry. That's why she chose ten. She would've integrated the anomaly into the structure at a point that would make the most of the outlier's uniqueness. She chose that picture to represent her turning point in spite of all her literary work. When I revisited the Ten, my perspective reddened by frustration and vulnerability, I held that picture in both hands, determined to see something I hadn't seen before.

I saw Aetna. Her self-portrait at the turning point, when she realized her wish to die wasn't something she'd get over. It was a truth made in her, out of her, as tumors are our own cells. She accepted it, started making plans. That was her crisis juncture. I was so sure of it.

Her portrait in that moment is not a portrait. Rembrandt's dusty Lucretias; those are portraits. Bags under their eyes, besieged by shadows, daggers in their pasty hands, aiming for their hearts. Millais' Ophelia, looking radiant while floating downstream and staring deadly upwards, hands upturned in benediction and submission. Artists love self-sacrifice. Why not a muscled Seneca à la Peter Paul Rubens, bleeding into a tub while dictating to a scribe? A Davidian Socrates at the top of his game, lecturing with passion on the nature of the soul: "And another thing!" he says as he reaches for the hemlock. If she wanted a portrait of suicide caught in the act, she could've found plenty.

There's no one in AS5. It's a crumbling building shouldering its own debris with casurina saplings shoving their way through the roof. But it's not a building either, or not just a building. As I wrote in my essay, AS5 materializes the feeling of wanting to die. It's a ghost. The spirit of the feeling that would one day overtake her, an apparition of one of her last great convictions.

I recognized the building right away. Nabi and I used to drive by it on the way to the marina. She'd remark on it sadly. Hurricane Fabian gouged out the roof. Casurinas invaded. Despite the efforts of volunteers like Nabi, who formed an interdenominational repair crew, the building had no hope. They gave in and tore it down.

It was a United Holy Church. It was blue, and in the photo you can see the cross-shaped vent at the apex of the roof. It used to have a cedar door decorated with a carving of a ship surging through angry seas. Now it's a vacant lot. It was called Faith Tabernacle.

The photo is absurd. Trees going through a church. A roof too weak to shelter. A tabernacle torn apart by acts of God. All paradoxes are absurd and necessary. A creature born with the survival instinct who would rather not survive. It's a contradiction, it's uncanny and beautiful, I am what I am not—and no one can explain it. Aetna felt absurd too. She was like the trees, undermining every structure. And she was like the structure, stone on the verge of collapse.

One other thing. Aetna lived in St. George's. Faith Tabernacle was in Somerset. An hour's drive each way. And there's no shortage of churches in St. George's. There's a United Holy Church out there on Water Street. And yet one church in all the world, one ruin, resounded within her.

I am her echo. Cracked, invaded, and absurd.

I held out little hope for Reverend Henry Cox, formerly of Faith Tabernacle, now pastor of Beulah Tabernacle. I called him and told him I was writing a book about a former member of his flock, Aetna Simmons.

The reverend sounded quite an old man. He paused for a long moment, thinking.

His words were: "Aetna Simmons. I know that name."

"Really?"

"Well, that's why you're calling, isn't it?"

I said I was just starting my research. I said I was having difficulty finding information about my subject. And I asked with anticipation twined around my throat if he had a few minutes to look at a photograph.

The good reverend said yes.

I was at his door in fifteen minutes. He had a cluttered study in the back of the church. He said, "You're the one who called me on the telephone?"

I'd put him in his late eighties. Glasses like binoculars.

"You're Barrington Caines' boy. The younger one. No. The older one."

You might find this amazing, but I didn't. It's the eyes. Once people see I'm too well-dressed to be a Filipino laborer, Masami and Barrington are usually their next guess. Every time, I consider saying no. But it's no use. And Cox looked so proud of himself. I didn't bother asking how he knew Barrington. Everyone knows Barrington.

"But you're writing about somebody named Simmons?"

"Yes, Reverend. Aetna Simmons. She belonged to the congregation at Faith Tabernacle. I was hoping this photo might jog your memory about her. It was with her papers when she died."

Reverend Cox brought the picture to his nose. Held it at arm's length. Settled on a middle distance and a faraway voice.

"This is the old church. My first real home. Faith Tabernacle."

Patience. "I'm thinking Aetna might've talked to you about this picture?"

"No no, lots of people took pictures, not me. I didn't like seeing it like that."

"It was important to her."

"Aetna Simmons," he said. "Well, the name's in there somewhere. Give it time. It'll come out. Lot of people come and gone through my congregations over the years. How's your mom and dad? You work down at their office now of course."

"Actually I have my own company. Do you know Myrtle Trimm? A friend of my family? I think she might know you."

Not really. Another arrow thrown into the dark.

"Where's she stay to?" he said.

"St. George's."

"St. George's. No, don't think I know her. Don't get out that way too often. So you've got your own business and you write books too, that's good! This lady Aetna Simmons would've been in my congregation when?"

"Recently. She only just died the other day."

"Oh, she *died*. So I must've done her funeral."

"I'm afraid not. She killed herself. Probably in the ocean. Her body never made it back."

He'd begun to flip through a large-print day-planner. Now he was still.

"Suicide," he said.

His chair turned on its axis. He folded his bony hands. Gave me a look that made me feel like a kid in Juvenile Court.

"Why," said Reverend Cox, "do you want to write about that woman?"

"So you do know her."

"I didn't say that. Suicide is wrong in the eyes of God, you know that. It's a trespass on the property of the Lord. Because our lives and our bodies were made by Him and belong to Him. We have no right to destroy what does not belong to us. *You are not your own*, said Saint Paul in First Corinthians, *you were bought at a price*."

I didn't say anything. Figured he'd wear himself out.

"It's an insult to Our Lord Jesus Christ. It is a slap in the face after the sacrifice He made. Jesus died so that we might have salvation and eternal life. If you refuse that gift, if you don't give Jesus a chance to save you from despair, then you're saying all He went through was for nothing. Now, is that what you believe, young man?"

"No, sir."

"That girl allowed the Devil to drive her to despair. Jesus offered her His help, no strings attached, and she ignored Him. You want to sell that story to the world?"

"Forgive me, Reverend, but that wasn't the entire story."

"She was not a member of this church."

A slam of the door could not have been any clearer.

But he was still going. "My concern is for you. I know you want to write a good book. I've written books myself, oh yes. And I've read more of them than I can remember. Whether you're reading or writing, a good book is a communion of the heart with the spirit of the words. That's why we read the Bible. Because God is in His words. Reading the Lord's words brings us much closer to Him. You're going to have to live and breathe this woman's self-murderous spirit. If you do your job right, and I know your family usually makes good on its ambitions, you will expose yourself to the Devil. Not to mention the rest of us you're going to want to read the thing. Is that really what you ought to do? Is that, young man, is that what you really need?"

I record this small tirade because it came from someone in awe of Aetna Simmons. So much in awe that he feared her and hated her. And feared for me as I dared to try to know her mind. His fear transformed him, this absentminded, fragile little man, into the orator who hid behind his field-goggle glasses. She didn't need Jesus to save her; she lived and died on her own power, frail and fallible as it was. Such courage was beyond the poor reverend's comprehension.

After making clear my responsibilities to myself and the good people of the world at large, the reverend said he couldn't force me one way or the other, but he hoped I would change the subject of my book. He bowed his head slightly, which I took as an indication that our meeting was over. Feeling cheated and put-upon, I thanked him for his time.

180

Then he said (offhandedly, but I think it was deliberate, that cheeky old goat), "Oh, by the way! I finally remember where I heard that name. It was from someone else. Someone else came asking about her. Not long ago, not long at all. But no, he didn't come here. He called me on the telephone. What was his name?"

The old coot tapped his forehead with dried-up fingers. I wanted to shake him, but I was frozen in place.

"He wanted to know if I knew how to get in touch with her, this Aetna Simmons. He thought I was her pastor. Don't know why. Don't think he said. Tell me, Lord, what was his name? Guess he didn't know that she'd passed on. I asked a couple women, happened to be here that day, but they never... Lord, what was that man's name? Now, You must've been here too, Lord, are You listening to me? Throw me a bone. Was it Derek?"

"Erik?"

"Erik. Thank You, Lord. Now, was that so hard? The surname's gone completely, I'm afraid."

Erik. More annoying than surprising. My nightmares: of course Masami was out to get me. Just her luck her covert operative was dumb enough to get found out.

The only reason I didn't give that little sycophant what he deserved was, you guessed it, Masami. Her strategy was obvious, but things were already precarious for me, I didn't know how much she knew, and I couldn't risk slipping her any more. You see, only someone who'd seen the Ten could've drawn a connection between Aetna Simmons and Henry Cox.

Now, I know what you're thinking. Aetna disappears, Clocktower and CAM send somebody after her. Her cottage, middle of the night—and there they are. The Ten. The infiltrator has a look, maybe takes pictures, leaves the notes where he finds them. Smart enough to leave no trace, he murders Myrtle. He tells Masami about the Ten, among them the picture of Faith Tabernacle. She gets Erik on the phone, but the reverend's either clueless or a terrific liar. Anyhow, Aetna's already dead.

Sensible, maybe. The sticking point was Erik. If Masami had to order something like breaking and entering, maybe end-of-life care for a nosy landlady, there's no way she'd let Erik within a thousand miles of it. That bye has clouds for brains and a tongue like a hummingbird's wings.

So I asked myself: if Masami's information didn't come from Aetna's cottage, where'd she get it?

The obvious conclusion was, she got it from me.

Not me as in *me*. She hired some kid to get into my computer.

This is not a huge concern. My computer's not involved in any sensitive business. (At least it wasn't till I sat down to write.) It's just the principle.

Anyway. Masami found the Ten on my hard drive. She saw the photo, thought of Cox, sent Erik. Less clear was when she did so and why Erik would ask how to get in touch with a dead person. Stupidity accounted for the latter. It meant Erik knew nothing. Masami sent him to find out what Cox knew about Aetna and me; but she didn't reveal who Aetna was or what I was up to. She didn't tell Erik what's at stake, she just told him what to do, and for him that was enough. Erik's a born flunky, a maestro of following orders. He lives only to earn praise from his august Momma-sama. That's how he managed to rise so high at CAM. But this errand required too much subtlety. He botched it with a nonsensical question. And what did I do about it?

What could I have done about it? Hacking my computer is like machine-gun warfare. Masami gets to disembowel me without looking me in the face. And that's just the way life is.

"Same old," said Nabi when I called to check on her at noon. Her voice was pallid. Her words were code for Martin, who must've come to take her out to eat.

"Don't bother coming in," she said. "It's slow." Translation: stay away.

"You're okay, though?"

"Sure! It's a lovely day."

Not sure what that one meant.

"Erik been bugging you?"

"Not to my knowledge."

"All right, I get it. Check you later. Love you, *nikkou*."

"Yeah, go on with your bad self," a.k.a. I love you too.

I imagine myself standing before one of Aetna's pages. AS6 blown up to my height: a magic mirror. Reaching up to touch her words. From the opposite side, her dark hand and then her face swimming toward me from the bottom of the sea. Her hand touches the surface, which for me is the page where I have lain my palm. We touch with the abyss of death and shifting words between us. I try to lure her courage into my heart.

∂

If it's in my book, it can get out of my head. So just this quick thing, then I'll get back to my invoices, so when those lot come back from lunch I'll look like a Managing Partner who's got it together. What I want is a vacation from bumper cars & I mean both of them, Lord have mercy. One's all sulky this morning, I mean still sulky. Sigh! Noon rolls around & he shows up at my office. I thought he wanted to "clear up" what he said last night in public & in very poor taste, but he looked sulky instead of sheepish, & just as he started saying let's go have lunch, the other one was calling me on my phone & who knows what he might've got himself into! I don't mean like what Iesha's worried about, I know that's nothing, but insurance & BRMS, etc, sigh! He just wanted to check on me (I mean K), but the other one was miffed that I even took the call when he's there trying to take me out to lunch (I mean M). Not that he (M) even knew it was the other one calling (K). & to make stuff more uncomfortable, he (M) wanted to go to that place on Dundonald calling itself TEN. I couldn't groan, I don't think M even noticed the story about that woman & the suicide notes when it came in the paper, gotta leave it to the other one to notice stuff like that.

So we sit down, I ask how his day is going, I wait for my husband to say he didn't mean nothing by it last night, & the man comes out with this:

"I just can't understand it. I'm serious, Nabilah. What is going on? What is it with the 2 of you?"

He meant the other one. SIGH! 2 whole days since the 2 of them talked to each other for about 2 mins, & Martin still won't let it go.

"1st you & the computer. Now him & Gavin."

"Honey, I told you that's nothing."

"Well, let me tell you what I see. (Like he hadn't already. In the car last night of all places.) I see the 2 of you trying to weasel information out of BRMS behind my back. Now, what am I supposed to think?"

"You're supposed to listen to your wife & stop worrying."

"It's him, isn't it. Trying to get you involved in something."

"Well, hello there! How are you?"

I've never been so glad to see my ex-boss from the bank. She came into TEN & of course we had to chitchat. Thank You for our

Blessed little Island, Lord. Interruptions like that can totally bust a mood, which was exactly what I needed. M quit sulking in a snap. He knows lots of people at the bank. Higher up than my ex-boss of course.

But she left & Martin said, "Was there somebody at that function you didn't want to see?"

"What?"

"Last night. Clearly you didn't want to be there. Was it cuz you didn't want to risk running into someone?"

"Who?"

"Well, I don't know. You sulked the whole night thru."

"I did not sulk, thank you very much. You were the one that got uptight, making jokes in poor taste."

& that (sigh!) put us right back where we started this morning. No, last night! That stupid invitation! But not just that one, I mean all those glittering evenings sucking up to so-&-sos, Martin don't need that. He's great at what he does, everybody knows it, & sometimes after work I'd rather have my feet up. Yeah I get to wear my dresses & laugh at people's gossip, & this is where Honey needs me most cuz people warm up to me quick. But did he ever stop to think maybe we weren't invited, maybe that's why we didn't get no invitation? "It got mixed up in my wife's papers. You know what my wife does with papers." Yup. & in front of an exec from XL Catlin. Lord, the way that man gets loud when he's nervous drives me fullish. I reminded him, in front of XLC's exec, of the time we were at XLC's formal thing & we met some bigwig from Sydney. He asked me my profession & before I could say anything, Martin goes, "She gets 6 figures for chopping up paper."

Aceboy loves this joke. He thinks it's the biggest crackup since Charlie Chaplin slipped on a banana peel. But that time? (Forgive me, Lord.) I turned to my loving husband & said sweetly, "6 figures to protect people from poky snoberses like you." I kissed him on the cheek, & while I wiped the lipstick off him with a tissue, brethren from Sydney laughed & so did I & Martin sulked. Excuse me, where would you be if you made some kind of note about a confidential case & neglected to dispose of it properly when the case was over & somebody found it?! Well, aceboy didn't like being reminded of all that in public at a "function" we maybe weren't invited to. He sulked & then he fished for reasons to get mad at me when we were going home. He brought out his "chilly headmaster" cuz of the other one & Gavin. Again.

Guess he just got off the plane. & there I go making excuses for him again. Sick of worrying about him, I mean Martin. & Martin's radar, Lord forgive us. Sick of worrying about K. & how much I'm been praying for these lot? You Up There paying attention?? Sick of them sniffing where they shouldn't & having to be afraid they'll stick their noses in the wrong shredder. & while we're on the subject, what You got against creating freedom? What's so wrong about what I did? If You in't got no answer, why don't You keep M & K out of it & keep them out of each other's hair like I keep asking? Is it cuz of Moses? I can't love who I want to cuz of what You told Moses, a magician with 2 wives?! You gonna teach my boys some self-sufficiency in that case? You know both of them think I'm got nothing better to do than buzz around after them, struggling to keep up with my little bitty wings. If they had any idea what I could be doing with my time...

Firewall Hacking Secrets. Email Hacking For IT Security Professionals. I'm done everything those books know how to teach & then some. Has either of dem byes been to computerforensicsworld.com? Do they know how to solve every problem & beat every counter-attack that site comes up with? Are they up to date on vulnerability research? Have they exhausted hackthissite.org & elite-hackers.com & completed every hack on hackaday.com for how many months running? No. I made a girl who follows sharks in caves in the Great Barrier Reef. In my mind I ask her why those 2 selfish men get to make me feel like a sinner & a traitor just for loving.

Let me ask You something. Does Seabird exist for You? Will she ever? Or would You say she's digitally real but doesn't exist? Or she exists as electricity & data but isn't real? She's got a license, birth certificate, passport, bank account. She's got history. Check her on Instagram. Check Facebook. People "like" & "friend" her all the time without knowing it. On her Pinterest You'll see all this beautiful furniture I've been wanting for my house. I could almost afford to

186

buy some if M wasn't obsessed with the wood & leather "clubhouse" look or K would get a bigger place & wasn't obsessed with books. She's got that Ted Baker dress I want, the Louis Infini luggage set, that cutie yellow Porsche.

She's posted about crawling thru the tombs under the Egyptian pyramids, spelunking in Borneo & Iceland & Thailand, cave diving & freediving & muck diving, shopping in Paris & Hong Kong & Dubai & London. No boys, no job, no awkward debt to her big sister, no parties unless she wants them, no bouncing back & forth between angry brothers like a tennis ball. History don't mean a thing to her unless she wants it to. & Lord does acegirl have Rock Fever! That's why she's "Seabird."

She never posts a picture of herself. Like a longtail bird never sits still for a picture. But if she did post a picture of herself, would she exist? If her picture was my picture, could I kiss who I want where I want without worrying Who's looking? There's pictures of Greece on Seabird's Pinterest. Plaka, Syntagma, Attica.

I hacked KEMH planning to give her an old moped accident from years ago, where she got lucky with road rash. But thinking about mopeds got me remembering how K let me use his bike while he was @USA cuz I couldn't afford a bike. But when he came home & our love grew up & started squeezing us real hard, Baby asked me not to ride on mopeds anymore, now he'd seen the craziness young people do on mopeds. I thought of how I'd asked my husband the same thing: no more mopeds, Honey, I'd rather go without the car so he could use it, & so Kenji let me use his car. Next thing I know, the hospital drama's gotten totally carried away, it starts with this scuba adventure where Seabird's exploring caves in Bermy's underwater mountains. She follows a grouper down into a hole, hoping she'll find a giant squid, she sees tentacle marks or something on the walls, so she follows them but dives too deep, the hole gets too narrow & she gets stuck & has to leave one of her scuba tanks down there, she comes up fast & ends up in the decompression chamber @KEMH…

That's Seabird for you. Doing stuff I'm scared to do. I made her to live & live & live. I did that.

Nikea saw me that time cuz I hesitated. Why? Cuz I'm used to underestimating myself, & that is what the bumper cars do for me. Next time that man makes a joke on how I make a living, I'm gonna say: What you don't know is I make living better than living. Or something. I'm sure the other one would come up with something wittier & snarkier & philosophical like that. I'm sure I won't actually say anything.

‽

Nobody's just one thing. It makes what people call *identity* pretty difficult to pinpoint without being at least a little arbitrary about it. In fact, maybe there's no such thing except insofar as people create it in their minds and on official computers. Knowledge of this is a kind of power and helplessness: all identities are false. It's why the idea of an impostor is so terrifying.

Not the pharmacist who pretends to be a scholar or corporate errand boy. That's just changing clothes. Think about that English lady who rented someone's house, legally changed her name to match the landlady's, got a passport under her new name, and sold the house that wasn't hers even though her name was on the deed. Now think of Aetna Simmons becoming Macy Moran. Only on paper but a very important paper. Aetna understood it all, the power and the helplessness, and that's how she made an art of what she did.

UnDoreen only thought she understood it. She considered what temporary Doreenness could get for her, that is, for her as UnDoreen. But in a true becoming, both RealDoreen and UnDoreen would be stamped out. The impostor would forsake everything she owned, every last vestige of the self she was born with, submitting to absolute assimilation, perfect Doreenification without remainder. RealDoreen in turn would cease to exist except as her own impostor, the very person she was not. Which would mean, in practical terms, *no one alive could identify her as the very person she was.* And this would apply to the impostor as well as RealDoreen.

The successful hostile takeover would've made sure of all of this. Aetna made sure of it. Aetna Simmons, whoever she was, sacrificed herself to it. But with a colonizer's arrogance, UnDoreen thought only of gains, not vulnerabilities. And so by sheer dumb luck, an accident of history and the fundamental, arbitrary impurity of all the races split a seam in what she mistook for changing clothes.

And this was all I had to go on. It was less than a hair's breadth from nothing. It implied there was very little UnDoreen wouldn't do even if she hadn't thought it through. And that's the most dangerous sort of person that exists.

But why be dangerous *like this*, why become an impostor? What kind of person does this to themselves and not just themselves but other people, strangers who've done nothing to them? Of course you'd ask me that. Or, I guess, maybe you would if you were who I thought you were. I'm sure you have your reasons.

Not that any matter of "identity" needs reasons. Nor have people ever needed reasons to destroy strangers. The English tenant, the house thief. What reason did she have to steal her landlady's identity other than money? What reason do people have to criminalize other people's identities? And when I say *reason*, I mean something that won't disintegrate when you think it all the way through; something that doesn't turn out to be just power-tripping, which itself boils down to fear that your own identity is as vulnerable as everybody else's. Which it is.

I sure hope you have your reasons.

I made coffee before I dialed again. This one needed all my wits. Then I got back in the car. As though I hadn't already flogged myself with questions until I was raw and all the questions were in dislocated tatters, I went through it all again.

Her every murmur heavy with darkness, it seemed her every sound pressed in on me. It was a physical phenomenon; all timbres are. But it was also, I think, fundamental bitterness weighing down her voice.

Then again, her idea of an icebreaker was proclaiming her bitterness over racist and misogynist injustices while being caught red-handed trying to rob a dead black mother. So maybe *fundamental* wasn't quite it.

Why would a postmodern graverobber hold Empyreal hostage? Revenge? For what? I didn't know the bitch. And yet, I thought with a quickening of dread, UnDoreen knew me. We cohabited some perverse wavelength by some sick accident. Why would she bother with Empyreal if she didn't know even more than she pretended? And where did that leave Myrtle? Even if this wasn't about robbery, even if it was just breaking in and looking and what by now amounted to vandalism, why Myrtle's house? Why would an UnDoreen want to get back at Myrtle?

Discounting for the moment the perfectly realistic possibility that UnDoreen was another pawn in Masami's conspiracy to destroy me, I asked myself what Myrtle and I had in common. Bermuda, I thought. So what, I thought. But if you set aside the possibility that

UnDoreen wasn't serious about anything (which, I think I warned you, I heard in her voice sometimes and it gave me the willies), there must've been something about Myrtle, about me, that aggravated or encapsulated whatever enraged UnDoreen deep in her heart of hearts.

The fact that something enraged UnDoreen most of the time was one of my few certainties. After she flattened me and pinioned my wrists, there were moments when I felt like I was being eaten. Almost unmetaphorically. She was indiscriminate: she and I were disgusted by each other and went at it anyway with extravagant abandon. Not in desperation. UnDoreen was the opposite of desperate. Every look and word made it clear she was above any need for me or anyone. Why devour something you don't need when it won't do you one bit of good? Because you're in the grip of rage that isn't going away.

None of that woman's paradoxes escaped me. Nor did this sickening irony: What were we doing, UnDoreen and I, except limbo at its fiercest and most ludicrous?

Incidentally, there's one more thing Myrtle and I had in common. But you knew that.

I reached St. George's in a tizzy. Her voice, that sound straight out of that hazardous body: the heat of all that rage I'd felt so sure I'd denuded was nowhere to be heard or seen. Not that she'd chemically doused it like a normal person. Clear-eyed self-control, that's all it took. It looked effortless. Maybe it was.

"Coming in or what?" She put her hands on my hips.

"Come outside," I said, against every urge in my body.

Her eyebrow went up, but she came out. We sat on the stoop. Surinam cherry bushes darkened the sunlight to maroon and murky green. Nothing moved, not even a lizard.

She was a liar. It was all I had on her, and it had to be enough. My plan was to make it sound like more.

"The thing is," I said, "you're not Doreen Trimm."

She was less astonished than I'd hoped. Make that a lot less. Make it totally unperturbed. "What else?"

"Give me the pearl, gorgeous."

"That thing's worth way more than one of your tall tales, babydoll."

"And who was it who asked me to help them find a sister they knew they never had?"

This amused her. Should've amused me too, a con conning a con, fondling my thigh while she was at it.

"Where is she, Kenji?"

Her breath in my ear. Her tongue. She wanted me to kiss her. I stood up and started pacing.

"Bottom of the sea." My voice was a discreditable croak.

I looked at Aetna's cottage, having no idea that it was for the last time. I see it now as in a painting. The hedges cluster round the small pink domicile in a closer, thicker formation than they ever managed in reality. The shadows are permanent, the light forever partial, the front door closed. There's a sort of *craquelure* over the entire scene, making it ancient.

"Tangled in mangrove roots. Inside barracudas and a million little fish," I said.

"Come on."

"What difference does it make?" If you can shout at a whisper's volume, I did so, but the predator got up in my face, snuffing out a flash of anger just as it appeared.

"That bluff's been called, teddy bear. She might've left the country, I'll give you that. So you can have a little time. Let's say Monday."

"Monday for what?"

"You want me to spell it out? What are you, bugged? On Monday I want to hear her voice."

"You realize how ridiculous that sounds."

"Quit playing around, all right?"

"You looking for a séance or some shit, this island's not the place."

"It's tiresome now, Kenji."

"Then give me what I came for, and I'll be on my way."

"Monday," she said in her infuriating deadpan way. "Because this smelly little backwater is so cramped and bored and twisted up that if I wanted to spread the word, say Aetna Simmons and some Tenderheart Bear poisoned her landlady, I wouldn't even have to try."

So she really was American. In a way, that explained a lot.

I said, "You have a hell of a lot more to worry about than a couple of dead people." And that puff of hot air was no defense against her sucker punch. I never even saw it coming.

"If you don't care about yourself," she said, "if being an accessory to murder is all the same to you, do it for her. Rescue her. That's what you want, isn't it? She doesn't have to go down that way, Kenji."

I managed to say, "What?" But the clout drained out of my voice.

"I understand why Aetna was tempted," she said softly. "But it was selfish of her to get you mixed up in this."

"I don't know what you're talking about. Really."

"You're a decent liar, Kenji. Except in certain vulnerable moments."

"I don't have vulnerable moments. That's just not something I do."

This didn't deserve a response and didn't get one. So close to me that I could feel her breasts through my shirt, she looked me in the eye and said:

"You say her name during sex. *Aetna.* You say it a lot."

The absence of breeze was a roar in the bushes. I thought I could hear ants storming up the stoop. The strength in my body left me with a deafening wheeze, the rattle that pipes make when they try to take in water but the tank beneath the house is empty. Shock and outrage? Sure. Indignation, the whole bit. What respectable person wouldn't? Here was this unruffled stranger, this impostor harping on "vulnerable moments" with impeccable impassivity—and I mean, the name, oh god. I couldn't find so much as a sniff of air.

She smiled and said, "I figured you had no idea."

I couldn't find the shards of my bravado either. I had nothing to say.

"Monday," she said. She went into the house and closed the door.

I rushed after her and knocked. I knocked and insisted, I banged and I shouted and for lack of anything to call her shrieked the name she'd stolen. But she was gone. Vanished like a ghost. I wouldn't have been surprised if the house was empty, if it had stood there empty since Myrtle's dead body went off to the morgue. I had no salient facts to fling at the impostor and dare her to refute, I had nothing more with which to bargain, no one answered my knocking, so I stopped.

I think I put my forehead on poor dead Myrtle's door as exhaustion fell on me. Like someone lost for weeks in a dark wood, I wanted to stumble to the cottage. I wanted to stand by the empty card table, sink into Aetna's absence, and see if I felt any sort of infusion. I don't know why I should've wanted such a thing because UnDoreen must have been bluffing about "certain moments"; she was just trying to rattle me. So I didn't go to the cottage. I found myself driving not westward but further east, deeper into St. George's and up a curving hill.

The Unfinished Church protruded into the blue sky like a broken tooth. If I were Thomas Hardy, I might tell you that I went among the stillborn limestone bricks, the arches that never had a chance to resonate with voices lifted up in song; I might say I found where the altar ought to be and that I lay down there, and when I closed my eyes I realized they were wrapped in fog. The sun would come down through the nonexistent roof and warm my face, but what the living took for the light of a mere star would be in fact the kiss of an angel. Aetna would appear, more beautiful than I'd ever imagined. She'd say it was time to go now that I knew the truth. And we would disappear.

Maybe more Hans Christian Andersen than Hardy. Or a schmaltzy way of saying that when I finally got out of there, I was ready to die of chagrin. I was at the church for all of five minutes. I sat in the car and watched the space where a spire never was. Embarrassment drove me into Hamilton in search of someplace sane.

A Front Street café. Armchair by a window. Tea I never touched. Outside, a bunch of tourists heading for a pub. Cruise ship in Hamilton Harbour. I succumbed to catatonia that blurred the view and swept away the noise. The death grip of longing clenched around my chest, and I couldn't shake it off or wriggle free, having no idea what I was longing for.

Rescue her. Those words changed everything. Did I cry out for her? Did I love her?

Sometimes it takes a stranger to make you realize things like that. Am I still in love with her?

194

How alike we are, all façade, all shadow. Few people will appreciate her defiant beauty. I've done that for her, and she's been a muse for me. It's because of Aetna that I stopped feeding time into the shredder of indifference and got back to work. For Aetna I've thrown my life into upheaval as I've been wanting and hoping and fackinwell *yearning* to do for Nabi. Let me imagine Aetna in place of Seneca in Rubens' bloody, painted tub, shrouded in her boundless curls. Instead of looking up, she looks down and to one side at the scribe waiting at her feet. One more word, he begs of her. But she's said all there is to say. She looks at him kindly, full of understanding, willing that as he once shared her desperation, he will one day know her courage.

࿏

SINCE YOU ARE STILL ALIVE, AND IF YOU HAVE NO PLANS TO
DO WHAT I AM GOING TO DO, THEN YOU HAVE NO IDEA WHAT
HELPLESSNESS IS. HELPLESSNESS IS LIKE RADIATION SICKNESS.
IT EATS YOU FROM THE INSIDE AND AT THE SAME TIME
POISONS YOU, SO EVEN AS YOU TRY TO HOLD YOURSELF TOGETHER,
YOU CAN'T HELP WANTING TO VOMIT YOURSELF OUT OF YOURSELF
ONCE AND FOR ALL. MY HELPLESSNESS IS SO SEVERE, SOMETIMES
I REALLY DO VOMIT. LATELY I'VE HAD ONLY ONE DEFENSE.
EVEN THEN, RELIEF IS TEMPORARY. I IMAGINE MYSELF GOING TO
LAS VEGAS AND BUYING A GUN. I GO ONLINE, FIND OUT HOW TO
USE IT. OR THE GUY BEHIND THE COUNTER SHOWS ME, A CHEAP
SHOT AT GETTING IN MY PANTS. I DRIVE INTO THE DESERT. NOT
TOWARDS CALIFORNIA, I DON'T WANT TO TAKE THE FREEWAY,
DON'T WANT TO RISK BUCKING THE SPEED LIMIT IN ANTICIPATION,
GETTING PULLED OVER AND ALL MY FREEDOM TAKEN AWAY. FIND
A DESOLATE SPOT, AND STOP. LOOK AT THE DESERT FOR A WHILE.
OR NOT. LOAD THE GUN AND PUT IT IN MY MOUTH AND PULL THE
TRIGGER. ALL MY SICKNESS VANISHES. I VANISH, NOW I'M
NOTHING. THERE IS ONLY NOTHING. SO MUCH FOR HELPLESSNESS.

AS6.
Pink paper soaked in words, ink, bitterness in handwritten caps (cf. Kurt Cobain). First-form or just ideation (*imagining*)? This unnamed *you*. Fake? But look closer.

You can read AS6 as the ghost of AS1. Haunted by the same frustration as Aetna relived it again and again. Making a living by courting the wish for death, a feeling so precise that it eludes all concepts. How often she must have turned back. Like Sisyphus. Knowing she'd gone wrong because she still wanted to live. Until one day she succeeded. Or not, and she snapped the drawing board across her knee and fed it to the first piece of Level 6 equipment she could find.

This is where drugs are useful.

I'm getting carried away, but you can see where this is coming from. AS1, AS6: one couplet haunts both documents, word-for-word identical. This is the strongest evidence for the Clocktower Hypothesis. One is a draft of the other, or both are drafts in preparation for another note that got lost or became evidence in some underwriter's report; either way I never found it. Another repetition: the word *helplessness* appears four times in AS6. In AS6 and AS1, helplessness is a *poison*, again the same word in both cases.

Both documents were meant to stand out from the others. Despite the pink paper in AS6, AS1 is more attention-grabbing, textually speaking. But the pink paper is there, same color as Aetna's cottage, to draw readers' attention to AS6 as the most honest of the Ten; the words set down by her own hand, by Aetna Simmons' own dark hand. AS1 foreshadows what happens in AS6. But only after AS5 and AS4 brought her an authentic philosophical understanding of what she was and what she wanted could Aetna be so honest and exhaustive in her honesty.

Which makes me wonder who *you* are, Aetna's nameless addressee. Who is worth the risk of honesty?

It's tempting to believe that if she really wanted honesty, she would've said so. Said it with her voice instead of silent squiggles. Of course, Auto-Tune and deconstruction made myths of honest voices long ago, but some people just can't let go of the idea. Denial is a powerful thing.

Was there a recording of Aetna's voice somewhere? Incriminating voicemail? A tape thrown out with the cat? That and a Ouija board were all I could come up with.

Except the Ten. Her authorial voice.

UnDoreen hadn't seen them. If she had, she wouldn't have been so ready to discard Czarina's body. But why blackmail me for that?

I learned she was ruthless when I collided with the armoire. Her co-conspirators would have to be ruthless too, I figured. I thought of Clocktower but also RealDoreen. RealDoreen didn't look ruthless, but if her mother shocked her with news of a lost sibling and then kicked the bucket, it would only have been natural if, distraught and confused, RealDoreen wanted the truth. With her background, she'd know how to find a ruthless gumshoe. But she would've told Neil Ingham. And I could tell from that flicker of ire: UnDoreen's stake in this was personal.

Journey abroad, deep cover, weeks among taxidermied cats and a dead woman's dust. She'd invested so much she'd mired herself in denial. She preferred it to coming up empty. So much was at stake, built around her like that oppressive hedge, that UnDoreen was unable to see, could not believe, even imagine, that Aetna Simmons was no longer of this world.

Selective insanity. Common in cops and clients.

I pitied UnDoreen. Tough, sexy, smart, and nuts. The fact that no one else seemed to give a damn just made her stubborn, her delusions grew into convictions, and then—picture this: she comes all the way from the US, bent on tracking down a ghost she doesn't believe in; she finds one person who is oddly sympathetic to her cause; she leaps to the conclusion that I'm in love with her quarry and, I guess, that I've got her squirreled away somewhere. Anyone with an obsession could've made the same mistake.

When my phone rang, my tea was cold. Nothing good was going through my head. Nabi said, "I've got till two a.m., come get me."

This was a shock. And I wasn't at my best. I mumbled something like, "But isn't it Friday?"

"Yeah, it's Friday. Iesha's covering. Baby, it's not a lot of time. I have to see you."

I ran to the car. People I knew saw me and said hi, but I kept running. From the Number One Shed parking lot to Bull's Head is five minutes, maybe less. Nabi hopped in and said, "You were in town already, sweetie?"

"Must've got your brainwaves. You okay? Did something happen?"

"Let's drive, baby, time's ticking."

She was as jittery as I was bamboozled. She got comfy, gave my knee a pat, looked straight ahead. By the time we left the curb, I couldn't take it anymore.

"Nabi, just tell me. Don't make me keep guessing, I can't do it, I don't have it in me, I don't know what to do."

"Okay, baby, take it easy. Let me get my thoughts in order."

I imagined her doing that bubble thing again. Or fluffing up a pillow on top of my chest, a muffler for the fatal shot. I reached for her hand. She gave it and was still.

"I do have. Something. We should discuss," she said. "I'm just not sure—"

"Nabi, come on, it's like you've got a noose around my neck and you keep dropping it."

"Baby, I'm sorry, it's just hard. No, let me finish. It's just that, well, Erik told me stuff that's pretty personal—"

"Erik."

"Right. And I'm not sure I should tell you. It might upset you. You've been so, you know. But I prayed on it, baby, and I've decided it's the right thing to do."

Green light on Spurling Hill. Horns blared and I forgot to move. I could only look at her and say, "Erik."

"Okay, baby, you can keep driving."

"Jesus Christ."

"Not in vain, baby."

"Sorry."

Nothing my brother had to say was news to me. Our rivalry wasn't new to Nabi either, but it still seemed to shock her that I hadn't been in touch with him. We were home before I could get a word in; and by that time, yeah, I was upset, for it was crystal clear that Erik was trying to spin a sob story to turn Nabi against me, some crap about my general foxy allure. I didn't mention Faith Tabernacle, didn't want to go there, and anyway I was too appalled by what sounded like Nabi taking his side.

"No, baby, I'm not, I'm just saying that in spite of all that stuff, he's reaching out to you. I mean, there's got to be a reason why he keeps calling even though you're ignoring him. He needs help, and for some reason it has to come from you."

"Damn right that bye needs help."

"Kenji."

"Did he tell you what he wanted?"

"Not specifically. But how he was talking, I think he just needs his brother."

I put my confused, exhausted self on the couch. "This is what's been eating you all this time? For four days? Erik?"

"Look, I know it won't be easy. But he's already taken the first step."

"Nabi, please answer my question. All right?"

She sighed and sat down. Her arms went around me, her little head onto my shoulder. But it was more of a pressing thing than a cuddle. She began a prolix description of the Thursday-night function to which she and Martin never did get formally invited but went anyway. He spent the whole evening carping about the missing invitation. In the car he wondered where it might have gotten to. At the party he made pointed jokes about it to people who couldn't care less.

"Lord knows I tried, but Kenji, I just couldn't bring myself to laugh. Martin didn't like that. I think that's where the trouble started."

The trouble. On that fateful evening, on the way to the lavish Furbert condo on the harbor, Martin was distant, even cold. He asked his wife why, in case she had any idea, that troublesome colleague of hers would attempt to "misappropriate BRMS resources for personal use." He meant Gavin, of course. Again. Nabi made him state the details plainly and expressed her disapproval of his attempt to make me sound like a thief. Rather than apologize, he belabored the issue: What interest does *he* have in criminal investigations? What does *he* know about the fine art of detecting? When did *he* learn to appreciate the nuances of insurance?

"I said it's for a novel. But Martin didn't believe me, baby. He thinks you're up to something and I'm helping you cover it up."

"Well, ya boy got something wrong wif him, then, innit."

This remark should've earned one of her exquisite scowls. Nabi didn't even blink. She just went on in a hollow voice. "He asked me why, if you're writing a novel, you'd need to know intimate stuff about a *specific* insurance company, stuff that only somebody with BRMS-type clearance could access. I don't know how to research novels, baby, that's what I told him. But he said that wasn't an answer. And he's right. Do you have an answer to that, Kenji? Not for Martin. I mean for me, sweet genius."

She looked through the glass door to the balcony. Beyond the balcony to the turquoise, sand-bottomed ocean with its dark splotches of coral. Beyond the ocean to the sky, a dashing blue, empty but for a few threads of cloud. She didn't look at me, though there wasn't even room for a napkin between our bodies.

I heard myself saying, "I want to know what really happened. Regardless of what I end up writing."

"Why?"

"What do you mean why?"

"Truth for its own sake? Come on, baby. You chasing this woman's ghost won't do a thing to help her, I guarantee. And in the meantime what's it costing? I've asked you to move on from this how many times. I don't want it to come between us—"

"What do you mean come between us?"

"And you just keep on going like there's nothing else for you to do."

"What do you mean, Nabi?"

She gave me a furtive glance, got back on the business about Martin, how I'd let my work with Aetna "go too far," i.e., "involve" Martin. In exasperation I began to pull away, but she didn't want me to, she kept pressing against me even as she grew more fidgety. She said the problem wasn't BRMS, just Martin. Martin, once he'd decided Nabi and I had something to hide, took that and ran with it. He was still running the same track he'd run already (this is Martin we're talking about) when he took Nabi to lunch the following day. Nabi shooed him off and tried to put it all out of her mind. But it felt "like hammerheads circling around me, and so I just had to see you, get it all out in the open." She got Iesha to cover. Fine. Called Martin around four. Only this time he wouldn't buy it.

"He asked if you and I are having an affair. Point-blank like that."

Point-blank. And Nabi didn't even look at me. She frowned at something in the airy, narrow distance between her left shoulder and my right.

This was the last thing I needed. My path to detonation wasn't long at all by that point, and as I tried to tell her yet again what we had to do, I began to make my way along that path. But Nabi didn't want to listen.

"No, baby, let me get this out. It was a shock, you know, him coming out with that."

"You're telling me." We'd had our secret for so long that while we were never careless with it, I suppose it had achieved a sort of unbreakable air.

"I told him no. Martin's like, *You sure?* I said, *Go on and call Iesha.* I asked him did he see something like, I don't know, evidence?"

So the bastard accused Nabi of "resisting" the Thursday-night function and being "dismal" at that stupid party even though he thought it was an important event. Her "reticence" that evening translated into her not being "supportive" of him and his aspirations. She blamed this on me, by the way. She said she couldn't get her cheer button working because she was worried about me and the deadly threat a writing project seemed to have become. Martin's other "evidence" turned out to be the Gavin thing and the unfounded conviction that Nabi had lied to him in order to help me escape his inexorable scrutiny. (How one gets to be team leader by slavishly dogging the stench of one's own prejudices I'll never know.) Maybe he expected that she'd burst into tears and crawl home to him on her knees, but my Nabi's all too easy to underestimate.

"I told him it was hurtful that he didn't believe me, accusing without real evidence like he didn't *want* to believe me. I said it was plain insulting that my word wasn't good enough for my own husband, and then I hung up. Kenji, I hung up on my husband." She said she'd called me immediately, shivering everywhere.

Pacing in front of the couch, I said, "Martin being obtuse and jumping to conclusions is old news."

"I've warned you time and again about his radar—"

"Martin being Martin don't mean nothing. And if you want a solution—"

"Time and again you ignore me. On account of Aetna Simmons and some you-gotta-do-it feeling—"

"This thing you have about my work, it's ridiculous. Nothing in the world would stand a chance of coming between us if you weren't hellbent on letting it."

"Yeah, well, what about that woman?"

"What woman?"

"That woman in St. George's. Iesha said she saw you with some shiny black thing outside of Gojo's. Shorts all up to here. Tight little somethin-some up there."

"That was Doreen Trimm. I told you, she and I were discussing Aetna's—"

"There you go again. Because of Aetna, you and Gavin put Martin on high alert. Because of Aetna, you're traipsing round St. George's with some little so-and-so come out of nowhere. Iesha said she gave you hungry looks."

I burst out laughing. Not because anything was funny but because it was horrifying. Everything seemed to melt out from under me like unwanted ice cream, and I had to sit down right where I was on the carpet. Nabi folded her arms. We'd arrived at the heart of the matter.

"You think I'm cheating on you because of how some stranger *looked*? Meanwhile you and Martin get to have your cake and eat it too while I sit by the phone and wait for you to need a *ride*?" Nabi tried to get a word in to calm me, but I was already waspish and getting loud: "How is it that you can get on my case about chasing ghosts when you spend more than half the time being openly unfaithful? At least the ghost won't do that."

She dropped to the floor and grasped my shoulders. "This is what I worry about, Kenji. This is what scares me more than anything, I'm serious. That you might refuse to let go of this woman till she leads you all the way to the end of her road."

"You're changing the subject."

"No, I'm not. Kenji, you think it's all roses having *both* you lot to worry about?"

"Get a divorce," I said. "If you want to be married, marry me."

Should've asked her long ago. And not like that. It took a death and the destruction of all I'd worked for. That's how scared I was.

The only explanation I have for that untimely adjuration happening in that disastrous way is the change in the falling question. The question that pumped my heart and breath had in a way always been Nabi, but it was also a state. Modal, ontological, whatever you want to call it. A state of suspension. But if *What are we* had no answer, the suspension had no resolution, and so the pumping question morphed into *How long can I bear it?* And when a question breaks out in those terms, *How long can I*, like breaking out in sweat, it already means you can't hold out for very long. *I had cried out for a dead woman.*

You don't get it. You can't. You've never had to *be* it. Terrified and stupid and to such extremes. And Nabi looking at me—tears gathered in her eyes but she just looked at me, didn't say a word. Then I knew I was going to start shivering, and that got me off the carpet, heading for the library. It no longer seemed to matter that Nabi'd blow a gasket when she found out about Hardy; I just knew I was in pain, pain in my very foundation, and that's what painkillers are for.

Nabi followed me. I had no idea until the thing was in my hands. She touched me, she touched my back, really a hint of a touch, almost a frightened poke, but I nearly dropped the book. I shoved it into place with *Desperate Remedies* and *Jude the Obscure*, I spun around and grabbed her.

I'm okay now. Not really. I am *jammed*. I am *rad*. I am *full hot* and a fool.

Now, where was I. Oh yeah. Untimely and disastrous.

I didn't grasp the extent of things. I still don't. Midnight passed too quickly. Nabi wanted to get dressed and talk a bit before I took her home. We had tea on the balcony with thousands of bright stars as the ocean breathed against the sleeping bay. We spoke in whispers as though we feared to wake the liquid giant that had us surrounded.

Nabi said she was under strain. I knew that. I knew she still wasn't giving me the whole story. I worried. Nabi isn't one to keep a bunch of dark secrets scattered about her person. Not like me, in other words.

She wanted to make a deal. If you'll permit me, I'll set down her exact words. I'll do my best to convey their tone. Just as they are seared into my memory for life.

"I will start thinking. About how I can. Rearrange my position. With regard to. To Martin. If you *seriously* look for another project. Something that's not Aetna Simmons. Or you know, self-destruction. You have to promise me."

There's this thing about hope. Hope hits back as hard as despair lashes out. The blows from both sides rain on the tired, mortal heart stuck in the middle, which at some point has to crawl into one corner or the other.

I said yes, it's more than fair, and like a black eye part of me puffed up with hope. I would get high on that hope. (Higher, that is, harhar.) Though Nabi must've expected it to peter out and be forgotten, I couldn't help myself. Even though I knew I couldn't keep my side of the bargain either. I had to find something to use against UnDoreen: Aetna, my darling, it all comes back to you. Meanwhile, Nabi dreaded her lack of a prenup. She spoke at length on logistical inconveniences associated with Martin's excision from her life—lawyers, family, the church, and so on—basically to demonstrate that what she asked of me wasn't half as much as what the deal required of her.

She didn't even mention my proposal. If I didn't know that Nabi didn't know enough to know better, I'd think she'd wanted me to think I'd hallucinated it, yessai.

Once upon a time, Nabi and I were on our boat. It was a fine spring day, the ocean was relaxed, and the *Ethelberta*, our small but plucky vessel, was in top form. Nabi was at the helm; we stopped a few miles off South Shore where we snorkeled with flying fishes. When we came up, we danced to Bob Marley and watched the longtails fluttering in playful pairs. They were beautiful and funny. We laughed at everything. When Marley's album ended, the water serenaded us and kissed *Ethelberta*'s bottom. Nabi spread some blankets out on deck. I turned to the cooler for a Coke. Acegirl started hollering, "Kenji, come here, come quick!" I thought she'd found a cockroach. I went armed with paper towel. But she was pointing out to sea.

I looked and there it was. Puff of water like an oceanic firework.

The hump with the blowhole, the fin—a hundred meters from us, maybe less—and then the tail, the expressionistic fluke of the humpback. He didn't do anything fancy, just came up to breathe and went back down to his esoteric underworld. Nabi and I stood there holding hands.

Why is it so amazing to see a humpback whale? Old Japanese: *isana*, brave fish. That's a whale.

Nabi was jubilant. She'd never seen a humpback in real life. I told her I see them all the time from my balcony; she should spend more time up there with me, forget Harbour Road. But she thought I was making it up, mistaking a rock or broken wave for one of those incomprehensible submariners. We stood watching the water, hoping the whale would come back.

"I saw him twice, Kenji. I saw the top of his nose."

"Wow, you did?"

"And then he breathed and we got to see the rest of him together."

She put her arms around my neck. May twenty-third. Next day was Bermuda Day, a Friday and a public holiday. So I was surprised she'd taken the afternoon off. She stood on tiptoe to whisper something.

I thought it was time. I thought she was going to say it, *Baby, I've left my husband.* Whales are supposed to be good omens.

But she said Martin had left that afternoon for a conference in Washington. He'd be gone until Wednesday. We had six days, counting the twenty-third of May. I laughed and swept her up into my arms and jumped into the water. Everything was blue and sparkling; everything we said was wonderful. But that night, anchored near One Tree Island, the two of us lying in the pointy end of the boat, Nabi said she thought I had something on my mind.

The sky was bright. We didn't need a lantern. My phone's got a star chart. We found every constellation. Nabi said she wanted me to be honest.

I said, "Have you ever thought about living where you couldn't breathe? Like the whale?"

"Why would I? If we couldn't breathe, we'd die. Baby, what's the matter?"

I turned to her with something squeezing tight around my heart. "That's how I live all the time," I said. "Waiting for you."

206

My breath permanently held. Hope is the rare chance to come up for air until the weight of the water drags me back into the dark.

No, you know what? That's not right. Hope is like that terrible Russian substitute for heroin, *krokodil*. One hit and you're addicted. Even as the stuff corrodes your flesh down to the bone. It's the kind of habit that has no cure except death. The bravest would give up.

తూ

He won't tell me what he's done, what he's seen, I got scared & acted like a jealous bimbo, nothing between the ears except 2 men & what they might do, where Kenji might go running off to next now that I've hurt him.

Kenji asked me something, sort of. I wanted I don't know. Lord Jesus, why now? It's too late, I have a husband who loves me, & he's the power & beauty in my Faith. I love him. I love Kenji, my best friend for always, & he is afraid, a monster chases him at night, an obsession he won't let me understand even though he needs a friend to pull him out of its dark maze. I need to stop him. I didn't lie to him, I can't lose him. Who would I talk to, who would inspire me & love me all the way thru & make me feel like the only star in the universe? But I did lie. I can't leave Martin. Giving up on him would be like giving up on Jesus, & I can't do that, He is part of me.

Lord have mercy. It's too late. It's too late now, Baby! If I had to say that to him, I would I don't know. Thinking about it makes me want to run after him, screaming every promise I can think of. I'll tell you everything, you can keep a secret, just let's be the way we were, the 3 of us, & don't tell Martin, Martin has to stay the way he is, but I love you, we'll be OK. But I can't.

If K adds any more to his conspiracy theory, it'll end up looking like that house in California where the poor lady kept adding staircase after staircase even though there was nowhere for them to go up or down to. I mean, 10 suicide notes (!) + the philosophy, psychology, whatever. Fine. Then + the insurance company + his momma + her "minions" + my husband! He's about to + me, thinking I'm trying to steer his bumper car away from the top-secret mission Martin's puttering off to in his own bumper car. Next it'll be + Dunkley's Dairy + Bermuda Bookstore + the guy who sells the cedar stuff down Barnes Corner. I know Baby's a genius, no one knows that better than me, but come on now! You can't file your own W-2, your boss has to do it for you, which would mean, if K's "hypothesis" was right, the evil insurance company knew what was going on & sent the evidence to the US government, & that makes no sense, but it's no use telling him cuz he in't listening.

Lord Jesus, Lord of lords, You know the 2 Kenjis, I pray for them every day. One thinks too much of himself to not wear designer clothes, but the other thinks the total opposite. If You made him walk the line between genius & crazy, what would happen to that 2nd one? I'd never forgive You, I'm telling You right now as Your biggest fan & Martin's too. Help Kenji. You know the way he sees it. To him, this business with the suicide notes isn't about money. It's about being misunderstood forever & ever, & Baby's had to put up with that all his life, so maybe he's made up these poor misunderstood dead people so he can feel them reaching out to him. I don't know what's worse, letting him run with this foolishness till all those nightmares make him ill or hurting him by trying to make him stop. Not that I've had any luck. He's not giving me the full story cuz he's JUST LIKE THE OTHER ONE. They're the fancy butterflies with their big flapping wings, & they think the little worker bee won't be able to keep up. The man don't listen! Either of them!

Gotta quit crying & get changed. I smell Kenji everywhere, I feel him everywhere in the burn inside my body, & Martin will be home any second. Iesha faked a late-night cocktail party with her managers so M got smug cuz he was already suspicious & said he might as well work late too. So I might as well go to my bed. Martin isn't gonna want to talk, he'll just keep on with the cold shoulder or "take up his cross" & pretend our "misunderstanding" never happened. K will go to bed & wake up screaming like something's eating him alive, & I can't think about it or I'll get all up a tree again.

❧

I was determined to spend all weekend in bed and medicated. I watched the *Saw* movies. All of them. Without a break. Couldn't stop laughing. I scoured the Internet for a way to Oscar-nominate them retrospectively. So wacked I couldn't eat a thing. I mean, three or four Zos at once could kill a guy; dat's why der vicked, don. I didn't take them all at once. I did start to plan a trip to my supplier in Boston.

My phones rang. I ignored them. My brother, several times. And a persistent somebody on the business phone. The latter left a message finally, pining for the girl with the green eyes.

And Nabi. Well, Nabi didn't call.

It was Tony Trent. You remember Tony. Big mouth, Paragon Re, likes to use my services to butter up choice slices of the reinsurance industry. Anyway, he was desperate. He thought some of his personal supply had been stolen.

Nothing of even slightly lesser magnitude could've budged me from my bed. By Saturday night I was in bad shape. Oblivious to everything except, in a handful of waking moments, a cozy separation between myself and everything else. Including my own body. I seemed to be in some kind of attic at a picture window streaked with old rain, looking at gray fog which I found greatly entertaining for its absolute lack of features. I drank disproportionately dark Dark 'n' Stormies. Very bad idea, alcohol and too much Zo. But I think I was going for a kind of balance. So the schlep on one side of the fog would be just as miserable as the lowlife on the other. I'd made good headway when Tony interrupted me.

Pompano Beach Club. Dark corner of the lounge. I'd told him I was sick. He said, "Man, you weren't kidding, you look like shit."

"Fuck you." And I told him if he wanted to see that green-eyed lass ever again, he'd tell me how he'd contrived this "theft," omitting no detail, no name or circumstance. He'd also make a perfect recitation of the fine print and pay a premium for dragging me out of bed in my precarious condition. And if I was in any way dissatisfied with his accounting or if I learned that he'd taken it upon himself to make a franchise out of me, I'd call my police contact: "And I hope you like the tennis courts at Her Majesty's Prison."

"Okay, I get it. Shit. What the hell makes you want to play it like that, man? What about customer loyalty and all that shit? All those referrals I've done for you over the years. Name one time, one time, when I've even come close to looking like I'd fuck you over. Never, right? Jesus, it was just bad luck. You *know* me."

All my clients think they're my friends. I let them think that. It's part of the service. We're not friends. I made him recite the fine print. Tony's been with me so long my boy knows it word-for-word by heart.

Now his "accounting." I'm going to distill it. When he finished, I went home and threw up on the staircase. Puke on my hundred-dollar shirt.

A week before Pompano Beach, Tony and some cronies were at some swankish bar. All of them noticed the woman. Surrounded by admirers, she was unfamiliar, but Tony recognized every face in her retinue. They were all insurance people.

Confident he could "outplay all of them, any day of the week" (Tony, with his gaudy array of American idioms, is happily divorced), my boy sidled up and proceeded to do just that. The woman had a "supermodel" smile of an enigmatic kind that wasn't actually a smile, and Tony found it irresistible. Her body was "aw *man.*" She was American, visiting Bermuda to "get the lay of the land" on behalf of her company. Tony never found out what she meant by that. "Could've been anything from reinsurance to asset management to, hell, investigative services," all of which fell within her alleged purview. You see, she introduced herself thusly:

"Vice President of Risk Management, Clocktower Insurance."

She asked intelligent questions about Bermuda's corporate scene. Her all-male assembly inundated her with gossip and inflated but well-intentioned data. She wanted to know what kind of "opportunities" Bermuda had to offer Clocktower.

Now, I could not grab Tony by the throat and demand to know why he hadn't told me this before. Not that I didn't want to, but it would've been counterproductive; there's no way he could've known of my interest in Clocktower. The woman hinted that she'd encouraged her company to pursue Bermuda's "opportunities" because she herself had recently concluded a successful venture of some kind involving CAM. Gossip ensued concerning CAM, Masami, and

Barrington. The VP of Risk Management offhandedly remarked that Masami had mentioned two sons, one who worked at CAM and another, more mysterious; at which point Tony, my devoted champion, seized the advantage by stepping forward with my name, adding, "I know him well." Thus Tony whittled down the congregation, so when he leaned over and murmured, "If you like to party, I know how," or something just as tasteless, he and the woman were alone. To enhance his credibility, Tony attributed his expedient know-how to his and the woman's almost-mutual acquaintance: me.

At this point I was entitled to throat-grabbing. I was too doped to do anything but sit there.

"What's this woman look like?" I said.

No reason for the feeling that I already knew. And when I learned the truth (the legs: unforgettable), I shouldn't have reacted. Tony looked alarmed. He said, "You *know* her?"

I lied. It was transparent. The shock, you see. She wasn't an investigator, not a hireling of any sort, but the mastermind and a hypothesis confirmed! I made Tony keep talking. Yes, he slept with her too, only she told him the truth.

Her name is Char Richards. The VP stuff is verifiable by Google. Her face, in all its perilous pulchritude, is absent from Clocktower's website probably because she isn't "Chief" something-or-other. If you want to be precise about it, and I think we should, she's Vice President of Risk Management and Director of Life Underwriting. According to insurapedia.com, that means her job is to: "ensure the integrity of underwriting practices," "drive changes to underwriting philosophies and methodologies," "act as an expert resource for underwriters on unusual or complex cases," and "serve as a primary resource for the establishment of standards and policy for the evaluation of risk during the underwriting process."

So for Vice President Richards, risk management does not mean what it means for Martin. It's simpler for her. In her ruthless world, *risk* means how much money it would cost for Clocktower to do one thing or another:

To honor or deny a claim, for example.

To fake a suicide note or let some kid toddle away with millions.

Put an author on retainer or shell out a fortune every time somebody dies.

Stand there watching when the author grows a conscience, or nudge the new liability towards expiration.

When she and Tony were alone, Char, high on Empyreal, couldn't resist sounding her own horn. It was she who played matchmaker to Clocktower and CAM, igniting a relationship that continues to this day in the mutually rewarding manner Gavin described. In answering fanfare, Tony bragged that I am one of only two Empyreal brokers in the world. All this to impress her with the drug's rarity and by extension the peerless luxury of a night in his company.

When he woke up, she was gone. So was a portion of his stash. She didn't use it to kill Myrtle, who by this time was already dead, but she knew how to set a stage. She didn't have to convince any cops, only make me believe that she had enough to blackmail me and thus make me reveal in my terror of a murder charge—what, exactly?

It hardly mattered. As soon as I found out the truth, Empyreal was secondary. My body remembered Char's heat and Char's grain, her weight and astounding strength as she thrust into me and pulled me into her, and meanwhile Aetna's blood was everywhere on Char and in her, staining her desire and her every move. Maybe it seems bizarre to you that I should grieve at all for Aetna, who would've meant nothing to me if she'd survived. But it kept me in bed with my pills for over twenty-four hours: I betrayed Nabi for the woman who drove Aetna to her death. And when I dreamed of Masami, I realized the feather wasn't a feather at all. It was a *wakizashi*. The sword of a *samurai*.

Menboku ga nai. Shame as the strength of the disgraced or captured *samurai* as he drags the *wakizashi* across his belly.

Sunday. I'm at home. How not-me is that.

If she broke a man's heart, she'd be ocean enough not to care, she'd be bird enough to disappear. & she'd never have the joy or bother of belonging to anyone. I mean "she," of course, who isn't really called Seabird except in my book & isn't really anything like what I call Seabird. Didn't start out that way, anyway. But she got to learn to fly, & now all I did was not say what cannot be said to K, & Lord Jesus I'm no ocean I am MISERABLE. Rather stick a pretty picture of an Infini-blue suitcase set inside my book, & I know my book would rather have that too. What hacker's dumb enough to put her issues in a book she loves too much to destroy? Well I can't help it, the one I should be able to tell I can't tell, especially now cuz when I didn't answer him I thought he might pass out.

Yesterday. Car boot sale at Mt O. Martin sold some old golf stuff. He also got up early & helped me bake & put the cookies in cute boxes. & eat some while he's at it. Honey was bouncy. Like he hadn't got home from work at 2 a.m. Like he'd forgot we'd quarreled. Course M never forgets, he just prayed on it & made up his mind to forgive. He was whistling "So glad I'm here, so glad I'm here, Lord," wanting me to sing bass while he tooted soprano, silly adorable man. It was fun, it helped us. Thank You, Lord.

But on our little Island, everything rubs elbows. Mt O's right near Kenji's place. 10-min walk could've taken me to him. Selling cookies with my happy husband at our church, I'm worried sick about my lover. K held me without saying nothing while I cried instead of answering. & I was such a coward I threw myself at him, thinking I was dragging us into some kind of refuge, loving with everything we got. & he forgave me too, poor Baby, he barely said anything else all night. & then I lied & then I had to make him drive me home. I couldn't see him in the dark. & he still didn't say nothing, so I said, "Chin up, Baby." & K said, "See you Monday." & this is what I'm thinking while giving cookies to Mrs Raynor's babies (making $0 for Mt O) & Martin's making the rounds of all the other cars, buying a little thing from each one, Lord bless him. I watched him, Martin laughing, everybody loving him. (Why can't he do this all the time like at "functions," I mean just be himself?!) I thought if I just ran up to Kenji for 5 mins while Mrs Raynor watched our car (she'd

214

have made more sales than me, that's for true!), just long enough to tell my Baby: Don't hurt, Baby, please. But that's nonsense. So then what? I can't say I'm sorry for everything we fought over, cuz I'm not. I mean I'm not sorry I did it, I'm just sorry we fought. But that's K's fault, not me. Lord, help him "let the dead bury their own dead." Don't let him do anything rash. Anything else rash, I mean.

Luke 9 in the car going home. Honey wanted to review before Sunday Bible Study, & Saturday p.m. we were going on his colleague's boat. So I read Luke, M drove. & for the first time (God save me), I read it without wanting to. Normally I love it, Jesus & all His friends, 5 loaves, 2 fishes. But this time I read, "Take nothing for the journey... If people do not welcome you, leave their town..." & I couldn't stand it, it almost hurt. No, mercy, it did hurt. It made me envious & angry. & I'd never noticed it before, but (say I'm wrong & I'll believe You, tell me all my sins are messing with my eyes) Lord Jesus, isn't this kinda weird:

"Whoever wants to be my disciple must deny themselves & take up their cross daily & follow me. For whoever wants to save their life will lose it, but whoever loses their life for me will save it. What good is it for someone to gain the whole world & yet lose or forfeit their very self?" ???!!! Doesn't that say the opposite of itself? Denying yourself is good & no good? I'm not mixing up translations, You'll notice there are no "..." How could I look at that & not feel like throwing up my hands? & that feeling scared me half to death.

I was scared to ask my husband. But You're supposed to have answers for sinners who pray. Poor Martin said, "It all boils down to choosing to go out & work on spreading Jesus' love or choosing not to & staying home, which is just selfish." Well, that sounded like an ultimatum to this acegirl. It never did before, but right then it sounded like merciful Lord Jesus saying there's only one right way to live & that's His way even though "what good is it..." & suddenly I thought that's a horrifying thing to say, I don't care who says it. It also sounded like no matter what I did I'd "lose or forfeit my very self." Then my stomach went all funny like the car was weaving out of control, but it wasn't. But just cuz I was terrified I almost snapped at poor Honey, who was trying so hard to pretend there's nothing to forgive. Then I felt bad for wanting to snap (I never snap) & thought maybe Jesus was right & I was lost already, my "very self" carved up & shared out between M & K. Then I felt horrible for thinking that about the boys who love me. & then I thought maybe I was really lost cuz I'd chosen Jesus & Moses & this Lord of theirs who said I couldn't love 2 gentle boys the same. & THEN (sigh!) I thought of Jesus saying, "Go... Take nothing for the journey..." & I thought maybe I should ditch all 3 (M, K, & Jesus too!) & go find out where I'd put the steadiness I thought I had inside "my very self." & when we got home I felt woozy & thought, How can I show my face at church tomorrow???!!!

Long evening on M's colleague's boat. I'll just say it: torture. Boat's moored up at Dockyard where Ethelberta is. So I had to look at her all abandoned & empty. Baby named it for some girl in a Thomas Hardy book, a poor girl who escapes to the city under a fake name & makes it big. Thinking of that girl right then, I felt sad & mad at the same time. Spent the whole party dreading Sunday. & watching the water turn black. & the dark darkening in Kenji's eyes. & thinking about when K & me & Ethelberta hung out off South Shore at night, just the 2 of us in a small boat on the big ocean & we felt safe like that.

Couldn't sleep when I got home. Worrying for K. Watching my husband snooze & worrying for him. Dreading Sunday. Dreading the sun. It came anyway.

After I've been on a boat, I always feel like I'm still on it for a little while. I pretended the feeling was bad instead of nice. Told Martin I was queasy. Sent him off to church with apologies for the pastor & the choir. Martin frowned, he knows we need to pray. But he also knows Bible Study couldn't manage without him.

So here I am. Alone in bed. Trying to feel like I'm in some wide open space. Not doing too spiffy at it.

છ

I woke up with a leg in the bathroom, rest of me in the hall. It was hard to breathe. My body felt like I'd need a crane to lift it. A pale patch on the carpet was a triangle of sunlight from the study. I don't recall anything more except an anvil's weight on my eyelids, and it took forever to get down a little air. What awakened me? A noise? If I'd lain there a moment longer, I may not have woken up at all.

Getting to my feet was a five-act comedy featuring wobbly legs, a wall that wouldn't stand still, the threat of vomit on the carpet, and the towel. I must've taken a shower, all I had was this towel, and since I was shivering it seemed to develop a mind of its own. Anyway, at some point I really did hear a noise. Even in my sordid state, I managed to discern a glimmer of the only explanation possible and strained to reach it.

Nabi. Come to rescue me. Ditching work on a busy Monday because she couldn't tolerate my distress, not even telepathically. Because I'd made a proposal and she had a response that couldn't wait. I didn't care that she would have to see me like this. I even wanted it, a vainglorious sop. I would weep for her forgiveness. Movement in the walk-in closet. I dragged myself to meet her.

One good thing came out of this. I lacked the breath to call her name.

She said, "You're not answering your phone."

She looked at me. Dropped what she was holding and my knees went out from under.

"What happened?" she said quietly. "What've you done?"

Not Nabi but Char Richards. Her astonishment could've passed for apathy. She stood above me in her high heels and pencil skirt, wondering if it was worth putting more time on this expiring meter, then crouched and—"Stay away from me," I gasped—and took the damn towel and tossed it in a corner, so there you have it. Happy?

"Is that your vomit outside?"

"How did you get in here?"

She looked at me like I'd asked how she found her foot each morning. "Can you breathe? You sound like you've got something in your—"

"Get out."

That was all I had in me. I was leaning on the doorframe, I think.

Next thing I knew, her nails were digging into me, she was shaking me. Something about a kit. Turned out she meant Narcan, which my supplier comps me every time (I keep telling him I don't need that shit), somehow she figured out where it was in the bathroom. And okay, I was like a rag doll, she made me lie back and shoved the Narcan thing up my nostrils. I lay there and she watched. A good twenty minutes. I'm hanging out for all to see and she just sat there. She counted my breaths, I think, as my respiration eased up to a serviceable speed.

"Should probably get an ambulance," she grumbled.

"No."

"What is it, Empyreal?"

"Leave. Go on." What did she expect? Thank you for observing the great humiliation of my life. It's so nice of you to stop by in the middle of my overdose. So convenient too, what with you being a blackmailer. If I'd had the energy, I would've chased her out with a Swiffer, screaming invectives and aiming for the head. But I was naked on the floor, confident I'd lose control of my stomach any minute.

Mortification hurts, just so you know. It can shovel you inside out.

Narcan is the devil in a teeny yellow tube. Just a whiff, and its instant-withdrawal chemicals attacked the fuzzy shields around my pain receptors. I couldn't stop vomiting. I imagined cutting my throat open.

Only one remedy. Zohytin for pain. Zo for terror and fury, Zo-hytin for shame. For oblivion. Or at least so I could form a thought. Shuddering in a bathrobe, groping for the library and Hardy, who understood the meaninglessness of suffering.

She was on the couch. Trying to guess the password on my business phone. "Your phone's in Japanese."

Her patience is scary. That's what it takes to be a hunter.

Most men would enjoy finding this woman in their living rooms. For me the shock felt like impalement. She tossed me a smile like I'd only been to put the kettle on. Seeing Hardy yawning open like a corpse under dissection, she laughed like the engine in a muscle car. I took my pill, shelved the book, availed myself of the nearest armchair. She assessed me like I was going cheap but what she really wanted was something in a lighter fabric. I couldn't take it. I had to close my eyes. And then the bitch who made Aetna want to die had fingers in my hair. She perched on the arm of my chair and touched my head. Not like you'd fondle a loquat before ripping it from its life-giving branch, but softly. Like it should make me feel better. And what was that? A joke, that's what. Even at the height of our hunger, she and I never touched each other without rage, without some disgusting contest going on between us. So her being gentle now was farce. And something told me she wanted me to know it. Why? Because it meant that she respected nothing, not even agony. And so her trick with the Narcan was just that; a feint, a one-up. Because she could. A sharp pain in my stomach almost killed the frail shadow of dignity she'd left me. I couldn't even try to shake her hand away. I said in a voice that scraped my throat, "Why are you—"

Right. I was too abject to finish. She shrugged. "We had an appointment."

Then she whipped out the dress. It was behind her, draped over the back of the couch. A little purple and gold sundress. Nabi bought it just to wear with me, and I swear to god that as I snatched it from Char's dripping claws, had it not been for Zo I would've slapped that woman to Peru.

"Size six," she said. "The clothes in the cottage are size six or equivalent. Where is she?"

"I told you to get the fuck out of here."

"Why'd you do that with the pills? Because you know you're cornered. She was here," said Char. Looking around. Sniffing the air. "Why did she run?"

"What'd you say to make her think she had to die?"

"When you knew she was gone, why did you let Myrtle Trimm call the police?"

"You've got it wrong," I began, but I shut up. Nabi's little dress crumpled in my lap, soiled by coincidence and a dumb misunderstanding. But you see, I couldn't give that woman anything of Nabi's. Especially her name. I didn't trust my head, everything was twisted up, so I said nothing. Raised the dress to my lips. Aetna and I were lost already anyway.

219

"How much did she tell you?"

I just shook my head.

"Where is she, Kenji?"

"Dead. And you as good as killed her."

She slapped me. Fack, she was fast. If it weren't for my complexion, I'd still have the wound to prove it.

"Wake up," she said. "Tell me."

"Or what? Tony owned up. You got the pill by screwing a junkie and plundering his stash. You planted it in Aetna's house the day after I met you."

"This Tony person," she said stiffly.

"Don't even worry with it. He gave me your name, your title, Clocktower Insurance. There's a picture of you on the Internet, Char."

She sat down on the couch. Not in shock. Just civil.

"You broke into Myrtle's house," I said. "You went in there and started throwing out the woman's stuff."

Stripping away the lies (some of them, anyway) that hid UnDoreen's identity (well, the name they put beside her picture at IntlInsuranceAssn.org) didn't amount to an excavation of the true essence (which probably doesn't exist) of Char Richards. She probably knew it was a matter of time before I learned her name. Maybe she thought I'd always known it. Still, you'd think my revelation would count for something besides another trigger for her understated laughter.

"What do you intend to do about it, teddy bear?" she said, leaving me no choice but to feign nonchalance about her freakish nonchalance.

"Nothing," I said with a languid gesture at the library. "I'm all tied up in you now, you know that. Thing is, you're tied up in me. You broke into my house too. That much I can prove. You didn't even wait a day before you started trying to threaten me."

We sat there smiling like a couple of potheads, each trying to outlast the other in a contest of phlegm. We cuddled our secrets and might've left it there, a pair of thwarted crooks making each other sheepish. Let bygones be bygones. The idea made me weary and disheartened. Char rubbed my thigh as if for old times' sake.

"I need to know, Kenji."

"I've shown you everything I can."

"Not yet. But you will."

She watched my hands clinging for dear life to gold and purple silk. She smiled a blues singer's smile. We spoke in bluesy voices.

"How'd you know where I live? I'm not in the book."

"I'll find a way, you know. I always do."

"You feel like talking to the cops, it's all right. It won't matter. Thing about this little backwater, everybody knows me."

"Oh, is that right?"

"Nobody knows you. They'll say you're just an expat trying to throw your weight around, undermine an upstanding local business-man. I'm just telling you how it'll look."

Her supermodel smile. Perhaps a bit diluted with the pity she reserved for those she deemed unworthy in the end. And one teensy-weensy unintentional flaw.

"Tell you what," she said, giving my shoulder a pat. "You want to negotiate. I get that. You're entitled. But you're in no shape for it now."

"There's nothing to negotiate."

"So what you're going to do is sleep on it." Another pat.

"Char," I said, "she died. I know it's hard to live with."

"I'll call you tomorrow. You tell me where she is and what you want." And a kiss on the forehead.

Char got up to leave. I made a stupid grab at her hand, then I had to rush to the bathroom. Nabi's dress tumbled to the floor, where I left it.

Char and I are two of a kind. That's the only reason I saw. Fascina-tion would've blinded any other man. But I detected a teensy-weensy tensing. Flash in the eyes as of a dagger concealed beneath a coat. That wordless flash was a promise to bring me down; and the same instinct, the same intimacy, that revealed it in the first place warned me not to underestimate it.

There was a hidden blemish on my garish sketch of my own untouchability. My word against another's would probably vanquish at Court Street and Victoria, but there is one person—one person alone could torpedo it and sink it. This person has more money and connections than Char will ever dream of.

How much did the dragon know about Aetna Simmons' death? How far would she go to keep it mired in shadow?

Just so it's clear. To ensure my own protection, I had twenty-four hours to instigate a game of wits against a diabolical power and emerge victorious. And I'd never been so sick in my life. Hanging out with my head in the toilet, I grew evermore disgusting to myself. It may sound impossible to be enraged and despondent at the same time, but I was, and the longer I sat there, the worse it got, building like the synchronous tension and weakness in my stomach, rising like the chill that came just before I vomited.

AS7, that's how I felt. That gush of ire like a retch or a long wail. This was the beginning of the protracted explosion of her suicidal rage. Violence and vengeance. You'd have to be high to miss the flying accusations. But Aetna also blames herself, maybe most of all, and cloaks her self-revulsion in vitriol aimed not quite truly outwards. It's her own fault that she's trapped. Trapped in what, she doesn't say, but this is the outcry of someone out of options. The capital letters. Is there any more flagrant representation of impotence and futility? Is there anything more helpless than a scream without sound?

Taken together, these capitalized words form a demented imperative. A note within a note? Two notes in one? Maybe for two different readers? Before drafting my essay I spent an entire night gazing at those capitals, straining to hear into their silence. A point of no return furiously scrawled blood-red on an abnormal canvas.

The W-2. With that, she signs her name. Clocktower's name. Delegates responsibility. Having no idea she'd send a minor pill-pusher to meet his demon.

Perhaps I thought things couldn't possibly get any worse. I can't convey how impossible it was not only to shove myself into a suit and drive to Hamilton without puking but also, reeling from my thorough disgrace, to steel myself for a confrontation I'd meant to avoid for all eternity at any cost.

I couldn't take the chance that if Char and Masami were in this business together, the predator might entice the *ikiryou* to attack. And I had no time, I was certain they would strike within a day; the assault could take almost any form.

Perhaps my strategy was to sneak into the mountain through a disused cavern. I knew it'd be impossible to infiltrate the dragon's lair and avoid the dragon, but I hoped to arm myself as best I could as I wended my way to my doom. Erik knew nothing, but Barrington would've been at her side as she wined and dined Jim Falk. Even if the glorified bellhop had no sensitive details, before he rang for his acknowledged ruler and befanged protector I might hound him into revealing useful vagaries. Did he know Char, for instance? Did Falk know her, or had her nefarious maneuvering slipped beneath his radar?

I had in mind a hazardous bluff: fishing for information while pretending to know all. This was unwise to say the least. Perhaps I thought I could convince Masami that threatening my credibility would endanger her own: if she knew about Empyreal, I knew about Clocktower. Maybe I supposed the shock of my appearance out of the blue, after years of painstaking evasion, would numb her percipience. Did I really expect Masami, force and begetter of nightmares, to unwittingly connive with me against herself?

It's true I can no longer quite discern my strategy. I'd understand if you surmised that I flew to Hamilton with no strategy at all, nothing in my mind except despair, wrath, and revenge, stricken by the realization that my peril and Aetna's were hopelessly intertwined as for all intents, I had no one else. How's that for risk management?

I arrived late in the afternoon. Just looking at the place turned my stomach. Bermudiana Road, dainty and smug between XL's glass monstrosity and a hunk of Bank of Butterfield's marble. The four-storied pointy structure with wings spilling out of it. The soft pink and yellow paint always makes me think of tongues and aging teeth. The building insists on local architectural traditions; stubborn about white cornerstones, arched windows, ornamental portholes, white roofs with ridges looking almost fluffy on the multiple turrets. Atrium with palmettos, fountains, and skylights, a gaudy diamond in a top-heavy crown lined with cedarish panels. Her office is the summit of one of the turrets. His is directly below, a private lift and staircase in between.

Aetna died for this. To protect this place, the mountain. So the goblins living in it could pretend to shine some inborn, gracious light upon the world, that their sheer relevance might seem to outdo everyone else's. Power, money, an army of yes-men. For that kind of treasure and the ideology of thieves, Aetna made a travesty of history. How many did they dishonor, undeserving and unknowing, for a little extra cash that they'd blow within a month?

All of it was an insult. By the time I met Barrington's sleek, upwardly mobile assistant, my charm reserves were drained. I demanded as the eldest brat of Barrington's progeniture to speak to him forthwith. The "executive assistant" jacked up her eyebrows, already loathing me, picked up the telephone, and murmured into it. When she hung up, she pointed to a heavy door.

I didn't knock, just barreled in, which made the shock much greater. They were all there. All of them.

She was behind his desk, he in a chair like a visitor or secretary, Erik-Katsuo standing. They'd all just finished laughing, you could see it on their faces. Laughing at me, I knew at once. Fresh-oiled snickering, secure in the opulence they'd cheated out of others by making Aetna lie to them. Flaunting it while she and I eked it out in shadow, hazarding, toiling, dying, so they could sprawl in the sunshine streaming through the picture window and stare at me. I knew Aetna like a lover. Through her I saw right through them. And still they had the gall to stare and (except Masami) feign astonishment, having never in a million bubbly, laughing nights suffered any premonitions of this awful moment, having never once known dread. The way Barrington looked at me, I might've been a mail boy who'd sauntered into a board meeting. Erik tried to cover his outrage with a sneer. He glanced at Masami as everyone, naturally, waited for her to speak. And when her eyes fell on me, I froze.

In that instant everything—my whole life, really, which she'd swept away with a shake of her head—rose up in front of me like a mirage. I watched it dissipate all over again, the ground beneath me disappearing to become the black place of my nightmares where I'd lived for far too long in the grip of that gaze full of hate.

For decades I'd imagined the day I'd stand before them with something that cowed them. And now look: here I am. Surrounded, all of them looking. And where's my blazing sword and dazzling shield? What do I have that will astonish them so blindingly they must avert their eyes, those stares tumble to the ground?

Ten suicide notes. A ghost. You, Aetna. And what's all this but confirmation that those people even have command of life and death? I stand there like a crooner who's lost the tunes and all the words in a stadium of thousands.

"Well, what is it?" she said. Her words went into me like needles.

"Money," grunted Barrington.

"No, never. Never," I said.

"*Mochi*, are you sick? He don't look too good, *okaa-san*," said Erik. He giggled.

"Out," I said. "This doesn't concern you."

"Stay, Katsuo," said Masami in brisk Japanese. "Kenji, what do you want?"

Not for a second did she take her eyes off me. Nausea shuddered through me as I drew myself up.

"It's come to my attention that this company has dealings, that is to say, does business of some kind, as it were, with Clocktower. The insurance company."

Heat in my face. My voice was thin. And Clocktower was not the place to start. I sounded like a total fool.

"Maybe, maybe not," said Erik (Japanese). "It's confidential."

"I'm not asking, idiot. I'm telling you I know that CAM does their investments." I insisted on English throughout this doomed exercise, probably just because.

"Yeah, and so what?" The little parasite clung to Japanese, glancing at his handler with every word that passed between us.

"Where did you learn this?" said Masami (Japanese).

"Doesn't matter," I said. "You take their money, you make it make more money, so when they make money, you make money."

"That's kind of what asset management means," said Erik.

"What's wrong with you?" said Barrington. He didn't mean Erik. "You forgot how to use the telephone? You come barging in here—"

225

"Quiet," said Masami (flawless English). "I still don't understand what it is you want."

Erik added, "Or why you suddenly care—"

"Quiet."

"It's for an essay," I said. "A story."

"Oh, for Christ's sake," mumbled Barrington. He clung to English out of ignorance.

"If Clocktower committed fraud to make more money, and—"

"What?" Erik and Barrington, the former's merry laughter. "*Onii-san*, let me take you out to eat, come on, you look like you could use it. We'll talk it all over, whatever's on your mind, you and Kiki and a little drinky-*chan*. Come on, come with *otouto*, Momma's busy—"

"What's that got to do with us?" said Barrington.

"And if you knew about it," I said pointedly. Letting the idea fester like a stench.

Erik exploded in giggles. Barrington went still. His face. Like I'd punched him in the gut. Like he had any right to pretend to know what that feels like. The man actually raised his arm, pointed at the door as though we'd all forgotten where it was. "Leave this building right now."

"Or what?" Me. "No Dad just—" Erik. We both spoke at once, but I was louder, I was shaking with anger. I turned on Masami: "How much do you know?"

She was calm as a sated *kami* in a shrine. She spread her hands, which meant she knew everything or nothing.

"Char Richards," I said. "Aetna Simmons."

"He's drunk," said Barrington. "He's on something."

Masami ignored him. She looked into my eyes and delivered her verdict.

It was the same look. When she gave me the sword that was supposed to be a quill. That look.

She said, "You have no idea what you are saying." And something burst in me.

"That's what you always say, it's what you've always assumed, that I don't have a clue—well, I know everything about this, *everything*, there are *documents*—"

"Enough. Your father is correct. You're ill. No one understands what you're attempting to imply. Go home and go to bed."

A hand on my arm, Erik. "Time to go, *onii-san*."

"If you speak about this nonsense to anyone again, you'll regret it."

She turned to the window. Masami turned her back on me.

I gave Erik a shove that sent him reeling, his arms wheeling like the helm of a doomed ship.

I ran to Bull's Head, didn't know what else to do. By the time I got there, I had three texts from Erik: *Need 2 talk!! Call me!!* Nabi was waiting. She'd been calling me all day, she said, message after message; was I still upset, had I been sleeping? I got out of the car, and only then did she observe: "Baby, you look awful."

"You drive, Nabi."

All the way home I had my head against the window. She pestered me till I mumbled about stomach flu, which after a long silence she insisted was her fault: "...didn't want to hurt you...last thing I'd ever...you're taking everything so hard...this suicide business..." She pressed the point till we were on the steps. The puke was gone. Her arm around my waist, Nabi noted my fine suit, alarmed that I'd dressed up and gone to town in my condition; there must have been some emergency—had our lawyer called? All I did was shake my head. She stopped with one foot out of her shoes.

"You went there," she said. "You saw her. Your momma."

"And the others."

"Baby, why? Why today when you're not well?"

"Because she knows something. He does too. All I did was mention Clocktower, and they threw me out. Leave the building, he says—"

"Clocktower? Excuse me, what about your promise?"

"Yeah, well, what about you? When's the hearing?"

"Bye, you best just rest yourself. If you think—"

"Look, I can't do this." Striding to the bathroom, I passed the library. Turned around, chose a shelf at random, swept the books onto the ground. One left: *Minima Moralia.* I grabbed it, stormed into my study with Nabi pulling at me, hurled Adorno's *reflections from damaged life* at the Tiffany lamp. It crashed onto the floor (I thought,

227

Freedom has contracted to pure negativity), I picked it up and smashed it against a wall and smashed again (*infinite abasement of living*), expensive glass flying everywhere (*and the infinite torment of dying*). I sat down, breathless and sick, and Nabi grabbed me by the chin: "Kenji, this is crazy, what're you *doing*, baby?!"

Well, the question seemed to me an aporia. I looked away, but Nabi's sharp inhale said she saw it all: fury and hatred, nausea, fear, and hatred, hatred. She saw me look around for something else to ruin; she plopped herself down on my thigh and held me, burying my face so all I could see were the fibers in her suit. She didn't ask anything more, didn't say any more, and I wanted to hate that too but couldn't, what with the effort of holding down my stomach and not screaming like some animal stuck in a steel-jaw trap.

In the bathroom I scarfed down the shit I'd hidden in my suit. Feeling unglued, I kept thinking I wasn't supposed to need so much shit on Mondays, but I couldn't face Nabi again without something holding me together. I sat on the floor in the shower with my face in my hands, begging the shit to hurry up and burrow deep.

She wouldn't hear any remorse, darling Nabi. She led me straight to bed. Maybe I remember her hand on my forehead, trembling. I fled into oblivion as fast as I could.

Given the aforesaid, I understand why Nabi's not answering back. Still, I don't want to understand it. I've just sent what appears to be the twenty-first text message to skitter from my phone to hers in this endless night.

The sound was like the wind rattling a window. It slogged through the quagmire in my brain and touched my consciousness only because Nabi already had. She wasn't asleep. She was playing with my hair.

"Can't be someone at the door," she said.

It came again, too insistent for the wind. I thought of Char, sat up. "Mercy, what time is it?"

"Quarter after one. Stay here, okay? Don't worry."

She quit biting her lip only because I kissed her there. I went out in my boxers.

The shutters were open; there was only a light breeze. I checked

them anyway, checked the peephole. Goosebumps sprang up all over me.

The presence of the man outside the door could only mean one thing. But instead of shoving my desk against the door (the wiser course), I opened it.

Yuuto Motomura. Masami's live-in butler and chauffeur. No Bermudian would condescend to such a gig. Every time his work permit comes up for renewal, she advertises, nobody applies. This is going on about thirty years. We bowed stiffly to each other. Motomura, the silent type, looked over his shoulder.

Behind him I could see the glow of headlights. Her black Prius idled at the bottom of the steps. I tried to slam the door but Motomura grabbed the thing (old fool still moves like lightning), and then all the strength I had couldn't budge that door. I shook my head. He looked at me with disappointment. That infuriated me, but I gave in. I held up my hand, indicating that he'd have to wait, and Motomura raised his chin. Two articulate grownups miming like a couple of spies.

I should note that these weren't habits of Masami's. Showing up at my door in the middle of the night or making Motomura do it for her. Till that evening I had no idea that she knew where I lived. Nabi was alarmed. She wanted to go with me, started to get out of bed. "So Masami will find out about us," I said. "You're ready for that?"

The look on Nabi's face as she shrank against the pillows. Such anguish that I wished I'd thought of snubbing her when she tried to lend me that crayon.

"That's what I thought." Dressed, snatching my phone. I walked out with that look of hers burning in me, worse than the worst gastritic pain.

The whole affair wrapped itself in the gray aura of the clandestine. It seemed she'd sealed us off from everything, perhaps so when she dragged me down to the deepest, darkest reaches of her lair, it would seem to all who had survived that I had never been at all.

Two of us in the backseat like a cargo of stolen statues. Motomura drove in silence. I was too angry to know how to begin, Zo

229

notwithstanding, and to my consternation Masami said nothing. She can't stand inefficiency. Excessive words are inefficient.

We left the southern coast for a dark and empty Middle Road. I figured we were heading for the cavernous mansion she'd installed in Warwick, where under one of the pagodas Erik had a wing all to himself. But the silent Prius glided past the site.

Like a chill wind from across the sea, she spoke.

"Are you very ill? Do you indeed require money?"

No apologies for the ungodly hour. No thanks for getting out of bed to drive around in pitch blackness. Besides that of rare street lamps, the only light came from the cruise terminal at Dockyard, mere twinkles from across the dark expanse of the Great Sound; and she wouldn't deign to turn on the lights inside the car and look at me.

She spoke quiet Japanese. For me: English, indignation. Like conversing through shatterproof glass. "So?" I said.

"The so-called documents you mentioned. What sort of documents?"

The clumsy adjective "so-called" appears often in my so-called conversations with this woman for the maddening reason that she refuses to believe a word I say.

My valiant parry: "First you have to tell me everything you know. Clocktower, Aetna Simmons, Char Richards."

"This is no negotiation."

"That's what you think."

Masami sighed. The kind of sigh that chills CAM employees to the bone, bringing nightmares of want ads and destitution.

"Char Richards," she said. "An executive at Clocktower." You could hear the redactions a mile away.

"How long have you known her?"

"Some years. Not in the way you think. These accusations, you believe that she's involved?"

"I know she is. As I know who stands to gain."

The light flipped on overhead, showing the dragon's eyes blazing with ravenous fury. Take it from me: this woman's hush belies a temper like the head of a match.

"Is this some kind of scheme to get back at your brother? If so, it is stupid, it is malicious and ridiculous, and you are only wasting everybody's time."

A red herring of course, intended to enrage me so I'd say too much.

I affected boredom. "This business would go sailing over that bye's head, you know that."

"Insulting your brother won't get you anywhere." Of course. Her golden boy.

"That idiot's beside the point. This is about you and CAM and Char and Aetna Simmons. And let me tell you something—"

"Quiet."

Zip. I shut up. Habit. Couldn't help it. Thirty years under her thumb. Could've slapped myself.

"*Tori wo nakazuba utaremaji,*" she murmured, whipping out her phone.

Proverbs at a time like this. Aetna's dead, a stranger wants to send my life up in flames, I'm sticking my neck out in search of answers, and this woman comes out with a proverb? *The bird who does not warble eludes the hunter's arrow.*

"Really," I said. "And who's that holding the quiver?"

She ignored me. Typical. Scrolling her phone, I thought, to create the impression that something more important awaited her elsewhere. But she held out the phone to me.

Missing Woman Leaves 10 Suicide Notes.

"She's dead," said Masami.

"Well, yeah."

"Your concern?"

All this intended to finagle information out of me without letting anything dribble back in return. Her MO? Sit back, take it all in, strike when the victim bares his throat. On any other night it would've made me laugh. But as a victim of midnight kidnapping who'd spent almost two days throwing up, I was pissed off, drained, foiled, utterly at her mercy. I said, "She died for a reason."

"Meaning?"

"You tell me."

She put the phone away, folded her hands in her lap. Again that look. I wondered if I was asleep or high and trapped in a new version of that hopeless dream. When next she spoke, she spoke English, soft as the movement of a reptile over leaves.

"So it's not only fraud you wish to lay upon my shoulders. It's also death."

"She wanted to stop. Char wouldn't let her—"

"Threats are dangerous for those who utter them all misinformed. Instead let us be clear. You believe that through Char Richards, Clocktower is involved in embezzlement of some sort. You believe this woman Aetna Simmons somehow participated."

"Falsifying documents. As if you didn't know—"

"And how do you know?"

"She worked for them, there are documents—"

"Which to your mind are false."

"No, you're twisting my words. You always mess around with what I say. You've assumed I'm a liar since the day I was—"

"She participated, then. Or at least she knew about this so-called scheme."

"She wasn't the only one. Difference is she died because of it. But you knew that."

Thought she'd sock me in the face. Barrington would've, I think. But the dragon lurked. Sat there with that look. Daring and disdain, challenging and withering.

"Okada Kenji, you are talking about your family." *Kazoku*: family. And she addressed me surname first.

"This quit being a family when it became a *kabushiki kaisha*!" A sort of "Co., Ltd."

"You really think your family would be party to such things?"

Without the naked fury that set fire to her eyes, the uninitiated might have mistaken the sharpness in her voice for horror. I thought she'd tell Motomura to stop and let me out, run me over, and scrape me off the tires back at home.

"Show me evidence to the contrary," I said (Japanese). With a sardonic look, I dared her to consider her track record.

"And you? Where is your evidence?"

"I tell you there are documents—"

"Again these documents. You have them?"

"No. You kidnapped me." (English.)

232

"You can describe them?"

"I'm not going to do that."

"Then this nonsense will cease at once. From now on, you will forbear to amuse yourself with affairs that in every sense lie beyond your reach. Motomura-san will drive us to your flat. You will give the documents to me."

"You're kidding, right?"

"You will give me the so-called essay that you have written. You will give me your computer. And if there's a publisher—"

"Of course I have a publisher. In fact, there are several interested parties."

I haven't talked to any publishers.

"Then I will speak to them."

"Hell no."

"You will not address me in that manner." English, and she was hissing mad.

"It's true, then, isn't it."

Yes, I was smug. But I can't pretend it wasn't still a shock.

"It most certainly is not true. None of your accusations are true. And I say to you that this so-called evidence does not exist," said Masami.

"Of course it exists."

"Then you are simply unprepared? You barge into my building, flinging accusations here and there, and you don't bring any proof? Very well, this shouldn't be surprising. I'll send Motomura-san to-morrow."

"To beat it out of me? He won't get anywhere."

"So there it is. Where on earth did you learn to try to bluff your way through things?" She gave a signal. The car slowed. We'd come as far as Paget. Something like ten miles from my place. I could see Hamilton twinkling across the harbor.

"You wouldn't," I said.

"Stop, Motomura-san."

"If either of you shows up at my place, I'll call the cops. You know it's true, all true. Otherwise you wouldn't bother with this cloak-and-dagger shit. And here's your minion from Clocktower scurrying around the place, pretending not to understand Aetna died because she couldn't wait around for you to hang her out to dry. What you did to her is murder."

"Quiet."

"It's worse than murder. You taught her to believe she had no reason to live!"

"I said quiet."

I shut up. It's incredible, really, it's disgusting, the lengths to which people go to hide things from themselves. Something pierced and made me wince. An old wound that never closed. And through it all, Masami breathed, quelling her anger with air. Quiet as the still, black water in the harbor.

"I certainly don't need to explain myself to you. But to make your situation absolutely clear, I will tell you. I came for you this way because I do not wish my son to shame himself in public."

She looked at her small, pale hands. Spoke as though I were a monster who'd corrupted her misguided progeny. As though I'd mangled somebody for whom she'd felt some maternal feeling sometime, way back when. Like she'd ever in her life known such inefficient sentiments.

"I am not the one who's brought shame upon this family." Harsh words in Japanese cracked my voice so I hardly recognized it.

"These delusions sadden me, Okada Kenji."

"Yeah, right. And anyway, how dare you—"

"Let me tell you what I know. With these accusations, this tragic fantasy, you intend worse than dishonor."

"Fantasy," I said.

"Fantasy, yes. With this pathetic fantasy, you intend to sabotage your family, the company which I have worked all my life to build for you—"

"Oh, come on."

"And to ruin yourself, most ridiculous of all."

"Even if that's what I wanted, it wouldn't hold a candle to what you've done."

"You don speak to *yo maatha* in such tone!" This from the peanut gallery. After thirty years, Motomura's English leaves something to be desired. "Is wrong! Very insorrent, ungratefuru!"

"Motomura-san," said Masami.

His eyes glittered in the rearview. A shake of her head. All of us were silent. And that said everything.

"You did know. Both of you," I said.

Pale hands, glittering eyes.

"The way they used Aetna. It started with Char. Or was it Jim Falk?"

Motomura looked away. Masami looked at her watch. I felt a sneer spread out on my face. In the air was just a hint of a little waft of victory. She couldn't do anything to me for fear that I'd do worse. She, Masami—yes, Masami, the dragon—didn't dare attempt to call my so-called bluff *because she knew it was no bluff.* She'd confirmed it herself. And if she was powerless against me, Char was too.

I'd won.

"So there it is," I said, snarky to the last.

Masami took out her phone. Affected unconcern, pretended the matter was of little consequence compared with whatever bits of data eked across her screen. "You have shown me tonight that you have nothing."

"Think what you want. Doesn't change the truth."

"You have no right to speak of truth. You have your fantasy and your perversion of your disappointment, that is all. Yet you will go to any lengths to publicly embarrass me, knowing full well the xenophobic currents running rampant in this place. And you apparently intend to stage this farce in writing."

This torrent of words? They didn't rush, their placid volume never altered. But there were so many of them! It meant she was enraged.

An inkling of a possibility of a tingle of glee. I took out my phone too.

"You intend to see your family disgraced and ostracized. You intend to have us ruined, perhaps driven out," etc.

None of this drivel had ever crossed my mind. Masami, however, is the type of person to chase down the remotest implications of whichever conclusion strikes her fiendish fancy at the time. Masami is Queen of uncontrolled extrapolation and hyper speculation. I knew this. And I couldn't help myself.

"You wouldn't consider that a kind of justice?" I said.

Motomura let out a growl. I really thought he'd spin around and grab me. I hopped out of the car, slammed the door, heard Masami snap a leash on him. As I dialed Nabi's number, the dragon, foiled for now but raring to fight another day, rolled down the window. A growing breeze took a nip at her black coiffure.

"You are the one who's set the terms," she said.

These were much as you'd expect. All my lies would be disproved, blah blah. In the instant I attempted to flaunt my campaign of dishonor before the public, her vengeance would swoop down upon me with the power of ten thousand angry ravens, etc. To wit, if I did anything to threaten CAM's good name or any of their clients, there would be repercussions. In short, I told myself, I'd won. I felt better than I had in weeks. Triumph as a shot of espresso, yet with all my might I kicked the low wall that was my only company there in the dark with the sparkling city mocking me from across the treacherous harbor.

When Nabi finally found me, triumph exploded from me like fire from a stricken match. I spilled everything. Redacting Char of course. I hadn't lost my head completely. At times raising my voice, the expletives just kept coming. By the time I got home, I owed Nabi a thousand sorrys, I was shaking, and I knew it was Masami who'd whispered intolerable things into Aetna's ear with a sibilant forked tongue. Poor Nabi thought I was in the grip of fever.

Words of advice: never tell yourself you've won. It's just not a good idea.

Just sent Nabi an obnoxious text: *Please.* Sat watching the phone like she'd actually reply to such twaddle. Beginning to wonder if she's made a clean break. Redacted me from her life once and for all.

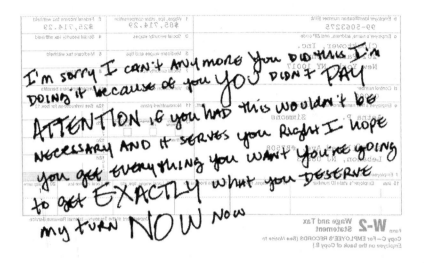

I'm sorry I can't ANY more you DID THIS I'm DOING it because of you YOU DIDN'T PAY ATTENTION if you HAD this WOULDN'T Be NECESSARY AND it serves you RIGHT I hope you get everything you WANT you're going to get EXACTLY what you DESERVE my turn NOW Now

AS7.

By hand on verso of W-2 tax form. Red ink. Fragment? Repetition (*now*) may be beginning of unfinished thought. Vagaries: addressee and what they want; the word *this* (possibly 2 different meanings?). What if *YOU* are not the same as *you*?

The Web has 2 sides too. The shadow side & the side with noise & color. I found these deaths on the colorful side. 13 years ago: 214 deaths in a 737 trying to get from Atlanta to Orlando. 11 of those deaths were a family heading to Disney World. The articles don't say that. Cuz by the time they reach the Web, deaths are numbers. Couple members of the family lived @USA, some in Canada, many were Bermudian, & they all met in Atlanta to fly to Florida together.

Why did You need all 11 all at once? You must've known there were really 12. 1 Bermudian who happened to be in England went direct from Heathrow to Orlando only to learn that everyone was dead. I don't want to, but I keep thinking of that airplane as a giant shredder. What do You plan to do about that 1 who's left? Why did You help midnight ice-cream cravings & not that 1?

Do You know Kenji's momma took him out of bed in the middle of the night? She knew he wasn't well, she just saw him this afternoon! Do You know that woman abandoned him on the side of the road in darkness? Did You know, Lord of lords, I had to take his car & get him, & Baby was so angry he was RUNNING to the top of Burnt House Hill towards Southampton? He was trying to laugh at her but he was talking too fast. I had to make him lie down, lead him to the couch & make him. Otherwise he'd still be pacing up & down getting mad enough to start attacking furniture: "She _____ thinks I'm _____ stupid, like I went to _____ Harvard to learn how to just NOT read between the lines & just not _____ ASK already. How could any _____ see what's there for anyone to see & not even _____ wonder?! Which _____ means she _____ did it. She killed her, Nabi, she killed Aetna. Aetna, OMG…"

I didn't say nothing about his language. If You'd been there, Lord, You wouldn't have said nothing either. In fact I can't help thinking if You'd been listening to what I've been begging for, Kenji wouldn't have gone thru all this. He jumped up & came back with that nasty genshu alcohol, & I couldn't argue quick enough, he drank it all one time even though his stomach…! He jumped up again for a sleeping tablet. Looks like it's finally knocked him out.

Lately it's like the only way I can protect us is to send Kenji to sleep. Sleep, Baby. Close down that passionate brain. Lock down those pretty eyes, flood your Crystal Caves with silence & the dead of night. & keep them closed, my reckless love, for both of us. Whatever made me think it was anything but depraved to tell Kenji to do that? Stop asking, Baby, quit thinking, throw out your sensitivity. Forget the guy who asked what some novelist's made-up countryside has to say about thinking & being ("phenomenology & ontology," course I remember, Baby). Time's up for being you, sweet genius. How could I do that to him. What choice do I have? To think of this while he's flopped out here exhausted, not even an inch away. To say it to him now, again (walk away, Kenji) now he thinks his own momma is some kind of murderer. He's holding onto my left hand with his 2 hands, I'm scribbling in my book. He forgets his momma is a woman, Mrs C is just a woman.

K forgets it cuz he owes her everything. That's sort of my fault, innit. Cuz of course Mrs C put up the startup $ for BHS even though Baby says not. So I mean I got to break out on my own cuz he took on that debt to her. The money's been paid back, but K still feels the weight of the debt cuz of how Mrs C is: she acts like a queen. & not just that. Since she gave us our livelihood, our life together here, K feels like she has that power over life in general. That's how much he's weighed down by her power over him. & it doesn't ease up in his sleep.

What if I said: Baby? None of this necessarily absolves your momma, I don't know what she's done, I don't know about the in-surance people or any of that, but Baby you don't know the whole story either.

Then what if I showed him my Goodreads page. He'll say: I didn't know you'd become a bookworm too, Nikkou, wherever did you find the time? I'll say: Truth is, Baby, what I like most about books is you talking about books. So when I was making this Goodreads page for Seabird, this book came up that had a lady scholar in it who cut up her Bible & rearranged all the Books of So-&-So in a new order, so all God's Words were the same but she could feel the creative part she played in making them meaningful. Part of the point of the book was it's the same thing with her body: her body is a Gift that was made a certain way, but now it's hers to make meaningful in her own way, you know? So I was like: I know that book! It's by Thomas Hardy…

What's making a girl out of stuff like Goodreads data got to do with K's momma? Nothing! Cuz Mrs C might be cold, but she wouldn't murder anybody. Also it'd make K smile. He'd remember telling me that when he got into Hardy, he learned that stuff that has always been a certain way is never only that way & never has to stay that way. I'd remember telling him: That means nothing's necessarily as bad as it might look. Then I'd find a way to say: Stop before you ruin everything.

It'd never work. It boils down to the same thing: Quit asking, just have faith.

If I ever got to sleep again that night, I don't remember. I'd wager that I didn't. Because Nabi definitely didn't. I know that because I remember how she looked the next day with piercing clarity.

Her eyes were wide and vitreous with the strain of cheerfully persuading herself that she was in no danger of nodding off in front of clients. Her smile was fixed and tremulous at the same time. I remember sitting on the couch, wearing the same clothes in which I had been kidnapped, wondering when it was that I had shaved, forcing down espresso as Nabi said, "Baby, that's not good for your stomach." She appropriated my espresso and drank it. It was my second triple shot anyhow. I must've made it while she was getting dressed.

She wore that mauve suit. The one I'll never forget. As I won't forget her twitchy, two-handed caress: my cheeks, my unkempt hair. Most of all Nabi's glassy smile as she scrutinized my face. Jesus, what I'd put her through. I must've spent the whole night pacing up and down.

She wanted me to sleep. I, an irredeemable reprobate, promised I would if she'd let me drive her to work first. Poor *nikkou*, my *hoshi*, looked almost tearful with relief. She said she'd do her makeup in the car.

Why didn't I hold her there until both of us were fast asleep, her little suit too rumpled to go anywhere? Wouldn't things have turned out better?

At that point, probably not. I should've kissed her longer anyway.

All the way to Hamilton, Nabi nagged me happily about sleep, sun, and soup. I didn't think much of anything about leaving her there as usual. I didn't think—as from Door #1 Nabi waved to me with a beautiful brown hand.

Cravings for retribution filled me to the brim. I dashed home, made myself look intimidating, grabbed my phone.

Here's what I knew from recent experience. Aetna was Masami's secret and the face of her guilt. A stranger, Char, was in on it, but Barrington knew nothing; Erik was a servant, not privy to details. The ghostly vision of *ikiryou* showed her that I'd delved into her shadows, come too close to what she had to keep hidden at all costs.

241

She sent Erik to Bull's Head to learn the extent of the danger. Be subtle, she said; and since he can do no wrong, she failed to see that what she asked of him was like asking an elephant to be tiny. Erik took liberties, lost track of his instructions as he'd done with Henry Cox. Enslaved to a Manhattan-sized ego, his attempt to take advantage of Nabi's trusting nature ended with the disencumbering of his manicured soul. He flounced away, his mission forgotten, only to discover his head on a bed of lettuce awaiting gravy. *Need 2 talk!! Call me!!*

I called him. I dared him to come to me, knowing that *ikiryou* could no longer touch me. I did it so I'd have someone to scream at. He'd run to Momma-sama but there was nothing she could do. Unused to helplessness, she'd go clean out of her mind, consummating my revenge.

That's what I imagined. As for what actually happened, that afternoon would see one of my vital palisades crumble to pieces, unleashing the phantasms in my substructures.

Why Fort Scaur? Because of all its paradoxes? Because it crowns the West End's highest hill, yet its devious construction prevents mariners from spotting it? Because it's full of hidden passages, yet it boasts a view of the entire island, north to south? Because it was a site of conflict between mighty powers light and dark? If that was the metaphor I had in mind, it failed. The British built the fort to guard against a Yank invasion circa 1870, but the invasion never came. When the Nazis likewise changed their minds, Scaur fell into disuse with a sigh of relief and became a public park, a ruin reclaimed by wildflowers and trees. Maybe I chose it because it's up de country, five minutes for me but far from Erik's blindly beaten path between Warwick and Hamilton. I wanted to preserve that triumphant frustration, that vertiginous, victorious rage. Because it was perverse, I determined to hold onto it. The bright unvanquished stronghold and its glorious vistas seemed to help with that somehow, perhaps.

Driving up, I recalled a certain clearing shaded by a poinciana tree. In a corner of the grounds, this circular clearing persisted without reason or assistance. Or so it seemed to the eight-year-olds who played "Oberon and Titania" underneath the branches heavy with red blossoms. Erik's plastic ray-gun was no use against our fey magic.

I pulled in beside his Fiat. There were no other cars; that's normal for a weekday. Just my brother's bluebird egg on wheels.

He said, "How's your convertibaby?"

"No touching. Let's go."

I led him to the clearing. He mooned over my MG the whole time, I just know it.

"Are you very sick, *onii-sama?*"

Erik likes to use this formal mode of address with me. It's sardonic. I'd rather tell it like it is. I call him *idgit*.

"You look a little better. There's this sort of gleam about you, *onii-sama.*"

Such poetic observations as we arranged ourselves on a park bench. I was a bit giddy from sleeplessness. I had all sensors on full alert while insisting on a high degree of numbness, all of which added up to a mild case of hysteria. Course I didn't know it then. I was high. I had to be high in order to stand up and not to scream. It made numbness into confidence and powerlessness a severe advantage. I said I was fine, never felt better in my life.

Then I put him on the defensive. "Whatever you're up to, leave Nabilah out of it."

"What the—? Hey and how are you too, *mochi*, I'm just fine, thank you, not up to anything. I only spoke to her because you wouldn't give me the time of day."

"Yeah, well, nothing's changed. I don't have time for whining. So if that's all you got, good morning and regards to your momma."

His hands were on me. One on my chest, holding me back, one on my shoulder sporting a pinkie ring and *eau d'Erik*. Thankfully the park was empty. How we must have looked, a parrot pleading with a crow; hibiscus and black dahlia jostling for position in a vase. He looked at me, all helpless innocence (typical).

"Well?" I said.

"I'm goin shru de trees, *onii-san.*"

"And what do you expect me to do about it?"

Erik shook his head. He never was good with sentences.

"If this is going to be like pulling teeth, let me remind you that you only have so many."

He squirmed, gathering courage. "I need to know what you're going to do, *onii-san*. How far is this going to go?"

"You tell me. She's obviously had you spying on me for some time. I'll thank you to let go of me."

He let go. He didn't deny anything. Just made a face and whined, "You said *fraud*, you know, at the office. That wasn't fair."

"Call a lionfish a lionfish."

"But they wouldn't do anything that wasn't for the best."

"You mean the best for them."

"You don't get it. You always…" And he sighed, indignation igniting underneath his seahorse-patterned tie. "It's bigger than that."

"Fraud and embezzlement, plain and simple."

"Don't use that kind of language. You've got no right without proof."

"There's proof. Just not for you to see."

"Why not, pray tell?"

"Because you wouldn't understand it, and you can't keep your mouth shut."

Erik's mouth dropped open as if to prove my point. Some exaggerated blinking, flabbergasted sputtering. "And you intend to do what exactly with all this? Assuming even a bit of it is true, which not one teensy morsel is, what are you going to write? Aren't you calling yourself a literary scholar? Or did you turn into Anderson Cooper when I wasn't looking? That the kind of story you meant, *mochi-sama*? You want to kickstart some investigative brouhaha? You really want to try to bring us down over this?"

"If I did, Erik, do you think I'd warn you in advance?"

"Come on," he said in a small voice. "It's illegal, you know. I mean blackmail—"

"Cease-and-desist already rained down from on high. Won't do one bit of good."

Again with the touching. His hand on my wrist. "That's not what I mean, *onii-sama*. Look, maybe you're on the right track. But if you are, it's for the wrong reasons."

"Do yourself a favor. Don't try to be profound."

"Let me finish what I'm saying, will you? Chingas, *mochi*, trying to say something to you is harder than talking to either one of them,

244

you know that? Course you do, you're doing it on purpose. Anyway, listen just a sec. That girl who disappeared? The one you mentioned? That's fishy, all right? I'll give you that. If she had something in the corner and it stank, someone needs to get it out, I agree. But that is totally different from CAM committing fraud, and *that* I guarantee you never happened. Momma would never. Ever. So you see? Our interests are the same."

"How exactly do you arrive at that conclusion?"

"If that girl was doing something that made it look like Momma was doing something even though she wasn't, I need to know. Do what you need to do, investigate, whatever. Just, you know, keep me informed. Before you go public. That's all I'm saying."

It wasn't, of course. When every last species of potential interlocutor goes extinct, still Erik-Katsuo will not have finished talking. An effluence of questions bubbled forth from him as though he were an overheated pot: what did I think Masami had done, how did she know that girl…stuff that Masami couldn't wring from me herself. And I made it just as clear to her sniveling toady that I would not hand out free samples of my work.

He gaped. "You want to go accusing us of things, you can at least have the decency to tell us what they are."

He was begging. I enjoyed it. So I threw a little bone. "Falsifying documents."

He thought I didn't notice, but the outrage fell out of his voice. "What documents?"

"I said no samples."

"For fuck's sake, Kenji, why are you doing this?"

"Because Aetna Simmons betrayed you. Clocktower and CAM and all three of you, even almighty Momma-sama."

That stung. I saw Erik's tongue get caught behind his teeth. "What do you care about Aetna Simmons? Nobody cared she existed till what, yesterday?"

"That betrayal cost her everything. The least I can do is rescue her, salvage her good name."

"You're telling me you know this person?"

"In ways you wouldn't dare attempt to fathom."

"Is that so?"

245

"That's right!" This gushing out of me as pride and gratitude flowed in, as I watched Erik founder and recalled Masami's stream of nonplussed babble. In a fit of nervous energy, I left the bench and stood in the shadow of the tree. The breeze plucked petals from its huge bouquet of blossoms. The uncertain light dappled the grass.

"So what's it going to say, this coup of investigative journalism?" said Erik.

"That Aetna was brilliant and fearless. That when she refused to be exploited, Clocktower and CAM drove her to the unthinkable. That it's time to take responsibility."

None of this appeared in my *Works of Art* essay. In fact until that moment, the idea of an *exposé* hardly featured in my thinking. Directly, anyway, most of the time.

"How in heaven do you know all this? What else did she tell you? What else have you seen?" On his feet now, mustering the nerve to try to get up in my face.

I said, "You're an idgit, you know that? You're knee-deep in this shit, and you have no clue what it is."

At that his whole aspect changed. His tirade was lengthy, the delivery impassioned. I half-expected it to end with Erik seizing an armload of petals, hurling them skyward.

Most of what he said, even his ardor, he parroted from Masami and Barrington. Their golden boy, who lives for nothing but their praise, hasn't a hope of appreciating the implications of his own words. Even if I wanted to remember them, I wouldn't clutter a page with more than a précis. I include that much only because it clarifies Masami's motivations.

Erik's monologue began with something to the effect that Clocktower's investment portfolio is "one of the biggest, most important new accounts we have." How new? He didn't say. I'd guess it's around four years old, given Aetna's timetable.

"And before you get on your high horse," he said, "you should know an investment of this magnitude makes a big difference to a lot of people." To Masami in other words. He invited me to "think even bigger." Imagine, he suggested, some multinational conglomerate holding company, world-famous (a name I'd never heard of), wooing Clocktower Insurance. Imagine what would happen if said conglomerate bought an interest in Clocktower and through Clocktower learned to love CAM, perhaps started an account for the whole conglomerate.

"You see where I'm going with this. Huge, right? Ginormous. For CAM *and for Bermuda* [his emphasis]. Think of the money that'd roll into this place. New jobs, tourists, all of it [with petal-throwing]!"

Put this in perspective. This idgit wants me to believe the CAM-Clocktower alliance could deliver Bermuda from the clutches of recession. Given what you know, would you wager an Okada-Caines could be motivated solely by the greater good?

I didn't think so either. Erik made a wan attempt to uphold his righteousness, but faced with my skepticism his inborn rumormonger got the better of him. He let slip that because CAM offered such puissant connections, the competition was cringing, the Premier was cozying up to Barrington. There were a lot of ifs and endless qualifiers but the end result could be, said Erik, Barrington as Minister of Finance.

"I don't think I've ever heard of anything more frightening."

"Phooey, *mochi*, don't make fun." He really said that. He was serious. Then he seemed to rewind and start all over again, his voice straining to approximate Barrington's Black-Power fervor and the conviction that somewhere, in some shadowy bend of the circuitous money trail, the lives of little children and the revival of Hawkins Island's Pirate Parties were at stake. Leaving it for me to discern the facts:

The Clocktower Account was a keystone of Masami's plan to rule the world, a sinister design that would remain secret at all costs. Though Erik knew nothing of Aetna's role and couldn't wrap his head around it even if he tried, he feared the unique circumstances of her death would call attention to her bizarre life; the life of a rebellious cog in said sinister design. As fear exacerbated his permanently dumbfounded condition, he flung out his questions willy-nilly and tumbled into a mortally perilous contradiction:

Erik wanted me to investigate. Masami: cease and desist. Blaring contradiction.

Never would Erik-Katsuo Okada-Caines permit his own desires to conflict with Masami's. Not even if it meant lying to himself and everyone who needed him to tell the truth. This just proved all his hyperbolizing was unhampered by understanding. It proved he had no clue what she had done.

Your revered Momma-sama drove a beautiful woman to her death for money and the power of a political insider. And you helped. A moment's thought with half a brain would show you.

That's what I botched my chance to say. Instead I went and got the tree involved.

Erik sat on the bench. The effort to convey the magnitude of Masami's magnanimity was just too much. The actual truth eluded him, of course. The scent of money and the glare of glory saturated his senses.

"Do you get it now, *onii-san?* All this is at stake. That girl could destroy it."

"You're disgusting, all of you."

"You know, she told me it'd be useless trying to reason with you."

"Reason? If you grew a brain and *thought* before repeating everything you're told, you'd see nothing you just said bears a remote connection to reason."

"Well, look, I give up. *Mochi,* if you won't do it 'cause it's right, do it 'cause I'm your brother. No need to understand why, clearly you never will, but I need to know what happened to that girl. Just tell me, that's all. 'Cause I need you to. Can you do that?"

"Because you need me to," I said, as the same old wound hit me with the same old burn. "And what kind of claim do you think you have on me? What makes you think any of you are entitled to ask me anything?"

"I'm in a tight spot, Kenji."

"Well, enjoy it!" I snapped. "How tight can it be anyway? It's all flag-waving and golden confetti, isn't it?"

"You make it sound so… Look, I need to know what I've gotten myself into. I mean what that girl could get all of us into."

"All of us? I don't think so." I turned and headed for my car, knowing I'd smack him if I stayed another minute. Erik grabbed my shoulder, I pushed him and he staggered, but he grabbed my arm instead, hanging on like Lyme disease, and I realized he was trembling.

"Revenge," he said. "Right? That's all this is."

Like it was such a measly thing. I pulled away and turned, but Erik grabbed me, started shouting, and with each word came more thwarted petulance, the tantrum of a pampered child. "You went looking for this, didn't you! Some way to hurt us even if it was all lies! Where the hell did you find that girl? What the fuck did you think you had the right to promise her? You talked her into going public with this, this, whatever you think is going on—"

Absolute nonsense. "I didn't need to, stupid. Aetna knew where she stood, she knew it was unacceptable. And she knew how to make you squirm, the whole fucking multinational retinue. You took away her freedom, her identity, her potential, and still you underestimated her. She had one thing left to use against you, and you couldn't conceive it, you're so fucking spineless—*she gave her life*—but you're all over the place now, innit, you're scrambling to the point where you want me of all people to cover your ass."

And you know what? She did all that for me.

The realization fell on me and took my breath away, or I would have declared it right there in our clearing underneath all that sunshine. Till it careened into a wall of silence, my little speech reverberated with admiration and passion, and the more I spoke, the more vehement I became, the more convinced: their desperation now— that feeling, too familiar to me, of the earth falling away—Aetna arranged it, all of it, for me. For me, at the price of her own life. My liberation—the least of her accomplishments, accomplished without consciousness—how could I not love her for it?

It struck all at once, you see, so I even stumbled when I snatched my arm away from Erik: Did Aetna know me after all? Had Masami mentioned a worthless elder son? Or had Aetna done some research when she learned who pulled the strings? Did she ask why I wasn't part of CAM? The chances were extremely low, but even if she'd never heard my name and whether she knew it or not, Aetna reached across the limits of time and awareness and secured the revenge I'd dreamed of all my life, never daring to believe it could become a reality. I knew then I had to finish it. On the far side of her sacrifice, it was up to me to cherish it, know it to the fullest, and make *them* feel the weight of her oppression.

I turned on Erik with all kinds of emotion. Love and anger. Loathing for my cowardice and the blood that ran in me, the name and the blood that had destroyed her. "It's ironic, isn't it," I said. "Aetna was one of those rare minds who understands the only truth is death. You turned her into a lie because she understood that truth. So you could lie to everyone, even yourselves. So you could steal. Like that would somehow solidify your relevance. If it wasn't fucking sick, it'd be brilliant."

I don't know why I bothered, it was all lost on him. I added, "Course when I say *you*, I mean them. The CEO and savior of our country. Not you personally. I know you don't have it in you to pull off that kind of stuff. You never have a clue what's going on."

"Course I do, *mochi*. This is all about Harvard."

Curving the Rs like an American. Biting the D like a snapping turtle. Erik's torpedo.

Harvard.

"Am I right, or am I right, Dr. Okada-Caines?"

My car keys, recently retrieved, fell in my pocket.

"That's what you call yourself these days, so I hear. Or at least you don't correct people if they make that mistake. Not even Nabi-lah-chan. She thinks you're some kind of genius."

I don't remember charging back into the clearing. But you will remember that I mentioned a tree. A tree becoming involved when I slammed Erik's head into it.

"We kept your secret, *onii-sama! Menboku o tamotsu!*" he cried.

I slammed him again. Maybe again. Or maybe I just breathed. Every breath felt like slamming and being slammed, I remember that. And *menboku o tamotsu*. Save face, my brother said. *Anata no meiyo o hozon*. Save your honor.

We stood a little longer, me with Erik by the tie, him glaring with pity and contempt, until so much welled in me it was either knock him down or risk letting him see it all. I chose the former. He fell on his backside with a squeal.

"She's brainwashed you completely, it's incredible," I grumbled.

"If she told you Somerset was east, you'd believe it. If she told you to drive around the island in reverse, you'd go and do it."

"You're going to pay for that, Kenji! Momma's gonna know you did that!"

"Course she is."

"Well, I tried, you had your chance." Brushing off his sleeves, his shorts, straightening his tie before even getting up. "It's up to me to look after her as usual, and let me tell you, *mochi*, you're going to tell me what I want to know one way or another, and it won't be hard to make it happen because you know what? You're just empty air wearing a bunch of colorful balloons. You're a goddamn poser, an impostor, and that's all."

"If I am, that's what she made me. Every time I found a chance, she murdered it, and you two dug the grave. You turned my whole stupid life into a waste."

Trudging to the parking lot. Behind me, I could feel the family's crown jewel smoothing out his hair, his shirt, straightening his golden tiepin as he called out to me. "Then why don't you just disappear? Something really is wrong with you, you know. You're like something in a haunted house, stuck in the past."

I flipped him off over my shoulder.

"Get your ass back here, Kenji."

Ignored him, made it to the car. And believe it or not, when I started my engine, that idiot was hurtling towards me and yelling. "No one's gonna believe you! You call yourself a writer, but don't think we don't know you've never published anything! Ever in your life! Whatever you write, it'll be worthless, understand? Just like everything you've ever done! It'll be your word against hers, against Dad's, the whole company's! Soon other people's too, people you can't handle! Momma says there's nothing more pathetic than a bored intellectual no one listens to. Let me help you, *onii-sama*..."

An entire fleet of dump trucks couldn't carry all the shit my brother flung at me as I got the fuck out of there. And now to hell with him, I can't wait any longer, it's time for my medication.

How do you confess something that will dull and soil the colors of everything you've said and every word you might utter? I guess

251

when I sat down to write, I took it for granted that I just wouldn't mention it. After all, I make the same omission every day. Done it for years. But writing is supposed to make emptiness its opposite or at least make it appear so: to explain.

If she won't let me speak to her, perhaps she'll let some words appear before her in silence. She need not take up their burdens as I have those of the Ten. To do so or not is a reader's prerogative, and I suppose she's had enough. But if she did look, she'd deserve to know the truth. As I deserve the agony of unmasking.

Some she knows. Some she could've guessed but hasn't. That's because she's determined to think the best of me. She could've googled Harvard's rules, found out the timing wasn't right, but why would she? Nabi's my best friend, she believed me, and I never wanted to lie to her. I'd already failed her, letting her walk away. This new failure just confirmed I'd never be other than a failure before her. Simple cowardice wouldn't let me face her. Let me get this over with.

Six years in Harvard's PhD program. That's what everyone believes except those who turned the final year into a deception. Harvard guarantees five years of support in the form of scholarships and teaching fellowships. After that it's up to you to win grants and loans and so on or work a full-time job while you write your dissertation. Manageable for Americans. But for those of us born elsewhere, who aren't allowed to work full-time, who are rarely eligible for American grants, whose tuition fees are always higher than Americans', and who have limits on our US visas ticking like time bombs? Try it sometime. See what the pressure does for you.

On top of that, I wasn't doing well. Nabi got married, rending something in me. I broke my arm, lost my part-time gig at the Faculty Club, started working for the chemist. Building a clientele took forever. For the longest time I relied on Masami to survive.

That made everything worse. She and the Americans never missed a chance to remind me that I lived by their good graces and on borrowed time. Spasms in my arm and shoulders from stress and wimpy painkillers. Books and heady concepts ceased to make sense as rationales for hanging on. Instead they made me angry and vengefully began to look like gibberish. I tore up some of them, made a pathetic fire in a corner of my apartment. Other nights down in the subway, watching trains go back and forth. Five years. My dissertation came to twenty-six pages of junk, not enough to coax any money out of anyone.

You've had more than your share of time, said Masami.

We've discussed it as a family, said Erik-Katsuo.

In our magnanimity, we've decided to let you do penance at CAM, said Masami.

Pay back all that money you wasted, said Barrington.

Like a *katana* sword through the gut.

The only reason I didn't lie down on the subway tracks: Nabi called me daily. Or I called her, and she answered, full of light. I didn't want to taint our laughter with complaints. *Nikkou* had her own problems. But I couldn't help confiding that my family had given up on me. Not the money. I lied and said it wouldn't be a problem, let her think I'd retain the illustrious title of Harvard PhD Candidate till the time was right to dazzle my committee with my dissertation's perspicacious resplendence. Every day I reached across the ocean to nourish the same lie while Nabi nursed me through the ordeal of my family's betrayal. I broke off all contact with them.

I eked a year out of my visa, bummed around Boston as a *ronin*, brokering for the chemist and thus—too late, Harvard had withdrawn my candidacy—I came into my substantial fortune. The visa expired. I led Nabi to believe that despite my new diploma (which she thinks I've stowed in a safety-deposit box), my foreign passport and America's economic recession barred my way to a professorship (which wasn't altogether false). With no prospects but the chemist's dreams of an exotic clientele, I bought a shredder. Nabi turned it into hope.

Years passed without any need for the ugly truth to show itself. No one asked about my history. They just assumed it. My countenance was a mask which eventually seemed not to enhance what lay beneath but to become it. I bought into the deception. The illusion gave me strength to go into crowded rooms and sunny days with my head up. So I let myself forget. No one said a word until that day at Fort Scaur. Erik had been saving it.

In 1620-ish, Francis Bacon wrote about a guy who tried to hang

253

himself *in curiosity*. This *certain Gentleman…fastened the Cord about his neck, raising himself upon a stool and then letting himself fall, thinking it should be in his power to recover the stool at his pleasure, which he failed in, but was helped by a friend then present*. The idgit *felt no pain*, he said, *but first he thought he saw before his eyes a great fire and burning; then he thought he saw all black and dark; lastly it turned to a pale blue, or Sea-water green…* Clearly this person was disturbed, but he was also a prophet. An oracle of the Zohytin lull, which this writing business seems to require more and more. First the numbing of the pain; then if you've taken enough, everything is bright. That PhD I wear around doesn't exist: fucking awesome. So awesome I'll be sure to forget it when Zohytin slides me down into its uncluttered darkness. When I wake, I'll see the ocean, the ambiguous blue-green of the Atlantic Ocean that from afar appears so calm and inviting. I'll dissolve in that soft color and the warmth of the water and its voiceless sighs; and as my cells mingle with oceanic molecules, components of my thoughts will separate and drift apart, their coherence giving way to nothing whatsoever.

The truth is I have no truth. Like my Aetna, I am lies stacked upon lies. But the foundations of her lies were death and poetry. The basis of my masquerade is shame. Hers was a sacrifice: she doused herself in shadows for the shadows' sake. My façade is flimsy, I maintain it out of cravenness. Her shadows are her creations, mine are stolen accidents.

If you haven't seen enough, here's proof. Once more, Aetna, I scrounge for traces of your tracks and strain to follow. Emulating you, I add a portrait of my ruin to its poor description. Not poetically as you did but as stark evidence of my indulgence and the beautiful, vivacious thing that I destroyed—all the hope I've ever known.

Erik was just the morning. Sometime in the afternoon, a photo arrived in Martin's inbox.

Cloudy day in Hamilton. A lane tucked out of the way. One wouldn't wander here, only descend upon the place with some specific purpose.

A truck stands at the curb. It wears a logo, but it's fuzzy in this low-res photograph. If you know what you're looking for, you'll make out a bull with silver horns. In front of it and at the photo's rightmost edge, there is a warehouse-like building, pale blue with a red awning at the entrance. Zoom in and you'd find the bull there too, glaring out of the red fabric.

Now the foreground subjects. It seems they've just stepped out from underneath the awning. The sidewalk is narrow. With a few backward steps they might have squeezed behind the truck and avoided the camera. But you see, their comfort zone is in each other's close proximity. Decades of tender friendship make it instinctive for them to act only on their instincts and their hearts' desires in one another's company. And there's a great deal that they can no longer disguise. It's become impossible because they are frightened. Each of them tries to rise to the occasion, protect and reassure the other, but at the same time instinct makes them huddle together and retreat into the closed, secret circle of their love. They cannot mask any of this; attempting to resist it only makes them feel more desperate, so they can't help but reach for each other as they've always done.

Our hands entwine, Nabi reaches up to touch my face. When the shutter snaps, our eyes are closed, our lips pressed together. Half a moment's withdrawal from the unasked and unsaid into unconditional consolation that solves nothing, promises nothing but the resolve to try another breath.

Treacherous and furtive, the camera captures the ambivalence of the fleeing instant. The tension in the shoulders, the urgency of the grip that draws the veins in the hands to the surface of the skin. Simultaneously the sure bliss of an authentic truth. Love radiates from this damaging image.

♊

That photo makes me look like a skank. Martin forwarded it to me, I said Bye-no-bye, no no no! I dived down to my secret cavern in the shadows: I'll find you, I'll hunt you down. It came from a scrambled address generated randomly by a disposable email site (st7andyk5xos@ppptietoja.com). With this kind of address, you can make it expire after 10 mins so when Martin tried to write back (right before dropping everything & bullying his way onto the next flight home!), the culprit had disappeared. I went deeper & found the IP address of the computer that signed up to disguise itself in throwaway masks. Turned out to originate from an account with a satellite ISP that gives global access to the account holder's executive employees. The account belongs to Clocktower Insurance. The computer's registered to someone named Char Richards, VP of Risk Mgt & Dir of Life Underwriting. Martin knows none of this. He told me to stop & doesn't know I disobeyed. Kenji thinks it was Martin who unmasked this person.

Baby, I'm so sorry, what if you were right, I wouldn't listen. That was my 1st thought. Lord what have I done? (My 2nd thought.) 3rd: Kenji Okada-Caines, I warned you about obsession getting the better of you, & if you got on the bad side of an overseas company, whether you were right or wrong, you should've hopped back off again like you were standing on a hot potato! If they had this person send this photo cuz you refused to let go, then my marriage is officially in trouble cuz of you & your obsession, & when you destroyed my marriage you destroyed my credibility. Did you even stop to think about that? People start believing my own family can't trust me, how are clients supposed to trust me with their confidential security? Why should they?! Document destruction is a trust-based industry, you know that, & you know how Bermuda works: reputation, reputation, personal & professional, it's all the same thing, & the photo went to Martin over the internet!!! Lord have mercy I mean how could you do something like this, Kenji? Any chance we might've had, you ruined it because of her. Maybe what we had wasn't perfect, but it worked, it was better than nothing, & now we don't have that, we may never get it back.

I said all that to him. My Kenji. We were on the phone, I called him as soon as Martin called about the photo. Course I had to be home when Martin got there even though it was a Tuesday & I dreaded what would happen. I panicked, I let him have it (I mean Kenji). He had a lot to say as usual. He's researched this Char Richards, she is "devious," not to be trusted. All the same (he says), she's not the one we need to worry about cuz clearly she sent the photo to his momma (!) & his momma sent the photo or told Char Richards to send it to Martin. "Clearly," the man says though the trail points not to CAM but Clocktower.

"Baby," I said firmly, "you have got to get past this business with your momma & start taking responsibility."

I thought he'd start shouting. I'd been shouting (not like me at all), & he'd been that way lately (Lord, the lamp!). But he said in this exhausted voice, "Nabi, you don't believe me?"

Lord forgive me, but that did it. I thought he was trying to skirt the real issue by acting like an injured little lamb. I pointed out to him that this determination to make the whole world complicit in his hangups is just plain fullish but even more than that: "The real issue is you thinking there might be some danger, & instead of backing away from it to protect those you love, you plunge yourself on in. I try to say something, you act up & just ignore it."

Ya boy got the nerve to respond, sounding dismayed, even frightened, "Why the _____ are you acting like you think I'm out to get you? Why would I do that, Nabi?!"

What am I supposed to say? He's so wrapped up in his own version, the truth would clobber him if it ever got thru to him. Oh Lord, I froze. & Kenji took it like it was some kind of answer when it was really that I couldn't answer! He said, "Nabi, I asked you to marry me."

& you know what I said? Nothing. You know what's even more disgusting? When K said that, I felt like ripping my hair out. You know those awful things on TV where the lions rip up the zebra & all the camera guys just watch? I felt like the zebra. Suddenly all I could think about was how unfair life is for zebras. It made no sense, I should've said Kenji forgive me, but I couldn't speak.

It's too late. I didn't say a word. He's the one who said, "I'm sorry, Nabi, really."

Then he said he wasn't feeling well. He hung up quickly & I worried, but I couldn't call him back.

Fact is I'd moved on. Martin was on his way. Lord have mercy, I felt him breathing down my neck while he was still somewhere over the ocean. ("We will discuss this in person, Mrs Furbert!") Last time we argued, M huffed & puffed like a headmaster trying to make me feel cheap. Well, Lord, I in't cheap. I love Martin, I love Kenji, but I in't no skank & that's cuz of HOW we love. I tried to prepare. Make a list of responses in my head so I could whip them out & not have to think. They were all wrong. I forgot them.

Martin crept into his own home like a burglar, & I should've got my You-know-what out of my chair, but all I could do was sit & look like I wasn't tired. Tired like ridiculous, overplayed, like the bumper cars flew off in separate directions & left me on the ground doing the splits. I guess that does mean cheap. I can't defend myself or promise anything. It's too late, Honey. I can't say that.

Thought he'd fold his arms & say I really shouldn't expect him to be surprised, something like that. He didn't. Poor Martin dropped his suitcase & his briefcase on the floor, dropped his blazer, & looked shocked. Radar, polygraph instincts...shocked. His accusations just the other day, the invitation—my Martin's got photographic recall, "no detail can escape"—yet somehow he just forgot? A stupid snapshot, somehow that's undeniable? He said, "Who ARE you?"

My husband. Yes, those very words, & his face like a pillowcase that's been peeled off & thrown aside. I had no answer, no I had too many, I couldn't say anything. Poor Martin left his bags on the floor, left his blazer, he went into his study & locked the door, & I didn't see him again that night. I sat in the chair in the dark, & it was like the 2 of them slapped out everything between my ears except Luke 9:

"Who do you say I am?"

I didn't go to my husband. I didn't call Kenji. I went to my computer, but I had nothing to do there. Seabird, was it really me that made you?

&

For years I nursed a secret. It outgrew
me little by little. It grew the way
hurricanes grow: heat and pressure,
ripple, wave, suddenly tsunamis and
whirlwinds decimate everything or gobble
it up, every resource even courage. And
now I'm backed up against a cliff while
it comes at me, and I'm alone, terribly
alone. I forgive everyone, and many will
think I'm taking the easy road. But the
truth is I'm out of hope. It's as though
I'm destined to choose badly at every
turn, to end up hurt and come out empty
everywhere and always. And if that's
true, it means there's nothing else for
me to do. I'm tired, and I want this.
Someone will forgive me. At last there
will be peace.

AS8.
Linen-ish paper, inkjet printing slightly bleeding. Literary prose
rhythms. Formal, old-fashioned (*terribly alone*), but serene. For everyone. A public allocution.

Having found man's life to be a wretchedly conceived scheme, I renounce it, and, to cause no further trouble…I am now about to enter on my normal condition. For people are almost always in their graves. When we survey the long race of men, it is strange and still more strange to find that they are mainly dead men, who have scarcely ever been otherwise.

The suicide note of one of Hardy's miserable, bumbling anti-villains. In this novel, Hardy's debut, the suicide note functions as the penultimate chord in the last, harmonious cadence. Justice is served, remorse is suffered, intent to self-harm is unequivocally declared, and the surplus son and suitor gets himself out of the way so that happily ever after can proceed without any pesky moral nigglings. You can tell he's reconciled to the outcome of his homemade noose and to the idea of a world *sans* him, which shan't be in the least put out. If there's any bitterness here, it's half-hearted, even tongue-in-cheek. The happy bride and groom never mention him again, and it's clear he wouldn't expect them to.

It's almost too neat, isn't it. Look closely and you'll see it doesn't even make much sense. Can a human be a human and have never lived? Can the still and empty grave have been this man's *normal condition* if all his problems amounted to hunger, love, and fear? Isn't this a string of specious excuses whose lofty tones cover up his pointless superfluity?

By the time he wrote his last, completely hopeless novel, Hardy was done with cover-ups. The suicide of the surplus son resolves nothing, accomplishes nothing, paves the way for nothing but dissolution. So when the surplus suitor dies in turn, nobody notices, the lady beloved having run off to seek unhappiness. That's how I read it, anyway: happily ever after is impossible, the lady beloved doesn't even want it—because the surplus son refuses to pretend that his subtraction is any more lofty or less remarkable than it is, and so nobody's off the hook, nobody, and remainders are guilty before the subtracted. His suicide note says, *Done because we are too menny* [*sic*]. Whether he means "too many" or "two things that are not men but too alike to men," he reduces himself to nothing more than surplus quantity, drubbing everybody else with the reality of their own insignificance. For anyone who's insignificant to themselves, happiness is a cover-up. Hardy never wrote another novel after that.

I'd never noticed any of this in Hardy's books before. Why my memory should alight upon it now I've no idea.

In twenty-four hours, three people swore to bring me down. Erik was innocuous, so when the last blow struck with such precision, I knew I'd been hit with some poisoned synthesis of other evil powers. But what's a puny ghost against a dragon and a hunter? I'd become one of the *ukabarenairei*, a tired ghost who hangs around the living out of dissatisfaction with its own expired life. It can't actually do anything. This kind of ghost lacks the vivid energy of *ikiryou* and the vengeful drive of *onryou*, so its movements aren't directed. It's just a *yuurei*, literally "dim spirit." It's a faint sense of a vague, annoying lack that you wouldn't even notice if not for its listless self-assertions now and then. It's a boring ghost, a pointless ghost. A ghost nobody wants, which no one has time for. One of those things that should not have bothered thinking itself up.

Suicide is the freedom to negate an inauthentic situation and not be suckered into another one. It's freedom that is free from being freedom to do anything. Freedom as negation is the negation of freedom: it just means there's no pressure anymore. Of course no one can experience this kind of freedom; once you're dead, you can't experience at all, and that's the point. Freedom from pain, freedom from relief, from dread and the worst of them all: hope.

That's one reason I love Aetna just the way she is. Dead and absent, bleeding out of the world, away from prying eyes, dated wounds, isolation, and desire. AS8 cries out to the Hardy fan in me (*alone, terribly alone...everywhere and always*). Structurally it's First Form: there's the long struggle with an unbearable problem; the sense that the problem isn't just her fault, yet only with her death can anyone escape it; she asks forgiveness, begs indulgence of her readers (text-book example); and she takes care, with poetic imagery that's all her own, to let readers know that she is rational and competent. You don't need to understand, she says, only trust that I know what I'm doing. Others might feel differently, but to this reader her intentions are unambiguous, especially as compared to the mercurial sentiments in AS1-7.

The sense that AS8 is an appeal to a wide audience may pose

difficulties for those who cannot help but question its suicidal authenticity. But to me there's no doubt. Even if Aetna composed this for Clocktower and the classic structure is but proof of her refined skill, it's clear that the end of her road is firmly before her eyes. AS8 tolls with finality.

My memories of that awful night are incoherent. You can guess what happened. Just look at the photo and where it ended up. Nabi blamed me, never considering the fact that only one thing could turn that picture into a disgrace. It doesn't deserve to be contemptible. Still, I can't blame her for thinking otherwise, considering what I am. Our argument was bitter, rage and panic shooting between us like ice-tipped lances. Such savage desperation had never entered our quarrels. We sounded nothing like ourselves; I said all the wrong things, but Nabi was cruel. Cruel. Her wrath cast everything in new, terrible shades that lurched grotesquely between tones, shifted this way and that in the noxious winds of doubt, subverting all perspectives and undermining everything I thought I knew. At the time it felt like the mutation happened suddenly. Like the swift dismemberment of a foot causing the world to tilt. But then it kept on happening: things I'd known, basic things, inverting, growing tentacles or monstrous heads, or vanishing until, dismayed to the point of panic, I really had to wonder about my sanity.

The night of the argument, something like three in the morning. My muscles were like Jell-O. Thoughts of movement made me dizzy. The air seemed very still, and that was fine, even awesome. But I was cold, my skin was clammy, and when I pulled up the covers, there weren't any. An idea dawned, unwelcome. I was in a bookstore, lying on the floor. The store was closed, and if I could get my eyes to open all the shelves would be black, tall and crowded like a sold-out gallery. The books would be big and small and thick and thin, each with two red bookmarks and a black cover. And underneath each cover there would be another cover. And another and another, each one black and empty. I hallucinated a giant *wakizashi* swooping at me with a roar. The sword was gray and sharp and smelled *Sea-water green*. So I went to sleep. I didn't want to wake up. But I felt like I had to in case Nabi called me back.

She didn't. I waited and waited and got so fucking despondent. I could only think of one person to call.

"You said you were gonna call me," I mewled.

"Something came up. Figured you'd call sooner or later."

"Char, the picture."

"Well." She was demure.

Why did I call? Char made an offering of me and Nabi to the dragon. Masami knew Nabi would fly to Martin with her conscience firing her rockets. I imagined a gift basket, champagne, crisp CAM letterhead: *Dear Mr. Furbert, Break my son the traitor.*

"You there, Kenji?" Curious, not concerned.

"I don't know."

"How much did you take?"

"Some."

"Does it sound like you're snoring when you breathe?"

She was placid. I was so messed up. I think I just said, "Char."

"You should throw up."

"No thanks."

"Seriously. I'm from Brooklyn, I know about this stuff."

"Char."

She sighed. "I'll come over."

"No, don't come." I wanted her to come.

"Then talk," she said. Like it was a simple thing. "Stay awake." She paused and asked, "Where is she?"

I remember my voice sounded out of reach and thin. It came out slowly like air from a pinprick in a tire. I think I was on the couch, blinking now and then at a black ceiling. I said, "*She suddenly thought one afternoon, when looking in the glass at her fairness, that there was yet another date, of greater importance to her than those; that of her own death, when all these charms would have disappeared; a day which lay sly and unseen among all the other days of the year, giving no sign or sound when she annually passed over it; but not the less surely there.*"

"Kenji."

"It's Thomas Hardy. Did you know he was totally misunderstood? He gave up writing novels in despair."

"Go and throw up, Kenji. I'll hold."

"No, I don't want to. You want to talk, you tell me why."

A puzzled silence or an exasperated one. I lay there panting and demoralized.

"Did Myrtle Trimm help you?"

"No. People's mommas never help me."

"I helped you."

"That's what you think."

"You have to stay awake, Kenji."

"Char, you have a weird variety of skills."

"You learn stuff because you have to. You know how it is."

And we waited. I was too out of it for flirting. I had no agenda. But as I strained to keep up whatever I was doing and Char strained her enviable patience, there came a silent moment when isolation took us by our throats.

"Why'd it have to be you, Char? Why do you and I have to have the same fucking infection?"

She replied, "I've been wondering about the reason you did this. What's it going to take, Kenji?"

"Aetna's dead, Char, really. I wish it wasn't true, I wish she'd waited."

"What do you mean?"

Indifferent as her namesake, a noncommittal singe.

"I don't know."

"You love her." Like she'd read it in a manual.

"Yes."

"She trusts you. You're determined. I get it. You like to make things happen indirectly. I respect that. That's why I spent so much time with you, not to say it wasn't an experience."

Press pause on this peaceful interaction. I'd encourage you to re-read Char's last statement. Of course I'm an experience, I know that, not that part. I mean the part where she lets slip that everything she did had but a single purpose. To test me, probe me, drive me to distraction, hoping I'd thoughtlessly reveal what she was so determined to believe I knew.

"We're the same, Kenji, but we're not equal. You're at the end of your rope."

No arguments.

"I don't want to do this," she said, quiet as a gas that seeps beneath a door, "but if you don't tell me where she is and how you helped her disappear, Clocktower will negotiate a contract with BRMS. We'll ask them to investigate Bull's Head Shreds. Publicly."

"Why? What for?"

"I don't know," said Char. Like this was a minor point and uninteresting at that. "Breach of confidentiality, whatever, I'll think of something."

"But we've never worked for you. We can't breach anything."

"So what? Once the rumor's out, it's out. Everybody knows you, right?"

Any other day, I'd have thrown back a whole arsenal of counter-threats. Maybe I did, but if I did I can't remember and they were ineffective.

"Proof means little in the end. In a place like this, suspicion is enough. And sensitive stuff like document security? Forget it. Once people start to wonder if they can really trust you, they won't take the chance. I have that on good authority. So even if the investigation never happened, the rumor that it might happen would ruin you. And her."

She said it so simply. Unblemished by resentment, impatience, or evil. However, there was this *And her*. This *And her* tossed out off-handedly: *her* was a pointed reference to Nabi—my Nabi, like a Taser to the throat—and so I made up my mind. In a single, mighty heave, I propelled myself into alertness, flung the tatters of my intellectual prowess at whatever the hell just happened and what the fuck was I supposed to do next, and hurled my strength into my flaccid muscles, springing from the couch and bursting free of lethargy. I tried anyway. Wasn't too successful.

More words might've been exchanged, I couldn't say. When I got myself upright, I got dizzy, dropped the phone, and so ended our negotiation. Really. That's what happened. I hope Char will always think I hung up on her in defiance.

The little bull with scimitars for horns. Scrabbling with slipping hooves at the narrow summit of a small iceberg. Surrounded by killer whales.

Because of ten suicide notes and a "gotta-do-it" feeling.

I lay under the weight of that awful truth, unable to find a decent breath. Then I stuck my fingers down my throat.

Back on the phone. No plan, just a cry thrown into the dark and the elimination of every other option.

He wasn't answering. It was barely after five, but I would've been awake if I were him. I cleaned myself up and drove to his office. Seon Place on Front Street. They've got two floors to themselves. The place was locked, the garage barred. It was too early. I leaned against my car in the shadow of the edifice's glass-fronted wings, which protrude symmetrically like the lenses on giant binoculars. Meanwhile a new dawn stole over the roofs of the reinsurance companies across the street. I was lightheaded and jittery. I recall the feeling that the morning was something I'd have to carry on my shoulders. Wasn't sure I was up to it.

I'd hung around about a half hour, pacing and wondering what would happen if I threw back my head and howled, when a door opened under the eyelid-like overhang.

It was the very man I needed and didn't want to see. Of course it was. The man who'd buggered me, maybe for life. One of two people in the world who could terrify the shit out of me. That morning I finally had the sense to let him. Not a pleasant feeling, I assure you.

Sunlight struck him in the face. A soft, golden color like a half halo. In the face of his new dawn, he blinked stupidly, the bastard, having no idea what it was. Instead he had the audacity to feel sorry for himself. His collar was open. Wrinkled shirt, no tie. Guess he'd spotted me from the top of the binoculars. Judging by his forlorn look, I surmised that he'd been there awhile, and this astonished me.

After cutting short an all-important business trip to scurry home and wag his bruised finger in Nabi's face, Martin was at work? At something to seven in the morning? I wondered if he'd bothered going home after all. Maybe he'd been already and they'd had it out with each other, and then he'd left, left her for good—and when I thought about that I felt a chill because Nabi hadn't called me once he'd left her alone.

The consternation showed on my face, I think. Martin's seemed to turn to stone. "You dare to show up here," he said.

"We need to talk about this."

266

"I beg to differ. You and I both know I'm under no obligation to make you privy to our plans. Neither is Nabilah."

For a fraction of a moment, his caginess summoned a phantom of hope. Martin Furbert, luckiest idiot who'd ever walked the earth, clung to BRMS like an overachieving intern, hanging onto the crystalline doorframe like it belonged to a strength-giving Fortress of Solitude. Was my best option really a Mexican stand-off with this guy or a sprint to his harborfront condo, where even as we gaped, Nabi might have been all alone in tears, waiting for me to rescue her? All this passed through my head in that fraction of a moment which, when it was gone and Martin shook his head in scorn, left me weak in the knees.

"No, you're right," I said, though it almost toppled me. "But there's another problem. I mean, for Nabi."

When I beckoned, Martin frowned. Distrustful, sure, that was his right; spies were everywhere. But he shuffled to my car, all rounded shoulders and limp arms like some kind of refugee.

Seeing him so sorry for himself—when his net loss would be nothing, nothing, because of Nabi's Nabiness, Nabi who signed a contract with the bastard in a church—this literally brought a cry into my throat. It landed heavy and rancid in my stomach when I swallowed it. I had to look away when Martin folded his arms; the two of us side by side, him looking at the ground, me fighting to hold my own against shivers.

I said, "You need to understand about this photo."

"No, I don't. I never understood what she sees in you, and I don't want to."

"Yeah, the feeling's mutual."

"Say what you've got to say and leave. I have work to do."

Stiff upper lip while my world ended. Martin didn't smell of liquor, smoke, or perfume. Team leader was haggard, but he planned to get himself through this like a wounded GI dragging himself up onto the beach, steel eyes riveted upon the fray ahead.

"Well, look, they sent the picture because—"

"*They* being a couple of actors who so happen to look exactly like you two, I suppose."

"No, we—"

"Or perhaps a Hollywood animator."

"No. Nabi—no."

Pretending the picture was a fake, the thought of denying Nabi, the idea that Nabi might deny we'd ever happened—it just never occurred to me until that moment. It brought a thick wave of nausea and hunkered down in my stomach to thrash around until I was alone and could wig out about it properly. Right now the point was Nabi in trouble because of what I'd done. I thought I remembered her saying it was Martin who'd told her where the picture came from. But maybe that wasn't what Nabi said, maybe I'd hallucinated everything Nabi said, I mean for years. Assuredly not wigging out (I had my forehead in one hand, my belly in the other), I said, "Martin, a vice president from Clocktower sent the photo."

This got him to look at me. I watched the investigator's relentless curiosity do battle with the studious indifference of the maimed ego.

"Clocktower," he said. Curiosity won.

"They sent the picture to put pressure on me by threatening Nabi. Look, they want to burn Bull's Head Shreds, they want to make it look like BRMS is going to investigate us for something they're going to cook up, and that's going to kill our reputation in the—"

"Wait, what? What? Hold on. Now, Clocktower. You asked Gavin if there were pending investigations, and there weren't."

"That doesn't mean nothing's going on, Martin. Look, I can't explain it all right now. The point is they're stealing money from their clients and investing it, they think I'm hiding someone who could testify to it; and even though I'm not, this VP they sent, Char Richards, doesn't want to believe me, so she sent the photo, right? So now you have to stop anyone at BRMS from thinking there's anything that Clocktower could accuse us of at Bull's Head Shreds and ruin everything Nabi's worked for all these—"

"This is all very dramatic," said Martin.

"Well, it's true."

"Gavin thought he was doing me a favor, talking to you. Somewhere he got the idea that you and I were friends." A cutting look as if, during all those strained dinners, crowded holiday gatherings, he'd ever believed it.

New tactic. "Look, even if there aren't any official investigations, cops or whatever, Clocktower's an open case for you, right? You've had your eye on them, right?"

I still had no proof of this. I only whipped it out during my plea for help because, Jesus, I don't know, it was a plea for help.

"You and I both know I can't tell you that," said Martin.

But when I pressed, Mr. Integrity threw up his hands and cried, "The answer's no! I have no interest whatsoever in this totally nondescript insurance company. You don't know anything about practicing business, so you're in no position to suggest that someone in my position ought in an ideal world to be interested in their, well, their position. In fact I can't make heads or tails of what you're saying. Someone wants to undermine my wife's little confetti-making enterprise because you don't like how a well-established insurance outfit handles insurance? Is that what you're telling me or not?"

I felt like pinning Martin to the ground and sitting on him and growling out everything, which only goes to show how mutilated it all was. "Should've known better than to think you'd have a clue."

"Oh, so I don't have a clue. I don't have a clue what goes on in my own house; that must mean I don't have a clue how to tell an insurance company from a lawnmower dealer. You think you can take me for some kind of idiot just because you dazzled Nabilah with whatever it is she thinks you bring to the table of life? Let me tell you something, Kenji, I checked out that company, you know why? Because if someone at the confetti counter needed something checked into, that person should've come to me from the get-go, not gone around me to my staff. She tells me you're writing a novel? About insurance? I'm supposed to believe that? And now what, with this photograph? Blackmail? The two of you *shred paper* for a living!"

Now Martin stuck out his finger. I'd always envisioned him as a finger wagger but only in the way you imagine monks to wear sandals even in the dead of winter. It was really true, however. The man wagged his finger at me. And I let him.

"Clocktower is clean," he said. "You two, however, are a different story. I asked myself why this little backatahn outfit keeps raking in high-profile clients."

"Because Nabi's good at her job?"

"I knew if anything besides paper-ripping went on there, I

shouldn't ask. I wouldn't have to. The truth would out. And I was right!"

"Oh god," I said. "Martin, it's not—"

"I know that," he said witheringly. "You two turned out to be capable of nothing more than rank adultery, as if that wasn't enough. You get caught, and you have the impertinence to try to mask what you did as something bigger, some conspiracy in which of course you are the victims."

That's right. He didn't believe me either.

"Don't go trying to turn what you did into something else. Adultery's adultery and betrayal is betrayal."

"It's more than that, Martin." Deep breath, and I said, "We love each other."

"Spare me. This is the two of you trying to find ways to laugh at me behind my back, just like always. This is about the fact that you're professional nobodies while I have an important, international career in which I actually accomplish things in the service of society, and you two just can't stand it."

Hoo boy.

"So don't go trying to hide behind whoever took the picture. I don't care why it was taken, Kenji. That's beside the point and it's disgusting that you'd think otherwise. Don't do it for her either, I mean quit trying to conceal her share of the blame. Neither of you deserve that. There's been enough lying anyway."

One guy could cancel out Char's threat. And here's the bugger telling me that I don't deserve to protect Nabi. Maybe that's true, but Martin was too wrapped up in himself to see that the threat was real, leaving Nabi without allies. That made me desperate to find her, wrap her in my arms, and swear, if she would stay, that I'd take on anybody and I wouldn't care what they did to me, I'd quit being afraid because at last I'd learned that terror was just the possibility of her being like me: hurt and furious and cruel. And if that happened to you, Nabi, you'd despise me and loathe yourself forever. You'd learn to hate, and Nabi, no—no, I couldn't bear it.

"Look again, dammit!" I said. "If you found something on Clocktower, they wouldn't dare go public."

And you know what that bastard said? "You even lie to yourself."

270

Again the throwing-up of hands. But listlessly. He turned away to his fortress of virtue, reducing me to begging.

"Please, all right? Please, Martin. Listen to me, man. This could be the biggest case of your career."

"I beg your pardon. This company is not some little corner-store-back-office gumshoe outfit. We do not go looking for 'cases,' as you call them. Clients come to us, thank you very much." Persuading a stone wall to lie down would've been easier.

"What if you could make the first move this time, Martin? Think about it. Clocktower—look, they're faking suicide notes so they don't have to pay death benefits."

"What? Are you crazy?" That got a whirl out of him.

"The evidence is there, Martin. You can find it yourself, you don't have to take it from me, you don't even have to tell me anything. Just get proof and tell Char Richards. She's behind the whole thing, sort of, maybe. At least, she's trying to cover it up, I think. Aetna Simmons. She's the key. If we can show Char that anything she dreamed up about us wouldn't hold a candle to the truth about Clocktower—"

"Threaten them yourself if you're so sure about all this."

"I can't! You're the one who's team leader, you could find the kind of evidence I could never get my hands on, and people would believe you! Don't let Nabi lose it all because of me."

"And have you ever considered maybe she deserves a lesson? Maybe you both do. Why should it just be me who gets hung out to dry? Humiliated, ridiculous. Because I wasted a decade of my life believing in a—in a joke."

The sun was out now. Front Street filling up with cars. A security guard came and unlocked the building from inside, calling a greeting to Martin, whose benevolent hand lifted as he pasted on a grin: "Morning, Will, how are you?" And I couldn't stand it, I grabbed him by the arm.

"That's what you think of her? A joke?"

"No, that's what I think of you."

I let that one go. I was shivering. My voice sounded like it had gone through a colander, leaving all gumption behind.

"Martin, don't you get it? Don't you know her at all? Besides a little bit of pride, you've lost nothing. She won't—"

Couldn't bring myself to say it though it stared me in the face. My chest cramped, my eyes blurred like windshields in the rain. In a broken voice I said—shit, I'll always remember; afterward I just wanted to die—"Martin, Nabi chose you. As her—the one she depends on—she chose you. Not me. If you think she won't stand by it, then you're stupid, and don't you dare let her down, you hear me?"

I threw myself into my car and roared out against the traffic. Ripping down East Broadway and then I couldn't breathe. Found the nearest parking lot and stopped and doubled over.

My panic attack was coming along nicely when she texted. *You ok?* Like she could sense my anguish from afar.

I called instead of texting back. "Nabi."

"Where are you?"

"I'm so sorry."

"Where are you, baby? At home?"

I was in a tiny lot on a hill near the city. My MG listed where a bulbous root had broken up the asphalt under one of the tires. Nose in a bunch of cherry bushes.

"The Arboretum," I said, mystified. Can you think of anywhere less relevant to my panic attack?

"Okay, ten minutes," said Nabi. She hung up, and I dug in my pockets for the painkillers I'd left at home. I checked the glove box, the cigarette lighter, the secret compartment under the radio, the other secret panel I'd rigged under the floormat in the trunk. I had my ass in the air, trying to infiltrate the secret spot of last resort behind the gas pedal, when it occurred to me a little old man was having his lunch in the car beside me, a woman unloading a perambulator from the next car over. I thought of asking her for Advil, Midol, anything, women are always ready for every eventuality. I said, "Good afternoon" to the little old man, "Excuse me" to the woman, and then a truck pulled in.

Big red truck with a familiar logo, empty bins knocking around in back. Nabi left it crooked in a couple of parking spaces. She was dressed for work, but her hair was loose and she'd forgotten her makeup. Her frown was the kind that makes a habit of itself. I knew it from my mirror, but it had no business on her face. I rushed to her and she wouldn't look at me, just said, "Let's walk, come on."

We went into the park. The grass was no good for her heels. I wanted to take her arm. But she hugged herself like it was freezing, not eighty-odd and humid. The sky was almost white. Bright sunlight seeping through thin sheets of cloud, trees too far apart to cover us. We walked in silence over a wide stretch of lawn, heading automatically for the copse we used to play in. The bench, the graveled path, shaggy palmettos draped over a little bridge. At a break in the clouds, sunlight bore down and startled her, our hands came reflexively together. But when our fingers touched, we were too chicken to hold on as we'd done for years; daunted by our lifelong comfort, we withdrew as if from fire, and I thought about returning to East Broadway, lying down somewhere in the middle; and then she said, "Kenji."

We stopped walking. Nabi started to say something, couldn't go through with it. Her forehead fell onto my shoulder, I threw my arms around her, Nabi hugged me tight, tight, and then it was like we heard something huge shattering above our heads. The instinct seized us both at once: run—but too late, there was nowhere. Just that copse, a miniature rainforest huddled around a bench, where Nabi's mother read as we played "Bagheera and Baloo." We arrived there breathless, I touched her tangled hair, Nabi stroked the black hollows underneath my eyes.

"I got so scared," she said. "After we fought. What you might've done."

We kissed for a long time. Like people in a desert stumbling on an oasis, dying of thirst and trying to make the water last.

"I've got to tell you something, baby."

I knew she'd say she'd left Martin, and I knew that was exactly what she wouldn't say. The hope in my expression demolished her control; tears sprang out of her eyes.

"I'll always love you, no matter what you think," she cried.

That wasn't it. I mean, it wasn't what she meant to say. It scared me. "Why would I think any different?"

"You don't know what I've done."

"You mean about Martin?"

273

"No, not Martin," Nabi snapped, "I don't mean Martin. That man and I couldn't find two words to say to each other. What is it with you anyway? The both of you think everything's only about you! Aw baby, you look terrible, you really should be home lying down."

Having bitten my head off, Nabi fussed over the sweaty sheen on my cheeks. I didn't know what was going on, I was well in range of another panic attack, beginning to wonder if I'd finished the first one. Then I started worrying that if I didn't speak up, she'd get angry and leave, so I started babbling: never meant for this to happen, she was right all along, my life is so pathetic that I just etc. But she cut me off.

"No, baby. No. Look, most of this is my fault."

"Yours? How? For what? For loving me? Is that really so shameful?" You can tell I was freaking out.

"Kenji, of course not. Baby, you're freaking out."

She sat me down on the bench. "Look, this isn't easy—" But I interrupted, told her I'd been to Martin and begged. When I finally shut up, Nabi looked at me like I'd stepped out of a coffin.

"What? What'd I do? Or not do? I mean, Martin's in the perfect place—"

"Kenji." Like a groan.

"Well, look, not even Masami would question him. Char sure as hell couldn't; and once he gets more evidence, with what I already know, we could—"

"Kenji, you don't know anything!"

Her voice in that moment. Left a scar on my memory like a third-degree burn.

"None of what you think you *know* is evidence, Kenji. It wouldn't count for *nothing* in an official inquiry. I've been trying to tell you nicely, but bye you just don't listen! You put us through all this because of something that you *guessed*. You guessed, based on literary carrying on, and that is not hard evidence, Kenji. It wouldn't count."

"Why not?"

"Well, for starters, you couldn't even prove Aetna Simmons ever existed! You couldn't find her passport, birth certificate, driver's license. Don't deny it, you said it in your essay."

I felt like a whoopee cushion that's been sat on.

"That bank account you found probably isn't even real. I mean, whoever you talked to was just telling you what you want to hear to get you off their back. And now, like sending my life up in smoke wasn't enough, now you want to send Martin's *company* after this? I mean, you want me to let him think it would somehow be *helpful* if he went chasing after, I don't know, a *mirage?*"

The great stomach of spacetime convulsed and overturned. Whooshing in my head as the bench, the soil beneath, Nabi's faith in me, everything turned over and dumped me out. Of course Nabi was wrong: I had the Ten, all my research, Masami and Char and what they'd done, it all fit together. Yet I couldn't shake the feeling that all of it was raining down around me into the abyss. The debris of surmises, shadows, tones, omissions, ten suicide notes, and besides that nothing but a too-familiar emptiness. My voice seemed far away, a forlorn cry left behind to haunt the world above as the rest of me kept falling.

"She was real," I said. "I bet Char even knew her."

"That woman who took our picture?"

"She thinks Aetna's still alive. She told me. That's why she sent the photo. She thinks I know where Aetna's hiding and that I'm just holding out on her. She's crazy but she's smart, Nabi. And she's got resources. Or, I mean, I think she does. She acts like she does, sort of. I mean, she must. Obviously Clocktower and CAM are on her side. That's why we need Martin."

The way Nabi looked at me, I don't think she saw me, but whatever it was she saw—something from the past or the future, I don't know, I've tried and tried to figure out what it might be, why she did what she did, why such a morbid thing would ever occur to Nabi, the light of the whole world. That horrified look and she turned away, her hand over her mouth.

"Nabi, what is it?" I took her gently by the shoulders. She began to cry. I said, "What's happened? What have I done? Oh god, Nabi." She shook her head, shrugged away my hands, and next thing I knew, I was on my knees: "Nabi, tell me, you're killing me!"

"Lord have mercy!" she breathed, taking my face in her hands. "I don't know what to do."

My breath went out in a rush of hysteria, which in my perspicacity

I mistook for relief. I gathered Nabi close and said, "We'll run."

She wriggled away with a growl. It bowled me onto my behind. Her reply almost convinced me that my heart had stopped.

"Kenji, what'd I just say about you and self-absorption?"

Feeling like a crumb vanishing into a dustbin, I said something such as: "But—"

At first she had no comment, intent on that time-telescope she wouldn't let me see. I moved, perhaps to brain myself against a tree, and the movement seemed to bring her back to where we were. She reached out to me, and I, glutton for punishment, put my cheek in her lap. She whispered a prayer, something like "little bee."

"I need you to trust me, baby. This won't make sense to you yet. Maybe it never will. Bear with me anyway, all right? I mean because you love me. And no questions yet, okay? I need you to tell me something."

But see, I was at my lowest. Well, maybe not, since the worst was yet to come. Anyway, I was beyond distraught. "What do you mean no questions? Of course I've got questions, I don't even know what we're talking about, where are you going with—"

"Kenji," she said firmly, "how far do you think Char Richards would go? Your momma too, if you were right about all this?"

"But I don't understand, I just told you Char said she'd get BRMS—"

"But would she do more than that? Would she do worse than that? That's what I'm asking."

Nabi gripped my hands. Her gorgeous brown eyes were full of frightened tears.

"Now take a deep breath, baby. Think. And give me your best guess. You're more equipped for it than anyone I know."

I was caught in the middle of a meteor shower, tumbling and being tumbled on at the same time. I couldn't think except about one thing, the same thing: Nabi, come back. All I could do was fumble for what to say to make it happen, panicking because I had no idea what she wanted. Hadn't she said the night before that nothing could be worse than disgrace?

"Nabi, I don't know."

"Think, Kenji!" Squeezing my hands like her life depended on it.

"I guess they'd go as far as it's possible to go."

"Hurting people?"

"Maybe, yeah, they could."

"Both of them?"

"Probably."

"You talked to her? Char Richards? Not just researched?"

What could I do except nod? Nabi let go of my hands.

"Nabi, talk to me."

She ignored me for the telescope. And the longer she looked, the more her face rigidified into a darker countenance that seemed less and less familiar. When she spoke, she was angry, and I wondered if an evil ghost had plucked me from my world and stuck me in a cosmic spin cycle.

She said, "What would they do if they found Aetna Simmons? To us and to her?"

"Nobody can do anything to her."

"You sure about that? What're you going to tell Char Richards?"

"I've been telling her the truth. Aetna's dead. There's evidence ten times over."

"Evidence? Kenji, for once in your life think outside the box you've made out of your own head. What if you're wrong?"

"I'm not wrong. She was real, and then she died. We knew that from the beginning."

"Knew it how? 'Cause you read it on the Internet? In a local news source that you've pooh-poohed all your life?"

"No, no, Nabi, you don't get it. See, there's real evidence. Written evidence. I may not know about much else, but I know about writing. Words and ideas. Aetna's words. Ten suicide notes."

"And you believe everything you read?" said Nabi softly. "Think about it, baby. First, despite a total lack of evidence, you decide this woman faked suicide notes for a living, including the ones you found. Then you turn around and say when it came to her own death, she couldn't help but tell the truth."

"That's what *paradox* means. It's a vital contradiction. Look, I know Aetna, okay? I know her as only the closest, most faithful and sympathetic reader can know an author: better than she knew herself. She couldn't lie to me even if she wanted to, and she doesn't have to! That's what I've done for her. She escaped those people, the ultimate sacrifice for the ultimate freedom, and I'm the only one who understands—"

"Yeah, and what if she didn't? What would they do? What would you do, Kenji?"

"It's a moot point!"

"What if you're wrong? What if she's out there all alone, no one to help her? What if she's just a nice, ordinary person, not some kind of evil mastermind but just one of God's children trying to get by? What could she do?"

"Why the hell are you taking this so personally? You want to talk about what-ifs? What if everything I say and do wasn't a personal affront to you? What if years of literary training were actual experiences that actually counted for something? What if I stood a chance of knowing what the hell I'm talking about?"

"Watch your mouth, Kenji Okada-Caines! This is your fault in the first place for letting that Clocktower woman think you know something. What if you really dropped some kind of hint and didn't know it? What if she found what you didn't want to see even though it was right there under your nose?"

Standing now and hissing at each other. Neither of us considered what might happen if the wrong person had followed us or a jogger happened to pass through our little copse and the jogger's husband's stepsister happened to work for CAM. I had no handle on the conversation, I'd given up trying to get one, I was at the end of my tether. As despair overpowered me, it became clear that only one person had a shred of sense.

"Aetna made sure no one could touch her."

"That's what you think, but what if she didn't? Kenji, what if— what if maybe you were right about everything except one thing: just the idea that she's, well, no longer around? I'm just saying what if, but Lord have mercy—Kenji, what if Aetna was alive and you knew where she was?"

Nabi fixed me with a beseeching look. My fortitude was gone, my discernment irreparably diseased. How much was true, how much did Nabi truly believe, how much was just hypothesis? I don't know, I still don't know. I shook my head but Nabi gripped my arms as though she planned to shake me if she didn't get her answer. In a ruined voice I said, "I'd call Char and tell her. Is that what you want me to say?"

"But why?"

"For you, Nabi. For you. For Bull's Head Shreds, your life's work."

"Kenji, promise me you won't."

"What?"

"I mean it."

"Am I going crazy? What the—Look, Nabi. No, all right? No. No, you don't mean it, and no, I won't promise, not even hypothetically even though I—"

"Please, baby."

"I said no. If you're trying to make me choose between you and Aetna—like if I said I'd rescue her, it'd give you an excuse to pretend I somehow love you less and you could go running back to Martin with a clear conscience—well, I won't do it, Nabi. I'd choose you. Even though I don't deserve it and you wouldn't—you'll never choose me. Even if she was your sister, it wouldn't matter."

"Yeah, well, what if it was me? *What if I'm Aetna Simmons?* It was me the whole time, that's right! Because I got sick and tired of the two of you—both of you fools thinking you're all that. Oh, Nabilah's just a worker bee, just confetti and a Bible Study partner for team leader. And guess what! You're no better! Swaggering around the place like just because you got to go away, you're the only one who knows how to line up words and make them do something. Not a thought to call her own in her pretty little brain, right? Well, got your chocolates, innit, both of you! What you gonna do about it?"

I sank onto the bench. Nabi burst into tears.

Nabi dead and bloated at the bottom of the sea. Nabi dressed for damnation, vomiting a storm. A gun in Nabi's mouth as cars fly past her in a desert summoned from a second-hand card table. Daily, my *nikkou*, cultivating despair.

Impossible. In her, it was valiant. But in you, Nabi, no, it's wrong, and just the thought of it is like inhaling death. That's why I couldn't move at first when you turned and ran. The air in me went still, heavy and fetid. And when like someone drowning I kicked towards the sun, you were halfway across the lawn. When I screamed, you shouted back, "Don't follow me Kenji I mean it!" but I kept running, and when I got to the parking lot you were already gone peeling off in the truck and I had to sit down I sat where one of your tires left a mark on the asphalt and Nabi I wept so help me I wept.

Mrs. Trimm:
You have done so much
Hope she comes home soon
Sees bares promises
Careful now Relax
Czarina: look to her.

AS9.
White copy bond, black ink, laser, huge font. Only note with addressee.
Clumsy trimeter. 2 instructions: to-do list or warning? Czarina???

Up became down. The proximal were unreasonably far away. The dead came to life and life succumbed to death. Ghosts took on solid form while the tangible world grew shadowy and insubstantial. Strangers seemed to know me best while the great love of my life became alien.

Haven't seen her since she ran from me and I collapsed in a parking lot. Haven't heard from her either, not for lack of trying.

It might interest you to know that the woman with the perambulator saved me from being run over that day, much good did it do anyone. This being Bermuda, she and two other young mothers, also with perambulators, surrounded me and insisted on helping me back to my car. They petted me and said there there sweetiepie, can't be as bad as all that. They refrained from asking me my name. When attempting to persuade myself that none of this was happening induced hyperventilation, one of the moms whipped out a paper bag, another started praying, and the third invited me home. I said thank you very much but, humiliated enough for one day, I turned her down.

Instead I managed to extract myself politely and crawl back to my empty flat. I took enough Zohytin to knock out a polar bear. I haven't been myself since. I've been sick a lot. Mixing Zo with rum to make it last doesn't work. Dreaming of blackness and *seppuku*. Asking why Nabi would want anything to do with Siamese cats, thinking if I could just understand that one thing, I'd know what to say to persuade her to answer me.

It hasn't worked yet. The fuzzy trimeter in AS9 doesn't help. Poetry isn't her thing, especially bad poetry. For content, AS9 has just a smattering of ambiguous well-wishes for the old harpy's future. It is true Nabi wishes everybody well, but she does so unencumbered by ambiguity.

In the heady first days of my discovery, when Aetna's texts danced with my intellect to the irresistible strains of my literary training, I saw in AS9 the strongest proponent of the Aesthetic Hypothesis; for there is no service that this note could have done Clocktower. Yet there it is: tying up loose ends, I thought, the last of the drama's rising action which will crest at what is now inexorable. Once I knew something of Myrtle, I saw that AS9 is also a vague and empty threat doubling as a helpless good-riddance.

But then Nabi. Then with everything I am, I rebelled against my own thinking. Nabi doesn't jibe, Nabi doesn't threaten, Nabi wouldn't *ever…*

So I got high and from that perspective discovered that AS9, with its wounded-adolescent style, contained coded instructions for a diagram that would make everything clear. A six-whiskered Siamese cat (six lines in AS9, take note) with one whisker outlined in the letters of Myrtle's name and another, opposite, in those of Czarina's. The eyes, nose, and ears consist of other initials such as A, C, M, and P. Clearly a capital N would have no place in such a configuration, which thereby proves once and for all that Nabi is just Nabi.

I was calm. It all made sense. And though my Siamese Hello Kitty resembled nothing so much as an uprooted potato, I congratulated myself on rising above the crisis methodically and philosophically. Until I wasn't high anymore. And the truth struck me so hard I couldn't get back up. Luckily I had my pills under my pillow.

I don't actually know Nabi. Nabi is Aetna Simmons? No. She wouldn't. Would she? She wouldn't have let me do all this—but Char said *You love her,* and I said *Yes.* Then who? Who was that in my arms? Who haunted my dreams after I traded her for Harvard? Who was that who said, under the trees which were our Neverland, *Why should we put an end to all that's sweet and lovely?*

Maybe that's not what she said. Maybe it wasn't what she meant either. I don't even know who I'm thinking about. And seven days without her. I'm really not very well.

After she left me. Two days in my flat thinking she'd call. She didn't.

I called Bull's Head Shreds. Wayneesha answered. She asked if I knew when Mrs. Furbert would be coming in.

Nabi never takes a day without informing all concerned and making sure everything's covered. Straining for nonchalance that eluded me completely, I expressed confidence that Mrs. Furbert would be there any minute. I asked Wayneesha to have Nabi call me when she arrived. "While you're at it, call me yourself, please, if you don't mind. In case she gets busy." Or refused to give me the time of day.

Nabi never called. Wayneesha didn't either. I called back the next day, Friday: Nabi hadn't been to work in two days. That evening I tried Iesha. She hadn't heard from Nabi in some time besides in church. Their parents hadn't either, but in Nabi's busy life this was not unusual. Martin didn't answer and didn't call me back. I called the pastor at Mount Olive, pretending I thought I'd find Nabi at choir practice. The pastor hadn't seen her in over a week.

I debated about Char. If it hadn't occurred to her to associate Aetna with Nabi, far be it from me to dispel her ignorance. But what if when the one who claimed to love her promised to betray her, Nabi thought her only hope was to throw herself on Char's mercy?

Images of Char. Black leather, studded whip, maybe a garrote. She was strong enough to beat someone to death. She'd been known to play with Narcan. Like she had any right to decide someone else's fate. Wracked by indecision, I left her a deranged voicemail. She didn't call back.

Beginning to wonder if I was the lone survivor of an apocalyptic cataclysm. Or if I was the one who'd left the world for its ghostly parody.

The following day I considered the police. Countless reasons why that would've been a bad idea. I reviewed all my research in the faulty light of new questions. Was she? Wasn't she? Until I couldn't see her face and was unable to discern any rational excuse to answer yes to either. No and no. That's it. Maybe I'm crazy.

I gave it one more night. Sunday, I staked out Mount Olive. The Furberts' Honda never showed. I pounded on the door at their condo on Harbour Road till a neighbor stuck his head out and said he'd seen the Honda heading for Hamilton. Bull's Head Shreds was locked and empty so, homing in on a conniption, I drove to BRMS.

Long shot? Not for Team Furbert. Gavin was in the driveway, sucking on a cigarette. Stressful moment while I fought the urge to rush him.

"Zapnin, bye?"

"Martin here?"

"Yeah, inside. What's—"

I barged through the door. I remembered Nabi saying BRMS had the sixth and seventh levels, flashed back to a Christmas party where

284

Martin bragged about his "top-floor" situation, and rode up to the seventh.

Big room with a bunch of desks. Each housed two computer screens and a teamster who watched in bewilderment as a stranger strode into their midst and assaulted the door to the private office at the back.

"Come in and make it happen!"

Some eye-rolling and I let myself in. "I need to talk to Nabi."

A moment before I understood what I was looking at.

Not just team leader in full swing, suit jacket and stiff Bermuda shorts, tie knotted impeccably, rising to hand me some papers like it was a busy Monday instead of a listless weekend afternoon, but also someone who'd received a nasty shock. Not "how dare you soil my sacred chamber," that kind of shock. Worse than that. And after what he said, I had to lean against the door.

He said, "I thought she was with you."

We couldn't talk there. I wouldn't. We went to my car, which I'd left behind a food truck across the street.

Martin hadn't spoken to his wife since Wednesday morning. Wednesday afternoon was the Arboretum debacle.

"Thought you'd run off to Greece. Course I checked your credit cards. Figured you were using cash."

"Nabi told you about Greece?"

He looked away. "Talks about you all the time. Shenanigans the two of you got up to as kids."

Yearning for the past and a fantastic future, both dead and impossible. My head dropped against the window.

"So you had a tiff," said Martin. I couldn't answer. "Probably gone to sulk at some spa in Martha's Vineyard."

"Which one? Can you check?"

"That was just a guess."

"Check anyway. Or tell me where to check."

"Clearly she's not interested in talking to you."

I punched the steering wheel. Martin looked at me like I'd grown an extra head. I shouted, "I just need to know she's safe. That all right with you?"

"Well, if she's on some kind of spree, it's your fault anyway. Look, this whole thing is just to make us beg. She wants us to panic, exactly like you're doing now, and beg her to come back."

I forbore to mention I'd already tried that. "That's not her, man, come on. Where else might she go?"

"And if she thinks she's gonna make me boo-hoo over her? After what she did? She's got another think coming. You and I both know I am not going to let that woman take me for a fool."

"What about Clocktower?" I said.

"What about it? Some of us have lives to lead, you know."

He said it smoothly, too smoothly. Even managed to smooth out his frown.

"Martin, if you know something…"

The timbre of my voice shocked him a little. The frown returned. He turned and looked out the window.

The shades were drawn on the food truck. A nearby car wore a parking boot. Martin said, "I got an email."

"From Nabi?"

He shook his head. "Colleague. Next-door office. Clocktower wants to hire us."

It was just as I'd described. Song and dance about outsourcing the disposal of Clocktower's sensitive documents. The due-diligence investigation is a routine preliminary to any sensitive hire, Martin explained, standard risk-management practice especially in "questionable circumstances." Like this one.

"Ms. Richards," he said (of course), "claimed she'd heard some kind of rumor that all isn't aboveboard at Bull's Head Shreds."

"There's no such rumor."

He just shrugged. "We won't take the contract. If my company investigated Bull's Head Shreds, anyone could scream conflict of interest and call everything we did into question. My colleague only sent me Ms. Richards' email because he thought I should know what people have to say about my wife."

"So what're you going to do? We can't stand by and let Char leak this shit to everybody. She came to you because BRMS could make these rumors look like they've got substance. You could also turn the tables on her, Martin. We have to find Nabi and stop this."

"She'll turn up."

Well, when that man looked at his watch, I grabbed him by the tie.

"What do you expect?" he snarled. "She dumps this in my lap, runs off to hide, leaves me to deal with colleagues muttering behind my back, and you want me not just to grin and bear it but to fix it for her?"

It murdered me to say it, but I was out of options. "It's too big for her, Martin, and these people won't give up. Look, this shit played out just like I said it would, didn't it? The rest of it's true too about the suicide notes. Come on, bye, tell me you've at least thought about it."

Hesitation: part of him never stopped thinking about it.

But he said, "I knew, you know. Not like you idgits could fool me. I had you figured out. But she tricked me. I changed my mind."

"Nabi don't play tricks." (Unless you count defrauding how many people out of their insurance money, which I didn't at the time, being for the moment in a "No she wasn't" mood.) "Why'd you change your mind? I mean about us."

This came out timidly. My insecurity was at its peak, and Martin gobbled it.

"The midnight calls," he said primly.

"I never called Nabi at midnight. We wouldn't have—"

"I know you didn't. One night when she was in the bath, I answered."

"You answered her phone?"

"I am her husband. It was one in the morning. Anyway, the person with whom I spoke *wasn't you*."

This insipid punchline appeared to give him a bit of a boost. I lacked the wherewithal to do anything except appear exactly as I felt (crushed) and gratify him by sniveling, "But who was it?"

He shrugged like he'd had his fun and was now back to being better than me. "That girl Pauline."

"Pauline who?"

"Pauline from your school days. She said she and Nabilah were reconnecting."

"I don't know no Pauline. There weren't no Pauline in our class. Nabi never said nothing about no Pauline."

For a snippet of a second, Martin looked like he'd stepped off a staircase into nothing. Unlike me, he recovered.

"Well, if you don't know, I certainly don't know."

I thought, *Pauline*. My powers of recall have known much better days. Pauline?

"The point is (A) now we know where she went. And (B) she never trusted you either." He said it like that. With the A and B.

"Course Nabi trusts me. We tell each other everything."

He made a noise, the kind that goes with sneers, and I took a dive off that staircase.

"Find this person, Martin."

"How? If she's with a friend, she's safe."

"No. No, see, you don't know that. Neither of us knows who this person is—"

"And I imagine that's the point. Wake up, you idiot. She betrayed us both."

I drove my fist into the dashboard as Martin walked away.

I called all the spas in New England. None had a Furbert or a Simmons. I tried Char again (nothing); and all the time Pauline, who the fuck is Pauline? Rhymes with Doreen? I exhausted every avenue I could think of and found not a trace of the one Nabi had chosen. Some black alley might've sucked her years ago into its gullet, and she never told me. Perhaps my own terminal darkness had infected her, perhaps I'd turned her into the woman who'd drowned herself in her own fathoms.

Or not, and *nikkou* wasn't a pseudo-suicidal pro-forger but had some other secret. Something she kept from me and Martin as she gave up on us both. Either way, she lied because she resented me; she built a door between us. *The books are black because they can't be read.*

It's not true, I thought. I thought: what will Char do if it's true? It's true or not depending on whether I'm stoned or hysterical (always one or the other). I said nothing to Martin; if she *is*, I must protect her; if she *isn't*, he doesn't need to know. It makes all the evidence make sense, even the lack of evidence—the computer was at Harbour Road, her passport was in her other name—and it makes all the evidence perfectly ridiculous. She said so: that should be evidence enough; the Nabi I know is incapable of lying. But Aetna is all lies, all shadow and deceit except when she is death. Whoever Martin spoke to was a liar too; there was no Pauline at Warwick. Evidence is just a reason to believe.

Trying to think my way into her shadow-world. Back to the Ten, seeking a sign, a tone, a word, a glimmer of sunshine in Aetna's endless night. And when I found it, I thought I'd have a stroke.

The letter P.

There: AS7. But on the back, in the cage.

Box E: AETNA P SIMMONS.

P for what?

HSBC said: SIMMONS AETNA P. The only record I could find. P for Providence?

It's not true. Nabi'd never heard of Aetna until she disappeared and I began my work. But if it is true, P for Pauline, then Nabi's not Aetna Simmons but something else altogether. Something I can't see. The text in caps in AS7—did she write that for me?

As Hardy says, despairing minds feed on compulsions. With each passing hour I fell into deeper misery. I was up all night on Sunday. Writing. Writing this, in fact. To her, sort of. That is, to you. Because I don't know who you are, you need to understand.

Monday morning, Wayneesha called. "Dr. Caines, *where* is Mrs. Furbert?"

She was close to tears. Nabi had promised to be there, day or night, when Wayneesha was ready to talk (I didn't know what this meant, I'd find out all too soon). But Nabi hadn't been to work and wasn't answering her phone. Clients were calling, employees had issues, decisions needed making, someone had to get in there and make them. Someone besides a nineteen-year-old receptionist. "Please come, Dr. Caines."

Why this child was the one in Nabi's office giving orders while the grownups ignored everything except their regular tasks, well, it's beyond me. Bryan and those lot could afford to be indifferent only because Nabi had rigorously streamlined their procedures, leaving little room for error. But even well-oiled machines need attention now and then.

I'm a businessman, yes? I thought, How hard can it be?

I stood in the doorway staring at Nabi's empty office.

"You all right, Dr. Caines?" said Wayneesha.

I wasn't, but I couldn't say so. To her other, plaintive question—posed in a lonely voice as if Nabi were a gentle and beloved parent—I could only reply that she'd be back any day.

Wayneesha showed me how she'd sorted Nabi's inbox. She logged onto Nabi's computer, showed me a dozen reminders that had popped up on the screen over the past few days. She gave me a mountain of phone messages, made me check the company's email address, and it was full of bills and invoices and question marks.

"It looks like a lot, but it's not really," she said. She asked when was the last time Nabi did such-and-such with some work-order forms.

I said, "Which ones are the work-order forms?"

Very long pause.

Then Wayneesha started talking. Work orders, barcode labels, CoC records, CoDs, invoices, transactions, billing cycles. She was very patient, enviably knowledgeable. And shit, I tried, but I was overwhelmed. When she'd been talking forever—not a word sank in, I was a step away from screaming—in swaggered the guy who drives one of the trucks. For an awful moment I feared the truck was missing, I'd forgotten all about it. But Nabi had returned it on Wednesday afternoon. Possibly the last thing she'd done before vanishing. I wanted to ask him about the timing, but the guy hadn't seen Nabi, only the truck. He had to hit the road but first he needed a battery for his handheld scanner-thingy and some receipt paper for his little printer gadget. I said, "Receipt paper?"

Wayneesha whipped a roll out of a drawer. When the phone rang, she and I looked at each other till she said it was okay for me to answer it, and the guy on the other end—I had no idea what he was on about, didn't know how to put the call on hold, I just looked at Wayneesha and she told me what to say, guided me to the relevant invoice on Nabi's computer. Someone barged in to complain about the toilet in the break room (this while I'm on the phone again, trying to reschedule someone's pickup and learn how to use the scheduling software at the same time), and Wayneesha whipped a plumber's card out of Nabi's Rolodex. She'd learned everything she knew, she said, from observing Nabi closely and asking detailed questions. I thought I'd done that too, over the years. Clearly I hadn't done it right. So the kid had to walk me through each one of Nabi's messages. When all I wanted was to hurl the phone across the room, I groaned, "Thank god you're here, Wayneesha," and that good-for-nothing child said she might have to quit.

"Are you crazy? You can't quit!"

Then the phone rang. The *Gazette*. Rumors, said the reporter, because of which Bull's Head Shreds could lose a huge overseas contract. I insisted on precision and learned that the contract in question was with Clocktower Insurance.

"What's your input on this?" he said. "Is Bermuda about to lose yet more international business because of local corruption?"

"The only corruption I smell around here is coming straight from you, bye." I had a splitting headache, a cold soda pressed to the back of my neck.

"Well, we're all in this together," said the imbecile.

"Then what're you trying to do, getting up in my face about nothing? First of all, I've never heard any unflattering rumors about Bull's Head Shreds anywhere in Bermuda or anywhere else. Second, we have no contract with Clocktower. We've never had one. Nobody's even proposed one. You want to bet what's going on here? Your sources on this matter are trying to make jackasses out of both of us. I suggest you find yourself some new ones."

I hung up on the guy. I put my head on Nabi's desk. And at the end of the day, when the sound of Nabi's telephone had stir-fried all my nerves, when I'd snapped at several employees and the colorful bars in the scheduling program began to swim together like rotten Neapolitan ice cream, Wayneesha informed me that she's pregnant.

I came this close to begging her to tell me she was kidding.

I got the whole story, all of it: morning sickness, deadbeat boyfriend, clueless grandparents-to-be; shrink who refuses to approve Wayneesha for an abortion; night classes at Bermuda College, where Wayneesha's trying to learn to be just like Mrs. Furbert, who'd taken the child into her confidence about diversifying into mobile hard drive shredding (no, Wayneesha didn't know any Pauline), which meant Bull's Head Shreds was on the cutting edge (ha ha awesome) of the tech and high-finance industries' most important support effort; and Wayneesha wanted to be there to be a part of it, a driving force in it, in fact, at Mrs. Furbert's side; therefore, like Mrs. Furbert, Wayneesha had no time for a leaky, foul-smelling, noisy, and expensive brat. The kid's made up her mind that Mrs. Furbert will be the one to see her through this; no problem is too daunting for Mrs. Furbert, Mrs. Furbert understands, she doesn't judge, she cares and she is wise, but now she's gone, and that leaves, well—somebody's teenager wailing into my shirt. I considered returning the favor, I was so burnt-out. Nabi would've bestowed a hug, but I was concerned that hugging or even being cried on might qualify as molestation or something else Char could use to cudgel us. I said lamely, "She'll be back soon."

However, I should mention that I made at least a dozen SOS calls that day. Some included invoice numbers. Nabi saw fit to answer none of them.

I can't promise Wayneesha anything, not without Nabi. But when eight o'clock rolled around and I'd texted the kid at least five times, I lost it and said she'd be officially in charge until Nabi returned. Yes, the sexually compromised barely-not-a-minor.

I was still in Nabi's office trying to make sense of her paperwork and getting nowhere. I'd had it, and that made me angry and ashamed and distraught. I'd built the place too, you know, with my savings and my risk, yet I felt so disoriented there, a ghost that can't get the knack of haunting. I'd lost track of the amount of Zo I'd taken just to keep my sanity, I hadn't slept or eaten in two days, and worst of all, the Zo didn't seem to be working: it made me sick instead of calm, and that made me panic. When I gave up on the paperwork and searched Nabi's computer for Aetna's traces (none), I felt like my heart was drilling through my chest; I couldn't browse the files in an orderly manner; I kept forgetting what I'd seen and reading things over.

Soon I slumped in Nabi's chair. The overhead lights were like javelins to the head. I turned them off. Closed my eyes in the dark in the place that's uniquely Nabi's.

I wonder if she found inspiration there. Make documents or tear them up, either way you change history. Whenever I try to make Nabi and Aetna bleed together, for some reason I imagine her there in that office. It's dark in those images. The only light is from that same, reticent computer glowing like a scrying pool. Perhaps it's end-of-month, and she has lied to both husband and lover, pretended she must stay late to balance the books. Perhaps it's really daytime, everyone's at lunch, and she's turned out all the lights in the windowless warehouse so she'll attract the shadows; and behind the scheduling program hides a word-processing document spattered with self-destructive sentiments.

It was a relief when Char called. The vacuum of that office was smothering.

I said, "I'll tell you everything."

No surprise to Char. She made no remark, just gave a room number at the Rosedon. Pitts Bay Road atop a hill. A converted English manor at the summit of a sweeping drive, like a *kanzashi* ornament secured with a silk ribbon. Flower-patterned curtains and velveteen chairs arranged before a painting of an English countryside gave a cozy atmosphere to the lobby's dramatic architectural curves. Char met me there and said, "You look rotten."

She, on the other hand, wore a filmy cover-up over a string bikini. She looked so good it was maddening and I wanted to hit something. She led me upstairs to a spacious corner suite with its own balcony, half arts-and-crafts, half colonial-plantation style. I imagined her kicking off her shoes in this pristine place after a long ride in a rented Twizy from a messy house, where for my benefit she'd doused herself in a dead woman's dust. She locked the door behind us, and like a spurned prostitute I said, "Why didn't you return my calls?"

She smiled like an anaconda who's found that perfect no-slip grip. "Don't worry, we're still friends."

"Did something happen?"

"No. I just wanted you to know what it feels like."

This with her hands all over me. The warm lamplight of this borrowed room. The burn of betrayal, fucking loneliness, frustration as the main force in a life lived in a chintzy little bowl stored on a shelf out of the way, and I was at Rosedon to beg. I seized her by the arms.

293

Too hard, she even gasped, but she slid her tongue into my mouth like someone sneaking a *petit four* from someone else's tray. And I was deplorable, I let the woman tease me, even open my shirt, only for her to throw me in a wingback chair and walk away, leaving me panting like a dog with my face in my hands.

She returned with coffee. Took the wingback across from me and waited.

"I have questions too, you know."

"I'll do what I can."

"Not good enough. You wouldn't give anything for free. Why should I?"

"Because I blackmailed you?"

"You keep it up and I'll have nothing else to lose."

This interaction was full of long looks. It drove me crazy; I wanted to grab my phone, pull up the photo Char had taken, shove it in her face and shriek, *Who is she and what have you done?!* Perfect way to get nowhere. Char was wary and curious, I was desperate and looked like a clown, and we knew full well we were both liars.

"All right," said Char. "Quid pro quo and all that."

She bade me start at the beginning.

"At least four years ago…it was your brainchild, I think. But it took at least two of you. And Aetna. Maybe someone at CAM. It might've started with Macy Moran."

I mentioned CAM on the off-chance that it might make me appear sympathetic to Char and her cohorts. She wasn't the type to let things slip, but still I had to hope. She was the first and only person not to exclaim in disbelief at the notion of fake suicide notes.

Her eyelids didn't even twitch.

"It's about doing your job," I said. "Eliminating needless expense is what risk management means." Like I'd practically written the book on the subject.

Unimpressed, Char said, "Where'd you meet her?"

"Bernews article."

"Excuse me?"

"Where'd you think she went? I mean when she disappeared."

"Took her money and took off."

294

"You haven't found her yet, have you?" Taunting not pleading. I hope.

Well, we're here, aren't we? said Char's eloquent eyebrows.

I watched Nabi flee across the lawn. The image still hits hard. Wooziness gripped me and I said, "Why? She just up and left. Why?"

"What's this about an essay?"

"You're not gonna like this."

I didn't mention names. I was vague about my sources. But Char got the gist of everything from Bernews to the Ten to the police file, landlady-extortionist, and *Aetna Simmons' Final Words*... As I talked, Char's eyelids answered, lifting or flickering, much to my surprise, in expressions of growing interest. Her verbal contribution consisted of the following remarks:

— "So you never even met her."

— "No, it did not occur to me to stick my fingers in a dead cat's throat."

— "Photos. Where do you think? A whole box labeled *Czarina*."

And finally: "Something is very wrong with you."

I said, "The real Aetna, the one who lived and died, she understood that identity's all just words. And she lived that understanding. And that's what she sold you. Her ability to not be anyone. And that mutability, that refusal to keep still, that's what she really was."

I'd thought Char would be a pacer. Big-boss types often are. But she sat in the chair, mug in hand, dubious frown. Watching me.

"Being and not being is hard," I blundered.

"Or," said Char, "you got carried away. Teddy bear, you're perceptive when you want to be. But you're also just another empty male trying to puff yourself up with visions of a helpless girl who can't do anything on her own behalf to prove you wrong."

Swift kick that left me winded. Char spoke of Aetna and me with equal repugnance. I said, "But it's not like that, it's—"

It probably was sort of like that. In that sense too I failed her. Aetna, I mean. Reading's always like that, isn't it? A little? But Aetna was never—Nabi, no, never—never just a mirror, some receptacle for my idiotic feelings.

"Char, I mean—she was helpless because of what you let you do with her. But she wasn't just some thing I found lying around—like some Sleeping Beauty napping in the casket in some episode of *Cold Case*. No. Aetna's words—every one of them was something she chose and arranged. All I did was read, read hard enough to find that truth, Aetna Simmons' living truth, a living contradiction. Why? Because I admired what she'd done, she alone, Aetna—not 'cause I'm fucked up, I know I'm fucked up—but because of what she did. For Christ's sake, Char, she isn't even here—at least, I don't think—and she's making me question everything, making me—"

"You got issues," said Char.

"You have no idea," said I.

Char looked at the ceiling. Her exasperated head-shake aimed at male-kind in general. "How'd she wind up with a W-2? It's up to employers to generate those and file them."

This I had not known. "You didn't file it?"

"That would've been stupid."

We tossed around ideas. I supposed Aetna faked the thing, an eloquent prop in the theater of the Ten. A subtle way of signing her name and Clocktower's to her death warrant.

"Why bother with subtlety? The point was to expose the whole thing and then die. She had no reason to hide anymore," said Char.

Subtle for subtle's sake. For art's sake. Not long ago, I would've declaimed it with conviction. But new, afflictive doubts—was she or wasn't she?—made it impossible. I struggled to focus and not to appear stricken; for although I had no answer, Char's question in itself was a triumph. It meant that she believed me, believed Aetna was dead, which meant maybe Nabi was safe. But Char was *amemasu*, a shapeshifter wrapped in fog, water, and night. I could not anticipate her, couldn't even ascertain her perspective. Why, for example, was she so interested in a doomed piece of literary criticism?

More than my knowledge of the scheme, more than Aetna Simmons, that scholarly buffoonery caught Char's attention and held fast. *Aetna Simmons' Final Words: Suicide and Suicide Notes as Works of Art.*

"That thing you wrote. Send it to my phone."

Char had me take her through it twice. All of it.

As I expounded on the significance of to-do lists, she said, "This was a lot of work. What made you want to do all this?"

What makes a candle burn up its own flesh?

I'm not sure I really said that. Maybe I only thought it. I remember the question in what alternately seems to be Nabi's voice and that of the *wakizashi*, the swish of sword through air.

"I've never read anything like this," said Char.

"These days, the academic perspective—"

"It's not academic. Man, you fell for her hook, line, and sinker."

More head-shaking. Then a moment of stilling. Steeling herself as if to look at a dead body, Char looked at her phone, at my intellectual blood-spatter.

"You love her. That's why you've taken her apart. Through her words. You dissected her."

I'd never thought of it that way. To do so and think of Nabi was no good for me at all. I said weakly, "Was it Aetna Pauline?"

But Char was somewhere else. The phone lolled in her hand, the screen shone at her empty palm. Her faraway look had deadness in it. Also a haunted bitterness so hard and fixed, so arid that in feeding upon itself, sometime long ago it had burst into flame. Since whenever it was, the moment of ignition, she'd never let it die. And most of the time she believed she controlled it, but the reality was she couldn't make herself stop feeding it. And maybe the moment of ignition had to do with differences between people, but it had more to do with love. The kind that hurts. Not slam-against-the-dresser hurt but hurt that keeps on digging at itself, taking me apart from the inside over and over. Char the impostor, who stole from widows and orphans, sat in thrall to the ghost of some such exquisite dissection, straight-backed and grimacing, not even half a minute. But I saw it.

It didn't shock me like it should've. Probably because I live with it all the time. Or she faked it to torture me. Or I made it up, driving myself batty with *Where are you, how could you leave me here alone...* Char's phone was right side up again already, her deep breath over and done with or imaginary.

She said, "Explain the narrative again. Want to make sure I get this."

She meant the Ten, the essay. Aetna's death throes clanging against my dismembered insides.

Ten suicide notes. Each one sealed and yet reverberant in the next and the last.

"The last. AS10. Well, this is, you know: wow, this is it. Perfection in the form of an unbreakable commitment. The others are full of masks. Images, tones, structures. In AS10, she strips all that away, the words run out of steam. Only bare thoughts left. Unvarnished, you know? And current. Forward-looking. That's how we know she was a young person. Old people kill themselves when they can't endure the weight of the past but can't escape it either. Aetna was different. She did it for the sake of the future, not the past. For death as absence and silence, everlasting incompleteness. That's what the dashes mean. Incomplete thoughts, things that want doing but—you know. She looks ahead into nothing—"

I never told Char what I left out of the essay. Not on purpose, I just didn't realize. Not until that night. After a day behind Nabi's desk proved to be as enigmatic as an ancient Bavarian grimoire, and I don't even know if the ancient Bavarians had grimoires. She wasn't, but *what if she was?* My stupid essay overlooked the futility of hope. I was so intent on narrative and resolution, making things make sense—oh god, I misread. I misread AS10's final wishes as imperatives. Misunderstood. It's not a to-do list.

It's a jumble of empty aspirations. Things Aetna must've known nobody could achieve except in dreams. Clichéd "instructions for life" like the sentiments of postcards. Such pointless things are analogies of existence.

The author of AS10 didn't necessarily want to die. She could've survived.

This occurred to me at Rosedon in the middle of a sentence. I didn't mention it to Char, having insisted all the time on the opposite. With a shudder of nausea, the best I could think to do was continue on that course: insist for Nabi's sake that Aetna Simmons left the living world long ago.

"You all right?"

"Lost my train of thought. AS10, looking into nothing. She welcomes it, the nothing, and she knows that means she's ready. For real this time, the end. She walks into the sea or heads for that gun shop in the desert. She's gone, Char. Texts always betray themselves. And

298

the real truth is I'm sorry but I wasted your time and that's everything I have to say, I don't know any more, I'm a hack, Char, that's all. I'm no threat to you or anyone." I wanted to go, but I thought I'd sway if I stood up.

Char paged through what I'd written. Frowning as if, having let it take her unawares and even get a jab in, she was determined to subdue it this time around. She dared it to defy her. As though what I had written were actually capable of something. I almost felt like laughing, watching her pore over it. Then I thought of how much I'd got wrong and felt like drowning.

"Char, when was the last time you saw her?"

"I've never seen her. We'd communicate online."

"You really hired her online?"

Char gave me a glance that said I should've known better than to wonder about the obvious and inconsequential. She turned back to my essay and said, "*Insurance association seeks innovative freelance copywriter for unique project in interesting locale. Details to be discussed with candidate.* You have any idea how many writers are out there waiting for someone to say, *Yes, and you're just what I need?* Nobody asked what the project was, just assured us they were perfect for it. She was convenient, she passed the background check, and she was just desperate enough. That's all."

It was all I could do not to dissolve, and I couldn't let it show. I recall hanging onto the armrests of the chair, trying to absorb its solidity into my voice, to mime Char's stoicism with the tired muscles in my face.

"And Char, what if—pretend she's alive. What would you have done if she'd betrayed you and gone off like you thought, but then you found her?"

She looked at me. The red eyes of a panther in a midnight wood. "If it wasn't for you, no one would've known what she was doing."

"Just say what if."

"I have people to handle it. Risky but not impossible."

I didn't want to squirm, but I mean, come on. What if Nabi *was?*

Nauseous, I asked Char if I could lie on her bed. She got a chuckle out of this. She stretched out beside me and I turned, I shoved my face between her breasts, I forced her to be still and hug me. It made her impatient, but she settled down. I pretended she was Nabi. Tried to hear Nabi's music in the bloodless intonations of the predator. But a shadow crept over Nabi's image, staining it black: the shadow of the woman at the Unfinished Church. All three of them were shadows, even Char, who studied her phone in my spiritless embrace. I took a peek and glimpsed Aetna's photo of Faith Tabernacle. I remembered Nabi going there to help out, wondered who else had done the same, and my head spun: maybe I was the hurricane. If Nabi didn't trust me, she used me and that's all we amounted to. I grabbed Char by the face, I made her look at me. My voice snarled, "Tell me," which made no sense at all. My fingers made rude indentations in her cheeks. Char extricated herself with little effort. She looked at me with loathing and triumph.

"You're bereft," she said. "It's fucked you up for good. That means you're perfect," she concluded with all the warm affection of a geometric syllogism.

"Perfect for what?"

She sighed. And set out to complete my estrangement from myself.

It was all about power for her. Maybe if she'd bothered to think about it, she'd have called it colonial power. Corporatocratic imperialism or something. But that's not all there was to it. Char's was the power of the wounded, righteousness of the wronged. It was also a base competitive urge and the thoughtless fury of vengeance. Thoughtless? Well, her way of overcoming her oppressors was going after those who were more powerless than she; setting up a secret fiefdom in a tiny country in the middle of nowhere, getting a desperate woman to do her bidding. Like Masami, really. Better to reign in Bermuda than be chained to a baby carriage pinned to the underside of some glass ceiling in the US or Japan. In fact, I wonder where Char found her inspiration.

But maybe I don't need to explain all this to you. Maybe you've got your own rationale for robbing orphans. Maybe I'm just wasting your time, how about that? I'll just tell you what happened. You need to know.

Char said, "Well, look at what you've done. In risk management, we answer questions with the simplest explanations that are easiest to prove."

I said, "I gave you one. For Aetna."

"Finally."

"I tried to tell you earlier."

"While you lied on every other point so you could get the research that you wanted."

"Well, you're the worst Doreen Trimm I've ever seen."

She laughed, a sort of humph. The closest I'd ever seen her to tickled pink. Probably because all she had left to do was plant her flag.

"Gonna give you a free lesson in opportunism. Something you need to work on." She tapped her phone and turned it.

Myrtle's postcard, *to my daughters . . .* This little thing, this scrap: one word—a misplaced letter S, an overdone flourish, perhaps a Freudian slip on Myrtle's part, in any case a myth—Char the hunter homed right in on it. She'd snapped a photo and zoomed in on the squiggle of opportunity.

"Things like this," she said, "that people leave hanging around. Little ambiguous things. Never pass up a chance to make a thing like this mean something. Even if it was really just an accident. Use whatever else you know to turn it into something deliberate and significant. Something kind of shocking, even. So those who think they know the person will start to doubt themselves. She was very good at this. If you'd get your hands off me, I'd show you where the original has a bit of unmarked space where she could've—"

"You kept the original? You kept Myrtle Trimm's will? What the hell for?"

"Why the hell not?" said Char. Like I was making a big deal out of nothing. Like there wasn't a RealDoreen for whom that postcard really did mean quite a bit of money. "The point is, when I found this, I realized I could use it," said Char, brandishing her photo of the squiggle. "I used it to try and measure your interest in Aetna Simmons. If you thought I already understood that she was just like you, a kid abandoned by her parents; maybe you'd let something slip about your relationship with her, how far you'd go on her behalf, that

301

kind of thing. A slim chance but a chance. Opportunity in a piece of paper left lying around."

I said, "You played me like a saxophone."

I snarled her up in my arms. Char struggled. Beneath her scary self-control I felt the latent violence that broke into my flat and slugged me in the face. She won. She said, "Quit it, Kenji," and got away. She rose and poured more coffee.

But when she turned back, she left the steaming mug on the dresser. She stood above me, looked at me. Like I was an ant she'd brushed off with a napkin.

"I've been wondering how Myrtle found out," she mused. "How did she learn enough to blackmail Aetna?"

"You better get back here."

"If Myrtle hadn't had that stroke, she might've ruined everything. Why'd I listen to that idiot?" Char grumbled. "Because no old lady came up in the background check..."

"Who did Aetna's background check?"

"Did it myself."

"So who was she? Who was Aetna Simmons?"

"Nobody."

The shrug of disdain, the muttering to herself, the admission about Myrtle's will, all this implied the hunter had relaxed her guard somewhat. Or Char was toying with me. Again. Because she could. But I sensed she wasn't lying at the moment. Granted, even at the time, I knew I would've been a fool to trust my senses; so I suppose I should call it a temptation. I was tempted to believe—simply because Char (impostor, thief, criminal mastermind) declined or neglected to say otherwise—maybe Nabi wasn't Aetna, maybe Nabi was the one who'd lied.

It tortured me to think of it, spread out on the bed in Char's hotel room, hankering with my whole body. I said, "I told you to get over here," an empty voice receding into emptiness. "Come on, Char. There's nothing else."

"Wrong," she said. "There's work to do."

Her phone monopolized my field of vision. The bright little screen, *Aetna Simmons' Final Words: Suicide and Suicide Notes as Works of Art*.

"This is good work," said Char. "You read through her. You saw through her to me."

"You want me to beg you, woman?"

"I want you to work for me. I want you to take her place."

Lying down and glad of it. Clocktower's phase-shifting face seemed to loom over me in the creepiest hallucination I'd ever had. Creepy because in another time, before I'd ruined myself, Char's suggestion would've sounded like good sense. At face value, her next question was even reasonable.

"She couldn't hack it. So what. Why should I give up? You've done most of the research. You understand the gig. You know how to hide in plain sight. Whatever you need in the way of information, leave it to me. You'll get background on each case in plenty of time for you to do your part. Delivery systems are already in place just like you thought."

So I wasn't all wrong, Nabi.

I said, "You're serious."

"Always."

"And what's in it for you?"

"Doesn't matter."

"I want to know."

"I'll be CRO before I'm forty."

She'd save so much money that the company would beg her to steal Jim Falk's position. Maybe that's his only role in this: a target. But the way Char said it, *CRO*. Sneered it, sort of. Or she didn't, she was as serious as a grave, and on account of my maudlin vulnerability I wanted to pretend her goals were loftier than that.

"A promotion," I said. "That's all."

"That's all? Better open your eyes, mister. There's a very nasty world outside your little island. And you know what? It's the real world. We don't play nice in America—"

"Last I checked, we don't here either."

"Well, you still don't have a clue. Men never have a clue. You have no idea how damn impossible it is, a black woman trying to eke her way up the corporate ladder."

She spat out the word *woman*. Like she spat out the word *men*.

"They tell you it's about the numbers, whatever kind of numbers you generate on the company's behalf. Then they tell you it's about the length of your skirt. Well, let me tell you something. My numbers can't just be good, they've got to be ten times as good as any white man's. My skirt better be ten times as accommodating as any white girl's. I can't just be better, Kenji, I've got to be *undeniably* better. And I can't just be a sycophant, I'm expected to grovel. And grin when I'm passed over for a giggling white bimbo who wouldn't recognize a good idea even if it didn't bounce right off her hairspray. Well, listen, I'm done with that. I'm not whoring myself to rich bastards anymore. I'm not letting any female whore her way past me. I'm done celebrating baby showers for people who think they should work less and get paid more just because they've generated yet more people. I'll get there my own way: by doing my damn job."

"And the rest of us can bow to the dragon or get eaten."

"Right. That's how the real world works."

When I think about her now, I recall this ravenous resentment as the first thing Char showed me. Right at the beginning when I took her by surprise, showing up at her crime scene with my crazy-rich-Asian eyes and designer jacket. Her voice at the Rosedon was as cool as it was then at Myrtle's door. Slippery and deep. Out of tune with the ferocity in her words. It meant there was more to her than ferocity.

I'd be damned if I could tell you what it was. Bitterness I get. Racism I get. Fucked and re-fucked. I get that. And the other thing that wasn't smashed-against-the-armoire pain. What I don't get is how Char got to be so cool about it. She was as dispassionate as she was furious; she took revenge by paying it forward with an indifference worthy of Manifest Destiny.

Maybe it was an act. Maybe she was on something I've never heard of. Maybe she'd never overdosed on literature. Whatever it was, I envy it. Lying on Char's bed in anguish, I *envied* her goddamn stolidity *so fucking much* I had to deal with fighting tears. And Char mistook my struggle for an attack of conscience.

"Look," she sighed. "We're dealing with people who either set themselves up to wait for somebody to die or didn't even know there was anything to gain from it. What if the insured lived to

304

be a hundred? What if the beneficiaries died before he did? They wouldn't see a penny. Happens all the time. Point is nobody's supposed to count on death benefits. That's why suicide clauses exist."

I was pretty far gone but not enough to think Char actually trusted me. Still, we seemed to operate on some ambivalent level that we were both prepared to pretend to mistake for trust for the time being. With Char, I think that's the best anyone can hope for. And because the unconfirmed possibility remained that Char's blindness and my own had helped Nabi escape attention, I thought I'd better make the most even of this fictive trust. If the idea was to end Char's pursuit of Aetna Simmons, what better, surer way to make it happen?

I said, my voice croaky and enervated, "That stuff about Bull's Head Shreds. The rumors, the investigation, all that's gone if I say yes. As far as you're concerned, Nabilah Furbert's out of the picture. Deal?"

That luscious fiend. She shrugged and flashed her crooked smile.

"Char, I told you everything."

"I know."

"So what else?"

"She'll be fine."

"You know something else."

"I said she'll be fine."

What choice did I have? I closed my eyes and said, "I'm not a forger."

"We'll stick to people with computers. Just get the words right. The voices. Like she did."

Steal their voices and change history. My hands went to my head.

Joining them, another touch. Char grinned at me like a shark, and all I'd gotten out of her added up to nothing. I said, "Wipe that fucking look off your face."

As we clawed at each other, I made myself pretend nothing mattered anyway. It was despicable, I tore her tunic to pieces. She raised my face to hers and looked at me.

"You should go," she said.

"Shut up."

"You're already done." Sniggering, knowing I would beg. "I'll be in touch. Go home and sleep. And lie low for a little."

"I don't sleep anymore, Char. I write questions without answers and get high."

"Then get high. Don't pretend you need me to warn you about that shit. Look, if it ends up that you can't do the job, I'll get someone else."

Just like that, no big deal. One way or another, I'd lost everything to her and it was my own fault. With an injured cry, I forced my way into her bikini. And though we grunted like boxers, in the end I was a broken pile of stones waiting for the sea. I tried to make Char hold me but she peeled me off and panted, "There. All right? Enough. Go home now, Kenji, please."

The next twenty-four hours I passed like a zombie, inundating my hard drive with this mess as though, wherever you've gone, you could magically see into my computer. As though you'd care to see into it. Maybe there's nothing intelligible here. Maybe you planned this—to do or make however much and then go, fly away, maybe never touch down ever again except perhaps on the surface of the sea, where the tides will make sure you keep moving. But it seems to me that's impossible. Or I never understood anything. I'm just casting pleas into the void.

I emailed Nabi. Texted Nabi. I called Nabi and begged her for a word. Two words, *I'm okay*, that's all. She didn't respond, and I don't blame her. She's better off without me even though life without her is a room full of smoke. When Martin called, I thought I was hallucinating.

"You heard from Nabi?"

"No. Who do they think you're hiding?"

"Fackin Santa Claus. The crew of the *Mary Celeste*, Martin, jeesums." And I had to explain about Aetna and the Ten. "Look, Nabi said—"

"And where do they put the profits from this racket?"

"Fuck you, bye. Where do you think?"

"It's CAM, isn't it. That's what this is really all about, isn't it."

"No. Call the cops, asshole. It's been almost a week."

"I'm trying to help, stupid."

"Oh, you're trying help. Finally you give a shit. Look, I've tried everything, I've called everybody, nobody knows where she is. You are her husband, Martin, call the fucking cops!"

"You do not want the police involved at this stage. You don't want the publicity."

He meant *he* didn't want it, fucking cad.

"What if she's in trouble?"

"What kind of trouble could she possibly—"

"If she was Aetna Simmons, and the whole damn world was out to—"

"She thinks she's Steve Jobs sometimes too, did you know that?" And he laughed in my face.

"You don't deserve her." I was fairly screaming, but my voice cracked and split like a pumpkin on Halloween.

"You know, I've never seen you drunk before, Kenji. Should be quite a sight. How soon can you get over here?"

Chez Furbert, like I'm at his beck and call. Something he has to show me, he says, right away and "time is limited."

It will take everything I have to describe it sensibly. By the time Martin called, I hadn't slept in five days. I couldn't think without Zo, and Zo was starting to scare me: no matter how much I took, I remained wretched, and it filled my mind with water.

Your condo. The capital city reclines across the water, visible in its entirety from your dining-room balcony. That massive dining room with its ostentatious chandelier; huge den with billiard table and a bar that runs the length of the room. You and Martin don't play billiards. One day I asked you why you needed all that stuff, you remember what you said? You said Martin has an image to maintain. I've always despised that condo. You never asked me to come to you there alone. It had to be my place unless you were having a crowd. Only then was it safe to have me.

Above the fireplace are framed photographs of the Furberts. You're smiling. Your smiles are uninhibited. I'm experienced with these photos; I knew I had to take precautions. I arrived with my nerves cushioned by cottony sleepiness, so relaxed I could barely raise my hand to the knocker. But when I walked in, the place was like an alien planet. The sunny yellow on the walls—I remember when you showed me the swatches, I helped you to choose, but it was like the sulfuric atmosphere of Venus. The Birdsey I gave you was suddenly a window onto someplace unfamiliar, a place where trees have claws and the ocean is slick as a dead eye, for I no longer know who you are. I ran to the powder room off your colossal kitchen, and between waves of sickness I asked myself why I'd come.

I was there because in my cloudy reception of Martin's phone call, I'd come to the following surmise: Martin wanted to talk about CAM because it's easier to get dirt on local companies than overseas outfits and because blackmailing CAM could inspire Masami to blackmail Falk, who would thenceforth cough up Nabi's whereabouts. This didn't make sense, but it was all I could do. In truth I was there to see the photos. I was there because I knew what the furniture would do to me. Because the color of the carpet, a pale silver, almost white, was excruciating. Martin made me sit in a leather chair he'd bought for her. He made me drink coffee, which I really couldn't stomach, since the idgit assumed I was hungover.

Meanwhile he paraded himself like a professor. His lecture was orderly. He used his hands no more than necessary, and he didn't even curse. As for me, well, you really can't expect that in my condition I'll remember what he said, not exactly. But certain words and the gist of his oration are still with me. Technically, I believe, it only happened this morning.

By way of introduction, Martin announced that he had something on which he required my "opinions." Initially he wasn't going to share this "discovery" of his, not with me. He knew I'd find out "in due course," and he hoped my enlightenment, whenever it occurred, would be "as nasty a surprise as that photo was for [him]." However, having done a lot of praying, he'd come to realize that letting the "discovery" hit me like a tidal wave was "not a Christian thing to do." In his magnanimity he'd concluded I'd be better off if I learned this thing from him rather than someone less benevolent. He, for one, would have preferred to learn of his wife's infidelity from her or even me rather than be "stricken by it from out of the blue." Then he looked at his watch and asked me to forgive him for keeping close track of the time, the reason for which I would soon learn. Dramatic pause.

"In short, you may be right about Clocktower Insurance. I emphasize the word *may*."

Pausing for my response. None. This was old news.

"I've found some evidence," said Martin. "That's what I want to show you." And to be fair, he gave credit where credit was due. It was really a member of his team who'd found the "evidence." Some kid named Nikea.

But before we get to that, he wanted me to know three things. First: except Nikea and Gavin, no one on his team knew he was interested in Clocktower or CAM. For Nabi's sake he wanted to keep it under wraps; he enjoined me to do the same. Second: when Martin considered the evidence, it led him kicking and screaming to the postulation that somebody at CAM may indeed have been involved in "something sketchy with someone from Clocktower. And with Aetna Simmons. Not necessarily faking people's suicides; we didn't find anything like that."

However (the third thing): "Masami Okada-Caines wouldn't take on a big account like Clocktower's without a due-diligence inquiry. If Clocktower was doing something underhanded, why didn't it show up in that preliminary investigation?"

This question wasn't a question but a rhetorical flourish tacked onto the fanfares Martin tooted on his own horn. So there was little point in stating the obvious: lo and behold, certain criminals were savvy enough to outmaneuver the team leaders of the world. Char, for example, could be dastardly enough to achieve whatever it takes to make herself untouchable. But thinking about this in Nabi's armchair gave my stomach palpitations. I know stomachs aren't supposed to have palpitations. Since I missed my opportunity to state the obvious, Martin ran with the assumption of his species' infallibility. Because everything in our fucked-up multiverse is absolutely contingent and thus could be anything at any time, he ran smack into the truth.

"Now, I'm sorry to say this, Kenji, but if you're right, somebody at CAM must've falsified the investigation's findings."

As much as I enjoy drama, I no longer had the energy to beat around the bush. "It's not just somebody. It's Masami."

Martin had a finger in the air in preparation for his ensuing point. He'd already drawn breath.

"Don't be ridiculous." He lowered the finger.

"Nobody else could make that kind of decision."

"Her reputation is spotless. You and I both know, heck, everybody knows her business ethics are above reproach."

"What do you care? She's not your momma."

"Masami Okada-Caines is a bedrock of this island's corporate community. Anyway, it's impossible. She's the one who called me."

Rewind twenty-four hours. I'm in my apartment doping myself up and spilling everything to my computer as your stand-in. Everything. Torments, lamentations, fuckups. Martin's at his office in obstinate denial. He gets a call from CAM.

The CEO herself. The dragon under the mountain. She says she'd asked an employee to call BRMS some days before, but she suspects this person did not obey. Martin confirms there's no record of such a call, but she says no more on the subject. She launches into her demands. She wants BRMS to handle a due-diligence update on (that's right) Clocktower. Team leader: shock and awe, etc. She wants a meeting right away; he sets it for the next day (this afternoon) so he can do some preliminary digging. He calls Nikea into his office, swears her to secrecy on pain of demotion.

"She's a gifted specialist in computer forensics," said Martin. "Now, just to be clear, we knew that whatever she found at this juncture wouldn't legally be evidence because of the circumstances of the search. But we're not going to court; we're just asking questions. Besides, often in this kind of search, Nikea finds things that lead to other kinds of evidence, you follow?"

I hope I had a snippy comeback. Anyway, Martin asked this person to infiltrate CAM's network and look for things pertaining to Char Richards, Clocktower Insurance, Bull's Head Shreds, and Aetna Simmons. It took an afternoon, that's all. Next morning, Martin called me.

"Char's not dumb enough to leave that kind of trail," I said.

"You mean she's smart enough to try not to," said Martin. Whereupon followed a long-winded explanation intended to showcase his

310

knowledge on the subject. Basically, nothing's safe. The best way to avoid leaving a digital trail is not to use electronics at all.

Yet when it came to Aetna, the gifted specialist came up empty. I brought up the W-2. Martin said the IRS had no record of any such thing.

"Like she never existed," he said.

There was a bunch of emails between "richardsc11" and "okada-cain", both @alum.wharton.edu. "Your brother went to Wharton," said Martin.

"So Masami stole his email address."

"He and Richards were in the same class."

"That must be how Masami got to know her."

"Kenji, they have a very close relationship."

"Martin, you must've noticed. He's with the other team."

"Not that kind of relationship. They're friends. Like I thought you and my wife—"

"We are friends, Martin, best friends. Don't bother trying to cheapen it."

"I don't have to try," etc. This went on until somebody looked at the clock. For the record, I'd like you to notice that he started it.

He brought out his laptop with a terrific sigh. Meanwhile, I explained. "This operation took intelligence. Masami has it, Erik doesn't. I know these people." Martin didn't answer, just gave me the computer.

"Thought you were trying to cover all this up," he grumbled. "I thought that was why you went to Gavin."

On the screen was a report by teamster Nikea, who in order to do all that hacking, wade through what she found, and compile the methodical document before me, must've stayed up all night. The report was replete with Martin's influence: years of correspondence culled, sorted, and summarized in three sections under headings chosen for their relevance to team leader's requests. The actual emails were included in support of Nikea's findings.

Section One intended to describe the logistics of the CAM-Clocktower embezzlement scheme. This section was almost empty. One message celebrated Masami's procurement of *the perfect little cottage.*

Otherwise the emails *implied that logistics had been verbally agreed upon.*

Section Two had meat in it. Every time there was a problem, a flurry of flustered argument flew between Bermuda and New York. Nikea summarized each one.

One problem was Myrtle Trimm. At the beginning of the project, Myrtle got fifty grand up front. In addition, Masami promised three thousand a month for a cottage advertised at less than fifteen hundred. All Myrtle had to do was look the other way. However, because she was Bermudian and a spiteful flibbertigibbet, not looking just wasn't an option. She peeked. She got suspicious. She sneaked into Aetna's place. She found something and threw it in Masami's face, declining to specify what it was.

It must have been damaging. For although Nikea wrote that the old witch couldn't squeeze any more money from Masami, I knew she got a lot more out of Aetna, who paid forty-eight hundred a month. So when Aetna disappeared, Myrtle went ballistic. She left harassing voicemails in the sacrosanct inbox of Masami Okada-Caines. She told Masami they'd continue their arrangement at the elevated rate, or the police would find themselves inundated with evidence: evidence of crookedness which Masami had concealed by exploiting innocent old ladies. Over the years, during several inexplicable bouts of inefficacy and abnormally garrulous supplication, Masami put all this in emails to Char.

When Aetna vanished, Char was first to hear of it; "okada-cain" neglected to keep track of the headlines. Cutting accusations as each correspondent accused the other of helping Aetna to escape, Char in her dry way, Masami in atypically whiny tones. The argument died when Char pointed out that neither of them could afford that kind of risk. She then expressed concern for what Aetna might have left behind. Harmful evidence was already on the loose—ten suicide notes of growing notoriety—and what if there were more? Masami was unconcerned. She evinced a deviant and naïve confidence that Aetna would resurface when she read about herself in the news.

Char conceded Aetna was a tool, a sucker, and a supplicant, but that made her just as susceptible to other people's promises as she was to her colleagues'. It was up to them to find her, find out what

312

she'd said and done, and find a way to (in Char's American phrase-ology) *neutralize any threat* that Aetna posed. Since Masami was dis-inclined to be helpful—an allegation which Masami answered with weak and wheedling protests—Char announced that she'd fly out and investigate herself. She interviewed Myrtle, who refused, pend-ing some exorbitant payment, to elaborate on her suspicion that her tenant *had never been quite right.*

After that, the emails ceased. Nikea conjectured that the authors switched to verbal communiqués.

Throughout Section Two, Nikea mistook Masami for Erik. Martin denied this, stubbornly overestimating Erik and underestimating the extent to which his forensic specialist succumbed to the influence of the *psychological context* described in Section Three.

The emails in this section were from several years before the scheme took shape. Obviously they comprise actual correspondence between Erik and his college buddy from an era long before his Momma-sama cloaked herself in his email address and birdbrained idioms. The stuff is vintage Erik: Char's the only person in the world who appreciates him, only person he can trust. He whined about me, about Masami and Barrington, his professors, everything. Eventually Char shot back that at least Erik's parents hadn't disowned and disin-herited him, going so far as to tell some people he was dead, cutting him off financially, kicking him to the curb almost literally, and for what?

Love, Char wrote, *that's all*. Char the hunter, *amemasu*. She went on: At least Erik wasn't female and wasn't black, so at least he had a chance of being able to make a living without selling his body, etc. *Control issues*, wrote Nikea. Clearly what Char saw in Erik was an opportunity to get to know Masami. Nothing more. And yet Char wrote *Love*.

The misanthrope to whom nothing was sacred. The vengeful, gluttonous, self-righteous bitch who purchased a living woman to generate dead people's paper trails and then used our love, my loving you, the only worthwhile thing I've ever done, to dangle you from the cruel end of a fishhook. Blackmail, *nikkou*, to make sure we won't get in the way. So Char can continue ramping up her numbers, bloating Clocktower's profit margins even though she's been found out. Our love, Nabi, our delight and our anguish, as just another deadbolt to safeguard the impunity of the powerful.

If I'd had anything left in me to vomit, I'd have done it then and there. "Love? Char? When? Who?"

"Nikea plainly wrote *Details unspecified*," said Martin. "And beside the rest of it, that's pretty immaterial, don't you think?"

I couldn't say this to your husband, but it wasn't just immaterial. It was the ghost of Char's humanity. Which from the looks of it was murdered not just by racial injustice but, well, like mine was murdered. From right up close and personal. Besides that, what she wrote, one long-ago day when the scheme was just the possibility of a seedling in the dark soil of her mind, is frankly worthy of me. I must paraphrase rather than quote.

Clocktower, she said. We decide how you measure your time. We do this by determining the dollar-value of your death and thereby of your life. Our position is that of a buyer. We can honor an agreed-up-on fee for your demise, or we may conclude it isn't worth the money and decide not to make the purchase. What seems to devalue a life is when the person who lives it chooses to curtail it. If you don't think you're worth your time, why should we? To put this another way: those who forge into the unknown instead of waiting for disease and cruelty, those who take control instead of letting us do it for them are worth less than nothing, not even a promise.

She said it all quite casually. I imagined the words rolling out in her dark voice as naturally as fog rolls in over the beach. It led me and Martin to further disagreement about Erik. The woman who wrote that, I argued, might play with Erik as a kiskadee plays with a lizard, but she wouldn't be so stupid as to entrust him with anything important. Martin clung to the simplistic counterargument that any messages to and from Erik's email address must have been sent to or composed by Erik. Mr. X-Ray Vision accused me of defending my brother at the cost of my own "dubious acumen." I retorted that I'd never waste my time defending Erik, who'd done me no such courtesy and never would. It was Martin who was hiding from the truth out of an asinine desire to pretend that the world ran like the clockwork in his head.

314

Our discussion had grown heated by the time I pointed out that neither emails nor report mentioned Nabi. At least not by the name which Martin and I normally attribute to her. This was a clear indication that Masami *alone* knew the details of the scheme in their entirety, including the truth about Nabi's involvement. My consternation spiraled till I knew beyond doubt that Masami was the one who'd lured you away from me, just to complete my destruction. So I told Martin in no uncertain terms that when he went to meet the dragon, I'd be right there with him.

I'm no longer sure how I arrived at these conclusions. At the time I was shouting. Martin yelled, "Absolutely not," and we did more shouting. It ended with the appointed time taking us by surprise, Martin running to his Honda and me to my MG. My car is faster.

౿

Sorry about the mess. It's my fault, but it's not just to do with me. No one will believe me or take responsibility.

Wish I could see you one more time, my lost love.

I'm sorry I lied —
Now don't be afraid —
Finish your education —
Always do a good job —
Allow someone good to love you —
Don't think of me —
Just live —
And say goodbye.

AS10.
A scrap (5.5x4" approx.). Stripped. Handwritten (black/blue-black). Final draft? (For fuck's sake who are *you*?) Is there ever such a thing? No one says *goodbye* anymore except in pop songs. At this stage there should be no more doubts (n.b., doubtful authority of *should*).

You're going to want to know: when did I give up? Was it with

Char? When I started working for the chemist? Or did I contrive to cling to some illusory purpose until this afternoon when I careened into the city, rushing rain made a river of the tiny expressway, and my MG skidded as I tried to overtake Martin but he accelerated and we very nearly crashed? Was it when he pounded on the *Close* button as I threw myself at the elevator's maw, seeing Thomas Hardy's heroine who flung herself into the wilds bereft of every hope?

We ended up in there together, muttering. "You better stay out of the way and let me handle this." "Because you've handled it so well already." "You need your head examined." "I'd suggest the same but air conditioning repairmen tend to be booked solid in the summer." And so on.

I cannot have believed that Masami would know where you've gone. Athens, Vienna... But those pictures, you see, the safe and easy happiness enshrined above your hearth. Someone should secure that. It was all I had left to do.

It so happened that Masami was outside her door talking to Motomura. They got to see us bearing down on them, tumbling over each other like boulders in a landslide. "Pay no attention to this person, Mrs. Caines!" said Martin, as I hollered something about life and death. Masami said, "Quiet." And we shut up.

"Thank you for coming, Mr. Furbert. It is fortunate that you brought my son with you."

"It is?"

"Motomura-san, we are not to be disturbed."

A silent door trapped us in the belly of the dragon's lair. A timeless, dark, and bloody place. It stunned me every time I had the misfortune to find myself in it, thankfully not often. The air was cold; it felt like Mars. A giant red and black Rothko had a wall to itself. In front of it cowered an antique globe worth a hundred thousand dollars. The whole place was like a Rothko, brooding and devouring, reeking of intimidation and foreignness. That's what they made her feel when she came here, so she plays it up and gives it back in spades.

The ashen harbor was relegated to the wall behind her altar-like desk. Tiny and far away was the strip of banana-yellow condos where the Furberts made their home. The view seemed frozen, captured

317

like a photographic image, beyond the reach of my experience of time.

Exhausted, I said, "I'm no threat to you or them. I just need your assurance that Bull's Head—"

"Please don't interfere. You are here as a courtesy."

"Who is Aetna Simmons?" I demanded.

Masami said, "I haven't the foggiest." Mild as a pickle in a jar. As I practically swooned into a chair, she said, "You will have a chance to speak when I address my questions to you."

Martin said nothing. Clearly he'd done business with Masami before. He'd met her at his wedding and other social functions. As he sat down, he looked like he was in the presence of divinity.

"Mr. Furbert, what we have to discuss will strike you as irregular. A due-diligence investigation of a firm with which I'm already in business. Of course our own risk management department conducted this analysis before we took over Clocktower's account. Their counterparts investigated us as well. All inquiries concluded to mutual satisfaction. Recently, however, certain possibilities came to my attention."

A moment before I realized that the chill running down my shirt was the dragon's gaze upon me. My plans included cajoling and threatening. Not going well. Martin saw me dithering and took advantage.

"Well, I'm sorry to say it, Mrs. Caines, but if Kenji told you what he told me, then some of it might be true. Specifically, there's evidence that Clocktower was involved in something under the table, aided by someone in this company."

"Nothing so crass as falsifying documents."

"As yet there's no evidence one way or the other," said Martin, earning a deadly frown. "But we can't rule it out. Respectfully, Mrs. Caines, it all hinges on Aetna Simmons. Who she was and what she did for these people."

The chill returned. "Well? Do you know the answers to these questions?"

"Why are you pretending that you don't? Martin knows—"

"I don't know any such thing," said Martin. "There is evidence enough to *suppose* that *someone*—"

"These falsified documents. What are they, if they exist?" said Masami.

Martin fidgeted. "You realize my work is just beginning. You and I have yet to draw up a contract."

"Come to the point, Mr. Furbert."

"It has been suggested to me, albeit without hard evidence, that these people are concocting the kind of documentation that would enable Clocktower's life underwriters to invoke, under false pretenses, legal suicide clauses which would preclude the payment of death benefits." He made it all sound very technical. Like something way beyond a confetti maker.

"Suggested by whom?" said Masami.

"Fake suicide notes," said the confetti rep. "Look, the show's over."

"Perhaps."

"You're not thinking there's some truth in this," said Martin.

"My son may be a vengeful, foolish liar, Mr. Furbert; but there is no threat to this company or my family that I will not address with the utmost seriousness. As you said yourself, we can neither confirm nor rule out any hypothesis at this juncture. But there's an aspect to this matter that to me is even more important than the methods involved or their ultimate objective."

She swiveled in her chair like a pilot in a cockpit. Beady eyes fixed on me like a bomber on an unsuspecting target.

"Ten days ago my elder son came in here railing about fraud, embezzlement, and one of my largest accounts. He refused to provide details."

"Yes, that's typical," said Martin.

"Therefore, that very day, I asked a trusted member of my staff to contact BRMS and learn if it would be worth our while for a neutral investigator to update our intelligence concerning Clocktower. This person responded to my orders with delays and excuses, and ten days later I have received no report. I must assume that either this employee forgot my direct orders and hoped I would do the same, which is inconceivable; or they willfully disobeyed me, which is so unwise that I assure you it never happens."

This diatribe was thrown at me like darts at a detested photograph. Masami turned to Martin and continued: "You will excuse me, Mr. Furbert, but I must be absolutely sure. I must be sure that Erik-Katsuo, my younger son, has not contacted you or any of your colleagues."

A smug glance thrown my way as team leader made a call to whomever passes for a dispatcher in his crystal palace. "I'm afraid not, Mrs. Caines. And I'm very sorry, but I suspect there may be more to this than procrastination."

She looked at him in a way that might just have peeled his skin off if she kept it up. "Be careful, Mr. Furbert."

"Yes, Mrs. Caines, I was born careful."

"For Christ's sake, Martin, you have the evidence right there." I couldn't stand it any longer. "This is not about somebody getting up the guts to disobey, which I assure you wasn't Erik."

"Quiet," said Masami.

"No thank you, I have more to say. Martin, this is an act, all right? Erik has nothing to do with this. She's just trying to efface the real issue with a petty one."

"Kenji," said Martin with a sigh intended to humiliate.

"Martin, open your eyes!"

"I apologize for this, Mrs. Caines. I made the mistake of having him over this morning—"

"The old lady may not have been a match for her, but you are, Martin!"

"And he stalked me, Mrs. Caines. He followed me out here."

"What lady?" said Masami.

"Myrtle Trimm."

"*Myrtle Trimm?*"

"Jesus, just stop, all right? You stashed Aetna in Myrtle Trimm's—"

"Myrtle Trimm was this company's first investor ever," said Masami. "Forty years ago."

"Then there it is," I said.

"It was not a matter of friendship. Nothing that would inspire loyalty. This was a woman who alienated her own daughter by constantly accusing her of stealing money. She entrusted her considerable inheritance to me only because she subscribed to the racial stereotype that portrays Asian people as servile and submissive."

320

"Well, you showed her, didn't you."

"If I may," said Martin, with noisy throat-clearing. "Mrs. Caines, you and I both know from long and trying experience that arguing with Kenji is impossible. Once he's ruled against you in that spiteful little courtroom in his head, you cannot redeem yourself except with drastic measures."

"Drastic measures. Like when you cut me off to get into that parking space."

"Excuse me, but the sign said *Visitors*, not *Interlopers*. Look, Mrs. Caines, regarding the matter at hand, I fully appreciate your priorities. In your position I'd have the same concerns. But whereas I think I can provide a pretty solid answer to your question even at this early stage, according to the man with the PhD the evidence I brought to show you is unconvincing. Ms. Simmons and Mrs. Trimm can't speak for themselves; Char Richards, who could answer you conclusively, is suddenly unavailable or at least not answering—"

"Char Richards," said Masami. So quietly that Martin stopped. The egregiously uninformed might've thought it was as if she recoiled from Char's name. "She's really involved?"

"No doubt," I said. Just to be mean.

"How do you know her, Mrs. Caines?" said Martin.

"Erik-Katsuo," said Masami. "She was his friend in business school. A close friend…"

"I would strongly recommend that you speak with him," said Martin.

Masami seemed for a moment not to see either of us. Silence and a punctured look passed through her and vanished like noctilucent clouds. She shifted in her chair like a hint of an earthquake, turning trauma into anger with a tightening of her lips. "We'll get to the bottom of this at once." Her hand shot to her telephone. She murmured, "I want Erik-Katsuo immediately, please." Then she let out a sigh. A puff of smoke from the summit of the mountain.

Don't think I don't realize this made everything worse. In front of me was Masami Okada-Caines sneaking up on the realization that she'd been deceived, something potent hidden from her. You are the core of it, whoever you are, I knew she'd go after you and devour you; and because you'd tricked her, you'd receive no mercy. Not even if you are the little girl who learned to eat with chopsticks at Masami's house, who always picked flowers and brought a card for her on Mother's Day. My mission there was quashed before I'd had a chance to begin, not because Masami was involved with Char but *because she wasn't*. This was baffling to me: Char was the daughter Masami never had, finally someone with the gumption to build her own mountain; it would take no imagination to envision Masami meeting Char at Wharton and, impressed by her shrewd energy, taking her under her leathery wing. But if Martin was right, the truth was even more unnatural, and I was in no shape to counter it. By the time I gathered myself and said, "Wait, let's think about this," Erik was bouncing in.

"Mr. Martin Furbert, it has been too long," he said, clasping Martin's hand with a fatuous grin. He gave a little start when he saw me crumpled in a nearby chair.

"*Onii-sama*," he said with a mincing little bow.

"I happened to run into Mr. Furbert," said Masami. "You may recall that on a very distant day I requested that you contact his company about the Clocktower account, Erik-Katsuo. He says you never did. Is that true?"

He bowed to her deeply, looked at me askance.

"It's true, *okaa-san*. I'm very sorry."

"Yet you agree that only an idiot, or someone who wanted to conceal the truth, would have disobeyed me on this point."

Erik winced at Momma-sama's disapproval. He had to think fast. This is not his forte, so over the years he'd developed a crude but effective strategy for situations that required hasty excuses. I knew he'd never deviate from it, but I was spent and struggling; despite my experience, I didn't see it coming.

It was a look I hadn't seen in years. The look that would come over my brother when he was going to tell Masami that I had spilled the Kool-Aid and he had to clean it up. A wily look. An evil look. Not always but often, he was the one who'd spilled. It passed quickly, this look—Masami never saw it—artfully replaced by a long-suffering expression. Numerous conclusions may be extrapolated from that look. All of them fell on me at once.

He must've told Char the entire ghastly story of the house of Okada-Caines.

"I'm sorry, *okaa-san*. I hesitated because I thought Kenji might be involved. I wanted to find out—"

"It was Kenji who brought the affair to our attention."

"He did that to protect himself. Once we knew about it, we'd be complicit."

"That doesn't quite follow," said Martin.

"Well, when it comes to him, who knows? Who understands the way he thinks? I mean, come on," Erik chuckled, "maybe he just did it to throw dirt on the fact that I landed this account."

"Which account?" said Martin. Erik bit his lip.

"Erik-Katsuo is our portfolio manager for Clocktower," said Masami. "Katsuo, you and your brother are barely civil to each other. How would he have known that I put you in charge of that account?"

"Because he's, you know, involved. How else would he have known all that other stuff he claimed to know?"

You'd think I would've chimed in. I was starting to feel like someone had arranged a felt curtain between me and everybody else. As they spoke, they walked away, deeper into the world that is closed to me. Or I fell away from it slowly, jettisoned from their company by a betrayal that should've been meaningless. But even in my growing disengagement and intensifying nausea, I discerned the only salient point.

Given the opportunity, Erik would wring you out and hang you out to dry just as he'd done to me. My stricken silence encouraged him and scared him. He gained momentum as he spoke, throwing frightened glances at everyone in the room.

"My friend Char? He seduced her, threatened her. She told me. I mean, it's how he is. Inconsiderate and hotheaded. He probably faked those documents himself. I mean, he calls himself a writer, he's good at feeling sorry for himself, it's really all he's good at, aren't I right, *okaa-san*? He did it to get your attention, that's what I think. He used me and Char to rig everything so we'd all profit from the scheme that he made up. And then he was going to leap out from backstage and announce that he was the root of our success. Just to make us look like idiots."

"Run that by me again?" said Martin.

"No, he's right. I'm Aetna Simmons."

A voice I barely knew though I've used it my whole life.

I'm Aetna Simmons.

I mean, I really am. Char asked me to take her place and I had to accept. She'll say there's no one to replace, it was me all along, and that's just fine, I'm tired.

"That's absurd," said Martin.

"Then why did you—" said Masami.

"I wanted to see how much you knew, that's all."

"I had nothing to do with this, *okaa-san*," said Erik. "I didn't call BRMS because I wanted to protect him."

"I don't think so," said Martin. "Mrs. Caines, Kenji didn't do this. He asked my team to look into it weeks ago. He wouldn't have done that if—"

"Well, if you'd done it properly, you'd have seen how it fits together," I said.

"Exactly," said Erik.

"No," said Martin. "Kenji, there's no evidence. Mrs. Caines, there's nothing to support this."

"What, you think I lack the ability? The courage?"

"No, you're just under some crazy impression—"

"Check my phone!" Slamming it onto Masami's desk. "You'll see all the calls from Char and ten suicide notes and at least one kid on a bike saw my car on Suffering Lane and Iesha Douglas saw me and Char—"

"That's circumstantial."

"Call it what you want!"

The curtain wrapped itself around my throat. A great surge of emptiness seemed to explode from me and douse the felt in its intolerable weight. I couldn't stand another minute in that place, my voice already sounded like an echo of an old machine that had worked itself to death. "Look, you win, all right? Everything's my fault, all of you were right, I've had enough."

"Sit down," said Masami.

"No, forget it. I have to go."

One person came after me. He only caught me because I stopped at a men's room to get as high as possible before hitting the streets of our misunderstood and lovely strip of coral.

"What are you doing?" Martin hissed.

"What do you care?"

"What if your brother takes this charade of yours and runs with it? What happens to Nabilah?"

Look, whatever it is you've done, Erik doesn't know about it. If he did, he would've betrayed you in Martin's presence. Or maybe he does know, maybe he found out somehow and to make me beholden to him or destroy me altogether gave me this one chance. Char will back him up.

This way, whether you are or you aren't, or for some reason I don't know you're protecting a complete stranger and that's why you left me, whatever. No one can ask anything of you. If they ask, point to my training, my wasted life, my confession. Martin heard it. Even if he claims not to believe me, he can't pretend not to have been there and he won't lie about what he heard.

"Nabi will be fine," I said.

"Don't be stupid. When Erik starts pointing fingers at you, what're you going to say? Aetna Simmons is dead, everyone knows it."

"That's right."

I left him there. I don't know what the three of them decided.

I'm Aetna Simmons. Why did I say that? I'm not Aetna Simmons. Why did Kenji have to go & do that?

I am in hiding with my book. The same person who pressured that poor girl to leap up to the sky & stay there. I'm not like Seabird, I'm too scared. I've betrayed 2 beautiful men.

No emails, texts, or calls from my husband. Millions from Kenji. Iesha won't tell him where I am unless I say. I don't know what to say. I ran to my sister's in a taxi. She lies real smooth like me. That's why it's frightening to hear her: "No, I haven't heard from her, but that's not unusual. She has a lot to do, you know. Have you tried the house?" Then she sees me going teary & gets stern: "Grow up, Nabilah. Make a choice & make it work."

She doesn't get it. My own sister. Why won't Martin call me? Has he given up? Kenji's messages are frantic. I won't leave Iesha's guestroom unless she makes me eat like a civilized person. I'm not a civilized person. Did I say I'm Aetna Simmons cuz it's my job?! I told Kenji he'd betrayed us, but he hadn't.

I have. I'm Aetna Simmons. Why? So he'd turn away in shock & forget what I had done. I'm not Aetna Simmons. I lied to conceal what we did.

I said the one way to be sure was to destroy her computer. I told her to leave it with me. I said I knew a way though it might take some time. Meantime to be safe, I got some data destruction software. I had it wipe her hard drive in multiple passes, & then I took it out of the computer. I took out all its memory too. I put the laptop's empty shell in a grocery bag & threw it in a dumpster round Mills Creek. I kept the parts that do the thinking to destroy properly later. But Martin's right, I make confetti, I'm a silly amateur playing around where it's too big & dark for worker bees, I mean I didn't think the software was gonna work!

What I did was worse than if the software hadn't worked. I wiped that HD, I wiped & I wiped. But before I did it, I used Macrium to make a clone. I did it just in case the sanitization software didn't get everything & I ended up wanting to start again from scratch. It's how they all do it: make a copy 1st so if you have to you can reinstall and start over. She knew, she was always involved, step by

326

step. We researched everything together. 2 girls, 2 computers, one getting ready to die, one starting a new shadow-life in The Art Of Vanishing in my office after dark, streaming jazz & learning all the way from scratch, nobody to say don't worry your pretty little head. & she escaped & I helped.

I never asked why. I was "the wind in her sails," & wind don't ask just blows. Worker bees get to work. Not like I didn't wonder, all the time I wondered, but I promised her no questions & I promised I'd be ready cuz it could happen anytime. & it did, a quiet sunny day after someone stole something from her. I don't know who or what, I didn't ask. Did the Good Samaritan ask the guy who lay there bleeding why he should help him?

But mercy, I betrayed her. I never wiped the clone.

After I left, that idiot had the nerve to call me. I didn't answer, so he left a message:

"Hey, *onii-sama*. I wanted to maim you, but oh well! Changed my mind. Even though I can't *believe* Char fucking slept with you. I could punch you, Kenji. Really. Day after fackin day I'm gone down Bull's Head to slap ya ass to the North Pole. But brah, you weren't even there, you left poor Nabilah-chan fending all by her little self down that backatahn place full of heavy machinery, and did I do you like you did me? Never even crossed my mind. Why? Because family don't do that to each other, brah. Anyway, it's all good. We're straight now. I never would've thought you'd step up to the plate for me, almost got emotional about it when I finally got out of there. I thought you were gonna blame me and I was gonna blame you and then there'd be no proving anything, but you did me one better. I mean, I thought you were spying for You Know Her and You Know Him and *they* were the ones who knew it all and put you up to pretending to know something so they could weasel the rest out of *me*! Talk about fucked up. Anyway, thanks for being a brother at long fucking last. I say we call this your *Thank-You* to me for the Harvard thingy. How about it, *Doctor Caines*? Check."

This is just for the record, you understand. In case you need to protect yourself. I don't know how helpful it would be, but you should have some record of what he said.

By the way—this is just a guess, I won't be able to find out whether it's true—I wouldn't be surprised if Erik paid Aetna and Myrtle out of his own pocket. In return, Char talked her superiors at Clocktower into starting a big portfolio with CAM. Erik made sure he got to manage it.

If that's what happened, Aetna might've told Erik when Myrtle started squeezing her for more money. My brother, given his upbringing, would've accused Aetna of extortion. They would've pooh-poohed in her face when she asked to leave that intolerable *dump* in Inman Square where they'd left her to rot out of revenge because she wrote. They wouldn't let her have a penny more even when she begged. Masami Okada-Caines would shake her head like spitting in her face and say it was her own fault and keep on doing it for years, however long it takes to squander a life away.

328

If it comes down to you and them, Nabi, or you and whoever; don't hesitate. Whoever it is, throw them over. And be all right. And trust yourself, acegirl. Trust your numbers, your instincts, your sharp business acumen, your years of experience. If they're telling you to get that HDS and mobile unit, you go on and buy that girt big truck.

Every time I said, OK Nabi-girl today you gonna sit down & wipe that clone just like the other one, I don't know, I couldn't do it. She doesn't know I couldn't do it. It's the 1st and only thing she ever asked me to do that I couldn't do. Not cuz of what's on it. I never looked to see what's on it. Acegirl never asked me questions either. None of this "Why, Who are you, How could you, etc?" So why now? Kenji. Cuz of Kenji I couldn't stop questions falling thru me like the rain that made the Flood. I plugged the clone into my laptop. Here is what I found:

Suicide notes. Some unfinished, some revised. Lots of revising. Hundreds of suicide notes.

DefinitiveBookOfHandwritingAnalysis.pdf.

Unsigned correspondence with disposable email addresses. & guess who signed up for those. Like she's only got one trick in her book. (Clue: I just might slap her if I saw her.)

3 emails from 4 years ago. Subjects: names. Bodies: blank. Attachments are details that go with the names. Finances, education, employment, spouses, parents, children, personality, major events in their lives. But Lord help us, these people are all dead. Their names go with the file extensions on the first suicide notes.

"W-2." But you know, not really. She never asked me to do nothing with the IRS, & if she actually filed this thing they'd be all over her, I mean she cut off the top row! No social security thing! Very tacky for a (oh Lord) professional forger. She left in the part where it says "Clocktower."

After the first 3 "profiles," she sent an email saying she didn't want them online anymore. After that her emails contain times & places, nothing else. Someone went to meet her, I guess, with the "profiles" of (mercy) her "victims." Here is what I did not find:

Why did she do this?

How in the world does somebody like her get mixed up in something like this?

WHY did she make me do this & then go & leave PAPERS lying around?!?

Why did Kenji have to want so much to read them?

It's like reading hieroglyphics from Pluto. Some language that's impossible. So the words don't look like words, they look like impossible pictures. Kenji's laptop & The Hand of Ethelberta & Bull's Head & bank accounts...? & that's just the email itself. It's got 3 attachments I'm afraid to look at. The biggest one, no, I can't.

But the one with no name. He let his computer name it "Document1." My finger moved & clicked like it was caught & pulled, like what his voice does to me when he speaks soft. & Baby wrote, "I tried." He wrote, "I cherish you." He wrote, "police" (!!). I'm telling you it don't make sense. Like our computers garbled the code on its way over. The file with no name is longer than the Book of Jeremiah.

I was vexed at 1st. Ya boy thinking he can talk his way out, bye's got some crust, I thought. Especially when it's talking, & him & his writing, that got us where we are in the first place. My best friend tried to undo the biggest achievement of my life. Course he don't know it's like that. You threw her in his path. Like You threw Bermuda in front of the Sea Venture. & the other woman, that American who cannot learn to keep track of her clothing, wasn't that Your idea? All these years of prayer & worship & he finally asks me to marry him long after it's too late so You just hand him over to some skank?! He made it all up, You say? To get attention? Well, why not?! How long have we been lying to each other? If he had that skank on one side & me on the other & if he was doing drugs & using BHS to launder drug money, that man was no friend of mine! But You know, I never saw him with no drugs, I never found them in his place, I know Kenji Okada-Caines would never destroy a book. He wouldn't ask me to marry him & then go putting the munch on some longtail. You're right, he made it up, he lied lied lied. He says "were" like our love is already over.

Guess I can't blame him for that. Even though life without him would be nothing but destroying machines, Yes Honey, Can I get an Amen. I know that. I know it's too late for any more than that. Worker bees can't walk out. They stick to their routine till their little hearts give out from exhaustion, but they Don't Give Up.

I keep reading & reading "Document1." Some parts are true, not made up. Parts with both of us in them. True down to what I wore, what we had for dinner, how I said my words, where Kenji put his head. Behind Kenji's words I hear his voice, his love & pain.

But some of what he wrote just can't be true. If it is, this email says Kenji's either breaking up with me or not afraid to hurt himself. These things are not possible. So why do I feel like I'm falling out of my own head? At the dinner table one of the twins said grace, I couldn't find my voice, dropped my niece's hand & ran & fell on the bed bawling like I'd gone crazy. Iesha's like: "Gonna be OK, happens to lots of couples, they survive," she doesn't know what I've done! K's not answering my calls, my texts, my replying to his email saying "What does this mean, Kenji?!?" He's not answering cuz I lied to him. I'm not Aetna Simmons.

I liked her. I enjoyed her company. I thought she was a good person. She believed in me. She never doubted I could learn to do what she needed. She's the only one who knows about my bumper car boys, knows I love 2 men, & unlike a certain sister in't got nothin judgmental to say. She's got so much she deserves to forget. & how many people get that chance, how many got a decent excuse to wipe the slate like she got, like she deserves? I believed in her. I Don't Give Up on people I believe in. I ridiculed Kenji cuz I believed in her. & what did she do?

She made innocent people look like sinners just so she could rob their families. & Kenji. My Kenji.

❧

Dear Nabi, dearest, dearest Nabi,

I hate to burden you, but you're the only one I trust. The attachments won't explain everything, but they do try. I tried. I can't honestly say I understand a damn thing. The only thing I know is that I cherish you.

Please destroy my laptop. I'd do it myself, only I haven't the strength. Destroy my phones too, if you would.

Now, it seems to me that you'll only be safe once the matter of Aetna Simmons is resolved in the public record. I could be wrong about that, you must always be careful, I've learned to mistrust everything I come up with, I'd go mad if I kept at it much longer. Do what you think is best, but I'd advise you to call the police and say I'm Aetna Simmons. I'll write a note to that effect (attached).

The keys for the MG, the *Ethelberta*, the flat, and the cabinets will be on the kitchen counter. They're yours now. So are all the contents of the flat, my bank accounts, my investments, and my interest in Bull's Head Shreds. Behind *The Hand of Ethelberta*, you'll find a certain switch. I don't have life insurance, it'd be useless to you anyway. Martin will help you. Take care of him. He tried to be kind to me. But above all, look after yourself and be happy.

I have always loved you. You were the joy in my life.

K

Document1.docx (403 kb)
TWIMC.docx (13.4 kb)
AS1-10.pdf (4260 kb)

His mouth was cold & dry, stained & stiff like an upturned shell left by a conch who's abandoned it or rotted. Nothing flowed back into me except the chill of a dinner forgotten on the table. Car says 1:17, but I keep running up the hill in darkness, & the cold won't leave my lips.

While I am moving my pen & holding my book & straining to see by this sometimey streetlamp, I won't be able to scream or walk back & forth outside. If I write everything down, it will become a bunch of letters, just a document, not the actual destruction of the world. I'll write what Martin told me, too. Just so it will take longer. Maybe then it will be noon.

I got Kenji's email around sunset last night. I tried to call him. But then Martin called me. This is what happened to Martin:

He heard Kenji tell a great big lie. He knew it was a lie cuz Martin always knows these things & Kenji was "not himself." When he met Martin at our house, Kenji was very sleepy, he was "irrational," "insisted on the opposite of what was there in front of him," & threw up in the powder room. At 1st Martin thought none of this was serious. He thought Kenji deserved it a little (!). But then Kenji shouted at his momma: I'm Aetna Simmons. No, Baby, that's a lie. But Martin knew he planned to turn the lie into the truth.

Kenji ran out of CAM & Martin tried to tell his family. The mother said, "Enough for today, Mr Furbert." She made Mr Motomura show Martin out. The brother thought Kenji was being "shrewd" &/ or a "drama queen." The father was on the telephone.

Martin worried all day, but at the same time he believed there was "a healthy chance" that his worries "would prove to be unfounded." He didn't want to look stupid if Kenji was just protecting Erik or "acting out" to get attention. But a strong feeling made those "healthy chances" seem like the masks of evil clowns. He thought it would be silly to ignore Kenji's "known penchant for overreaction" & the "expert opinions" of his relatives. But the feeling wouldn't go away, & Martin knew it was the kind of feeling he should trust. When the sun began to fade, Martin found himself in the living room, unable to make up his mind. Then (he claims) he saw our wedding photo above the fireplace. That decided it, he told me. Well, whatever, but at least something got the man off his you-know-what.

He called me. (I mean Martin.) I didn't answer. I was reading "Document1." Kenji wasn't answering, I didn't know what else to do. I didn't think I could just show up at his place cuz what if all this was Kenji breaking up with me while trying to save us both some dignity? That's just an excuse, I was just scared. "Zo was starting to scare me…it filled my mind with water," Kenji wrote. But no gut feeling came to link what Kenji wrote to Martin's one & only phone call after days of silence. No sign, no Gentle Voice, no warning from whatever I've been praying to. Since I didn't answer Martin texted: Go to Kenji NOW.

I called him back in a freakout. He didn't say hello, he said, "Kenji's not answering his phone. I'm at his place right now, it's dark, there's no one here. Nabilah, where would he go?"

Martin didn't have to tell me what he was frightened of, & I couldn't say it even though I thought I knew it was impossible. Martin said, "He says he's Aetna Simmons. Where would he go to make that true?"

All I had left of Kenji were words turned into digital signals turned into pixels. I scrolled thru the Unnamed file, I babbled, "I don't know I don't know."

"Think!!" Martin shouted.

I shut my eyes & thought about my Baby, & I kept seeing his face as he knelt on the ground in so much pain. Come on, Baby, reach out. But he had! He WROTE that Aetna's truth was in her writing, & he thought the truth was courage, & the place where he imagined her showing the whole world that she was not afraid…

"The Unfinished Church?"

It was just a guess. Martin was doubtful cuz he hadn't read what Kenji wrote, so we argued & I panicked & Martin got fed up & said, "Just go!" He promised to send the ambulance & meet me at the hospital. Iesha lives in Smiths so it would take me 20 mins. I stole her car keys & I ran.

St G was pitch dark. Sir George's heart under the obelisk, the ghost of the Deliverance, the slaves in unmarked tombs behind St Peter's church, no cars, & so few lights. A whole city of ghosts. I was all alone, counting on the ambulance to show up right behind me, but it didn't, of course not, it had to come from Paget. The Unfinished Church was a hunk of darkness on a dark hill. Halfway up, there was one tiny light.

Kenji's car. The inside light. The door hung open, I parked behind it & got out calling his name. Silence like the bottom of the sea. I checked the car (empty), grabbed Iesha's emergency flashlight, ran up the hill screaming for my Baby. There was no moon, there were no stars, maybe that's why it felt like the universe was already empty, I was too late always too late, I saw where Kenji threw up & kept climbing, & if it wasn't for the flashlight, I may not have found him, it was so dark! The dark of hurricanes, when the electricity goes out

& your house falls silent, all those quiet sounds you didn't know it made just disappear, everything looks the same whether you close your eyes or open them, no God lives in that kind of dark.

He was lying by the stump of what never got to be a pillar. Stupid not-a-pillar must've struck his head when he fainted. I'd never seen so much blood, & it was Kenji's blood & I couldn't wake him up. He wasn't breathing.

All that time in church did one thing for me. The choir & Bible Study group called for volunteers to learn CPR cuz there's so many elderly at the meetings, so the trusty Furberts volunteered. What do I get for my trouble but a broken heart in a broken church under a burned-out sky, the man I've prayed for all my life dying in my lap? I had nothing to stanch the wound, the hot blood of my sweet genius spilled onto the grass. I put my mouth to his as we'd done in all those overdue nights.

Used to be a blaze in Kenji's kiss, the urgent glowing of a wish that just won't stop. But his lips were cold & purple in the shadow of the ruin. I wanted to exhale every ounce of life from me to him, one great big whoosh. That's not how you're supposed to do it. Small puffs, chest compressions. But no matter how much I begged & puffed & screamed & puffed & shoved Kenji in the chest, he wouldn't answer me.

The ambulance came. EMTs took over rescue breathing, so all I could do was stand there drenched in Kenji's blood. On the way to KEMH they got him to breathe a little by himself, but he couldn't keep it up & I just couldn't stand it, they ended up giving ME the oxygen! The hospital lab found enough "hydrocodone" in my Baby "to kill an elephant" (Martin said that's surely an exaggeration) & I blurted out "Zohytin" & kept blurting, "I don't know what that is, I don't know what that stuff is, I didn't know he was taking medication, I don't understand what he was doing," & they said Zohytin is a super-strength form of hydrocodone that doctors give to people in constant unbearable pain. That's when my knees gave out. Too bad there was a chair or maybe I'd have fell & broke something & Kenji wouldn't have to spend the night alone.

They hooked him up to a Naloxone IV. It has to keep flowing until he can keep breathing. The Naloxone should reverse the Zohytin, turn it off. But Baby took so much! Best case the reversal will be hard on him. Worst case Naloxone won't be strong enough, I leave everything to my sister, the end.

They wouldn't let me see him after they took him away. Just cuz I missed my chance to be his wife. Martin & Iesha tried to take me home. I wouldn't go, they went for Kenji's car & then Iesha's car, came back & tried again but I wouldn't budge. I told them to leave. Martin kissed me on the cheek & I felt faint cuz that's how Martin fed Kenji that poison. So did Iesha & Aetna Simmons & Kenji's so-called family & most of all the "One" who abandoned us. Now I'm in Kenji's car in the lot outside the hospital, smelling his smell & putting my cheek in the places where he put his hands, covered in his blood & drowning in his absence, wishing I could undo it all or take his place.

&

TO WHOM IT MAY CONCERN:

I have lived more than one life. Altogether, they proved to be too much.

You know me as a partner in Bull's Head Shreds, son of Masami and Barrington Okada-Caines. Others know me as Aetna Simmons, forger of history. On behalf of the life insurance industry, I created suicide notes that by means unknown to me appeared at the scenes of recent deaths, *ex post facto* enabling my employers to invoke suicide clauses which obviate the payment of death benefits. A former tenant in a cottage belonging to Myrtle Trimm at Suffering Lane, St. George's, I fled my home and employers when an attack of conscience forbade me to continue to my work. I apologize for the inconvenience subsequently incurred by the Bermuda Police Service.

And now I choose the *samurai*'s escape. No one but myself is to blame for the misfortunes suffered by those who know me and bereft victims whom I will never know. As proof of my misconduct, I enclose ten suicide notes of my own authorship.

Kenji Okada-Caines

Back in hospital before visiting hours. Considered faking chest pain so they'd take me "backstage" & I could escape & find Kenji. Too chicken to try. A waiting room, his Unnamed docx on my phone: Kenji's "fleshless visions." Noon finally. Nurse said I couldn't go in till I'd traded my bloody shirt for a clean gown. She said Kenji was breathing but "feeling a bit ill." "Precipitated withdrawal": if Zo knocked out his nerves, Naloxone shocked them all awake. The "discomfort" could last a few hours or days. "Like an overloaded fuse, only it will right itself."

Well, if that was supposed to prepare me, it failed. Regardless of what Kenji's done, he doesn't deserve eruption after eruption, jackknifing over & over, vomiting brutally even when the diarrhea started, I couldn't watch & I had to, it's the most awful thing I've ever seen. & when he finally got to lie down, pain in his whole body made him cry out & thrash around. Big bandage on his head, bunch of stitches just above his temple. I stayed all afternoon, wiping his face & trying to hold his hand. He never noticed me. It's the same now that he's home. Pain & sickness are his world.

Let me back up, I'm all over the place. KEMH kept him 2 days. Then they wanted to get rid of him cuz withdrawal isn't "life-threatening" so his insurance won't pay for any more hospital time. The ambulance took him to MAWI, the mental hospital (!). "Policy," they said: he hurt himself so he's crazy, he could do it again or try to hurt other people. Kenji wouldn't hurt a fly, but they wouldn't listen so I followed him to MAWI. Soon those lot were complaining cuz Kenji is so sick, they can't evaluate him like this, they're not trained to deal with "life-threatening illness," KEMH should have kept him. Sigh! Squabbling between the hospitals & insurance co. Kenji ended up discharged from both. I wanted to give everyone a slap upside the head.

Martin was good enough to pick us up. Kenji was severely carsick, M & I practically carried him inside. He was in the bathroom for hours, his body trying to rip itself to shreds, he almost didn't make it to the bedroom before he passed out. We sat with him, watching his breathing.

Me & my husband in the room where K & I made love.

We didn't have a clue what to say to each other.

"You're welcome," said Martin. Stiff as a martyr in a bad religious painting.

"Thank you for taking 5 mins to make a phone call, Martin. Thank you for not turning a blind eye to a fellow human being in trouble."

I don't know why I chose that moment to pick a fight. We did it in whispers, K didn't know a thing, poor sight.

"He really is unbalanced, you know," said Martin.

"& you & I are models of stability."

"Just as an example, he thinks you're Aetna Simmons."

I didn't say anything.

"I think he believed he was doing this for you. To shield you."

I played with one of Kenji's curls.

"You don't have anything to say, Nabilah?"

"What am I supposed to say?"

"Where did he get that idea if he's not seriously out of touch with reality?"

"He's not crazy."

"So?"

"I don't know. You don't have to stay."

"But you will. & it would be inhumane for me not to be OK with that."

"Honey, not now with the sarcasm."

"He'll have to go away. Rehab, you know, abroad."

"Martin, please."

He got fed up & left. But before he went, he whispered in my ear like a cold breeze from a haunted place.

"You lied just now, Nabilah. You know plenty more. He came clean as best he could. But you lied to him too, I bet. Makes me wonder if you know how to do anything but lie. Well, let me tell you something. I may have let you make a fool of me for years, but you & I both know I'll find the truth, you understand? & I mean all of it."

I've never been frightened of my husband before. Never been scared of Kenji either. I am now.

I made sure Martin's car was gone, locked the front door, zoomed to the library. I found that awful Collected Works of Thomas Hardy

& dumped it in a trash bag. I found The Hand of Ethelberta, that's Hardy too. I pulled it out, behind it was the switch, one of those flat switches.

4 shelves full of books swung backwards into a closet. I stood there doing nothing for the longest while, staring at this thing straight out of "Narnia," thinking could this really be the place I'd been coming to for years? The closet was too low to stand up in but quite deep, it went pretty far back into the wall. Inside there was a little lamp & some wooden cabinets. I remembered the key. Right on the kitchen counter where K said it would be, an old-fashioned brass key I'd never seen before. The cabinets were full of small velvety boxes & in the boxes were ugly poisonous shadows of a bright & beautiful stranger.

I went a little crazy when I swept them all away. Each of those tablets was another layer of deception. I ripped a drawer out of a cabinet, turned it upside down over a trash bag, same with the next drawer, every drawer (except the ones full of cash, those made me have to sit down) like I could make a truth out of him with a spring cleaning. I took the trash bags to the dumpster up the road, sealed the closet, sat on the floor with my back to Kenji's books, & cried.

Any minute, I thought, I'll wake up in Kenji's bed, he'll say there's no such thing as Zohytin or Empyreal, just a silly nightmare, Nikkou. He'll hold me in his arms while my heart learns the steady pace of his.

But then the real night came. I got in bed with him. Kenji had a fever & goosebumps at the same time, he was shivering like crazy, spasms arched his back & bent his legs & threw them down again. The internet said I should rub his abdomen "in a circular motion." I did that, he didn't notice. Not asleep, just under fire from inside. My phone found an article called "Brain Injury From O2 Deprivation Following Opioid Overdose."

Brain damage. My sweet genius. A genius regardless of what Harvard had to say. Well, I panicked. I shook him, kissed him, pleaded with him. Kenji came around so slowly! When he opened his eyes, it was like no one was inside them. He said my name but wasn't sure. He looked around, saw the Miró, his breathing became thick & hard, he stiffened everywhere & shut his eyes like he was wishing everything away. I said, "It's OK," & his eyes flew open.

"What're you doing here?"

"We didn't die, Baby, we're home."

Kenji pulled away & turned, I thought he was going to vomit in the trash bin by the bed. But instead he started sobbing! I tried to touch him, he shrugged me off, I tried again & he said, "No Nabi, just go, go now, Nabi, please." I whispered, "It's OK," & Kenji screamed, "I SAID GO! GET AWAY FROM ME!"

I ran out, hid in his study. Kenji cried so much it made him sick. The sounds from out of him hurt something awful inside me.

& that's how both my boys learned to hate me in one day.

I've forgotten how to pray, forgotten how to sleep. Kenji didn't sleep all night, he vomited & vomited, diarrhea & everything. He shooed me if I followed when he staggered to the bathroom. I threw out the bag of vomit in the trash bin by the bed. I put a new bag in, flitted around straining to hear & not hear into the bathroom.

Dawn made everything gray. That corner of the couch where I told Kenji loads of silly things I can't remember. Kenji's desk, his pens, his empty notepad. Kenji's closed-down laptop, the "birthplace" of "Suicide & Suicide Notes," "Document1," & mysterious unfinished drafts—maybes & if-onlys that wouldn't stand a chance without him, & there I was among them. The TV is dark, but it remembers us laughing. The books dream his touch & his excitement. The whole place is hollow & haunted.

"I wonder what to call you." I think maybe he meant me! I'm not like Aetna Simmons, I'm not like Seabird or Martin. Maybe I thought about it in a time of frustration, but I can't run off & abandon people. Kenji should know that already. My phone showed me the Unnamed like it's just another file. Just another couple kilobytes & not Kenji wondering how long he could stand it. I looked for warning signs to beat myself up with. I looked for stuff to make myself feel better. "AccuWeather," stuff like that. I saw how much I didn't see. I saw that this is all her fault.

She knew that book about the girl who reorganized the Bible. I knew it was Hardy's book. I said I have a friend. In one look, she knew all about my friend.

I pretended I hadn't seen the look. I acted like it wasn't a look that saw too much. Not like Martin's "polygraph" look, weirder than that. Or less subtle or something. It wasn't till much later that she admitted that she knew, she'd seen into my heart with that one look. Guess it was her job (!) to pick up on people's secrets without needing to hear much else about them. It wasn't her job to make my Baby "fall in love" with her & lure him into wanting to be nothing but wind over water!

Except it kinda-sorta was her job, luring people into thinking about suicide. Making people think other people wanted to die. She did it to strangers, professionals. Her words were that strong.

But only if you couldn't hear them. Kenji fell under her spell cuz he couldn't hear how scared she really was. She was a "guilty remainder." Scared of being alone, scared of her own emptiness. I know cuz I could hear it. But she turned that fear & emptiness into power with too-long "fleshless" arms like radiation. None of us knew her, & look what she did to us.

Poor K was SO SICK we didn't get a moment's rest this p.m. & I am terrified. Changing the trash bag for the umpteenth time I found myself looking for excuses (!) not to go back in the bedroom, scared of the smell & liquids & convulsions, I mean Kenji's never sick, Martin's never sick, I'm never sick! Panic tries to tell me what's suffering in that bed isn't really Kenji. His head hurts bad, he squeezes it like it's a blister. I'm scared to touch it, scared to hit the stitches, so where I'm touching him isn't really where it hurts. & I know he's the real Kenji, Kenji who knelt at my feet in the Arboretum doesn't notice I'm beside him. Whispering, "It's OK, it'll go away," I'm the one who sounds false.

Was I ever not false & helpless even in my "prayers"? Were they just me pleading with my useless self? Is that the whole story of me & K: "false & helpless," "always already gone"? Just cuz I "signed a contract with Martin in a church," I can't love both them byes with all my heart? Kenji must know better than that. Making himself suffer cuz I don't "belong" to him doesn't make sense. (Do I "belong" to M or God or anybody, aren't I my own self?!) Loving Aetna Simmons cuz she don't belong to him or anybody don't make sense either. Some parts of the Unnamed are for me, but what if that part was for her: "already gone"?

No, K thought I was her. That's my fault. If the real her knew a real man loved her, a good man, she'd get spooked & take off just like she did, I guess. Which one of us does Kenji wish I was? Do I wish she was never born? No plane crash, no suicide notes, no mysterious theft, no Art Of Vanishing, no Seabird? If there'd never been any of that, could K & I have just kept going nicely like we were?

Begging night to end. Like that gray light coming back will make everything OK. Kenji still can't sleep, can't stand the light either. I turned on the bedside lamp like always & he groaned.

"No, turn it off, turn that _____ off. You want to do something, turn off the _____ water heater, I can't stand that _____ noise. (The water heater makes one click twice a day.) & get rid of these _____ sheets, I can't stand it. & on the bookshelf there's—"

Poor Baby couldn't even finish talking, the pains in his stomach & his back are HORRIBLE. They ripped his thought away, even that thought. I held him like we were a snail, I was the shell, I pressed his belly with my hand.

"Quit that & go," Kenji gasped.

"It's gonna be OK. Everything feels bad right now, but it's—"

"I shouldn't feel anything. I shouldn't feel ANYTHING. I shouldn't have to think anything."

He meant cuz he should be dead. My Kenji. Mercy, it's too much. I can't do this, I can't see Kenji like this!

"I couldn't even die."

"Kenji, you mustn't die."

"I couldn't even do that."

"Don't think about it anymore. I love you. Think about that."

Baby turned to me, he was in agony but he tried to wipe my tears away. The emptiness in his eyes filled up with the pain of wishing, his hand shook, I leaned into it & saw him drain out of himself like a soul ditching its earthly shell. His voice sounded like somebody stuck it in the Panashred.

"I asked you to leave me, & I meant it."

"No, Kenji."

"Don't you get it? I can't anymore."

"I need you."

"No you don't. No you don't, Nabi."

He turned away, didn't want me to touch him. The words & tears & kisses I poured onto his shoulder with his back to me obviously seemed empty to him. So I mean he's writhing in pain, I'm wracking my brain for a way to make him choose living, Kenji's fighting to resist everything that has to do with living, "the crew of the Ethelberta" in the most horrible stalemate I can think of, & what makes it worse is that we love each other!

"Stuff in the book. Big Hardy book. Please, Nabi."

"No, Baby, no more of that."

"Please! I'll get it myself."

"Kenji, no, lie still. (Mercy, I haven't told him about Hardy!) Let me do my thing. (Whatever that may be!) I'm scared too, Baby, but—"

"Then go to your saintly all-put-together husband."

"It's not about my husband, Kenji, you wrote, 'What are we?' Well, I don't know, I just know even after I promised before God that Martin's my whole life, I kept coming back to you. 'Acegirl keeps showing up,' you wrote, remember? Even across the ocean I had to hear your voice each day. Even with a good man for a husband, I can't hardly last 3 days without seeing you up close & feeling that you, Kenji, you are here with me."

Maybe the words got buried in my hiccups, I don't know, Baby looked at me like I was babbling Icelandic.

"If you ever loved me, Nabi, bring the book."

Sigh.

I ended up sort of pinning him. It wasn't hard. My leg across his waist is too heavy for him now. I put kisses on his head, my arm across his chest. Kenji gripped my arm like I'm a prison fence. He turned his head away & suffered.

She came to BHS instead of those guys up de country cuz I'm a woman. Like that's supposed to mean I can understand better how to wipe a whole person away & not let it hurt. She comes in my building saying delete this & that, so I say: Sweetie, I know you said no questions, but say we actually succeed at this, what you gonna do once you got no passport, no bank accounts, no birth record, no nothing, once you're dead to the whole world? She didn't answer me.

I don't know what she was thinking, whether it was just about the airplane or she wanted to protect Char Richards that much that she wanted every trace of what they did to "un-happen" (?) or she hated Char Richards so much that she wanted to blow up everything they'd worked for. Did acegirl think her own suicide would somehow make up for the other ones she faked? I don't know, I don't care anymore.

I remember I said, like I'm her "spiritual adviser": Let's think this thru together. Must've hit her up with some Biblical foolishness.

"Pray, Love, Shop, You Go Girl!" Whatever it was, it worked. & it wasn't a big deal, telling somebody keep on breathing when they can't help but keep breathing. "Pray, Love, Don't Give Up," that's just the kind of thing church-loving Furberts do. & now I almost hate myself for it cuz I went off triumphant & made "Seabird" her new life, she's trotting around with her new passport, but I can't think for the life of me what I said to make Aetna Pauline Simmons change her mind about the meaning of "Vanishing," I'm just too much in a panic, so I mean I can't make the man who loves me want to live!

He's lying beside me breathing hard & fast, refusing to look at me, while I scrawl my freakout in my book cuz that's all I can do. Doesn't he remember the drop-off boxes? 40-50 lb apiece, I'm seen him lifting 2 at once cuz he likes to be the one to carry them to Max Sec from out the front just so he can walk past my office & give me a smile. That's not a little thing, I swear I thought Kenji knew it's an amazing thing. So why didn't he write it in "Document1," some example of how strong he is, how strong we are, how our love is always alive everywhere? I try reminding him, "Kenji, you know the drop-off boxes...?" He can't hear me, I don't think. Pain is deafening.

Morning turned the sky the color of a dirty burlap bag. I freaked out till 8:00, left K rolling around, slipped into the hallway, called my GP. "No, not my husband, a close friend." Sigh! Whined about the hospitals & freaked some more till Doc agreed to a house call.

Kenji begged her for Zohytin. He pretended a hospital @USA Rxd it but he'd lost the Rx (!). Doc refused. K begged for Vicodin. She refused, he said Anything!, Doc said Tylenol. I SOSed Iesha, she went to the pharmacy. K was overwrought. Me too, thank you very much! I tried activating my Managing Partner setting. I told Baby (it was true) Doc said I'd have to call the ambulance if he kept refusing fluids or (blubbering again) he could get heart failure (!!!!!) from dehydration.

"Are you threatening me, woman?!"

"No, but Baby you gotta try, blah blah."

"Who the _____ do you think you are, telling me what to etc."

My best friend & lifelong love thinks I'm the Evil One. No one knows how much this hurts. No one.

Supermom Iesha offered to give him what for. She didn't see it'd only make things worse, but thank goodness she backed down. She showed up with hugs & advice & home-fried chicken & Gatorade. She also brought the stuff I'd left at her house & FORGOTTEN when I ran to the hospital with nothing but my phone & trusty book: My briefcase. My laptop. Aetna Simmons' HD clone!!

It looks on the outside like any portable HD, but I almost shrieked when I grabbed it from Iesha. My poor patient sister, she has no idea! I shoved the thing in the cutlery drawer in Baby's kitchen. I turned down Iesha's offer to pray together, I said I hope my nieces never learn to love like me. Iesha must think I'm gone off my head.

Kenji wanted to keep the Tylenol beside the bed, but I said no, no way. He said, "What do you care," & well I'd been had it with the cold shoulder, I took my book & put myself on the couch. I thought: I hate this. I thought: If this was Martin (this would never be Martin), I'd talk everything over with K. Then I panicked cuz I'd left my Baby struggling alone, I rushed to the bedroom, he was curled up in a ball, he shook me off when I touched him: "What can I do? Just tell me what to do."

He didn't answer. All he could think of was Zohytin, I just knew it, & it wasn't fair, but I kept thinking: If you were always already gone…

Martin came to check on me at noon. We sat in the living room & said nothing.

Well, I guess Martin said, "How's he doing?"

Little question like that closed my throat. I shook my head. Tylenol wasn't helping, Kenji couldn't keep it down, I'd spent the morning squeezing his hands against the pain. Truth is I could only hang with Martin cuz everything got so bad Kenji had sort of fainted. Almost gave me a heart attack, but it was the closest thing to sleep he'd had in forever. I leaned close to hear his breathing ("every sound a terror & a treasure"), to hear Kenji breathing & remember him not breathing ("living on the edge of a precipice…").

"How are you doing?" said Martin.

Well! Ya girl was barefoot, my kimono rumpled & soggy, my hair like I'd stuck it in a hurricane, my nerves like I'd stuck them in an electric socket. I was scared to fall asleep, I felt like everything I said & did was the wrong thing, I kept reading in K's Unnamed file that my life wasn't what I thought I'd been living, I was scared to think more than 5 mins into the future, & suddenly I felt it all at the same time. I keeled over on Martin's shoulder like a falling-down tin shack (the kind of shack that don't exist anywhere on this Island!), hugging this set of Kenji's PJs I've started carrying around.

Martin didn't hug me. He was stiff. That's how he gets when he's afraid. He cleared his throat & said, "Well, we've been busy at the office."

The world carried on making money & buying stuff, enjoying sunlight on pink sand while K & I hung in this backbreaking "limbo." I heard a sound, hopped up. Baby was covered in sweat & didn't know a thing, but I dripped some water thru his lips, & as he coughed he moaned something.

Now, Nabi-girl, be fair. You can't be sure what Kenji moaned, it was very weak, poor sight was definitely past thinking. & if he did say what you think he said, it's partly your own fault cuz of the stupid idiotic confusion you started when like a stupid idiot you mixed up your priorities.

Still, did I get vexed. Man, did I get vexed. Cuz I thought Kenji said her name. I mean "Aetna."

I stomped back to the living room with the image of her stupid face burning in my head. If my head had poisoned rocks in it, I'd hurl them at that face. Chances are there's only one other human being alive who's seen that face & knows to connect it with what Aetna Simmons did.

Martin (he's not the one, he never laid eyes on her), staring into space all forlorn, he don't know what Kenji wrote, not "Works Of Art" or the Unnamed. I said Kenji told me (lie, he wrote it) that his brother was involved in this thing with Clocktower, & Nikea had his emails. I said I want to see them.

I know from the HD clone that after the first couple "victims" someone emailed times & places where Aetna went for info on the dead people that she was going to "impersonate." Places like Harbourfront (!), the Arboretum (!!), etc. I didn't say none of this to Martin, I said I want proof that Kenji's own brother conspired with the demon-fish who preyed on my Baby when my back was turned (I didn't say it like that). Martin brought up Nikea's latest update on his phone. ("When do you think you're coming home?" said Martin.) Since Nikea started watching, Erik's been deleting stuff like crazy, shouting out to Brooklyn floozy, but she (floozy) is ignoring him. ("I've told them I'll have to postpone my next trip," said Martin.) I thought: Erik saw her, Erik spoke to her, she was what she was partly cuz of Erik, & when she slipped thru his fingers Erik told Kenji NOT to stop hunting her. "You sure their bosses weren't in on it?" I said.

Martin sighed. "They weren't in on it. But Mrs Caines is dragging her feet on the investigation. We still don't have a contract. It's understandable, I suppose."

Putting it in my book feels like watching myself in a movie starring strangers. I'm appalled at myself now, but at the time I totally wasn't. I thought: Watch yourself, acegirl & said, "Even the police gave up. Maybe there's sides to this that should be left alone."

"Kenji didn't think so."

"He's got no choice now, innit. Honey, if & when you speak to him—"

"I hardly think that's a good idea."

"Well, even later. Don't bring up any of this. It hasn't done him any good."

My voice was too high & crackling like the sound of marbles spilling all over the place. But my husband didn't say, Don't worry, your dearest, dearest friend will pull thru, he's got a good long life ahead of him. Martin said, "I told Mrs Caines what he did up on the hill."

"What'd you have to do that for?"

"He's her son."

"That never made no difference! The last thing Kenji needs is that woman coming around—"

A cry from Kenji's room. I ran, I know this cry, it's what comes with the dream of that woman & the sword & the black books with red tongues, it caused another HORRIBLE attack of throwing up. I had the bright idea of a damp towel for Baby's forehead, but the dampness killed the wrinkly attempt I'd made at bandage-changing. This was a last straw for me, I don't know why, maybe all I could think about was throwing rocks at somebody, but when poor Kenji fell back, panting, I ran out to yell at Martin. "You hear that? That's a lifetime of bad dreams & it's her fault!"

"My guess is it's your fault. You lied to both of us, & he's too carried away to handle it."

The room swam like Martin had kicked me in the face. He said sit down. I sat down gasping on the floor. My poor husband stood stiffly over me.

"I just want all of us to be OK!" I said.

"What about doing the right thing?"

"That's all I ever wanted, Martin, you know that."

"Then tell the truth. If Kenji hasn't lost his mind, why in the world does he believe you're Aetna Simmons? He believes it enough to stake his life on it, Nabilah. If that's some gross delusion, if the man needs psychiatric help—"

"He's hurt, not crazy."

"Is he? Because he came to my office, did you know that? So what

353

I heard with my own ears was either: (A) Kenji in the grip of some dire misapprehension of which you just didn't bother disabusing him because, Jesus save you, all you care about is concealing your own transgressions, or (B) Kenji going seriously insane & spouting demented rubbish."

"No."

That's all I could say. No, Martin, no, Kenji, my sweet genius. It was like something popped inside me. Maybe the imaginary hot air balloon I'd dreamed up to follow Seabird in sometimes. Like my part in what she'd done could float away over the sea & learn spelunking.

If Kenji thought he was insane, if my Baby thought his big bold brain had given out on him, well then he really wouldn't want to live. & I'm sure he saw online in his research, people who try to do like he was trying to do often retry & succeed. The probability is more than 50%. I've checked.

So when Martin cornered me with that, I felt like I really had vomited that hurricane. (I thought: "destruction in creation's name... potential that art shares with death"!) But the truth that spilled out of me in Kenji's empty living room at poor frightened Martin's feet wasn't the whole truth. How could I tell Martin what Kenji wrote & felt, how could I talk about Inspector Bean & Brooklyn skank? Baby didn't write any of that for Martin. I didn't tell the whole truth about Seabird either. I left out one detail.

Besides that I told Martin everything I did. My husband looked at me like I was something on the bottom of his shoe.

"You promised. Nabilah, you swore to me you wouldn't."

"It was already too late. But it was just her, nothing else. Everything I did, it was all to try to help—"

"You abetted a CRIMINAL. You HELPED these PEOPLE commit FRAUD. You PARTICIPATED in the very type of offense that I spend all my waking hours fighting to PREVENT!"

"And what would you do in my place? Turn her away?"

"This could finish me, Nabilah, you're my wife for God's sake."

"Answer me, Martin."

"It's a compulsion with you, isn't it, that's what it is."

"You call yourself a Christian, Martin Furbert—"

"Don't you dare try that with me! Don't you DARE! Did you even give a thought to the people you love? Then again, I guess that's never been priority for you, has it."

Martin walked out & slammed the door, Kenji screamed from the bedroom, "What the _____ is all that racket?! Can't a _____ die in peace in his own _____ house?!! Take it outside, both of you! Get out of here & LEAVE ME THE _____ ALONE!!"

So here's me in the hallway like "a ghost nobody wants." Between the bedroom where my lover didn't want me & the door that slammed when my husband walked out on me. Mid-afternoon & it was dark like end-of-day.

It can't be true what Martin said, that this nightmare of death & pain is all my fault. It's true I didn't say I'm Aetna Simmons just to protect Aetna Simmons. I said it so what I'd done wouldn't unravel: my gallant rescuing, my Artful Vanishing, my shadowy triumph. "Like my Aetna, I am lies stacked upon lies. But the foundations of her lies were death and poetry. The basis of my masquerade is shame." Kenji wrote that. But was it masquerade if I was doing it to help, I mean cuz helping's what I always do, that's how I really am? Would I have let Martin go on thinking Kenji's crazy, Martin who just blabbed to Kenji's relatives? Would I really let my Baby start thinking he's insane just to keep up the illusion that "I'm Aetna Simmons" if Martin hadn't called me on it??!

All I wanted, I mean ALL I wanted, was for one of them to cuddle me & say we're OK. I was ready to believe him, whichever of them did it. Whatever happened after that, I figured I could handle it. But the truth is I'm scared of missing one of Kenji's breaths. I stayed in the hallway cuz I'm scared of messing with them too. If I tell Kenji the truth, it could kill him. If I don't tell him, it could kill him. Hope he plum forgot it all? Really? Wish brain damage or amnesia on my Baby? Now I'm frightened of the one Kenji called "the only one he trusts." I'm frightened cuz he thought that one was me.

355

"Aetna Simmons" who's not Aetna Simmons anymore.

Was she worth it? We learned, we flew thru shadows, we took on the bank & TCD. Seabird was a fun thing. We had a connection. I mean I thought we did. It was me that talked her off the ledge! With the power of prayer & shopping! But maybe it wasn't real, I mean our "connection," me & her. Kenji said to me once with that soft laugh I miss so much, "You wanna know a thing that's awesome about you? Everyone's your friend right up until the moment they've proved they never were. Don't ever change, Nikkou."

Sometimes I think about hunting her down myself: Aetna Simmons, look what you've done, look what you made me do!

She'd say: I'm sorry but you knew the risks. (How was I supposed to know she'd sink her teeth in my Baby?) Or she'd get all up a tree & jump out of it in remorse. (The ledge, remember?) Or she'd take off without saying nothing. (Track record!) Wherever I found her, she'd jump ship & run, knowing I can't tell nobody what we did. (Except apparently a BRMS "Team Leader." Sigh!) Or she'd get sorrowful & say: Won't you let me meet your K, let me tell him it's better to stay alive, all that rah-rah-keep-on-movin stuff you sold me that you can't remember now cuz you can't hardly think of nothing except Kenji not breathing?

Stop ya noize, acegirl, you know "the great impersonator" wouldn't risk that kind of commitment. "The real Aetna, the one who lived and died, she understood that identity's all just words. And that's what she sold you, her ability to not be anyone." Char Richards, that floozy born of Satan, got to hear Kenji say it with his voice. But he wrote it down for me. He wanted me to be the one to think about it. & I think Kenji pegged Aetna Simmons to a tee.

Every time we met up, she tried her best to make sure I wouldn't remember her.

I never noticed it while it was happening, at the time I was just happy to be going in the shadow world, just like a foolish worker bee dipping in a flower. But later when I read stuff like "Aetna in place of Seneca watching the cutie scribe," it popped into my head that "Aetna Simmons" was perfectly, consistently, "Bermudafully" polite when she spoke. She always answered back exactly as you'd expect a decent person to answer back, I mean exactly. Like I think

Baby would say she spoke only in cliches. Phrases everybody uses like…whatever, I can't think of any, but stuff we hear all the time. Stuff that wouldn't stand out. Words that you could never say "Aetna Simmons always says…"

Maybe she really was a polite & decent (?) person who just wasn't creative with words? That's what I would've said to K if he'd come out with this a week ago. But we know Aetna Simmons was creative with words! We know her job was to fade away behind the words. So she had to be unmemorable as herself, right?

That's why I think she never wanted to laugh. Laughing is a thing that's worth remembering. She didn't even like it at 1st when I laughed. But I like laughing, I wanted to make Aetna Simmons laugh. I worked at it. & she did her best to make sure I did the chopsin. That means she must've asked me questions, just not memorable questions. "Nice weekend, then?" Maybe not those words, maybe not even that question, maybe I blabbed about my weekends cuz that's what I do (I need a nap or something, mercy).

If I'd known what she was running from, would I have helped her? I thought I did know what she was running from. No, I knew I didn't know. I knew it wasn't the airplane. Poor thing wouldn't have said "no questions" about the airplane. That was all over the news till I Vanished it from every digital archive. & if it was about the airplane, the theft (somebody robbing her for a change!) wouldn't have mattered.

I didn't know her at all, did I.

4-ish Martin called. Still vexed. I said, "Honey I'm sorry," but he cut me off: "I'm at work, Nabilah." He just wanted to "inform" me that he'd done some digging, & although my "little operation" clearly "had some measure of success" with Aetna's police file, a paper copy still existed, which Martin took to mean that I'd "failed to cross (my) T's as usual," & in fact all my "efforts at concealment" were the kind of thing that he & his team eat for breakfast.

To think I'd been fool enough to hope that after Seabird flew away I could use my shadowy "talents" to help Team Leader with shadowy questions.

"Thank you, Martin," I said in the yawning pause.

After one day working on this, he'd not only found the police file but also found out how it got to where it was & spoken to Commissioner Wallace himself.

"Good for you, Honey."

That made him more vexed. So what he said next was hurtful.

Wallace told Martin that somebody told him that if he made his Inspectors stop investigating Aetna Simmons' death, he could count on a favor from the future Minister of Finance. That would've been a bribe, the commissioner said no. He only canceled the Island-wide search, cutting the investigation short, but that was obviously just to save resources. There was nothing to investigate anyway, he said, cuz clearly Aetna Simmons killed herself. It just didn't hurt that the future M of F (Mr C) so happened to have a firstborn (K) who, according to a "certain source," had an affair with "the Simmons girl" years ago, an affair that "culminated in an illegally terminated pregnancy"!! Martin's words, quoting Wallace, quoting this unnamed "source." None of it is true, Kenji loves me & only me, & besides I know exactly how Aetna Simmons spent her nights, & it wasn't with him! The "source," guess who it was, wanted to save a certain family from any risk of embarrassment as future M of F prepared to hit the campaign trail, where Wallace thought this person deserved a fighting chance. Clearly there was nothing to investigate. So why risk the reputation of good people who wanted to do something worthwhile for Bermuda? Obviously, since Wallace was completely transparent about this with Martin, there was nothing wrong with his decision whatsoever. Some people just amaze me. E.g., who was it, this "source" who MADE UP this horrible malicious evil TOTAL-LY UNTRUE gossip?

Erik-Katsuo Okada-Caines, that's who, the "needy little brother" I'd forced on Kenji weeks ago when "poor Kiki" came crying to my door.

I'm disgusted. So is Martin. He didn't believe the malicious evil totally untrue gossip, he knows Erik was covering himself, but my husband pretended to believe it. He reminded me what Erik said about K & the fish-demon, & that kicked off the biggest argument we've ever had, & sometime Martin said, "Did you ever really love me, Nabilah?"

Really don't need this right now.

"I do love you, Martin."

"Well, he's convinced that you're in love with him."

"Hard to say this to you, Martin, but I do love him."

Confused pause. Poor Honey.

"Have you told him the truth?"

"Not yet. Honey, you're both wonderful people."

Martin laughed! A nasty laugh. "Do you ever mean anything you say?"

"I mean everything I say, thank you, that's why I never promised Kenji anything."

"I beg your pardon. I didn't realize you were free to make promises to him, considering a significant promise you made to me!"

"What about what you promised? Respect & all that—"

"When have I not respected you? I tell everyone how proud I am of you, my wife, a self-made professional. I've always been supportive."

"Supportive, huh?" I recalled the jibes (confetti, etc), my supportive & respectful spouse claimed he'd never jibed, those were "light-hearted aphorisms." I said I beg to differ, things got a little berserk, & he came out with this:

"Maybe I envied you a little, how everything comes easily to you—"

My turn to say, "I beg your pardon." But Martin didn't listen.

"How at ease you are, especially with him, since you know you'll get everything you want. The two of you treating life like it's one big playground. (Not true.) But I never did anything to endanger any part of it, Nabilah."

Oh, Martin.

Silence fell on us like a bunch of overripe coconuts.

"Look, call me if you hear anything. About CAM or, you know, related matters."

"Why are you still looking, Martin? You said Mrs C wasn't interested."

More coconuts. Then he sighed.

"You & I both know I'm a man of integrity. (Me: Of course, I've always admired etc.) No, just listen, Nabilah. Whatever he might be, there's no question that he'd sacrifice everything for you. Other people, his family, self-respect, whatever. Understand? You better make sure you deserve it."

That night everything changed. Putting it in my book will make it more real or less real, I'm not sure. I'm worried that my book, so full of songs & kisses, is getting used to being a burial ground for things that could be demons. But that's why it's gotta take them. Things like the Unfinished Church. Water in Kenji's lungs. Martin running blindly into the night. So they can get out of my head. "Writing's a different kind of thinking." I can't look at my hands when I'm writing.

So let's see. 1st it was: "Are you sure Hardy's empty? You sure you had the right book?" Then I had to tell Kenji I threw the thing away. Baby didn't want nothing to do with me after that. I sat outside his door holding my head while the news destroyed him.

Then the doorbell. Sigh! My face was a mess, my kimono was sweaty & tear-soaked, I couldn't make myself put down Kenji's PJs. I also smelled. But I thought maybe it was Martin. It was evening, about 7:00.

It wasn't Martin.

"Oh no, mochi, you look awful, look at your hair!" Erik tried to hug me, that horrible malicious gossip.

"Kenji can't see nobody! Especially you! Martin told me what you said. Your own brother. The commissioner of all people!"

"Aw, mochi, it's been so hard on you, I can't imagine."

No one else bothered to say that. Not my husband, not my sister, they sort of thought I'd brought it on myself. Not even Kenji. Tears starting already, mercy, my nerves are fried, I needed a hug so bad, & Kiki was Kiki & his hands were shaped like Kenji's, his shoulders too. My head fell on Kiki's shoulder, my face in Kenji's clothes on Kenji's doorstep, Kenji's little brother patted me on the back.

"Mochi, listen. They're on their way. Momma-sama, Motomu-ra-san, my dad, & I've never seen her like this, mochi, I'm telling you. I came early, I drove like lightning to warn my brother, he's gotta be prepared."

Prepared. By Erik. I wriggled away.

"Prepared." Yeah, right. This is the guy (& I'd just let him hug me!) who handed "the impersonator" faces of dead people & instead of owning up about it let his brother hurt himself. "You mean you wanna put your words in Kenji's mouth so he'll go on taking the blame in front of your momma. Well, that in't happenin no more."

"Nabilah-chan, I'm telling you this as your friend. Say what you gotta say to me, but don't go trying to play it tough with them. You're too little. You don't know how. Kenji needs somebody here who knows how to handle them. Now, you gonna let me in or what?"

"No."

Erik laughed. That's when I noticed he was different. Starting with his laugh. He looked the same, slick & colorful in his snazzy suit, & the sun was heading west over our heads, making his gold Bermudiana tiepin sparkle. But his laugh was mostly snort, it rounded out with him sucking his teeth, no giggle in it. So I mean, it wasn't a Kiki laugh. & the way he stood, hands in his pockets. Like they told us not to do at school cuz it messed with the crisp look of our uniforms. Shaking his head at the ocean like the ocean was the "little" one "trying to play it tough." Like Kiki himself wasn't the opposite of tough, jealous of his brother & whiny about it to boot.

Was that why I didn't slam the door in his face, cuz aceboy was so different? Was it cuz I was too chicken to do such an un-Christian thing? Even his voice was different. Lower. Quieter. Not softer, Erik always had a hard voice, hard like a cymbal or a school bell. Now it was hard like ice.

"You know, mochi, soon as I heard Professor K was onto this, I figured he was out to get me. I wanted Char or, you know, somebody to throw him off the trail. But she thought he could lead us to wherever that stupid woman went & disappeared to."

He meant Aetna Simmons. Using my Baby as bait for Aetna Simmons.

Course I had to bite my tongue. Ya boy went on shaking his head at the ocean. "I think she got distracted. Char, I mean. One day you'll have to explain why women fall all over that so-&-so."

"It wasn't about Kenji, just her being a fat old demon who eats everything in sight."

I never would've dreamed Kiki could growl. Kiki-chan who air-kissed the maitre d' with his pinkies sticking out. "Mochi, you don't know _____, OK? Tucked up in your little warehouse round backa-tahn, which my Momma-sama bankrolled from the outset (not true,

362

but I had to let it go), you just don't know what it's like to have to fight thru a world where people don't need reasons for stomping on other people. But a small-island half-breed who's gotta play the global stage, or a black woman with—"

"I'm a black woman. You don't see me going around leaving my shorts on the floor."

"A black woman & a single mom & a lesbian."

"What?! Go head, bye, don't even worry with it."

"Yes, girl, I'm telling you. Char's a divorcee with a feisty little girl, & they hate each other's guts. Besides, Char in't got no Momma-sama to call her own. Her family owns a major, I mean major gospel record label, & they kicked her to the curb when they found out she loved a woman—"

"That in't got nothin to do with nothin."

"Disowned, disavowed, disinherited. Like she never existed. & so, saddest thing ever, mochi, Char started to hate the girl she loved. Later being pregnant made her hate being a girl herself. Now the only one who understands her is me."

"Come on, bye. Boohoo for Brooklyn skank, so she's got a right to steal people's inheritances & poison Kenji with self-hatred? I don't think so."

This acegirl might be a softy but I was down to my last drop of nerve. Char Richards didn't have no "demon's preternatural energy," she told Kenji "we're the same" just to make him think he's as worthless as she is, & whatever "wavelength" she made him think they "cohabited" was just the simple fact that she knew all about him before he even learned her name thanks to the biggest gossip who ever walked the earth! & I was gonna tell Erik about himself, I had my finger sticking out & everything. He was talking over me, sputtering about my use of the word "skank." & those hybrids like the Prius, they don't make a sound when they go slow. That's why we didn't notice the footsteps on the stairs.

Kenji's father: "Nabilah?" (Like I was a surprise. Guess I was, but SIGH!)

Kenji's mother: "At least there's someone watching him."

Me: "I'm sorry, it's not a good time. Kenji can't see anyone."

363

Erik: "Que sera sera, mochi-chan."

Mrs C: "I will see my son."

Mr Motomura bowed at me. Didn't say a word except what he said with his hands: Move aside or else.

I didn't move. I am Kenji's acegirl, Kenji's line of defense, the 1st & last.

Me (pretending like my heart's not stampeding from chest to head & back): "Kenji was in respiratory failure. Technically he's stable now, but he's not out of danger. Dealing with visitors will upset him."

Mr C: "We're not visitors, we're his family."

Me (last drop of nerve): "Well, I'm the one who loves him."

Mr C: "Is that right? Where, may I ask, is your husband?"

Mrs C: "Quiet. There's no need to broadcast our trouble to the world. Nabilah, will you at least let us come in and discuss with you what has happened to my son? Because he's an adult, the hospital is prohibited from giving any information even to his mother."

Me: frazzled hair, naked toes, Kenji's PJs in my fist. I must've looked like a fresh-caught mutt that grew up feral. I started thinking: Mercy, what if E was right & I can't handle them, Masami Oka-da-Caines & her army of angry boys & me, just me? When I looked at E, he shrugged. & Mrs C sounded freakishly reasonable, not angry (unlike me), not frightened (unlike me), & she's always had this power in her voice, this weird energy even when she's quiet (definitely not like me), I can't explain it but I feel it, I feel everybody feeling it.

I only know one person who stood up to it. One skinny little boy never forgot to squeeze my hand to tell me I was safe from it. With the "Co, Ltd" ganging up on me, the empty cavity I was carrying inside felt a whole lot emptier.

I remembered KEMH wouldn't let me stay with him at night cuz I'm not family. I remembered what he wrote & realized that his family has the power to hurt Martin & BHS, but would they? Is Mrs C that sort of person? I got confused, I felt weak with missing Kenji & Martin. Maybe that's how they got in, I don't know, so much else has happened, a whirlpool of things happening so I'm not sure who I am anymore.

Erik pulled out the kitchen stools for his momma & daddy. Kenji's kitchen only has 2 stools. As Mr C sat down, E showed him something on his phone. Mr C shook his head at me & laughed, a snort-laugh just like Erik's not-a-Kiki-laugh, & in a flash I knew what they were looking at.

I remembered my own voice tearing Kenji apart. Remembering it thinned me so I felt like I was just a see-thru surface disguising an empty cavity. I said weakly, "Erik. You sent Martin that picture?"

"Technically that was Char."

"But you told her. Martin's name, Martin's—"

"What picture is this?" Mrs C.

She snapped her fingers twice, E put his phone in her hand. I kissed my Baby in the palm of her hand.

Guess I got a little loud. But how could anyone with feelings strategize like that? All E wanted was to "throw K off the trail," he'd said so. But to scar our love with shame, maybe break it: "That's your idea of a DISTRACTION?! Hoping Kenji & me & Martin gonna be too hurt to care about investment portfolios??!!"

Mr C: "You should be ashamed, young lady. Your husband, too. Instead you're trying to tell me how to run my family."

Mrs C: "Did I not tell you to be quiet?"

Me: "Kiki, look at me."

He looked like an immigration officer in a mean & dirty city. He looked like he didn't care, didn't know me from Adam, colorless & stiff & hating me for all of it. Mercy, there was no Kiki here! The way his eyes glinted, it was almost like there never was! He got his phone back from his momma & said: "Family first."

"Kenji IS your family!!!"

Mrs C: "Nabilah, that's enough."

"But look at what he did!!!"

Kenji, my Kenji—he put his hand on my shoulder.

I spun around & squealed. My Baby came to rescue me! I threw my arms around him, pinning us to the wall that held him up. His eyes were like the windows on a ruined house, empty & packed with ghosts. He had a scary drained-to-the-point-of-going-crazy look intent on the terrible effort of being there. But he was there, right there with me. & the arm that wasn't bracing him against the wall was holding me to protect me. I could feel against my cheek: Kenji's breathing "scurrying thru the labyrinth of horrors," Kenji facing down the woman who'd terrified him all his life, battling death & his own body & the people who'd hurt him so bad, & all for me! I didn't care what those lot thought of us, I held him tight. I wanted to be the thing that held him up.

He said, "Whatever you're doing here, it's got nothing to do with Nabi."

A flicker of fire! A match snatching at a spark in a windy night. It made Kenji squeeze me a little, I know it did! But even if the squeeze was my imagination, the flicker burst my heart like a piñata. I went up on my toes, kissed my Baby on the cheek. Kenji looked at me like I'd stabbed him in the back.

Mrs C: "Kenji, explain what happened, please."

Kenji didn't answer. He looked at me, looked so lost & torn apart the soft strength-giving thing I'd meant to say flew out of my head.

Kenji's daddy: "We've got a special hospital lined up. Switzerland."

Kenji's acegirl: "No, you can't take him away!"

Kenji's brother (!): "Onii-san. Brah, you gotta sit down. Dad, the stool, you gotta let—"

Kenji: "No. No. You threaten Nabi again & I'll—Martin's gonna make you lot wish you were never born."

Kenji's momma: "Calm down & listen. We're here to help you."

"Martin knows everything! Enough to ruin every one of you!" Kenji was shivering like a leaf about to fall. I wedged my shoulder under his shoulder, threw my weight into it. I saw us as he saw us: beaten up & rumpled, panting like something was chasing us thru an uphill maze, us 2 in our soggy sleepwear, bus-stop pink & baby blue, while those lot in their power suits "pressed in on us like labyrinthine walls"!

Mr C: "Who's threatening who, you idiot?"

Mrs C: "Quiet. You will come home with us, Kenji."

Kenji: "Isn't this payback enough?"

Mr C: "You think our wanting to help is payback?"

Kenji: "I in't going nowhere. You gotta kill me first." (!!!!!!)

Mrs C: "All right. Enough." She stood.

Me: squeak of surprise as Kenji gripped my elbow. Like maybe he meant to stuff me between him & the wall or maybe he had no idea that he'd done anything. Then a lot happened at once.

Behind Mrs C, Erik stepped forward. I thought he was gonna touch his momma's rigid shoulder, but he stepped back again, wide-eyed. Mr C: "Bye, you are one mistake after another." Me: "No Baby I miss you!!" Kenji looking at me, Kenji didn't say a word but he was begging me, begging for I don't know what. Confusion like a knife in my belly, Kenji's shoulders sagged & his momma said:

"I've only ever done what is best for you, Kenji. In return, you have disgraced this family, as your father says, one disgrace after another. You've attempted to disgrace my life's work, Caines Asset Management, & you've done so without remorse, without a thought to the consequences for others. You've attempted to do this thing to yourself, fully aware that such an act would stigmatize our family. I'd rather have discussed this when your health is restored, but your refusal to help yourself by allowing anyone to help you, disdaining your family even when you need us most & doing so in the cruelest, basest fashion—"

Me: "Mrs C, this isn't the way—"

Kenji: "It doesn't matter. Get out, all of you."

Mrs C: "When we leave you here, Kenji, it will be for the last time. If that is truly what you wish, you'll no longer be a son to anyone."

Kenji looked at his momma, Masami Okada-Caines looked at her firstborn baby. I tried to tell myself that what I saw flying between them wasn't hate.

Me: "You don't mean that, Mrs C."

Mr C: "Stay out of this."

Kenji: "It doesn't matter." He dropped my elbow, put his hand to his stomach.

Erik: "He messed up your family too. Admit it, Nabilah-chan."

Me: "Not true, Kenji—"

Nobody else heard Kenji gasp. But they must've seen him start to double over slowly, they couldn't have missed the look on Kenji's face that meant he wished his heart would stop right then & there. It didn't help that 3 of us spoke at once:

Me: "Baby, come back to bed."

K: "Go home. Let Martin protect you."

Mrs C: "I'd advise you to keep your remarks to yourself. You too, thru years of thoughtlessness, consistently cause our family to lose face in both our countries."

Kenji looked at her one last time. Mrs C didn't notice, she was talking to Erik (!):

"& this reckless scheme of yours. Dead people, for Heaven's sake! 6 months' suspension, relieved of all accounts, sans remuneration, effective immediately."

Erik! He was sorta smirking, I think he assumed Mrs C was scolding K, but when she mentioned accounts, I bet that smirk fell kerplunk right off his face. Not like I actually saw it, cuz Kenji lurched out of the room. I lurched too, hanging onto him, but at the bathroom door he pushed me back into the hallway. He slammed the door & locked it & threw up.

& Kenji's family? Their voices stalked us all the way. Those lot kept right on squabbling without missing a beat.

"Suspension?" Erik.

"While your brother is reduced to this." Mrs C.

"But I did it for you. For you & Dad & CAM."

Me: banging on the bathroom door (with blubbering).

"It doesn't matter, it doesn't matter!" Kenji choking & retching.

Mr C boomed like a magistrate: "You did it to get in that woman's pants."

?!?!!!

No. NOOOO. Do not need this, I thought. Didn't know whose pants he was talking about & didn't wanna know. With those yucky words in one ear & the sounds of Kenji's PAINFUL self-rejection in the other, I dashed to the kitchen to get rid of those heartless people.

Mrs C: "Will you be quiet? You insist on making preemptive remarks, but I assure you their shock value is nullified by their vulgarity. One more outburst & you'll be waiting in the car."

She meant Mr C! He didn't say nothing, Mrs C was dangerously vexed. She didn't look vexed, mind you, & if I didn't know English & just listened to her voice I wouldn't have thought she sounded vexed. It's just the words, like Baby wrote, a "torrent of words" from Mrs C means she is way past vexed & into rage. & she had more to say:

"If I have permitted you—without putting a stop to your ridiculous playacting, without even making comment—to abuse every homosexual stereotype (now she meant Erik!), I did so for one reason alone, though it was clearly a mistake. Do you know what that reason is? It is that your duty as my son is to continue the Okada line. I trusted your ability to win Char Richards as you obviously hoped to do—"

"My God, how'd you even—" Erik, so shocked he had to whisper.

"I'm not blind, Erik-Katsuo. In fact it seems I am the only person here who is capable of seeing past the end of their own nose. You have not only failed in your filial duty, you've permitted Char's corruption to blacken your ambitions at terrible risk to CAM. Your comportment as a giggling buffoon damages our menboku every time you are seen in the conservative streets of Hamilton or Tokyo. You know this, Katsuo."

"But okaa-san, I never wanted to deceive you! (Sigh! & if it wasn't for that hug I wouldn't have let E finish, but he needed to get this out & clearly Mrs C did too, & OK so the idea of interrupting when Mrs C was dangerously vexed plain petrified me.) I just wanted to show Char that even in Bermuda you can find the courage to love who you want to love. Seriously, that's all I wanted. You know, with all the boys. But if Char found it in her to let me into her heart (like an everything-eating demon's got one of those), I'd dump whatever boy & go on & love Char Richards like she deserves to be loved."

E's voice was full of feeling. Not intense enough to be like K's but just enough to make me think of Kenji's voice & how this HELL that he is going thru is just DESTROYING IT. It hurt so bad to think about it, what with Baby spewing his guts out & nobody in his family even noticing he was gone.

So yeah I know this was a big moment for E & all. Ripping off the Kiki costume that fooled even me & K. Going public with his "love" for fish-demons. Getting suspended & learning from his momma even the "golden boy" can mess things up big-time. Not to mention finding out that she'd been watching superspy-style to the point that she knew the Kiki costume was a costume… And yeah all this prbly said a lot about K's momma. (She said to E: "All your posturing & caricaturing demonstrates a disgustingly veiled disrespect for sexual

369

difference. This despite the trouble I took to have you somewhat liberally educated.") Real instructive & all that, sure.

But at that point all I heard was Erik not saying a word when his father lashed out over our picture. I said, "All that pretending just to tell that blankety-blank that she can love whoever, & she in't even here to help you take the heat. But you want me to feel ashamed for loving Kenji, enough to let her so-so picture ruin our lifelong—"

"Quiet." Mrs C. I went quiet.

But I have never been so angry. I felt like something huge that's caught on fire. Like a building. Something you want to get out of the way of when it's caught on fire & only defiance is keeping it upright. I prbly looked like a strangled chicken, I sounded like a strangled chicken, that's why they all looked at me. Erik looked disoriented & sort of compressed. I think he would've said something or maybe thought of saying something, but his momma said, "Go sit in the car."

E & Mr C went to sit in the car. They didn't look at me, didn't say nothing. E looked miserable & shocked. Mr C, I have to say he looked relieved. Mrs C said a word in Japanese, & I guess Mr Motomura went to sit in the car too.

To be honest, I didn't see them leave the flat, I assumed they did cuz Mrs C is Mrs C & I stood aside to let them leave the kitchen. But as soon as they'd done that, ya girl was at the bathroom door, "Baby let me in," burning cuz of all that he'd endured all for me, words that nobody's baby should ever have to endure. I had my forehead & my shaky hands pressing the door. Kenji was still being frighteningly sick. I tried to melt the door with tears. Then I felt something beside me.

Mrs C slid up without making a sound. She didn't touch the door-knob, I was squeezing the doorknob, but she lifted her hand. She put her hand on the door.

So it was me & Masami Okada-Caines, a closed door, & the sounds of suffering.

I forgave her a little. For a sec. There was pain in the way she held her mouth, fear in the shiver of her forehead. When Kenji retched, she blinked & it was like a wince.

I said, "You & Mr C gotta give Kenji a chance. Take some time, try to understand."

"If he would allow us, I'm certain we'd understand."

"But see, it's complicated."

"Yes. He's fortunate to have you as a friend."

Much good was it doing him, I thought. Mrs C dropped her hand & turned to me.

"Nabilah, how much do you know about this business with Char Richards, these so-called documents..."

"Aetna Simmons," I said, feeling sapped.

"You must understand. It puts me in a difficult situation. It wouldn't do for the scheme to continue. Especially in the event that he (she meant Kenji) went somewhere with his accusations. But I cannot simply go to my contact at Clocktower & claim that one of his VPs is defrauding their clients & embezzling on the company's behalf. I cannot accuse his people of trying to use my firm as a so-called laundromat for ill-gotten gains. As my husband would point out, people are already too eager to believe that Bermudians are capable of nothing else."

"That's beside the point now, Mrs C."

"Indeed. My concern is different. If I emulated his finger-pointing tactics, Clocktower would have no choice but to mount an internal investigation or hire a firm like BRMS to do so, in which case the inquiry would doubtlessly be successful. Char would never work again, CAM would lose Clocktower's portfolio. If he went public with this, the same results would issue."

(She never said, not once, but she meant Kenji.)

"In neither case could I appear to condone fraud because of nepotism. I'd have to fire Katsuo."

"That's kinda how it should be, isn't it?"

"Is it? Well, you're not a mother. If you tried to think as though you were, would you be able to punish your son for wooing Clocktower in order to please you & propel his father's ambitions? Would you alienate your child for that? If it meant not just destroying his career but also turning him out of your house, publicly denouncing him, & distancing yourself from him, could you bring yourself to do it? My clientele would expect no less of me. Do you understand?"

"Not really." (Couldn't tell if Baby was coughing or sobbing.)

"Although Katsuo's actions were deleterious to some, his intentions were noble. & I must think of CAM. It's a private company, & it's going to stay that way. Someone has to carry on. I've been preparing Katsuo for years. There's no one else. Our colleagues need not learn the reason for his sudden absence. The other thing must simply be forgotten."

"But that's not fair."

"Katsuo must endure his suspension. As I will have to endure it. At first I considered excising both sons from the family register in Tokyo. Both of them set out to ruin me. Perhaps it would be best if history believed I never produced children. I changed my mind however."

"You're still a mother."

"Exactly. It would be too much. But he (still Kenji) obviously desires that his family should be excised from his life. Far be it from me to dishonor such impassioned arguments as those he made tonight."

She had a little frown, that's it.

"Do you understand, Nabilah?"

I was too shocked to say anything, I just shook my head. What with everything else, I can't remember what she said next, maybe nothing. I keep seeing her walk away, her perfect haircut & gray suit getting smaller & smaller.

Courage, acegirl. Baby's got a fat lotta nobody on his side.

All these "visitations" were HORRIBLE for K. He unlocked the door but couldn't get up from the floor. He sat opposite the toilet, his head against the wall. The instant I barged in I threw myself down & hugged him, Kenji gasped cuz of how hard I hugged, & I know I'm the most pathetic female on this earth, but I hung onto whatever I could reach of him. He was burning up with fever, my head felt like I was ready for a straitjacket. "Baby, let's call the hospital. I'll go with you, it'll be OK. You're not alone, Kenji, OK?"

"Go home. It doesn't matter." His voice was almost gone. It made me think how easy it could be to lose him, how I almost did lose him to Aetna & Char, other people's ambitions, & The Last Loss that means lost forever!

"What're you talking about, 'doesn't matter'? Kenji, listen. Don't leave me. You dragged yourself out to get me cuz you know I can't make it without you."

Never thought of Kenji all drastic like that before. He started pushing me away, he wouldn't let me kiss him! Then his hand was a claw at the back of my head, pushing my head against his chest where his hectic breaths went in. & isn't this how it's been forever, us 2 clinging to each other despite ourselves?

"I can't go on like this, Nabi. (Oh, Baby.) I keep telling you it won't make a bit of difference."

"Everyone's just scared. Your family didn't mean those hurtful things. But whatever. I'm gonna take care of you."

"Yeah, you say that, but you…"

"You think I don't mean it, Kenji??!!"

"You're better off without me. A junkie weighing you down."

This is what the man says while he's passing his fingers nice & gentle thru my hair. Then doing it again & again so I'd feel like I matter. I couldn't understand how he could just not believe me! I could only think about terror of being without him. I cried, "Forget the junk. You know what I learned out there, Baby? I am not no 'courageous & decisive spirit turning terror into courage.' Yes, Baby, I read it all. But you didn't write it all. You remember once we couldn't help it even though it was Thursday? I called you to come get me & we watched that scary movie but I was a fraidy cat & hid behind your hand, & you laughed real soft, remember? You asked

373

should we turn it off & I said no cuz all the screaming & chainsawing & carrying on was raining down on us & it was totally OK for me to be the silly fraidy cat I really am instead of Managing Partner, lead soprano, steady wife, computer guru, whatever else. It was OK cuz you were with me, Kenji. You remember? Well, I am nothing but that fraidy cat. Those other things, they're just 'crumbling facades,' all I've been doing for however long is running from one to the other to the next & back. Except when I'm with you. Kenji, I'm nothing except with you."

I was too loud, Kenji wouldn't let me look at him, I didn't mean to compare the O-C family to a slasher movie, it just bumbled out.

"I've got to get out of your way, that's all, Nabi."

"Kenji, I'm telling you I can't lose you."

"It was just a movie, Nabi!"

"Kenji. Kenji, why won't you hear me?"

"Let me go. You have to."

But he buried his face in my hair, & I felt him fighting exhaustion & how hard it was, for the first time I understood how hard, how much I never understood even though it happened in my arms & kept on happening. I kept hearing the way Kenji said "Martin" in front of everyone, I felt Kenji's hands clinging to my back & faltering, Kenji too afraid to hear my voice. I kept seeing him backed up against the wall, fighting to stand still & not collapse in his own kitchen. & all this time, that's what it was like for him, holding us together by deferring & deferring, like his own feelings didn't matter just cuz Martin's family. The labor of being there for me.

We gave up trying to leave the bathroom. Something like 11 p.m., poor K was almost screaming with the stomach cramps, & the doorbell yet again! I wasn't planning on answering, but the so-&-so kept ringing. I ran out to scream at whoever.

Didn't think of Martin. Figured he was still vexed. I threw open the door & we looked at each other. The night, the outdoor sconce above his head, dark kitchen behind me, the horror of my hair, my terrified look…Martin's terrified look, I must've given him a fright. I thought I whispered, Honey save us! Then I figured out I hadn't, I was relieved that I hadn't, I realized I was losing more marbles by the minute, & I sort of "fell into his arms."

Martin said, "Lord forgive us." & kissed me, a big kiss. A passionate kiss. I needed this. Yes. I kissed him back.

It shouldn't be wrong to love any other living thing. But it is sometimes.

"Come in," I said softly.

Martin wanted to kiss me again. There in Kenji's kitchen. I don't know what I thought I wanted. I made him sit on a stool, I mean Martin. He looked stunned.

Martin in the car, Martin in the church, Martin opening the oven, Martin at a harbor-side table in the sun, Martin on the beach under the stars, Martin in our bed asleep…

I checked the bathroom. Kenji sprawled in the empty jacuzzi with his eyes closed, breathing quick & shallow. I left the door open.

I offered to make my husband a cup of tea. It seemed like a sane-ish thing to do. Poor Honey still looked stunned, his tie was balled up in his pocket. "Any improvement?"

The naked hope in his face had nothing to do with K. I felt mixed up & messed up, I fiddled with the kettle & asked why he wasn't home in bed (I mean Martin). Honey'd left his blazer someplace, he looked at his shoes, & I knew that rigid-shouldered pose. He was thinking of a prayer.

He took a breath. He looked at me. My Martin. He said he'd found Doreen Trimm-Eastbridge (PhD). He'd left her a message & she'd flown to Bermuda. Like, the same day. This evening, 8:30, she's tapping on his door.

I imagine this small frumpy white lady with the puffy face in the buzzing offices of Martin's team. It's after hours, they're going strong. Cheap suit, too tight on her. It's wrinkled cause she's just stepped off the plane. If Martin is a kiskadee, sleek & shrewd & courageous, then Dr Eastbridge is a sparrow. I bet she's trying to sound English & forget that she's Bermudian. She says something stiff & formal such as: I am here pursuant to your inquiry concerning Aetna Simmons, but she's actually freaking out. Martin offers her a chair & a look that says: competence, reliability.

Here's what she told Martin.

Even before Martin got in touch with her, Dr E heard from her cousin, Neil Ingham (Private Constable), that "somebody" was asking questions about Aetna Simmons. "Somebody" said he was writing a book, but cousin Neil had doubts about this "book" cuz this "certain somebody" was the son of a CEO & potential MP. Few weeks later, a certain corporate investigator emailed Dr E about the same thing, & she got even more suspicious. She decided to come home & find out what her momma had gotten herself into.

Martin said something like: Forgive me, Dr E, but you don't seem too surprised. You really think your mother had it in her to be part of something "underhanded"?

I think Dr E was thinking that's for true & take her that. But she didn't say so. She got a frumpy white lady's version of the look that Kenji gets when anybody points out something that's been obvious to him for donkey's. She said, "Why do you think I became a criminal psychologist? To try to understand her."

At first this seemed extreme to Martin cuz poor old Mrs Trimm was never formally accused of any crime. But soon he understood where Dr E was coming from. Since she felt like she could trust him, Dr E told him things her momma said over the years.

From the beginning, Mrs T sensed something strange about the tenant in the cottage. A sort of oddness stank out of the place that the tenant rarely left & nobody visited. Mrs T told Dr E: Czarina didn't like it. Dr E is sensible & ignored this. She told her momma to leave the tenant be. That might be why Mrs T became a thief: she resented Dr E trying to tell her what to do (Dr E's opinion). Mrs T went fishing & bragged when she hooked something (talk about poky snobers): the woman poked underneath her tenant's mattress! Martin said Dr E said her momma told her that she found enough paper under that mattress to stuff a couch. Prbly exaggerating, I mean Dr E never got to see it for herself, but the papers, the documents, were neatly laid out between the mattress & box spring, one beside the other & plenty of them too. If a couple walked away (thought Mrs T), nobody would notice. She stole 10. 10 papers. 10 suicide notes.

Now, in Dr E's professional opinion, somebody who sleeps on a bed of suicide notes prbly needs help. In fact years before, when Mrs T described the guy who brought the tenant to the cottage for the first time (Erik), Dr E guessed he got stuck with a "balmy relative" & chose the cottage in St G as "discreet storage" for this person (Martin's words). Mrs T thought there was more to it than that, but Dr E didn't want to hear it. She thought it wasn't a landlady's place to do or say nothing one way or the other.

So when her momma invaded the tenant's privacy & made off with her stuff, Dr E hit the ceiling. She reminded Mrs T of the time the cops came: Mrs T decked (!!) a garbage man who tried to take the dead stuffed cat off her doorstep. She got off with a warning cuz she's old & Dr E called in. But this time, Dr E said, you get caught with stolen property, I'ma let de man deal wif you (man meaning cops). Actually she said (I mean Dr E told Martin) that she couldn't lie & pretend her momma hadn't told her what she'd done. She'd confessed to a crime, & Dr E had a professional reputation to consider.

So Aetna vanished, Mrs T got scared. She thought Aetna was hiding from something way worse than embarrassment. She called the police but feared that they or "other people" might find the documents she stole & start asking questions. So she took the suicide notes back to the cottage.

Why didn't she put them right back where she found them? Cuz when she looked under the mattress (which was neatly made up), the rest of the papers were gone. Mrs T figured poor Aetna found her out & hid them someplace else. She searched the cottage but didn't find nothing. She called the phone number Erik gave her but could only leave a vmail, tried going thru the CAM switchboard but could only leave a vmail for his secretary. & after that she didn't know what to do, the cops were on their way, she was all up a tree. So she dropped the 10 on the edge of Aetna's desk & went to meet the cruiser at the top of her driveway.

Except for the bits that made the news, Dr E has no idea what her momma said to the police. She heard K & M were on the case & flew home. That's how she learned someone broke into her late momma's house & "absconded" with several "prized possessions." (She says "prized possessions" like it's a set of antique china she's talking about, not a houseful of dead cats. & the woman calls herself a shrink.) Dr E's "instincts" as a criminologist made her wonder if these "happenstances" might be connected. The taxi driver who brought her from the airport was waiting to make sure she got inside OK, so Dr E got right back in his van & rode it into town. She went to Martin for advice.

Honey likes giving advice. He's good at it. He also believes in justice. Not the better-build-an-ark kind of justice but the kind that goes with kindness & humility. He's not a policeman, which means he can be free with the second kind.

So he didn't let it show that he was mad enough to want to call Mrs T "a nosy dirty-fingered pond frog." He didn't tell Dr E that what her momma did wrecked a bunch of strangers' mixed-up lives & destroyed my beloved genius. He didn't wag his finger & inform Dr E that her 80-something-yr-old momma was part of a den of thieves & an extortionist who drove her poor tenant to "drastic & foolhardy criminal behavior." He felt no matter how much evidence he uncovered, he'd find it impossible to expose the truth anyway. He kept that to himself too.

He said, "Your mother is with God. Pray for her. A lot."

That's all. Course Dr E's not stupid, just confused & (said Martin) "full of undefined guilt." She sensed that he knew more & wanted him to share it: "CAM sent two top executives to my mother's funeral when I wouldn't spare the time. They sent their son [K] to learn what she was about. Whereas when she was alive, she tried to tell me & I wouldn't listen."

Martin was sympathetic to Dr E but refused to give her any details of his investigation. It's off-record anyway. He didn't tell her that either.

"She really did die of a stroke. I checked," I said.

Honey didn't ask what I meant by "checked." His mouth moved, his voice didn't. Poor sight. I asked him (again) why he continued to investigate at all. He said a lot remained at stake.

He said (I kid you not), "How else am I going to get to know you?"

What's a wife supposed to say to that? My husband was miserable. But well, I was miserabler.

"Do you realize what this means? (Martin's panicky little chuckle gave me not-nice goosebumps.) All this nonsense stemmed from a bored old lady's meddling. All of this, that's all it boils down to, just a meaningless, misguided—"

"No Martin, that's not true."

Martin hasn't read what Kenji wrote, what Aetna wrote, what I wrote, Martin hasn't seen my book. But if he had, he'd know why I can't believe all we've been thru is just "nonsense." Guess Baby did mention the "meaninglessness of suffering" according to his favorite dead white Brit. But thinking about that "meaninglessness" & thinking about Kenji, Kenji's family, what Kenji did & what it cost him, I just couldn't do it, I couldn't let those words in. Honey tried to argue about "purpose" & "waste" (not like him, too philosophical!) but I had to cut him off: "I disagree, Martin, & that's it. Look, I'm sorry, it's not your fault, but I'm got no more tears in me right now, it's not that I don't want to talk, but...tomorrow, all right, Honey?"

"But I'm not finished," said Martin. Like a little scream.

"Keep your voice down." I turned to go & close the bathroom door.

Guess Martin thought my turning was trying to say something, I don't know. I don't know what the frig I was thinking at that point, but I went down the hall & Martin followed me. He didn't know poor K was in the bathroom. He grabbed my hand & spun me (I mean Martin).

"Nabilah, when are you coming home?"

& he didn't keep his voice down. He was distraught.

"You just asked me that yesterday. No, this morning," I whispered. Frantic & stupid.

"Yes, well, I want to know," not-whispered Martin.

"Well Honey, I don't know, I mean, he's—"

"Then I'll stay here. We can both stay until he—"

"Martin," I said.

Midnight in that apartment & I was a hopeless mess. I heard Kenji turn on the water in the jacuzzi.

"Martin, you really still want me?"

"Of course I do. I love you, & you know it."

He had my hand, he had my arms. My elbows. Around my waist. My husband. I stared at him like the most vacant-headed ninny that Superman ever plucked out of the flames. He drew me close.

"For he has rescued us from the dominion of darkness and brought us into the kingdom of the God he loves, in whom we have redemption, the forgiveness of sins."

I am a selfish woman.

I am silly & weak.

I am a hot air balloon goin shru de trees.

I thought I wanted to be free like the air.

Sometimes what I think just isn't the main thing. I guess I never really appreciated that.

I absolutely meant to bawl some more & beg for comfort. But when I went in the bathroom, I didn't see Kenji.

I saw water.

Water turning the floor into an ocean. Water pouring out in waterfalls like when the ocean fills a crater in a reef & then escapes.

I saw Kenji's hands. Curling at the edge of the jacuzzi. Pushing, pushing up to push his body down into the water. & he was weak enough, it wouldn't take much, all he had to do was breathe while he was underwater. I couldn't even scream, I was just thinking WATER, & I think I saw him do it, I saw the water sort of convulse & I plunged in & I grabbed him, my Kenji, my love all my life, he fought me, he resisted me! We thrashed, we banged the tub & faucets, I ended up grabbing his hair, his chin, hauling like CRAZY till I pulled Kenji's head & arms & shoulders clear out of the water & he hung over the edge, water gushing out of him. I grabbed his armpit so he couldn't sink, I turned off all the faucets, I pounded Kenji in the back with my 2 fists while Kenji hacked & heaved the water out. & while I pounded I was screeching like a madwoman.

"ARE YOU TRYING TO KILL ME IS THAT WHAT YOU WANT KENJI?!"

"Go! If you ever gave a flying fuck about me!"

"NO I WON'T GO KENJI!!"

"Please! You will anyway. You have to. You promised him, I know you did, & I can't do it anymore!"

Selfish woman.

Martin drew me close. I mean before. Out in the hallway. I put my hand on his chest. I said, "I need to think. I need some time."

I think that's when the real bad feeling started. Cuz I prbly knew deep down: time's exactly what I didn't have. Martin & I were right outside the flippin bathroom, & he (I mean Martin) never did get around to whispering. He cried, "How much time, how long?" & I thought of Kenji falling for how many years. The bad feeling was a chill behind my eyes & in my throat.

"Can you be patient, Honey?" I mewed. I steered him gently toward the front door.

"But what's to think about? I don't, I mean, I guess…all right."

He wilted. Martin never wilts.

"Thanks, Honey, thank you so much. Now go on home, OK? I've gotta check."

I turned & left my husband to let himself out. & while poor Martin ran blindly into the night (I found the front door hanging open later), poor Kenji went in the water, the water rushed into him, & I plunged into the water, I ripped the drain plug out, ripped off my wedding ring, my engagement ring, I threw them in the water, the water falling away, my rings ran down the drain with all the water. & I said, "Look!" & I said, "LOOK!"

Kenji looked at the water tumbling down the hole. I grabbed his head & turned it, I felt myself cracking.

"Kenji, come back, come now, come quick!"

"Why did you do that? You shouldn't have done that. Why did you do that, Nabi?"

"Cuz I wanna live!" I wailed.

"But Martin."

"Sent him home."

"But he's your family, he'd take care of you. I can't. I can't do anything."

"Yes you can. You're my safe place, Kenji."

"You don't even know me."

"Yes I do. I love you."

"But what does that mean? We keep lying about who we are, we don't know, I don't know who you are, if all we know is that we're liars maybe nothing we say means anything ever. Even if what you said means something, it doesn't solve anything, I mean LOOK AT ME!! & what if it doesn't mean anything?!!" Mercy, he was shrieking.

"But you know it's true. Even if we never said it, we would know it's true. I know you know that, Kenji." I made him look in my eyes. I had a clamp-grip round his underarm & the back of his neck, I risked one hand. I touched his cheek.

He dropped his head. So I couldn't see his face no more, only his dripping curls, his shoulders shaking.

& then he gave a racking cry of rage cuz he knew that what I said was TRUE & even suicidal courage might just have to cave to it. The cry left him panting with defeated little moans, it left my insides twisted up & scarred.

But I held the back of his neck as tight as I dared, I said, "You're right just loving by itself don't fix nothing. But don't it mean we're strong enough to take a shot at getting better? We gotta trust it, Baby, trust each other, not lie anymore."

Soaked & shuddering & wheezing, I mean both of us. Kenji didn't lift his head, didn't pull away either. & then his smashed-up voice:

"Not out of pity, Nabi."

"No, Kenji."

"& I mean, you'll stay?"

"I'll stay."

"Meaning like you won't leave?" Almost screaming again.

"I won't leave, Kenji."

"Don't do it just to keep me here."

"How about cuz life without you never existed for me & never will. No more falling, Kenji. Hold onto me."

Now he let me lift his head. I'll never forget that look, Kenji looking at me like he couldn't process what he was seeing, my beautiful broken genius. I felt the crack in me break open into zillions of cracks. Then I was a bawling heap of rubble in Kenji's lap in the jacuzzi, kimono & all, my Kenji sobbing violently into my shoulder as the water tumbled down the drain, so much lost time.

A ring's just a symbol. A seriously expensive symbol but just a symbol. Martin hasn't called today. Prbly still bleeding from last night. Nobody from Kenji's family called either, & that gets to me. I keep hearing Mrs C say that impossible thing to him, I know my family would've tied up all the airwaves with apologies. I worry what it's doing to K inside, but he hasn't mentioned it.

I'm the one he's worried about. Sometimes Baby looks at me like he's not sure he's not looking at a ghost.

But when he feels bad, he reaches for me on purpose. He let me talk him into sipping water too.

I don't know what I'll do later. Trying not to think about it.

A new day was almost gone when I woke up. Fresh sheets, clean PJs, Kenji's head on my shoulder. & I know my Baby's breathing, I know how it feels to hold him when he's fast asleep, & right then that feeling was better than anything I'd ever felt, I even cried, it was so good. Then I tried pretending this was any other Monday, maybe the Queen's Birthday so we could stay in bed.

But my Love had a week-old beard. Totally not like Kenji. I woke up cuz he sighed & it tickled. He'd lost weight, under his eyes were the salt traces of tears. My rings weren't on the nightstand where I put them.

No, this wasn't just any Monday (or Wednesday or whatever it is). This was the 1st day after Kenji, my Love who wanted to die cuz of me, ended up having to choose to live. Also cuz of me. That's not something you can just sleep thru. & the black fuzz on his face reminded me how fragile Baby's always been. Just a little brush by time changes the whole shape & texture & color of his face every single day.

So! This acegirl had things to do. Didn't know what they were, but I knew they couldn't wait. Baby kept on sleeping when I slipped out. I did some mopping in the bathroom, but halfway thru what I was doing I zoomed to the kitchen, grabbed everything that's sharp, all the knives & forks & the thing that spins inside the blender, & then Aetna Simmons' HD clone popped up in the spoon drawer! Mercy, I'd forgotten all about it, I dashed around the kitchen trying to figure out where to put it, I hid it in the most unlikely place. My heart kicking up a racket, I zoomed to the living room & locked the cutlery in the secret cabinet that used to have the drugs in it. I in't writing where I put the key, so duneenwurrywifit! I zoomed thru all the other rooms prowling for stuff that hurts, stashing a letter opener, a stapler, all our razors. I stood in the hallway fanning myself with my hand. I wracked my brain for stuff to batten down or purge. Like my blood was all up in my head & on the run.

I don't know what made me think of BHS. For a while there (2 weeks-ish?) it was like I'd forgot my "enterprise" existed! I zoomed around looking for my phone, found it in the hallway in a corner on the floor. Wayneesha burst into tears & I did too.

I said Kenji's real sick, I said hospital sick, I said I can't leave him, today's only his 3rd day home. Wayn said the psychiatrist said no, abortion's illegal without a yes from a psychiatrist, & what with the high-tension adrenaline zooming around in me I found myself promising to lend her $ to go to NY for a weekend, find a clinic, & do what she had to do if it was really what she wanted, but she had to step up to the plate for us.

"Interim Manager. Dr Caines says you can do it." Baby hadn't said that, but he'd written something like it. Wayn jumped at it of course. "Don't you let us down now, acegirl. Now look, I gotta go." I heard a swish from the bedroom.

"Wait, Mrs Furbert, tell Dr Caines we're praying for him, see? Bryan just came in & you know how I write down what you say, so he saw. He says he's gonna light a candle at his church."

If anybody's up there looking at candles, I'd just as soon "They" keep "Their" hands off my Baby, considering how well "They've" done for him so far. I didn't say that. I said a nice thank you.

The swish was Kenji turning over in the bed, looking for me. I tried to keep regret & fear out of our long look. Baby couldn't manage that no more, keeping stuff out. So even the way we kissed had changed. Cuz now I knew he'd never kissed me without regret & fear, I had to make each touch more reassuring & steady, more complicated than I love you desperately, please stay!, which (face it, acegirl) when I lay down & kissed my lifelong love, was really all I could think of. Kenji let me do it, Kenji kissed me back at last! But he whispered, "I can't ask you anything now. It wouldn't be fair to you."

386

I knew the thing he meant. Thinking about it made me panicky again. (CHECK: bug spray, cleaning fluids, hide keys for bike & car, anything that could be rope.) Baby didn't mean we need anyone to tell us it's OK to love each other, he meant he's too afraid to ask me to count on him for the future. Too afraid of himself. Cuz he's not counting on himself! I kissed him in a panicky way that I knew would freak him out eventually. So we cut it out. Kenji slept. & I thought, holding him: How did we get so afraid?

Maybe it wasn't fair, but I homed in on Aetna Simmons.

"Aetna Simmons." The idea that wasn't an actual girl that gave Kenji the "courage" to leave me forever, to face the pain & terror of dying & whatever (maybe nothing!) comes after that, & killed his courage for doing anything else, even thinking about the future.

"Aetna Simmons." The actual human who legally in't got that name no more, who's gone off traipsing God knows where, she did that to my Baby by choosing the words she chose, selling them like she did, & not hanging around to answer for it when the chips were down. Instead she talked me into making her an "Unsolved Mystery," luring my delicate Love into her clutches long after she'd quit caring whatever the Hell happened to whoever got in her clutches! I bet she don't even know you can get "Heart Failure From Physical & Emotional Stress During Opioid Withdrawal" (!!!!!!). Bet if she knew, she wouldn't care.

Sometimes I think I should call the FBI. Or whatever. But that's stupid. Healing's more important. Getting Kenji to want the living kind of courage. His eyes half-opened (not for long) cuz he felt how my touch changed when that girl got in my head. & I thought all in a flash: I'm gotta throw away that weapon too, I'm gotta rip the saw out that chainsaw. Acegirl, you gotta show Kenji that there was no courage in what that woman did, what she did wasn't suicide. & that's just for starters.

She tried not to be remembered. But I do remember.

It was winter, so it was already dark. Everyone was gone. Then came the stranger with our Yellow Pages ad. Just so happened I was poking round Wayn's desk for something.

She didn't say nothing, we just looked at each other. But with that look, Jesus (I thought) let me know she was a nice lady in trouble. So here went Smiley-Face: "How can I help you?" She was scared but I was patient. We stayed in my office talking till my husband got worried & called.

After that, when we met up, I told my boys I was figuring out a new billing system, & billing can't be done off-site cuz of security (true). Neither of my sweeties minded driving in to pick me up however late. She must've passed them on the street, walking to the bus. Maybe sometime Kenji's headlights tripped over her shadow.

She was shy, but we got comfy quick so we could focus. We had a job to do, & at first we didn't have a clue, but she didn't mind trial & error. She had a sad smile.

All I had to do was what I did every day. No different from destroying other people's voided checks, expired memos. Just like Bookmart had no use for last year's waybills, Island Press had to bury all those fliers that forgot the "er" in "Masterworks," soon BELCO wouldn't need to know about her anymore. She'd just be excess data in HSBC's computer. Same job but with computers. In their shadow world.

It wasn't the same. Thanks to the shadows, it wasn't a job. It was burrowing into a cocoon & coming out with big dark wings!

She never mentioned friends. I tried inviting her to dinner or the beach, just the 2 of us. It was dumb. I mean hello, it's Bermuda. People would see us & recognize me & I'd have to introduce her & they'd remember & that'd just defeat the purpose.

She didn't say nothing. Poor thing, too sad to refuse & too nice to be snippy about what a dumb idea it was. Then I realized I'd messed up & changed the subject. I kept chopsin foolishness till one day (finally!) a joke about somebody (K?) made her crack a giggle.

I said, "Anytime, acegirl, day or night. Nobody has to know."

She worried that if she called, it'd put me in an awkward place. But I said if we do our jobs right, then with God's help that won't happen. Well, I didn't think she'd call, but she did! Lots of times. Always after Honey/Baby went to sleep.

It was just chitchat. Anyone could tell acegirl was lonely, so I just said whatever popped into my head. Stuff from Bible Study, gossip from choir, things Baby/Honey said. Name a book, you'll hear her open up. Baby loves books, so I talked a lot about him: Thomas Hardy, critical theory, speculative realism. I could feel her wanting to say something back to him. I just knew if they met, their thoughts would build on each other till they left the galaxy & the atom in the dust. 2 of a kind, my sweet genius & my co-conspirator. One night she murmured that she understood that I love him, she said his name. Kenji. Next thing I know I'm bawling about bumper cars.

So she & I were bound by the ribbons of our secrets. One time I took too long in the shower, Martin answered my phone. I didn't know he'd done it till the next day when she told me. He said, "Good evening, who is this?" in his preacher voice & frightened her, poor sight. Well, mercy, she couldn't say her name! She was too shocked to think of anything, it'd been ages since she'd spoken on the phone to anyone but me. She blurted out "Pauline" & said she was my long-lost sistren. That was a lie, but when she told me I couldn't stop laughing. Mostly out of relief.

As time went on, she grew a burdened look. It got restless & haunted. Soon I could tell she was wearing herself out trying to be brave. Then one night...

Well, she always hated spending money. I hope it's cuz she was saving. In the end I couldn't let her pay me, I said, "Sweetie, I should be paying you." But anyway, one day I gave her a sistrenly lecture on paying her rent in advance, & she got upset. She said nobody deserves to take anything from you before you're ready to give it.

I was never sure she really wanted what we were trying to do, I mean wanted it with her whole heart & soul. That night I got less sure. But she wouldn't let me stop & soon we couldn't stop. TCD had forgotten her. Her birth certificate, school records, credit cards, phone bills, online orders, all the news stories we could find about the airplane, etc, etc (who knew an ordinary person took up all those bytes!), all of it dissolved in the shadows. Then the theft. She got angry. It was time.

I never got to see her in the sun. When I think back to the night she came to say goodbye, I feel like something in her was already sort of thin, sort of withdrawn like the moon on a foggy night. We hugged, I straightened her sweater. She reminded me to erase the time we'd spent together from the BHS security system's video archive (I didn't need reminding, she was just "sistering" me). Then she reminded me to forget her, never look for her. We started getting teary. We couldn't make a scene so I put her on the bus.

She made mistakes, got in too deep. People used her. When "someone" stole from her too, it was the straw that broke the camel's back. She almost told me about it, but instead we FOCUSED. She turned her anger into energy.

As for the "stolen goods" (sigh!), I'd prefer to think she was too focused to keep copies. I've thought about this a lot: she faked the W-2 so flags would go up when she filed it, the American government would start asking about Clocktower, but by that time she'd be long gone. Tip the first domino, get out of the way, let revenge take its course while she got on with starting over. That must've been her plan.

But she got scared, got tired. Realized how small she was or something. She gave up on the idea of filing it, that's what I think.

She recycled it instead, drafting something on the W-2's back, & she meant (she must have meant) to THROW IT AWAY but Mrs T got to it first. She got scared that Mrs T would show it to Erik. If that happened, he & Char could figure out what she had planned.

That's the best I can come up with. It's mostly holes, innit. From the looks of things, acegirl printed mockups for all her "assignments" & then made a girt big pile of the things under her bush mattress! So I guess she wasn't focused after all! Sigh! Girl, come on! Why keep the flippin things? To send to somebody? To torture herself? I don't get it. It makes everything we did…

Well, Honey was being cynical, missing the point, she got out, that's what matters. Just bad luck that Mrs T was Mrs T & she stole what she stole & Kenji…

So maybe Martin's right. We'll never understand, everything is meaningless.

We didn't wake up again till night. I got Kenji some water & a little juice. I put my head on his chest & Baby stroked my arm. He's got a special way of doing it. I don't think he knows it's special, but to feel him do it now, just like he's always done it, after clawing his way back from the edge of death just cuz I asked him to, it flooded me with love & hope.

I asked if he felt well enough to talk a little. If we do it now, like this, we'll be safe, I thought. "It's about Aetna Simmons."

Kenji didn't say nothing, just stroked my arm. I started thinking maybe he really had forgotten, & it made me panicky again, wondering how sick he really was. I looked at his face.

He hadn't forgotten.

"I in't Aetna Simmons, Baby. I just said it cuz... Well, lately I'm not sure why I said it."

He still didn't say nothing. My Kenji stared into some darkness that I couldn't see, looking like he'd woken up on the Sea Venture. He stroked my arm the whole time.

Finally he looked at me. My Love's exhausted eyes looking trapped in that darkness.

"To rescue her. That's why," he said.

"How do you know that, Baby?"

"Cuz you're you." Kenji moved so our faces brushed each other, & he whispered, "So, I mean, you didn't write any...anything?"

"No, my Love. I didn't write any suicide notes."

His breath stumbled over my forehead. He kissed me there & then just hugged me. Hugged me like in desperate relief, sort of.

Should've left it at that, maybe. K was prbly at capacity just with that. He didn't ask what rescue meant, didn't ask nothing.

But it was up to me to cut the last blade down, the sharpest & the fastest.

"I wrote something else," I said.

My book was in the nightstand on my side. Normally I wouldn't put it there, normally it lived in my Porte-Documents Jour. My book is big & fat. It's got handmade pages from on top of a bridge that goes over some pretty Italian waterway with curly boats on it. Beauti-

391

ful leather cover, black cuz it's from K. It's got 2 red ribbons attached inside as bookmarks.

When Kenji saw it, something scaly rose out of the black pools of bad dreams. His hand went to his stomach, he looked like all he wanted was to go unconscious. & then (timing, acegirl, gotta work on it) I thought of my own words from just a little bit ago. Words that K wrote down & thought about even though I said them to put him on the wrong track: "The books are black cuz they can't be read."

I think K & I put it together at the same time. We stared at each other & my book.

"...ribbons that start out red but change color, wriggling & flowing like the tentacles around the jaws of the sea-dragon, the very sea-dragon who attacked the diver cuz she stole the magic antidote for the agony of grief..."

Over & over with terror & blood.

"Mercy, Baby, what's this mean?"

"I don't know." He said it twice. He breathed thru nausea, his eyes shut. He said, "I bought that for you, didn't I?"

"20 yrs ago. Writing in it ever since. On & off, you know. Sometimes I stick stuff in. Like look at this, Baby."

Emails from Baby @harvard.edu stuck in beside emails from me. So I could pretend we were saying with our voices:

"'Loquats are out. Found a serious sweet fat one with 4 seeds in it down on the Railway Trail in Somerset.' I tried to draw the loquat, see? 'Estimated actual size.' Then I remembered I didn't have no scanner or camera-phone to send it. I wrote, 'I miss you.'"

"Nabi." Poor Baby. He shook his head like, Don't.

So ya girl keeps on going! I felt like I was chasing a seagull with a butterfly net.

"Stuff I should've said to you but ended up keeping in, a lot of it's in my book. So's Aetna Simmons. (Deep breath, acegirl!) I want you to know. I think it's important. Kenji, Aetna Simmons didn't die. I'm the only one who knows."

His eyes opened. He said thickly, my poor Kenji, "You what?"

That "Sea Venture" look hit me like a giant bee sting, but too late to turn back: I put my book in Kenji's hands.

Nobody else has been allowed to touch my book since the last time Kenji did. All those years ago. We held it up together with a pillow's help. The red bookmarks (I always thought they were so classy!) hung back over the spine.

Kenji asked me to read for him, my words in my own voice, straight out of my body woven together with his, so each time I took a breath, Kenji couldn't help but feel it. I couldn't help but feel how what I did & said touched him, whether he tensed or stopped breathing. I handled turning pages, flipping past the stuff that wasn't hers (Martin, hymns, Iesha, Kenji, Kenji...) unless I couldn't help it (always Kenji), & sometimes Kenji asked me to turn back. "Go back to the part where you taught yourself Python/Java/broke into whatever/built them a new website so stuff looked like it was normal but really you were in the shadows changing everything..." Another time he looked at me. I worried cuz of what his eyes were doing, but Kenji said, "You learned all this by yourself." I almost burst into tears cuz my Love was proud of me & too confused & beat up to show it except with pain. He said, "Go back to the part where we were talking hard drive shredders & you sang." So I did. Kenji said, "Read it for me." So I did. Partway thru, Kenji said, "Nabi," & I said, "Look at what you do to me," & then it took an hour to calm each other down. Those were the easy parts.

Aetna's Instagram & stuff, Aetna & Jude the Obscure, those parts made Kenji sick. He said, "Take this (the book), take it," & threw up in the trash bin. I figured that's why he lost his temper. He groaned, "Who are you?"

"I'm me, Baby. I'm here. Just breathe."

"Then who's that? (Mercy, he meant in my book!) That took years, a _____ lifetime! To cultivate a mindset that could _____ erase somebody while she's sitting there in front of you!"

"I didn't just erase her."

"No. No, you deleted 'Aetna Simmons' from the world. You replaced her with something. A bunch of memories of what never happened. Memories of some made-up somebody who'd done all that daredevil _____ that Aetna never did. & you stuck a name on that, that construction, & you stuck her body on it. A body that the rest of us idiots think is dead. That's what you did."

& Kenji retched, he had gritted teeth & a gloss of sweat when he lay down, but as I wiped his face I couldn't help myself, I whispered, "Should've known you'd understand, should've known you'd see exactly. Somebody had to help her, right, Baby?" Inside I thought: At last somebody knows besides me! Finally someone to help me bear the weight of her secret! Not just anybody either, the only one who understands both me & her. I put my book aside, I felt dizzy with relief, I wanted to flop out in Kenji's arms, let Kenji carry all of me.

But Kenji said, "Help her?! She was raw material for you, that's all. So you could change yourself into this—this unnecessary, narcissistic, _____ incredible metamorphosis—into something mighty & elite & terrible."

I was halfway between the nightstand and flopping out. I stopped in the middle, squished between horrified-insulted, horrified-ashamed, & just plain shocked. Kenji lay on his back with his hand over his eyes.

"It wasn't like that," I said.

"Yeah it was. You wrote it. All that _____ about creation, making something into something else, the Art Of Vanishing. Like you think you're some kind of god. & all that time, Nabi, you—you wouldn't let me—Aetna was my inspiration, my opportunity, my vengeance, and Nabi you willfully destroyed... You told me not to give up, but you only meant it as long as you thought I'd never succeed. When I started to think I'd actually get somewhere, for once in my life achieve what I set out to do, you let me think I was crazy. Just to cover your own _____. Or maybe CAM put you up to it. Did they? Or you came up with it yourself, right? So you'd always have a reason to go back to him?"

"Baby, you're not making sense. It was never about you."

"I could've helped you. I understood her. I would've understood."

Never crossed my mind, but it's true. Kenji would've noticed stuff in her that wasn't just face value, stuff I never thought of. & as soon as she said no questions, I guarantee my Baby would've let her have it with the questions.

"Instead you let me think I had nothing," said Kenji.

I wish he'd screamed it. Seriously. He didn't have it in him. Everything just drooled out of him. Yeah, some of it was crazy, but it all made sense, I mean from Baby's point of view. It's just I never bothered thinking thru that point of view.

Me. Kenji's acegirl & his love.

If it was anybody else, it would've floored me long before today, that's for true. I would've told the shameless so-&-so to sit in a church & read the part about Judas & ask themselves some questions. I snatched Kenji's hands. His eyes were the scary kind of tired. I said, "Forgive me. Please, my Love."

It was like he had to dredge his voice out of the sand. "Do you know what I had to do? What I had to promise Char so she won't hunt you down?"

"It's in my mind every second, all the time, what you did. Don't worry about that woman, Baby. I'll make everything right, I promise."

"I made a deal. If I don't keep it, she'll find us. She'll know that you're my reason for not keeping it. She'll infer that you're neck-deep in this. She'll use her suspicions to disgrace Martin & pressure BRMS to make him betray you. Maybe he won't crack, but I know Char. She'll crack something."

"You don't know her, thank you very much, & she do not know you."

"If she figures out what you've done, she'll ruin us. & Martin. & Aetna."

"Well, she won't figure it out. She may think she's all that, but I'm here to tell you she don't know nothing about handling herself digitally. Listen, Baby, you won't have to. OK? I promise when you're better, I'll figure something out. You just don't worry about nothing. You just—just love me, Kenji. Love me & don't let go."

"But this is what I meant, you don't trust me. You trusted Aetna, a total stranger. What you did, Nabi, that's computer crime. That's what you did for her. That's why she pretended to give a _____ about you. Anyone who looked for her, the most they'd ever find is you. For her, that was your only purpose, & you knew it. You knew that _____ spineless _____ planned to hang you out to take the heat. She used you and you let her. & I—& Nabi, I—I stuck your neck out. When you tried to tell me, I couldn't stop, I wouldn't stop."

"Only cuz I didn't really tell you anything. We were hardheaded about not talking to each other, but that's cuz we love each other!"

"We think so, but what is that? What are we but a couple of impostors?" (!!)

His eyes sort of hollowed out. I got scared he might turn his face away from me, I couldn't handle it if Kenji did that now, I tugged his hands like a lost little kid.

"You don't think we can get better? Kenji, come on, give us a chance."

He couldn't answer. He lay like a dead tree washed out to sea & washed back up.

He hated all of us for a sec. Me, her, himself. But he didn't take his hands away.

Maybe he understood it wasn't all my fault: Baby knows I'm a silly goose & a hacker, but that's a far cry from what she did, & it's not my fault she didn't tell me what was going on. Or maybe he was just tired of fighting dragons.

Or the truth was something else. Kenji turned my hands over & looked at them.

They're bare now. They go naked. Their emptiness gave me a shudder, but I hid it. Kenji looked at my eyes, didn't say nothing.

He let me hold him. We kissed, we took our time. He laid his head on my breast.

Watching Kenji sleep. I want to stay awake in case he dreams. Or doesn't dream but wakes up thinking about a future as a man without a voice, trapped in the minds of dead people. When he opens his eyes, I want to be the 1st thing he sees.

I also made him a promise. It's time to wrack my brain to figure out how to keep it. Once he was deep asleep I made myself some espresso.

My Love needs to know that what I say really means something.

Mercy, 3 days? 5 days gone? This acegirl don't even know. I'm had to start sneaking to get a moment with my book! Haven't even had time to miss it (sorry book!). I'm so busy I in't answered none of Wayn's texts (poor child hasn't phoned, so hopefully she's OK?).

It started right after I showed Kenji my book. I'd planned to stay up all night, but! So much for espresso. I have this hazy memory of my book & pen going away. I woke up in some nice arms, Kenji mumbled, "Go back to sleep," & he did too. Later I got up for Tylenol, he mumbled, "When's the last time you ate, Nabi?" I got an orange too. My Love was having quite a bit of pain, but he said, "You in't getting enough rest. Think I don't know, innit. Come on & lie down." Stuff like this went straight to my achy little heart. It's all Kenji wants to talk about. Even though poor sight's still throwing up (they say it can go on for weeks!!). The difference is in his eyes.

Every now & then, Baby & me look at each other & I see something like a new star being born real far away. That kind of thing needs watching, so you see I'm very busy.

Once or twice in these chockablock days, I thought I heard a noise. I was too blissed out to know for sure. I texted anyway: Did u come by? I'm sorry, I was asleep!

No answer at 1st. Couple days later Martin texted: ILY.

I answered: ily2 hope ur ok.

Next morning he answered back: Morning.

I answered: Morning honey.

We're scared of being apart. Couple mins, OK. More than that, I start to worry what Kenji might be up to, I think he starts to worry what I might be thinking of, & then we both get antsy & that's not good. So we bathe together. Plus there's the issue of the bathroom & jacuzzi. I have panicky flashbacks every time I look at them. Kenji doesn't seem to mind them, maybe cuz he's so exhausted by the time he gets there.

Anyway, we're in the bath. I made it hot cuz K was feeling "like a football after a football game." He's admitted that the pain goes right down into his bones.

He had his arm around my shoulders, his shoulder under my head:

perfect recipe to make me fall asleep, just what I didn't want to do, afraid aceboy might sink.

He said, "You wrote that you gave her a new name."

Kenji with his eyes closed, a frown below his stitches.

"A name that nobody & nothing in the world, not one damn computer, not even that book of yours could link up with the name Aetna Simmons. Nobody except you."

I began a fresh study of the stitches.

"What's her new name, Nikkou?"

"I shouldn't tell you that, my Love. I promised her. She asked me to forget her."

"So tell me the name & then forget her."

When we've been thru a hurricane & the electricity's been out forever, so we've been living in the dark, running to & from the tank with a bucket on a rope & existing on canned peaches & cereal, & then all of a sudden there's a surge, just for a second, a throb goes thru the house (lights flicker, fridge groans), & everything might go dark again right after but we've got hope now, we know it's trying: everything that ever had a spark of energy, everything that ever lived is trying to come back...that's the throb I heard in Kenji's voice right then. From that moment, I knew I can't let myself miss out on anything he says, any word, ANY little blankety-blank word could bring the fire back!

So I thought it might kill me to stamp out that early spark. "It don't matter what her name is. It's better you don't know, my Love."

"No, it'd be better if I were the only one who knew. If someone figured out what happened."

"No one's gonna do that, Baby."

"Well, if someone tried. Char's not stupid. Char won't hesitate."

"Thought you weren't gonna think about her no more, Love."

"Just tell me," said Kenji softly. "You see, I'd rather... If somebody started asking around about Aetna Simmons, they'd find me before they found you. I'd try not to tell them. But if I had to, I would. There'd be no need for them to find about you then."

I don't think Kenji knows how huge it is, him saying that. He just said it. Thinking about me, not about himself. But what I heard louder than the foghorn on a megaship was Kenji thinking forward. Like

Baby thought he might have a future after all. Here with me, with the strength to protect me. I put a teary smackeroo on him cuz what's a silly girl in love supposed to do? I said, "Let's keep her as my secret. If Char Richards or anybody like Char Richards ever shows their stinkin ugly face round here, they gotta deal with me. OK, Baby?"

"Well, no, it's not OK. You know everything, Nabi, you saw her face—"

"& I in't talking about that either, so duneenworrywifit."

"But Nabi, you're the only one who could put Aetna Simmons back together with herself. That means you're not safe."

"I already promised we're gonna figure something out. Now slow down, OK? Trust me."

I kissed him all over his face, I found his lips with mine. My ditsy little soul felt like fireworks in the sky.

I'd already sent the email. The other night when that espresso let me down. I'm thinking now we should've talked it thru 1st, K & me. Oh well. I didn't tell him. I'd put too much on him already.

I told him later.

Late afternoon sometime I was giving K a belly rub. Should've noticed he was deep in thought, but my eyes were closed.

He said, "What you told me about Erik. What you wrote. What Erik told you about Char."

Again with blankety-blank Char! I woke up real fast with some firm words to say. But Kenji's eyes were closed with a frown-ridge in between.

"The idea of some woman erasing herself over & over. Char prbly enjoyed it. Unconsciously, you know. The idea of making Erik pay Aetna to do it. & the idea of me, I guess, erasing—"

"Baby, I emailed Mr Falk."

Another shock, poor Love!

"I was gonna tell you later. If anything comes of it. If not, we'll try something else."

Baby said, "Jim J Falk. Clocktower's Chief Risk Officer."

"That's the one, sweet genius. You wrote to me about him."

"Yeah but, but…"

"I emailed to say I'm concerned that a VP on Mr Falk's team

wants to use my company, Bull's Head Shreds, to destroy evidence of fraudulent practices. I implied that I'd refused to sign a contract with this person but instead decided to tattle, urged on by my conscience. I invited Mr Falk to contact me for further info. & I cc'd you & Martin."

Kenji struggled up onto his elbow just to put his hand under my chin. He looked at me like I was a funny thing he'd picked up on the beach.

"That was rash, Nabi. And devious. Also pretty savvy."

Now he looked like he was wondering if the funny-looking thing he'd found might be a diamond, & that puffed me right up. I made my announcement.

"The whole thing has to stop. That's it. That's the only way we can be positive we're safe," I announced.

If Mr Falk even sees my email, let alone reads it, it'll be a miracle. (Plan B? Pending.) I knew Kenji knew that, but an email is still something, & what Kenji needs is hope in any form. He watched his little worker bee chatter on about taking down an international high-finance racket. He looked doubtful like he thought maybe he should grab me before I buzzed into a praying mantis. But this ace-girl was soaring.

"Kenji, you really think after what you wrote I could fail to understand what it means to spend your life writing suicide notes? Pretending there's some mistake in wanting to be alive? Baby, forget it. I don't care what I gotta do."

"Well, I do. I'm not worth any kind of risk."

"That's where you're wrong. Kenji, just one of your breaths means more to me than anybody else's life."

"You shouldn't say stuff like that."

"I'm saying I love you."

"We don't know what's going to happen."

He was getting upset. Like really upset. He lay down, I pulled his hand out of his hair, his voice made me think of too much water.

"Nabi, I betrayed you."

I didn't know what to say, I didn't want to say anything. Like I don't want to say anything about Martin or worry over what counts as "betrayal." All that mattered was Kenji's voice climbing & con-

400

stricting cuz of that helpless rage that scares me like nobody's business.

"Never before. & never again. Right?" I said.

"Yes. Only Char."

"OK, then let me tell you we're OK. WE'RE OK." We were scared stiff. Kenji let me envelop myself in his body, I closed my eyes & tried pretending we were like those snails that find a nice wall to stick to & sleep the summer thru. But I heard myself beg, cowering against his chest, "Please believe me. Please, Kenji."

He whispered, "All right, Nabi." Cuz he knew I was afraid. I know it's not enough.

Later Martin texted me a moon. I texted: sweet dreams honey.

How much of all that was bravado? How much was the espresso kicking in just long enough for tappity-tap + Send? None, I thought. Kenji knew better. I've never been sometimey when it comes to sleeping, I never have bad dreams, I'm not a ceiling-starer. But I popped up in some crazy hour & bugged poor K till he woke up. Baby wasn't even all that surprised.

"I've gotta ask you something, Kenji. It can't wait."

We let a little just-in-case light sneak under the door. Besides that it was pitch dark.

"You gotta follow the question all the way thru like always. Wherever it goes, Baby, OK?"

I reached up into the dark. I found Kenji's face exposed to the night's most slippery hours. He held me so I lay on top of his lungs.

"Kenji, would I, like if I'd known…I'd have shown that girl the door & nothing else. Wouldn't I?"

It came out feeble. But Baby knew I meant Aetna Simmons.

He said, "It's OK that you're not psychic."

"Yeah, but I should've asked her, innit. I should've asked her SOMETHING. Sure, we don't ask clients why they're destroying what they're destroying, but document destruction isn't the same as breaking into immigration & all that. I care about our business enough to understand that. I'm got common sense. So what happened, Baby? I mean, like, in my head."

I could never ask anybody else something like that.

I already knew the answer too. But I hoped Kenji would answer something else. Something to prove the real answer wasn't true.

He said, "Pride." So gently!

"You said it in your book. You wanted to show me & Martin a thing or two."

My cheeks were on fire. But Kenji didn't sound disgusted, he caressed my face & stroked my back & said, "The fact of where I went to school doesn't mean I've ever thought I'm better than you. I've always known you're stronger. Upstairs & inside. Whatever the Hell I did to make you think otherwise, I'm sorry. I never wanted you to feel condescended to or stifled or like the scum of the earth, like you're throwing yourself at the walls in a padded soundproof cell day after day."

402

Shame made me fidgety. "It wasn't that bad, Baby. I got no right to judge you."

"Whatever, just don't hate yourself for anything. Don't hate anything ever. OK?"

"But Baby, do you think if I'd asked what she was running from, I mean if I'd known Aetna Simmons was guilty of something awful, something bad enough to run from..."

"If you'd known she was a forger for an insurance racket, you'd have told her to get crackin."

"You really think so, Love?"

We lay quiet in the dark. I don't know why I kept pushing this question. Cuz it's the question of what I am, I guess? So like: me + Kenji = ? Me + Martin = ? Cuz me = ??! Who's got time to worry about "me = "? This worker bee's too busy buzzing. But what if I filled every second up with my own buzz cuz even though I didn't know it, deep down I was scared of the answer to "me = "?

I said in an all-new kind of panic, "Kenji, you know me better than anyone. So I mean, look. You started working for the chemist cuz you were desperate. I wasn't. It just didn't occur to me that anything I did would ever hurt anybody. Kenji, if I just didn't let that occur to me, how far could I have gone to make myself feel liberated & empowered or whatever even if I did have all the info? You know what I'm saying? Could I risk everything we have just to show what I'm made of?"

He thought about it. Long & serious like he always does.

"Turn the lamp on, would you, Nikkou?"

I turned it on. Orange light on one side of Kenji's face showed that new star struggling to learn to twinkle, trying to fight its way out of his ancient black hole. Darkness swallowed the other side. His love beamed thru the darkness & the light in waves of mysterious energy like they're always finding out in space but here, right here in the quick parting of his lips & the tremor around his eyes. It rocked me with a shockwave every day of my life & sometimes I didn't even know, I was so busy buzzing, I didn't even know it was the kind of energy that could burn him out forever. What kind of acegirl fails to see that? What kind of "me" just fails to see it?

"My friend, this is an existential crisis," said Kenji.

"I knew you was gonna say that, bye." I felt like bursting into tears.

"I think Martin would prescribe going to church."

"Prbly. What do you think?"

"I have a lot to learn about you."

He thought long & serious about that too.

He said, "You still got Aetna's hard drives, Nabi? The original & the copy?"

"Yeah."

"Where?"

"Where I keep them."

"Where's that, Nikkou?"

"Pretty briefcase you got me."

"You've been carrying those fucking things around with you all this time everywhere you go?!!"

"I couldn't leave them hanging around for poky snoberses to—"

"Fack! That's why you started looking at hard drive shredders, innit," Kenji breathed.

Now, which one of us set out to make BHS a laundry service? Clue: it wasn't K. All he wanted was to help me build something, just so happened that drug money was all he had to do it with. But which one of us set out to spend however many hundred-thousands to make our "confetti counter" cover up a crime, & which pathetic stupidhead never even thought of it that way cuz she let herself stay ignorant & figured she could do no wrong?

"Told her to leave me her laptop," I mumbled. "Figured we could get a HDS & after a while I'd sneak it in with some work order. Told her if it took too long to get our own, I'd sneak off overseas to somebody who's got one."

I never thought the words "computer crime" till Kenji said them. Seriously.

My jaw shivered. My sweet Kenji said real soft, "Hey, acegirl, come here."

I'm a traitor. I am blind. I hid my face in Kenji's neck. Where his breath moves & his pulse flutters & his voice lives. "I'm the worst Managing Partner ever!"

"The best, you mean."

"The worst criminal too!"

404

"Hey now, you weren't trying to be a criminal. You thought you were helping her. Even if you had other motives too, you really did want to help her. Didn't you?"

"Yeah," I whimpered.

"Course you did. My Nikkou."

Kenji kissed me on my head. Like he could hear all the rubble in it flying around & smashing.

"Once you decided you were gonna help her get away, you didn't just follow thru, you went above & beyond."

"To cover my own blankety-blank."

"Yeah, that too. I'm glad you didn't neglect that."

Even though I lied to him for it. Kenji kneeling in the grass, Kenji drowning in poisons. I couldn't even ask the question that I knew hid behind my other questions. Could I hurt BHS without realizing? What about: Could I hurt YOU, my Love, without letting myself realize??!!

He didn't make me ask it, he didn't ask it. He asked, "Nabi, is there a way to shred hard drives without a shredder?"

"Power drill." I sniffled.

I couldn't think about no power drill. This "existential crisis" blew up literally right that second into a life-&-death-level freakout: me & my pride & not asking enough questions, all my buzzbuzzbuzz sent Kenji up that hill to DIE.

"Kenji, how is it that you still love me?!"

He said, "You're all I care about. You're all the reason there is."

His voice was steady. & I could tell by his breathing he was doing his genius thing, & all this decked my bravado: What if I can't protect him, what if I can't prove to him that it is worth it to keep struggling, what if I get in the way of my own efforts to protect him…???

Nothing lay between Kenji's chest & my messed-up head, so the sounds that only he can make went deep in me. His life throbbing thru him filled my head & throbbed thru me & throbbed in everything. The air, the dark. The walls. The light under the door. I listened all night long.

His new thing was this power drill. Day after day: "Let's do it today, Nikkou."

I miced. "Too sleepy, Baby, wanna snuggle here with you."

He admitted that sounded nicer. Only to get right back on the other thing.

"Do you own a power drill, my Love?"

"Well, no."

We couldn't buy one on Amazon. Well, we could. But after we'd paid more than any drill was worth to get the thing across the ocean, we'd still have weeks to wait for it to land & clear customs, etc, etc. Kenji didn't want to wait that long. But going out to buy a power drill didn't even need discussing. It's Bermuda, our track record sucks, the last thing we need is someone being able to say they saw me buying a drill, & Kenji isn't well enough to go into town. Standing up makes him dizzy. Nausea makes him angry & depressed. I'm scared to leave him alone, scared of finding him with a pen or something in his throat.

"Don't we have one down Bull's Head?" he asked.

"Prbly. But I'd have to tell Bryan I'm taking it, cuz he'd miss it. Cuz remember I put it in the contract for those lot: all Bull's Head Shreds equipment stays at Bull's Head Shreds, & it's Bryan's job to make sure—"

"OK, OK. Did I sign that contract?"

"Yes, you did."

"Fack."

"Anyway, I want to keep Bull's Head Shreds out of it. From now on, you know. We made that, Baby. We depend on it. It's ours."

Kenji kissed my hand. He refuses to let me stay ashamed. I give into him easy, I don't like guilt, I like smiling at my Baby. He was on the couch. His 1st day sorta but not really out of bed, he was in his PJs on his back under a blanket. I'd talked him into trying out the living room. It's way brighter with the sliding glass & white-tiled balcony & sea & sky. I cotched beside him & we held hands & ate the plain white bread I'd made. Now & then I nuzzled his cheek with mine or under his chin with my lips, I couldn't get enough, cuz that morning Baby'd shaved his beard off (with help & supervision!) just like he always does & just cuz he wanted to!

"What about Martin? Team Leader got a power drill?"

"Yeah, he likes being prepared. But Baby, I don't want him involved."

"Why's he gotta be involved?"

Sigh! So that's how my Love & me wound up sneaking into my own house in broad daylight. Kenji didn't want me going by myself. I didn't want Kenji staying home & looking at the ceiling by himself. We called ahead to make sure nobody was there. I'd texted Martin already that morning to say hi, so he had no reason to think anything "unusual" was going on.

We bundled Kenji up in a sweatshirt. We took South Shore Road so I could show him the ocean & beaches & lighthouse & bay grapes & banyan trees, all the stuff we've been looking at forever but it's different now. Now I'm saying, "Check all the tents down Church Bay, Baby," meaning Don't you want to stay & enjoy stuff like this, stuff that's all about life & color & noise?, but without actually saying it cuz saying it would be too much. Now I'm sneaking glances at Kenji in the passenger seat of his own car, he's looking out the window & I can't tell if he's seeing the blue-gray sky & snow cone guy or not, I'm worrying like maybe I shouldn't have pointed out the tents cuz it means it's Cupmatch weekend coming (& it's true all the other cars got their red&blue/blue&blue flags flying for the Cupmatch teams), Bermy's favorite long weekend that K & me never spent together cuz, well, it was a long weekend.

"Feel OK, Baby?" & he took my hand in both of his. He didn't say nothing, maybe he felt carsick, the more we drove the more he looked like he was concentrating like crazy on looking at my fingers & then not looking at them.

Anyway, we got there, Martin's car was gone, he was at work. I sorta wanted Kenji to stay in the car cuz he's slow-moving, poor sight, & he could honk if there was "trouble" (???). I also didn't want him staying in the car in case he started to feel bad & went & sat down in the road instead. Kenji really wanted to stay in the car, he was breathing real deliberately, he said, "It's just the pictures." & that settled it, I wanted him where I could grab him, I dragged him in the house.

I offered to get a chair, but we thought we wouldn't be too long. K leaned on the counter & I felt him watching me like he was scared to look anywhere else. I thought the drill would be in the junk drawer with the stuff Martin uses to hang pictures. It wasn't. Sigh! So I tried the cabinets. That kitchen's got a lot of cabinets. I started with the less used ones high up, no luck. Poor Kenji sat down slowly on the floor in a corner, & I started on the lower cabinets.

Part of me kept thinking I didn't really want to find it. But I did want to find it cuz Kenji wanted to find it & I knew that hardheaded bye would insist on going into town if we didn't find it. Maybe I thought if we found it, got that much out of the way, I could snuggle him into forgetting what he thought he wanted to do with it. I looked under the sink.

"Oh look, Baby. DeWalt. Don't they make drills?" It was a black & yellow bag like an overnight bag. It had the drill, all the little pieces to go with it, & a screwdriver set too. & now I think about it, I must've been the one who bought it, prbly for Martin's birthday or something (this head & soul of mine need a vacation). "OK Baby, we're good to go."

Then the front door opened.

"Nabilah? You're here? You're home?"

Martin.

Do you, Martin Alan Furbert, take…

Martin.

He came around the counter, spotted Kenji in the corner.

My boys gaped at each other. The 2 boys gaped at me. The 3 of us who've known each other for how long, & the shock of being together turned us all to stone.

"Good afternoon?" said Martin.

Like that, like a question. Not sarcasm, just shock.

"Hi Honey. How are you?"

Kenji murmured, "I'm so sorry. I'll go. I'm really sorry—"

"No, Baby, stay right here. It's OK, really."

I set my hand on Kenji's shoulder. He was trembling & everything, instantly almost-off-the-charts distraught. Some days it takes nothing whatsoever to upset him. Like when he fell asleep & let the cup of tea I'd made for him get cold, I think the word for that is "inconsolable."

"Martin, you doing OK?" I said. Too loud, I think.

Martin nodded & shrugged & tossed his hands in the air all at the same time. He looked thin, poor Honey. Tired. Not as thin as K & not even half as tired, but anyway I just don't want to think about the silence.

Martin: "Well, I was actually just coming to call you. Coming here. That is. To call you. Instead of calling from work. & then after that I was going to go back to work. Cuz it's a work day."

"Nabi, I should go," K whispered.

"No, Kenji, don't move a muscle. Oh really, Honey? What about?"

M & K were back to staring at each other. Not like cowboys in cowboy movies, more like stray cats staring at oncoming cars. Except both of them were already in pain. Cuz of me.

"Martin? What did you want me for, Honey?" I said gently.

He cleared his throat & said, "Well."

He looked at K & cleared his throat again. My hand on K's shoulder was a clamp, the other hand had the bag with the drill in it. Of all things, Martin came out with: "Char Richards."

Kenji closed his eyes. Like the executioner's right behind him with the axe.

"I understand she's left Clocktower," said Martin.

My hand gave K a squeeze. He blinked at Martin, blinked at me.

"You didn't get the email?" Martin took out his phone.

I said, "No, we…" We'd been zonked most of the time. Kenji held onto the hand I'd put on his shoulder.

"One of Falk's secretaries copied all 3 of us. 'Mrs Furbert. The employee concerned in your inquiry is no longer with the company. Regards.' So I did a little digging. You may be aware that I have certain official-unofficial contacts with access to sensitive information. They're unofficial in the sense that I can't share what they say or who they are with anyone, but I can use what they say to point my team in the right direction, if you follow me. They're official in the sense that they're intimately connected with law enforcement—"

"Char's dead, isn't she," said Kenji.

"What? No, she isn't dead. What gave you that idea? Actually, you know what? Don't answer that," said Martin.

"Honey," I said gently.

"She's joined the FBI," said Martin. To Kenji, really. Then my husband looked at me & said, "FBI."

Kenji groaned. Martin looked at the kitchen counter like he wasn't sure it really was his own kitchen counter.

I said, "Just like that? Any so-&-so can just up & join the FBI?"

"Typically, no," said Martin.

"& she can't have got fired all that long ago. When'd you say the secretary wrote you?"

"They wrote to you, Nabilah. They copied me. Nabilah, you start a stone rolling down a hill like this & don't keep track of it?! Don't answer that either. Richards wasn't fired, she resigned. You're right she left the company mere days ago, prbly after you sent that reckless email. I'm not claiming there is any correlation between the 2 events—"

K: "Course there is. Char wouldn't risk triggering an investigation. She doesn't want anyone presuming to decide her fate. If she was gonna take a dive, she'd want to do it her own way."

Me: "Excuse me. You do not live in no demon-woman's head, thank you."

M: "She's an expert financial auditor. There's no doubt she'll be a certified fraud examiner within weeks."

Me: "Prbly got lots of practice. Looking for ways to portray people as embezzlers or gambling addicts or whatever. So it'd make sense that they'd you know."

"Do themselves in," said M.

I gave him my kick-under-the-table look. K was rubbing his head & frowning at the drill bag. M has a way of not noticing looks or kicks when they're inconvenient. He looked at the drill bag too.

"I've inferred from what I've heard that as soon as she decided to resign, Richards offered her services to the Bureau & was recruited on the spot."

"Power means more to Char than money. Sticking it to whoever," said K.

"Yes, well, it seems to me, though this will never be confirmed, that they recruited her on the spot not only cuz of her credentials & the Bureau's sorry track record as an equal-opportunity employer, but also cuz she offered in exchange, on the proverbial silver platter, the names & details of multiple corporate executives whom she claims are guilty of insider trading, inflating expenses, selling nonexistent shares, & so on. & not just in the insurance sector. Not just men either, contrary to what you might—"

Kenji grabbed the drill bag. "Can we borrow this? I mean, I guess, can I borrow this?"

Me: "Baby, wait. Sit down. We gotta process this. Obviously the Bureau (!) don't know about Aetna Simmons. Or about Erik. Or I mean anything about Bermuda, right, Martin? Kenji, bye, gimme that thing." I put the bag of sharp hole-making things on the counter.

Martin: "One would infer that since what Aetna Simmons did would be of no help to anyone besides an insurance company, it would hardly be in Richards' best interests to mention her or Erik. For the same reason, I should think former-VP Richards would avoid drawing any connection between herself & Bermuda."

My sigh of relief nearly floated me to the ceiling. Then it went all the way thru my toes into the floor.

"Thank you, Martin," I said.

"Not a problem," he said softly. He put his phone in his pocket.

The knot in Martin's tie was a little off. Not askew, just not precise enough for Martin. I pulled the wraparound bit down about 2 mm to finish covering the knotty bit. I'd forgot about my rings, but Honey saw of course, he looked horrified. Kenji in his corner had his head in his hands. Martin & I looked at each other, poor Honey bursting to say something & wishing with all his heart I'd say it for him. Something to do with hope.

I said, "Thank you. We should go." I put my hand in Kenji's hair. "Seriously, the drill & stuff. Can we use it?"

Martin sighed. Not like my sigh.

"Just don't tell me what it's for," he said.

"I'll bring it back."

"You will?"

My husband of 8 years looked at me with hope & terror. I glanced at Kenji on the floor, the man who loves me more than his own life looking at me with hope & terror.

I'd never imagined this. I'd been trying not to think about this. Trying like crazy.

I looked at Martin & told myself I wouldn't cry.

I said, "Yeah, I will, but I won't stay."

Kenji let his breath out. Martin looked at the floor.

"I'm real sorry, Martin. I'm real grateful—"

"If we're finished, Nabilah, say it. Say it or make a promise. Don't expect me to do it for you. & don't make Kenji do it. Whatever you do now is entirely your doing," said Martin.

His face was trembling. Kenji's too. I felt like I was dying. I know I've got enough love & laughs & strength in me for both of them, I know I do.

Then again, maybe I'm wrong. Maybe I'm just arrogant. Maybe being arrogant almost made me a murderer.

& by the way, acegirl, who are you kidding about the strength? You looked at Kenji, you looked into his eyes, you lifted up his chin so you could see his love & soak it up & turn that strength of his, the courage to go on loving you, into courage of your own—but a whole different kind.

"We're finished, Martin. I'm sorry."

You wouldn't have thought anything, not gods or anything, could love with the love that hurricaned in Kenji's eyes right then, acute just like the storm, lavish like leaves & grass & snails & whistling frogs & things the rain brings out of the woodworks, mixed up & excessive like the colors that the sun flings all over the sky for no reason, & the thing is, he couldn't help it! Kenji wouldn't have done it if he could help it, he wouldn't have exposed himself like that in front of Martin, especially not in that moment. That was the kind of moment where Kenji would've held everything in, swallowed it & hidden it & even smiled at me, just so no matter what I did I'd feel like I was doing the right thing. But he can't do that no more. Doing it all those years used him up to the last drop, so now my Kenji is too weak not to show the helpless strength of his love. & instead of holding it in, he surrendered to it, he had to, he surrendered everything, & the strength not to resist it anymore filled his eyes up, & if it wasn't for that strength, I kid you not, I would've puddled on the floor in the awful silence.

"Yes. Well," said Martin.

& in the other awful silence.

"Please go now. Both of you," said Martin.

Kenji flung out his hands. I pulled him up, & he made sure I didn't fall.

We couldn't say anything. We held each other around the waist as we walked down the drive. Kenji walked me to the driver's side of his car cuz he saw I was dazed, but he didn't say nothing, he was dazed. By the time we got to Middle Road, I couldn't see. Kenji said, "Pull over, Nabi, quick." & I did & I crash-landed in the arms of the best friend I almost killed.

We didn't even think about who might be watching, we couldn't have cared less, Kenji kept crying, "I promise! I promise!" as we blocked up the entrance to the plant nursery, Kenji's expensive car all slanty half in & out the street cuz the driver kept on crying. & Kenji held my face & Kenji kissed me everywhere that there were tears & Kenji said, "Nabi, we have to go get rid of everything. We gotta go & do it now."

"No Kenji, take me home, hide me forever," I moaned.

"I will. I promise you I will. I love you, Nabi, I'm so sorry about everything, that's why you gotta help me, I can't do this by myself, I've gotta make sure you're safe. I need us to be sure, Nabi, as best we can."

His feverish look said clear & deafening he couldn't rest till we'd done whatever he thought we had to do. Cars & bikes must've been wiggling around us, people trying to pass the plant nursery, but we lot didn't have a clue. I whined some more, & Kenji whispered, "I know. It hurts real bad & you just want to fall asleep in the darkest possible place. Believe me, Nikkou, I know. Just this one thing. I can't do it without you. Then we can sleep & then, you know, if you want, face the rest of it together."

"I won't get thru one more second unless you're here. Now. Every now. You understand? Kenji, I'm serious. Do you understand how much I love you? Do you finally?"

We flooded each other, I felt weak like I would faint, Kenji breathed into my mouth again & again, & I couldn't help throwing myself open, surrendering to the aching wish we'd always known & never understood cuz our love is better than both of us. & Kenji put his forehead against my forehead, Kenji said, "I understand."

Then there was this BRRRPPP!!! from the water truck that was just trying to pass the plant nursery or visit the plant nursery. Baby & I jumped a mile, my Love wiped my face with his hands, his ace-girl hollering, "Don't go calling me an impostor ever again, don't go acting like one either!" & Kenji said, "OK," & said, "Get us outta here, Nikkou." & ya girl made a squealing U-turn in the plant nursery & cut off the water truck & a minibus full of tourists to get back on Middle Road. My sweet genius was in the middle of telling me his idea when he spied Southampton Post Office & we peeled in. I jumped out, grabbed an armload of the phone books they had in the doorway, threw them in the trunk.

However many trips to & from the car, Kenji wouldn't let me make a single one of them alone, he refused to take one step empty-handed. Besides our other stuff, it took 2 of us to carry the charcoal from the shop at the marina. K looked terrible by the time he plopped on Ethelberta's bench, feeling sick & fighting it. It was too much, he knew it & wouldn't stop. I plopped beside him, but he'd only let me hold him for a minute.

"Sun moves so fast," he whispered. He kissed me, anxious & badly out of breath. He went & started up the engines, I cast off the moorings. He didn't want to stop at the gas station ("We lot gonna be out of gas long before the boat"), but I insisted on that one thing. We didn't know how far we'd be going, not like accurately.

So while Ethelberta glug-glug-glugged herself up to the brim, Kenji & I made a point of not seeing how much it cost, I leaned against him & said, "Don't do it. Just let me wipe everything from the past 2 months or so. I bet I can make it so it was never there." Baby just shook his head.

We drove around Bermuda's curly tip. The sun chased us southwest. I wanted Kenji close to me, the 2 of us squeezed onto Ethelberta's driving bench. I made him promise to keep an arm around me at all times.

My need for him scares me, how it's exploded. It's physical need but not just about attraction, it's psychological & I guess spiritual but not only about love. Maybe it's not even new, maybe I just hadn't noticed it. That scares me too cuz I can't afford not to recognize what Kenji's feeling anymore, cuz I need him & it scares me…

The ocean was restless, steely blue, it frightened me like it never did before. It's too big for us, it has no sympathy for us, what if it doesn't accept our secrets, what if it swallows us instead before we've even had a chance? & once we left Dockyard there was nothing to see ahead but ocean, & I could only look ahead. I was tired fit to cry, but I was driving. Over the Rim Reef & Terrace Reef we went (according to the sketchy maps we'd glanced at on our phones before we sailed away from all the cell towers). Outside the reefs, the ocean rocked us & spat on us. The swells got bigger & grayer, the sky got grayer & thicker, the sun & ocean closed in on each other. Ethelberta's pointy end climbed & dropped & climbed & dropped.

I worried Kenji might get seasick. I don't think he knew his fingers dug into my hip. I called out, "OK, my Love?" but Baby didn't reply. He gazed at the horizon with the wind pushing his black curls & slapping him in the face, with all the rage & darkness of his history, all his fragility & all that's left of his life that he threw into his riskiest gamble ever: me.

Letting him down scares me more than anything.

Baby's idea was to go to one of the downed airplanes or modern shipwrecks that "encircle the whole Island in waste & failure & buckling corpses" as he put it (sigh). My idea was to do it around Challenger Bank, an underwater mountain about 13 mi offshore. Its highest point is 50 m below, & it's full of unexplored caves & sinkholes. Baby's idea had to do with hiding in plain sight. My idea had to do with vanishing. The wrecks are only a few miles off Bermuda in just a couple m of water, shallow enough for scuba tourists. The mountain gets far fewer visitors, & none of them except the whales can go as deep as the water goes. I got Kenji to agree with me pretty easily. (Right now I think he'd agree if I said let's buy a submersible.) I told him outright I don't want him thinking about "waste & failure" & staring at airplane skeletons in the middle of the ocean with a power drill in his hand. & hey, who knows if we'll get lucky with a sinkhole?

I didn't talk about the sinkhole for chuckles, I'm too freaked out for chuckles, I feel like half of me just broke off like a piece of sandstone cliff, & I know the missing half isn't just Martin, that's the thing, it's a piece of myself that's turned into a shade, the piece that thought ya girl had it all figured out. Life in general, stuff like that. & Kenji's right it hurts like a phantom limb, & I think Kenji has to be the one to do something about it, that's just how it is. He could do something about it if he was himself, but Baby's not himself, & if he'll ever be himself again depends a lot on me—Kenji is everything now, he is everything—but maybe it doesn't just depend on me, & what'd I just say about me anyway?! As I drove our little blue boat straight into nowhere, I worried like crazy about my wounded Love "dissolving in oceanic molecules," going overboard by accident or on purpose. I clamped my arm around his waist & took up one-handed boat steering.

Ethelberta's GPS thingy told us when the mountain was maybe underneath us kinda-sorta. I slowed the engines down. Baby put his nose in my hair, gathering strength, & then he started pulling away to get ready, but I held onto him. We're not very good at the GPS thingy. We're used to using Bermuda to navigate, but we couldn't see Bermuda. Either cuz we'd gone too far or the gray in the water was seeping into the sky or the sun couldn't stand to look at us no more. We were the only boat out there. I doubt even the whales were there.

& another problem. Kenji didn't have to see my face to see the problem, he felt it in the way I held him without looking up. Or he'd seen it already in what I'd written, & he understood it cuz of what he'd written. He reached over & cut the engines. A gust of silence swept in. Without the reefs to calm them down, the waves sent our little boat swinging side to side.

Kenji said, "You don't want to let her go. You think Aetna Simmons was the biggest adventure of your life. You think she took you out of yourself in a good way. I get it. But you got lots more to do, Nabi, OK?"

"You too, Kenji."

"& I'll love you like crazy all the way, just like you are, all complicated like that."

He brushed my lips with his but quickly. We went to the pointy end where we'd put all our stuff. On one of the cushiony benches, we made a stack of phone books & wrapped it in duct tape.

This year's phone book has a cover picture of the Arboretum. Baby & I looked at each other when we saw it. It cut into Kenji's voice. His voice cut into the dirty-cotton clouds, the ocean's splish-splosh as we swung:

"Aetna first. You get the rest."

I kept him in tackle range while I got out a screwdriver. I got out her HD.

The HD of Aetna Simmons, the original. A small rectangle I'd wormed out of its laptop body. Silvery on one side, green on the other, 6.8 cm long & not even 1 cm tall. Kenji held it in his hand. "This is everything she did."

Well, technically, it used to be. Till I erased it all with sanitizing software. Poor Kenji seemed to have forgotten that. I didn't say nothing. He held the HD in both hands.

"Every death. Every becoming. This blunt thing. This rigid thing." He sounded weak & sick. He stroked the HD. Just once. Maybe instead of aluminum & nickel phosphorus, my Love saw the dark shapeshifting ghost who threw herself into the ocean in his imagination when it ran off all harum-scarum. Maybe the look of agony on Kenji's face was cuz he was at a crossroads, & in the dark in front of him was the decision to lose Aetna forever or join with her forever & lose everything else, & I in't having none of that.

"Let me do it, my Love."

"No, Nabi."

Kenji duct-taped the HD to the stack of phone books. He put on a snorkel mask like I'd told him, he plugged the drill into Ethelberta's outlet, he stood in front of the bench & used his knee to brace the phone books against Ethelberta's hull, he pointed the drill at the HD. My Kenji. & no, this isn't the proper way.

"Stay back, Nabi."

I told myself I wouldn't think about Python & shadows, the woman clutching our ad from the Yellow Pages, Kenji writing & writing.

"NABI?!!"

Like jumping up in the middle of the night, except the cry was my name too. I rushed to him, I slid my arms around him, Kenji holding a power drill like it was a pistol & shaking head to toe. I put my lips to his back, I put my hands over his. I squeezed, Kenji squeezed. The shrieking of the drill ripped thru both of us.

We drilled 10 holes in her HD platter & controller board. I don't know if we meant 10 or it just happened. I had to tell Kenji to stop.

He didn't want to stop. His voice was all torn up. "Get the others, Nabi."

Aetna's clone. Aetna's RAM. The storage chips & SIM cards in our phones. HD from my laptop. HD from Kenji's laptop. "Aetna Simmons' Final Words," Pauline's phone number, Char's phone number, Erik's incriminating vmail: "Aetna Simmons" was all over our flat little silver boxes which looked almost just like hers. Like our hearts & lungs & nerves are almost just like hers. I held Kenji from behind & Kenji held the drill & the drill butchered everything we'd done. So I can never get it back, all those bits of code I wrote, all the notes I took on what I learned. Kenji's archives from Harvard, the unfinished thoughts he never went back to, they won't get to be anything now, Kenji's unnamed confession, Kenji's suicide letter to me. I begged him not to, I cried for the Harvard stuff & the unfinished things that never had a chance, but it was like my Kenji was consumed by our destructive frenzy. He didn't say a word when I put the SIM card from his "business" phone under the drill with all our other ghosts & maybes. I wanted to save our laptops, what was left of them, I told him we could put new HDs in easily. But Kenji, oh, my Baby, he threw everything overboard, every last microchip. We weighted down each thing with bunches of teardrop-shaped bits of lead, fishing sinkers held on with duct tape. Kenji threw the things in all different directions, he threw them as hard as he could.

He threw hers last. The original. I imagined it sinking, sinking, sinking, & nothing about its body would help it stay afloat, sinking into a sinkhole that got too narrow as it sank, so the little box got stuck sinking in the sinkhole, more waste, another corpse. & Kenji watched it sink. He kept watching after it was gone.

He wouldn't let me do any throwing. Baby said the worst was yet to come. He said I should save my strength for the worst. He refused to lie down after everything disappeared under the water, but he wasn't doing well at all. He said, "Please Nabi, get us out of here."

I tried to turn an exact about-face. Then I realized I should check the GPS thingy cuz the ocean's got its own mind, the ocean could've spun us around without us knowing. I turned us so the GPS said we were heading sorta north. & mercy I have never been so relieved to see Bermuda in my life, I even said, "Kenji, look, it's Bermuda!" even though none of us felt like talking. I saw Gibbs Hill Lighthouse 1st. Then lights in the houses along the shore, then Pompano Beach & the last bit of sunset in the sky. Kenji was at the wheel with me & then he wasn't.

He was vomiting over the side. & the thing is boats don't have brakes. Ethelberta took a century to stop.

It was like the ocean grabbed him by the throat & tried to yank

419

him in. Worse than that, it was like the ghosts we thought we'd killed rose up out of the ocean & wanted to make Kenji one of them by ripping him out of himself & eating him. I hunkered down, gripped his shoulder, braced his forehead, "Baby, we're safe." & Kenji heaved, the darkening Atlantic all up in his face. We hung over the edge, half in the boat & almost in the water. I said, "Don't give her any more of you. Don't grieve for her, she doesn't want it. & don't be scared for her either, my Love. Forget her. That's what she wants." I tried to sound brave instead of hanging-off-a-building terrified, not thinking of how Martin didn't come to the door, didn't watch us drive away. I wanted to be solid instead of shrill, but I wasn't, not when I said, "I in't letting you go," meaning get the Hell back in this boat or we're both going over!

Kenji let me draw him back in. But mercy, he was crashing. He vomited in Ethelberta's emergency bucket until he had nothing left, & still the sickness flogged his hidden parts. When it finally took a breather, we headed for the wheel, but on our way there Baby sat down hard on the floor without meaning to! I got him up again but barely, Ethelberta's got these movable vinyl panels that can make the whole pointy end into a lounge bed, & Kenji collapsed there, Zohytin's vengeful ghosts overwhelmed him from inside.

We lay face-to-face in the middle of the sea. We used our double-wide sleeping bag as a blanket. We couldn't talk, I just stroked the back of Kenji's neck. Ethelberta cradled us, the ocean rocked us not too gently, making a sucking sound against the boat. & no, there was nobody at the wheel. & what did I just say about the ocean's mind? It's stupid to not pay attention, people die from it, K & I know that better than anyone, but for once I felt like I was making the right choice about what to ignore. Night coming fast & cool. Our little Island sinking into darkness, shrinking to the size of the light from the lighthouse. The light reached for us & pulled away, passed over, slipped away, came back. I gave Baby a kiss & went & got one of our storm lanterns so I could look only at him. When I got back, Kenji had his hands over his face.

I let him mourn. I know what I said about not grieving is impossible. I kissed the creases in his face & didn't make him tell me who his agony was for. An image of her hand & our Yellow Pages ad got into my head, just her hand & the torn-out page. Then the little yellow house & Martin's face when he made us leave it. & those images stuck. I know they could get infected, I know how we'd feel if they got infected, I know cuz of Kenji's nightmares & the Unfinished Church, & I clung to him & mourned. The lighthouse waved its filmy hankie in the sky & took it back.

Baby didn't even twitch when I started the engines. Could've set a course for home, but something in me understood it'd be dangerous to stop, we couldn't make ourselves try again if we gave up. & if we tried to do it at the apartment or marina, people would hear us or smell us & say something.

I know when my sweet genius envisioned this "operation," he was thinking of Bermy's more remote outlying islands, the kind that're just rocks barely big enough to stand on. But the only one I could think of after Kenji fell so heavily asleep was this cute little place he & I enjoy on weekdays when nobody else bothers. I don't know what its name is, it must have one, Bermudians name everything, but anyway instead of heading to Dockyard I took us under Watford Bridge, & there it was.

If we had the energy, we could cover the whole rock at a stroll in about 3 mins. It's got a couple casurina trees, beautiful formations of black stone in the water, a little beachy semicircle nestled among the stones, cozy bit of seagrass easy to anchor in. That's it. It was too dark to see any of that stuff when we got here.

I do see a resort when I look across the water to the main Island. So I mean, this place isn't ideal. Any old so-so tourist could look across & see our little fire if we ever get around to it. You're not supposed to light fires on the beaches, I hate it when I stumble on the stinky remnants of people's charcoal. Anyway, when we got here, the sprawl of pink bungalows was just a sprinkling of sparkles in the dark. It felt like we were in the middle of nowhere. Knowing the resort was there made me feel something like loneliness.

I knew I wasn't lonely. In the pointy end my lifelong love was running a fever. That meant he was fighting with every cell in his body, fending away the past, all for me. But watching Kenji fast asleep, the lights from the resort over his shoulder, quiet little sconce-lights that jumped into the water & wriggled toward us without reaching us, I felt a new kind of confusion, totally unfamiliar like something mythical, nightmarish—like an invisible monster pouncing on me from behind.

I started worrying I'd passed on my existential crisis to Ethelberta! Ethelberta was built for pleasure & sunshine, not for covert missions of destruction, not for imaginary monsters that each of us tried to fend off all alone. Ethelberta was for me & Kenji to be comfy in together & no one else.

Sure I know what I gotta do, but it's scary & I'm small & tired & hurting! I took one look at the 40-odd-lb anchor & knew I'd drop it if I tried to lift it by myself. Instead I slipped my legs under the sleeping bag with K, sitting up & leaning on Ethelberta's padded backrest. The water lay flat like it had drifted off to sleep in the embrace of all the reefs & little islands that are Bermy. Kenji moved his head into my lap without waking. I turned down the lantern so it wouldn't hurt his eyes, then I couldn't see his face but my fingers found him by themselves. I was stroking his cheek when I realized that weird confusion wasn't as sharp or pressing as I'd thought.

I opened my book. On the bench between the lantern & where we rested in shadow.

The last thing in my book was "Existential Crisis 101." So I started with "How Not To Get A Power Drill In Bermuda" aka that very morning. Which is yesterday morning now.

I wrote all night. I wrote thru dawn. I kept an eye on the resort, the bridge, the black stones in the water easing out of the dark. If the boat drifted too far from the island or too close to the stones, I got up & moved it to a safe spot over the seagrass. Then I wrote some more.

It was weird, I was sleepy, but I didn't seem to get any sleepier. I didn't want to write what I was writing, I even cried some of the time (like when I wrote that K said, "Can we…I mean, I guess, can I…"), but I couldn't stop writing & knew I shouldn't. Baby woke each time I moved, but he was dangerously tired, exhausted in every way, I just had to say "We're OK" & he drifted off again. Like we're home right where we are. We're not home, we don't have food or different clothes or anything. Sometime I got up to pull Ethelberta's sunshade over the pointy end. When I sat down, K said, "I'm real sorry about this, Nabi."

He lay on his belly, I rubbed his back. "Rest, my Love, don't worry."

"What're you writing?"

Baby knows I can't be trusted when it comes to my book. I'm addicted to my book, I write stuff that can't be read.

423

I said, "Martin. You know."

K & I looked at each other for a while. He took my hand. The one that wasn't writing "see his love & soak it up…that strength of his, the courage to go on…"

"Take as long as you want, OK?" He meant it, he knows what writing is. But I can't make Kenji wait for us like that no more. He closed his eyes & a line showed up, left of his nose. That line means a headache, I brought Tylenol & water, but he shook his head. I rubbed his back until he slept.

Then I scrawled for both of us. Cuz of what we'd come out here to do.

I wrote all day. A day & night of writing!

Kenji sat up slowly when the sun was almost gone. He was dizzy, he didn't think we could lift the anchor either, even with the 2 of us. If we weren't pooped we would've laughed at all the moaning & groaning we did just to get into our bathing suits. We tied Ethelberta to a sticking-out bit in a stone formation in the water. Our knot was pathetic, our arms were too tired. & we still had to wade onto the beach, hauling charcoal on our shoulders to keep it out of the sea.

I told Kenji he could help carry the charcoal only if he let me set it up, gather sticks, & deal with starter fluid by myself. Poor Baby had to agree, he sank down on the sand, I could tell he ached all over, he looked like part of him was having trouble waking up. So I built our "funeral pyre."

After that, I was too shaky to get a match going. Kenji had to do it. Kenji lit the fire. Then he held me in his arms. We watched the smoking pile of sticks.

Kenji said, "I'll do it for you if you want."

I wanted to say no, I should be the one to do it.

But this will be a break, & I am brittle, & I've learned to feel it. I shrank against my Baby.

"Together?" I said. What a wimp.

"OK," said Kenji softly.

"Only way I can get thru this is if you're here & now with me." & yeah, I said that already. Won't be the last time either.

"I'm here, Nikkou." My Love.

So with his knee touching my knee, Kenji's hand in one of mine, I opened my book in my lap. I found the page where she showed up with our Yellow Pages ad.

"OK but 1st you have to kiss me, kiss me so it'll be all we remember," I blurted out.

I'd wrapped him in a beach blanket. Kenji wrapped me in it too & looked at me with love & sorrow. & then he closed his eyes.

His breath, his love & sorrow, the warmth in his body filled up the whole moment. I could hear his heart or maybe it was my heart or the rhythm of the tide all around us, all I want is more of it. I nearly cried when Kenji drew back hesitantly, & it had been some time already, I know cuz the fire had grown up & become light. It got into his eyes & revealed the deep young star that was quickening his breath.

I tore the page out of my book. Kenji took it from my hand before I could change my mind. He said, "Don't look, Nikkou."

He put it on the fire. A piece of my book. Straight out of its delicate insides.

The shadows are hungry, the shadows are burning: Seabird, "Aetna Simmons," nights in shadows with dark wings. The smoke is making Kenji sick, he keeps clearing his throat & swallowing. But he won't take his eyes off the fire except now & then to peek at me. Like he's forcing himself to look at the fire, like it's punishment.

I peek at the boat. If one or the other of us falls asleep, neither gonna be fast enough to catch Ethelberta if the tide comes up too strong & sudden. Soon as we left Harbour Road, we were marooned, that's one way to see it, but I can't look at it that way. This acegirl gotta make sure we're fast enough for Ethelberta cuz I'm the fraidy cat who's gotta be the harbor now. That's why I wrote all day & night. I'm having trouble stopping, I'm too used to my book, I write stuff as it's happening just cuz I can't stop. So it's no "document," it's not a memory, it won't survive. That means my book isn't a book anymore, it's something else now. A shadow on the sand? A reflection in water?

"You doing OK, Baby?" (A little while ago.)

Kenji shook his head. "Don't look, Nikkou." He put another couple pages on the fire. Stuff to do with bank-hacking & HD shredders. Kenji takes what I've done & feeds it to the fire. & it hurts like heartburn: what happens in our chests when we don't get enough to eat. At one point Kenji put some bits of my book on the fire, then he crawled to the ocean & vomited. I went to him & brought him back to the fire.

My Love's face is the scene of the battle between Hell & Heaven. The night & firelight & shadows thrown out by the firelight attack each other, leaping, crashing, & falling right there on Kenji's face & inside him.

"Lean on me, my Love, come on."

"When you're done writing." Baby turned aside to cough. & I realized I'm doing it again, fiddle-faddling!! But the limbo is death & always was. Focus, acegirl. Make it true, what you said to him: We're safe! True so Kenji believes it.

I tore out some more pages. "All right, Baby, let's do this."

Kenji took the pages. He read by firelight. "You sure? This stuff's from years ago. We only need to burn stuff that mentions—"

"I think we should do it all. It makes things look one-sided when they weren't."

Shadow & gleam fight over Kenji. History & future, breath & time, fire & water.

I rubbed his shoulder. "Just get me a new book, Baby, get us matching ones."

I tore out the pages with Martin & the drill. Kenji read them twice, I think. He cleared his throat a couple times. Then something occurred to me.

"Let me do those ones, Baby."

I took the pages back, I took them to the flames with my own hands.

I groped for Kenji's hands. Kenji put his arms around me. I kissed him where the light fell on his face, I kissed him where the shadows fell down into him. We watched pages become ruins become ashes, then they weren't there anymore. How do we build a harbor out of ashes?

Kenji whispered, "The crew of the Ethelberta."

He said it like he'd never seen that phrase before, like he didn't write it himself. Baby was the 1st to write it, I just shared it, but he

426

looked at what's left of my book like he'd forgotten! (This was a couple mins ago, the past comes on so quickly!)

"I like that," said Kenji.

Me (no more crying, acegirl): "Somebody should see about the anchor in that case, innit."

The faint sound Kenji made was laughter or the opposite. I've been extra attentive to sounds ever since. All kinds of sounds, water against the boat, water against the beach, fire against the air. & nobody stood up to get the anchor. We kissed while I tore out the page Kenji was looking at.

"Don't look, my Love."

"You neither, Nabi." Kenji put the paper on the fire, & then I turned him from the fire, we kissed & sank into the breath passing between us.

The leather cover of my book won't burn. That's why we're ripping pages out a couple at a time. Nobody feels like looking for the emergency knife we feel sure Ethelberta has. The whole crew is too emotional to remember where we keep it. So we can't cut the binding or slash all the pages out at once. & anyway it's too painful to think about being violent with my book, worse than trying to do it gently. Baby & I didn't have to talk about that to agree on it. I have a feeling something will happen to my book's black mask & red ribbons while I'm driving Ethelberta home.

Kenji curled up on his side on the sand. He laid his head down on my knee.

"Hear the whistling frogs, Baby?" I caressed his complex cloud of curls.

"I hear you. I see you, Nikkou, everywhere. Don't let me fall asleep."

My book will notice one more thing. Then it's going to stop, & I'll just take care of Kenji. In the dark & in the light.

Maybe it's cuz of the water or the frogs, but I notice that the pages make a weird sound when they burn. It's almost like no sound at all.